P...
One Hot Cowboy Wedding

"Funny, frank, and full of heart… One more welcome example of Brown's Texas-size talent for storytelling."
—*USA Today Happy Ever After*

"Alive with humor… Another page-turning joy of a book by an engaging author."
—*Fresh Fiction*

"Will make readers laugh along with the large and colorful cast of characters… The couple's relationship is hot as the Texas sun.
—*RT Book Reviews*, 4 Stars

"I didn't want to put it down… I'll be hunting down more cowboys by Ms. Brown."
—*Night Owl Reviews* Reviewer Top Pick

"Classic characters, a dash of spice, and a healthy addition of southern twang. It's a winner."
—*Long and Short Reviews*

"Delightful… The hunky males who occupy this corner of Texas and the women who have corralled their hearts combine plenty of sass and spice in this sweet Western romance."
—*The Reading Addict*

Praise for Carolyn Brown's Christmas Cowboy Romances

Also by Carolyn Brown

JUST A COWBOY
AND HIS BABY

CAROLYN
BROWN

sourcebooks
casablanca

Published by Sourcebooks Casablanca, an imprint of Sourcebooks, Inc.
P.O. Box 4410, Naperville, Illinois 60567-4410
(630) 961-3900
FAX: (630) 961-2168
www.sourcebooks.com

Printed and bound in Canada
WC 10 9 8 7 6 5 4 3 2 1

*If you love sexy cowboys and sassy ladies,
then this book is for you!*

Thank you to all my readers!

Chapter 1

EVIL SHOT FROM HIS DARK EYES. THE AIR AROUND HIM crackled when he raised his head and glared at her. He'd been bred, born, and raised for that night and she didn't have a chance against his wiles. He was bigger than she was and he knew it. He was meaner and he'd prove it.

Gemma O'Donnell didn't give a damn how big or how mean he was. She intended to be in control from the minute she mounted him. The message from the set of his head and unwavering stare said that she was an idiot not to shake in her cowgirl boots. She glared right back, her dark green eyes meeting his near black ones and locking through the metal bars separating them.

He dared.

She challenged.

She hiked a leg up to the first rung on the chute, and two hands circled her waist from behind to help her. Her heart slipped in an extra beat at the cowboy's big hands touching her, but she attributed it to nerves. She glanced over her shoulder into the sexiest brown eyes she'd ever seen, all dreamy and soft with heavy dark lashes.

"Thanks," she said.

"My pleasure. Go get 'em, darlin'." His voice went with the rest of the package: a deep Texas drawl that sounded like it should have been singing country songs in Nashville, not riding wild broncs on the PRCA Million Dollar Rodeo Tour.

Dammit, Trace Coleman. You pulled a slick one, but it's not going to work. You are not going to throw me off my game, she thought as she slung a leg over the top and locked eyes with the wild creature again. She had a horse to ride and even though his coat was as white as the driven snow, the look in his black eyes said that he could run Lucifer some serious competition when it came to meanness.

His name was Smokin' Joe and he was a rodeo legend. Cowboys said that he could see right into the soul of a rider and could feel the fear he'd struck in their hearts. Well, Gemma wasn't afraid of Smokin'-damn-Joe. He wasn't a bit meaner than the bronc out on Rye's ranch that she'd trained on, and she'd shown him who was boss. Smokin' Joe was just the next bronc in a long line, so he could take his evil glare and suck it up. Tonight she was the boss. She didn't care if the other riders had made bets about how quickly into the ride he'd throw her off into the dust. She'd show them all, cowboys and bronc alike, that a *cowgirl* had come to town.

She had two options.

Number one: Stay on his back for eight seconds and show him she was the boss.

Number two: Wreck.

There was no in between, and "almost" did not count. Gemma didn't allow herself to think the word *wreck*, not even when the almighty Trace Coleman produced a smile that would part the clouds. He was well over six feet tall, with dark hair and light brown eyes. She'd done her homework on all the cowboys. She knew most of them personally from the rodeo rounds, but she'd only known Trace by picture and reputation. Both of which intrigued her to no end. When she'd seen him in action in San Antonio, the heat level of the whole great state of Texas jacked up twenty more degrees. His swagger, his broad chest, and his body had said that Gemma was in deep trouble. But it was that deep sexy Texas drawl that brought on images of tangled sheets, lots and lots of heat, and a warm oozy feeling called an afterglow flitting through her mind.

Trace might have just meant to be charming and helpful, holding his hand out to assist her in climbing the chute, but Gemma wasn't buying his brand of bullshit. He wasn't stupid, and the twinkle in his eye said he knew exactly how his touch affected a woman. Besides, his gaggle of rodeo groupies were proof positive of that. In San Antonio, Austin, Redding, and Reno, Gemma had seen them circling him like a chocolate addict set loose with free rein in a candy store. Oh, yes, without a single doubt Trace knew how to turn a woman's mind to mush, and she'd lay dollars to horse apples that he played it to the nth degree.

Just like Smokin' Joe, Trace Coleman had met his match. Gemma intended to win that big shiny belt buckle in Las Vegas come December and leave Trace Coleman along with his scanty-dressed groupies in a cloud of dust. She had a big construction-paper lucky horseshoe tacked to the door of her travel trailer, and every time she won, she rewarded herself by pasting a small shamrock on it. After the final ride, it would be matted and framed and hung in her beauty shop, and all the cowboys who'd given her a hard time could crawl up under a mesquite bush and lick their wounds.

Any other time and any other place she might have

flirted with Trace. Cowboys were definitely her thing, and he sent out vibes that dug deep into her gut. But this was the rodeo circuit. For the next six months, Gemma O'Donnell had her job cut out for her and there was no room for Trace or any other cowboy.

Damn his sorry old hide, anyway! He was the top-seeded contestant in the tour and ten thousand dollars ahead of her. Staying on Smokin' Joe's back a full eight seconds could knock Trace off that pedestal in a tailspin—if thinking about his dreamy eyes didn't ruin her score. She took a deep breath and put him out of her mind. If he thought his cute little grin and deep voice could mess her up, then he could smear ketchup on his chaps and eat them for supper. And slap a little taco sauce on his spurs and have them for dessert.

She closed her eyes.

He will not bother me. He will not get into my head. He will not throw me off my game.

She kept the three sentences running on a continuous loop as she slung a leg over the top of the chute and got ready to mount old Smokin' Joe. She couldn't very well ride with her eyes shut, so she opened them, only to see Trace standing beside the bucking chute with a cocky little grin on his face. Light-brown chaps parenthesized a package locked behind his zipper that looked so inviting that Gemma almost drooled. She envisioned peeling his tight jeans from his body, leaving him wearing only boots, that cute grin, and a Stetson that sat just right.

"God Almighty," she whispered.

Someone called his name and he turned and walked away. But the backside was just as hot as the front with his chaps framing the cutest butt she'd ever seen. Lord, if she could stay on the horse eight seconds it would be a miracle. If she got a score high enough to beat him, it would be pure damn magic. She blinked and imagined Trace tossing his hat toward a pitchfork in a hayloft and coming toward her with those brown eyes speaking volumes about how hot that hayloft was about to get.

Stop it this minute! You've got to stay on this horse eight seconds. Sweet Jesus, you haven't ever let a man upset you with just a touch before. What in the hell is the matter with you? Get it together, Gemma O'Donnell!

The familiar whoosh filled her ears. When she had first started riding, her brothers had told her to focus on the ride and block everything else out. She'd imagined holding a conch shell up to her ear. Nothing could break through her concentration once she got her whoosh mojo going. And she was almost in the zone.

Folks around Cody, Wyoming, were big rodeo fans, so the stands were packed with a loud, rowdy crowd that night. But Gemma didn't look up into the crowd, even though a rider likes a whole arena full of noisy fans as much as a country music band likes to play to a lively audience. If she looked, it would break her focus, and she'd already drawn the meanest damn horse in the rodeo. Which was good because if he bucked hard that meant more points. She rolled her neck, limbering it up for the ride and reminding herself to keep it loose. It only took one drop of fear to lock it in place and then *boom*, whiplash would put her out of the next ride over in St. Paul, Oregon.

The announcer's voice was full of excitement. "Gemma O'Donnell, our only woman contestant in saddle bronc riding, will be coming out of gate six. Gemma comes to us from Ringgold, Texas, and I hear she can ride anything with four legs. She told me this afternoon that her big regret in life is not pursuing this dream before now and letting Kaila Mussell take home bragging rights to being the first woman to show the boys how it's done. Keep your eyes on gate six and let's make some noise for Gemma, who intends to be the second woman ever to win the bronc riding contest when the dust settles in Las Vegas in December."

When she settled back into the saddle, she was fully well in her riding zone. The announcer might as well have been reciting poetry, because all Gemma heard was each heartbeat in her ears as she eased into the saddle. She tried to psych Smokin' Joe out. It wasn't against the rules, and he'd done the same thing when he glared at her through the bars. She leaned forward and whispered softly in his ear, "You do your damnedest, old boy. Buck the hardest you've ever done and I'll do my damnedest to stay on your back. I need the scores, so give me your wildest ride. Don't you hold back a thing because I'm a woman, darlin'. I could ride you with my eyes shut and eating a hamburger with my free hand."

She measured the hot pink and black rein and got a death grip on it. Her saddle had been tweaked by her brother Dewar and the rein braided by her brother Rye. The gold lucky horseshoe pin had been fastened to her hot pink hat by her brother Raylen. All of it was important but especially the saddle. To a bronc rider, a saddle or stirrups can be off one-quarter of an inch and it might as well be a mile. It has to be absolutely perfect, in tune with the rider and so comfortable that she could sleep in it.

She shoved the heels of her boots firmly down into the stirrups and put everything out of her mind but the "mark out." The heels of her boots had to be above the points of Smokin' Joe's shoulders before the horse's front legs hit the ground. After that it would be an eight-second line dance. Smokin' Joe would buck. Gemma's legs would go back and come forward, spurring him on to buck even more. In the end one of them would win, and Gemma was absolutely determined that Smokin' Joe would lose.

If she missed the mark out she'd be disqualified, so she got ready.

Rein in hand.

Determination in her heart.

"Eight seconds!" Trace's deep voice said from the top of the chute.

She could have shot him, dragged his sorry carcass out to the back side of the O'Donnell ranch, and poured barbecue sauce on him for the coyotes. She vowed that she would get even. He had the next ride of the evening and paybacks were a bitch. He should have thought of that before he broke her concentration.

She pulled up on the multicolored rein.

Everything stopped and she was in a vacuum. Even the dust out in the arena was afraid to succumb to gravity and fall back to earth. The noise of the crowd hung above the arena like a layer of foggy smoke in a cheap honky-tonk, but Gemma couldn't hear it.

She settled her straw hat with the lucky gold horseshoe pin attached to the brim on the back of her head, touched the horseshoe for good luck, and nodded. Three rodeo clowns stepped away from the gate. The chute opened and a blur of white topped with snatches of hot pink whirled around the arena, kicking up dust devils in its wake.

Time moved in slow motion. She could hear the crowd going wild and the announcer's excitement, but the roar of blood racing through her veins kept all of it at bay. The dry dirt clouds filling her nostrils were like drugs to an addict, and with every breath she took in more, the exhilaration so great that her heart was on the brink of explosion. The horse attempted to twist itself into a pretzel, but her body responded with the right movements instinctively. The next move put both his back legs into the air and she felt like she was on a little kid's slide. The dirt arena came up to meet her and then *boom*, Smokin' Joe was a damn camel with a big hump where his back used to be. But she stayed loose in the saddle, moving her legs the right way for balance as if she'd been born to ride Smokin' Joe that day in Cody, Wyoming.

She didn't hear the buzzer saying that she'd stayed with the ride until the end. When one of the three pickup riders reached out and looped an arm around her, she hung on to the reins until he yelled and then she let go. She slid off the bucking bronc's back and let the rider carry her to safety in the middle of the arena.

"And that's how it's done, cowgirls and cowboys!" the announcer screamed into the microphone. "With that kind of competition, Trace Coleman had better be ready to ride like the wind. Let's hear it for Gemma O'Donnell, a small-town Texas girl who just showed the legendary Smokin' Joe who is the boss. And the judges are tallying the scores. While they get the final number, give it up one more time for Gemma O'Donnell."

She inhaled and waited.

High seventies would be wonderful. Anything more would be icing on the cake. She'd gotten a seventy-eight in Reno, Nevada, two weeks before, but Trace had walked away with a seventy-nine. He hadn't ridden yet in Cody, and she had no doubts that the number one pick for this year's bronc rider would score high.

"Eighty for the lady! Put 'em together, fans, for the little lady from Ringgold, Texas. Next up, the man of the hour, Mr. Trace Coleman, is climbing into the bucking chute behind gate eight. Will Gemma give him a run for his money today, or will he take home the purse and the bragging rights as first place in the bronc busters for a while longer? We'll see here in a few minutes when he comes out of the gate."

Gemma exhaled loudly. She rushed to gate eight and climbed up the side right beside two cowboys. Trace had settled into the saddle and had his own special red, white, and blue rein in his hands.

He looked up, said, "I'll show you how it's done, darlin'," and winked. He touched a gold hat pin that looked like a miniature ranch brand from where she stood.

So he was superstitious too, was he? Did he eat the same thing for supper every night of a ride? Did he wear the same socks and boots to every rodeo, no matter if the socks had holes and the boots were scuffed?

Luck be damned. Payback time had arrived.

She blew him a kiss. All was fair in love, war, and bronc riding. It was probably even written in the fine print at the back of the rule book.

Not to be outdone, he caught the imaginary kiss mid-air and stuffed it inside his black vest pocket.

—m—

Trace had known he'd met his match the first time he saw Gemma O'Donnell. Her name had come up in rodeo conversations for a couple of years, but he'd never ridden against her or even in the same rodeos as she had. Not until she showed up in Rapid City, South Dakota, four months before. She'd flown in and rode one mean bronc that night, had a big wreck about three seconds into the ride, and was gone the next day. He didn't do much better at that rodeo. He lost control five seconds after he came out of the chute and Dugger McDonald from Cheyenne, Wyoming, took the purse home.

But that Irish beauty had haunted his dreams for the past four months. He'd watched her determination and her form, but he'd also seen her walk away when she'd been defeated, head held high and back ramrod straight, no tears for the loss but a purpose in her stance that said she'd be a force to be reckoned with before the dust all settled in December.

He'd meant to make her nervous when he circled her small waist to help her up the side of chute number six. The way she'd put shame into old Smokin' Joe's eyes said it hadn't worked a damn bit. But it had sent a sizzling jolt through his body. One more touch like that and he'd have to shuck his chaps because what was framed in front would be pretty damned obscene.

Since the rodeo in South Dakota when he had seen her spinning out of the chute in a blurring burst of hot pink he'd had trouble sleeping. And that was before he'd even touched her. She was smoking hot and now his hands felt like they had red coals of fire in them. He did not have time, money, or the energy for any woman and certainly not one like Gemma O'Donnell. Hell, he didn't even have the energy for the groupies that hung around the trailers after a rodeo. He had to concentrate hard on winning right up until Vegas the first week of December.

He had hoped he wouldn't see her again after the South Dakota ride, but there she was in San Antonio the next night. He'd come out the winner that time and was more than a little disappointed that she didn't stick around for the dance following the rodeo. Then in the middle of March she'd showed up in Austin, Texas, to ride like the devil and snatch the purse in a gold match, making them even.

Poor old Dugger broke his arm in a practice session and that put him out of the running. In May she came to Redding, California, and whipped him by six points, but that was a silver competition, and in Prescott, Arizona, they both wrecked and a newcomer by the name of Coby Taylor grabbed a silver purse right out from under them. Again he'd thought she'd give up, but she showed up in Wyoming pulling a travel trailer behind her truck.

That meant she was in it for the long haul.

Trace would have his hands full for sure.

He was ten thousand dollars ahead of her and he needed this ride for a nice comfortable lead. He measured the rein one more time and shoved his boots down into the stirrups. He hadn't even met her formally, so why the hell did she make his brain go to mush over one little touch? He'd had less reaction to Ava, the only groupie who had ever wound up in his bed.

He shook his head and tried to free himself of the image of Gemma with her red hair, green eyes, and lips that would run Angelina Jolie some stiff competition. He was riding Hell Cat, a big black horse with a solid reputation in the rodeo rounds. That was fine by Trace. He needed a real bucking horse that night to beat Gemma's points.

He didn't like losing at all, but to a woman? That was a tough pill to swallow. Hell, he'd never even competed against a woman until this circuit. And now he'd been whipped twice by that red-haired piece of Texas baggage that was trying to get into his head by blowing him a kiss. Well, she could damn well take her sassy little butt back to her part of Texas because he was about to show her exactly how to make more than eighty points.

He tightened his hold on the rein and nodded. The gate flew open and Hell Cat went into action, twisting, turning, bucking as if he were trying to throw Trace all the way to the St. Paul rodeo—airborne, with no stops. Trace kept one hand up, held on to the rein, and did what came natural in his movements. Legs forward, legs back, spur, go with the movement of the horse.

The buzzer sounded and a pickup rider was beside him with an arm outstretched. Trace grabbed it, slid off the horse, and hit the ground running. When he was away from the bucking horse, he stopped and waved to the crowd. Everyone was on their feet screaming and yelling. Folks did tend to like a winner.

While the buzz left his ears he headed for gate eight and listened to the announcer say, "And that, cowgirls and cowboys, was Trace Coleman from Goodnight, Texas, who just did his bit in taming Hell Cat. He's our final bronc rider of the night, and to beat Gemma O'Donnell he has to have at least eighty points. And the judges are totaling their points now. Remember, that's fifty for the horse and fifty for Trace's ability. And the winning number is, oh my goodness, Trace, sorry, old man, she's whooped you right here in Cody, Wyoming, but just barely. You've got seventy-eight points, so Gemma O'Donnell takes the saddle bronc riding purse home tonight and you come in second. Next up is the bull riding."

Trace nodded toward the judges' stand and then tipped his hat to the roaring crowd still on their feet and making enough noise to raise the dead before he slipped back behind the bucking chutes.

Eight seconds could damn sure change the whole world and knock a rider off his pretty pedestal. He'd have to work harder, keep his mind on the ride better, because if he didn't final and didn't win the big event in Las Vegas, he could kiss his Uncle Teamer's ranch outside of Goodnight good-bye.

He'd planned on sticking around Cody for a few hours after the rodeo to toss back a few beers and bask in the glory of the win before he began the thousand-mile journey to St. Paul, Oregon. But suddenly a party didn't look so inviting and he was eager to get on the road. He made up his mind that as soon as the rodeo personnel removed his saddle from Hell Cat, he intended to load up and point his truck and trailer toward the west. By the time the sun came up tomorrow morning he'd be more than a third of the way there.

"Hey," Gemma said so close to him that he jumped.

"Good ride," he said stiffly.

"Not my best. I could have done better, but thanks," she said.

"Guess that puts you where I was yesterday." Trace's drawl was deep and very Texan. He slumped down on a rough wooden bench beside the chute he'd ridden out of just minutes before, stuck his long legs out, and crossed them at the ankles.

"Guess it does, but the night is still young. Anything could happen before the finals." Gemma sat down on the other end of the bench, pulled a knee up, and wrapped her arm around it.

"What are you ridin' for?" he asked.

Vibes bounced around in the space between them like a bucking bronc without a time limit. He wanted to move closer to see if the flames were hotter the closer he got, but he sat still.

"Glory of being the second woman to win the title. And you?" she answered. Her voice had just enough grit to be sexy, and it went with that red hair, those full lips, and green eyes.

"A ranch."

"One of us could be very happy when December rolls around."

"And the other one is going to have a few dollars in their bank account," he finally said.

"You going to St. Paul or Colorado Springs?" she asked.

"Both. You?"

She nodded.

"Which one?" he asked grumpily.

"Both! It's a lot of driving, but it's doable and I need the money to put me in the finals."

Gemma didn't look forward to a thousand miles in two days to St. Paul and then thirteen hundred back to Colorado Springs. But at least there were five days between St. Paul and Colorado Springs so she wouldn't have to drive for hours and hours on that stretch. She hadn't been a greenhorn when she started the circuit. She'd known there would be fast drives as well as those that could be taken leisurely. It was the way of the rodeo circuit. Drive hard. Hurry up to get to the next rodeo and wait for the eight seconds to ride hard. Then get in the pickup truck and do it all over again.

Tonight she got to put another shamrock on her construction-paper lucky horseshoe. There were still miles and miles between that four-leaf clover and the one that she was saving for when she won the Vegas competition. There would be a lot of riding, a lot of driving, a helluva lot of waiting, and a lot of missing her family and friends, but the night she got to glue the biggest, shiniest shamrock on top of her horseshoe would make it all worthwhile.

Gemma stood up and settled her hat on her head. "Well, I'll see you there."

"And I'm going to win," Trace said.

"Don't bet on it, cowboy. Tonight is just the beginning of a long line of victories. You might as well go on home to Good-bye, Texas, and forget about it."

"Goodnight!"

"Right back atcha." She grinned.

"No, not Good-bye, Goodnight."

"What?"

"I'm from Goodnight, Texas, not Good-bye."

"Tomato, tomahto!" she quipped in a slow Southern drawl.

She'd done her homework and she knew exactly where Trace Coleman hailed from. She knew his statistics, how tall he was, and when his birthday was. And she had not made a mistake when she said "Good-bye." She'd made a joke. Evidently he didn't think it was funny.

He quickly stood up and fell into step beside her. "So you're in it for the long haul for sure, no matter what?"

"Yes, I am, so let's clear the air and get something straight right now. If you ever try to ruin my ride with a comment again, I'm going to leave your body so far out that the coyotes will starve huntin' for it."

He chuckled.

Instinctively she reached out to push him, but he caught her arms and used the momentum to pull her tightly to his chest. She had intended to send him ass-over-spurs into the dust like she did her brothers when they were all kids and she pushed one of them in anger, but suddenly she was listening to his heartbeat. She leaned back to look up at him and his eyes were fluttering shut. She barely had time to moisten her lips before his mouth covered hers in a sizzling kiss that left her wanting another and yet wanting to slap the shit out of him at the same time.

"If you ever try that again, I'll…" she stammered in a hoarse whisper.

"Darlin', either fight your way to the top with the big boys or go home and lick your wounds. I'm not one bit afraid of you," Trace said.

"That's a big mistake, Mr. Coleman." She turned and walked away from him briskly, fringe on her chaps flopping with each step, leaving no doubt that she was stomping instead of walking.

Coby Taylor moved out of the shadows and said, "Sassy bit of baggage. Sexy as hell but needs a bit of taming."

"You'd have better luck trying to tame Smokin' Joe or Hell Cat than that woman," Trace said without an ounce of humor.

———

Gemma retrieved her saddle and carried it to her trailer, stashed it in the special place in the closet, and took the shoebox from the shelf. Damn that Trace Coleman anyway for making her so angry.

She touched her lips to see if they were as hot as they still felt and was surprised to find that they were cool. She'd show him that she didn't have to fight her way to the top, that *he* had to fight every day to keep his place because by the middle of the circuit she intended to be so far ahead of him that he couldn't even get a whiff of the dust she was leaving behind.

She opened the shoebox and a smile replaced the frown drawing her dark brows together. She rifled through the small paper shamrocks until she found the one with Cody written in glitter and gently turned it over to smear glue on the back. Then she stuck it on her horseshoe and stood back to admire it.

"There, one more step toward the big one," she said.

Lick her wounds, indeed!

Chapter 2

TRUCK ENGINES RUMBLED OUTSIDE GEMMA'S TRAILER window, and the weatherman on her radio alarm was all excited about the heat wave. "It's going to be sunny and hot today in Montana, so load up the cooler with water bottles and don't forget that sunblock."

She cut him off midsentence when she slapped her palm on the snooze button and crammed a pillow over her eyes.

She mumbled to herself, "I don't give a damn if it's sunny and hot. What the hell do you expect in July? Snow or sleet? There are still miles and miles of road between me and the next rodeo, so it doesn't matter jack squat to me unless it decides to rain in St. Paul. God, I hate to ride a bronc in the rain. Saddle gets all slippery."

The alarm was set to go off every minute after she hit snooze, and the weatherman was still going on about the heat when it went off again. "I'm telling you, folks, this is the hottest summer in years. We are breaking records here in the northern states. It's normal to be this hot in Texas in the first week of July, but not in our part of the world. No rain in sight for the next week."

She hit it again and threw her legs over the side of the bed. Another day of white lines on the highway and telephone poles lay ahead. She hadn't planned on the sheer boredom of the long, long rides. She listened to the radio, played CDs, talked to herself, called her family members, but it was still mile after mile from one rodeo to the next. Add that to constant analyzing of what she'd done wrong on the last ride and how to correct it on the next and the days dragged on and on like a turtle race.

She rolled the kinks out of her neck and stood up. The trailer looked even smaller that day than it did when she left Ringgold the week before. She wished she'd brought the bigger one. But one person didn't need a trailer big enough to sleep four. At least that's what she'd decided after looking at both of the trailers a dozen times.

"I'm an idiot. I could have a bed, table, and even more storage room if I'd brought the big one," she talked to herself.

In her tiny new world, she was confined to living quarters less than half the size of her bedroom at home. The kitchen and closet that held her clothes and gear covered one side of the trailer. She had a two-burner cooktop, a dorm-sized refrigerator with a freezer packed full of steaks, a microwave, and a tiny sink that served as a place to wash dishes as well as brush her teeth.

At one time a set of bunk beds had occupied part of the space on that wall, but Dewar and Rye, her two older brothers, had removed them and built the closet with a special compartment to house her saddle. A tiny bathroom with a shower and toilet, only to be used when she couldn't find a truck stop or a campground with the option, and a booth-type table that dropped down to make a bed took up the other side. Dewar had taken the table out and had a special mattress made to fit on the platform he and Rye had built for the space, but it dang sure wasn't as comfortable as her big king-sized bed at home where she could snuggle with six pillows if she wanted.

She glared at the clock on the microwave. It couldn't be six o'clock already. She'd only shut her eyes a minute ago. The damn thing was lying or maybe the batteries were old and didn't work right.

"Coffee! I need caffeine!" She filled a cup with water and stuck it in the microwave for instant coffee. While she waited, she popped the tab off a can of Coke and guzzled part of that down and then brushed her teeth. When the microwave timer dinged, she removed the cup, stirred in coffee granules, and took a sip.

The KOA campground in Three Forks, Montana, had shower facilities so she grabbed her shower bag from the closet, stuffed in a pair of cutoff jeans and a bright pink tank top, took a couple more gulps of coffee, and slung open the trailer door.

Cool morning air greeted her. It wasn't all that hot. That crazy weatherman should step out of the house in Texas in July. Then he'd know what hot was for sure. When she left Ringgold, the lizards and scorpions were having races every time the back door opened to see who could get into the house before Dewar and Gemma slammed it shut.

The campground was one of those areas that looked like a picture on a postcard, and she was glad she'd finally given in to exhaustion and stopped for the night. She'd been so hyped up when she left Cody that she planned to drive all the way to St. Paul on the jacked-up adrenaline surge from winning the competition. At midnight she'd begun to flag and stopped for a cup of coffee and a fried apple pie at McDonald's. At one thirty she saw a billboard advertising a campground only a mile and a half off Interstate 90. Next exit, it said, so she took it and followed the signs. It had been dark when she checked in at two a.m. She'd been too tired to notice the gorgeous surroundings and was asleep five seconds after her head hit the pillow.

She sat down at the picnic table right outside her door and enjoyed the view of the Bridger Mountains off in the distance. Big puffy clouds looked like fluffy icing on the top of cupcakes. The sky was that gorgeous shade of blue that only came in the springtime in Texas. In the summer, it was washed out by the heat and days would go by when there was never a cloud in sight.

The aroma of bacon and real coffee wafted out from the kitchen window of the camper next to hers and her stomach grumbled. She promised herself a bacon, egg, and cheese McGriddle from the next McDonald's out on Interstate 90. But for now she needed to wash the rodeo dust off her before she started driving again. She stood up and headed toward the building housing the bathrooms and showers.

The hot water felt so good that she stood under the shower and let it beat down on her sore back muscles for a long five minutes. Eight seconds wasn't so long when she was out exercising horses at her folks' ranch in Ringgold, Texas. It wasn't very long at all when she was talking to her sister, Colleen, on the telephone or playing with her niece, Rachel. But slap her butt on the back of a bucking bronc and those eight seconds were equivalent to working a whole week with no rest. Everything ached and the next day, the day before Independence Day, she would be doing it all over again. She'd be right back in her spurs and looking down from the side of a chute into the rolling eyes of a bronc. And then five days after that she'd be repeating the same process in Colorado Springs.

"I wonder if Dewar could rig up a Jacuzzi in my trailer. I could do without the bed and sleep on an air mattress if I had a tub with jets to laze in after a rough ride," she muttered.

She turned the water off and ran her hands through her thick hair, squeezing out as much water as possible. She wrapped a towel around her hair, bent forward, and rubbed even more moisture from it. Then she flipped it over her back, dried her body, and dressed in the cutoff shorts and tank top. Her rubber flip-flops made slurping sounds on the concrete floor when she carried her bag and towels to the vanity. Then she leaned forward and checked her roots.

"Still good," she mumbled.

She had dark hair by nature, but she was a hairdresser and she wanted something different for the rodeo tour, so the day before she left Ringgold she had dyed her hair a gorgeous light auburn. It went with her complexion and gave her even more of a kick-ass attitude than she'd had before—if that was possible.

She was smearing sunblock on her nose and face when she felt a movement against her leg. A burst of pure adrenaline sent her into a jump that landed her in a squat on the vanity with one foot on each side of the sink. She caught a glimpse of herself in the mirror, and she looked like a big-eyed owl perching on a tree limb, but she didn't care. Public bathrooms bred spiders and an occasional mouse and she hated both of them.

They were sneaky creatures, always appearing when they were least expected, and they weren't afraid of the devil. She didn't care what her daddy, Cash O'Donnell, said about them being more afraid of her than she was of them. Spiders she could abide at the distance of ten feet if they weren't wolf spiders. Those suckers had been injected with kangaroo DNA back on the fifth day of creation. They could jump more than ten feet and they always jumped toward her, never away from her, which proved her dad was dead wrong about their fear of human beings.

When she looked down from her perch, she didn't see a spider or a mouse but a small dog looking up at her with dark eyes. It wagged its tail as if to say that it was sorry.

"Bet you always wondered if humans could fly, didn't you?" she giggled nervously as she eased down off the vanity. Her flip-flops slapped back down on the tile, but the little dog didn't move.

She squatted down and reached out to touch the tiny critter and it didn't growl or snap. The tag on the brown leather collar made introductions.

"Hello, Sugar, where did you come from? Do you live here on the campgrounds?"

The dog's tail flipped back and forth even harder as she licked Gemma's palm. She scratched its ears a few seconds before straightening up and heading for the door.

Sugar followed her—tail still a blur of movement.

"Did someone dump you?" Gemma asked.

The dog was a slick-haired red Chihuahua with all the markings of pedigree. She had a sharp nose and big soulful dark eyes. Surely someone had lost the friendly little thing and would come looking for her.

"Sugar," a man's deep voice whispered outside the door. "Are you in there?"

Gemma stopped and the dog sat down at her feet.

Gemma had heard that drawl before. Her imagination was playing tricks on her. That could not be Trace Coleman's voice, could it?

"Sugar," he whispered again.

Gemma rounded the privacy wall, flip-flops smacking on the already hot concrete with the dog right along beside her. The owner was searching behind a short hedge with his back to Gemma. He wore red-and-green plaid cotton pajama bottoms and a red tank top that hugged his muscular frame. His flip-flops were green and his dark hair hadn't been brushed.

"You lookin' for a dog?" she asked.

Trace Coleman turned and her heart thumped.

He gave her a brilliant smile. "Good morning, Gemma. Yes, I am looking for a pesky little Chihuahua."

Sugar meandered out of the bathroom and sat down beside Gemma's feet.

"I'll be damned," Trace said.

"This is your dog? I would have figured you to have a pit bull or maybe a Doberman."

"No, just that sassy little Chihuahua," he said. "She usually doesn't take to strangers."

"We aren't strangers. We shared a bathroom." Gemma was amazed that she could say two coherent words.

Trace was a couple of inches over six feet tall. He weighed two hundred and ten pounds and it was all muscle with no spare fat giggling anywhere. His face was a study of angles covered with a full day's dark scruff. Jet-black eyelashes and equally dark brows framed brown eyes that looked as if they could see to the bottom of her soul. That kind of cowboy surely did not have a Chihuahua named Sugar for a dog.

He reached down and scooped Sugar up into his arms. "You going all the way into St. Paul tonight?"

Gemma nodded. "I am. Don't care if it's midnight when I get there. I can sleep as late as I want in the morning and then check out the grounds. If I have to drive until noon tomorrow, it's not the same. I like to wake up on the grounds on the day of the rodeo."

She would never admit that she was as superstitious as a football coach; that she always ate a hamburger from the rodeo grounds on the day before she rode that night; that she touched her lucky horseshoe hat pin just before she nodded for the gate to be opened; and that she would never think of wearing anything but her hot pink cowgirl boots. Or that the times when she hadn't come out of the rodeo with the purse had been when she'd gotten there late and tired.

"Me too." He nodded. "Had breakfast?"

"I'll stop at a McDonald's and grab something." She turned and started walking toward the trailer.

"I made pancakes and bacon. I haven't eaten yet because Sugar decided to slip out the door when I opened it to look at the mountains. We could heat up the pancakes in the microwave. It's the least I can do since you saved me from having to go into the ladies room to rescue my dog."

She hesitated.

"Oh, come on! I'm not going to poison you so I'll win at St. Paul. I can do that without any help," he said.

She stopped. "Don't kid yourself, cowboy."

Trace's face lit up in a sexy-as-hell smile. "I'll take that as a yes. Sugar, we've got company for breakfast. It's the first trailer you see over there. I guess that'd be yours beside me? I pulled in right after you did last night. Your lights were still on but they went out before I could walk Sugar and grab a late-night beer."

When they reached the trailer he opened the door for her and stood to one side. "It's not much, but it's home for the next few months."

"It's bigger than mine." Gemma looked at his feet and his big hands.

Dear Lord, what am I doing? That old wives' tale isn't true, and what's wrong with me? I say the word bigger and my mind goes to his body, not this trailer. I've got to get my mind out of the gutter. But he does have some big hands and some big feet, so I wonder. Stop it, Gemma! Right now!

The aroma of fresh-brewed coffee and bacon met her. She dropped her bag inside the door and scanned the place. She was facing a booth-type table on a pedestal that could be lowered like hers used to back before she took it out and replaced it with a platform bed. At the other end of his trailer she could see a bed with tangled covers.

She couldn't take her eyes off those gold-colored sheets. He'd look like a hero on the cover of a romance book with his brown eyes and hair against all that gold. She could just see him with the sheet covering the bare essentials and a look in his eyes that invited her to join him. Would he be as good a lover as he was a bronc rider? The past had taught her that cowboys were sometimes better at riding bulls or broncs than they were at having sex. But there was something in the vision of him in that bed that said Trace Coleman would set those sheets on fire.

Trace made sure the door was shut tightly before he set Sugar on the floor. The dog raced back to the bed, hopped up on a stool at the end, meandered across the bed like it was her personal domain, and finally snuggled down on a pillow.

"Have a seat. Breakfast will be served as soon as I wash my hands."

Lucky dog! Fate is a bitch. And I'm telling Liz tonight that I don't believe in her tarot cards or her fortune-telling. There hasn't been a blond-haired cowboy that made my heart race since she told me I'd have my very own cowboy by Christmas. But just looking at the dark-haired one's bare feet sets my underpants on fire. And he's the worst cowboy in the lot because falling for him could jeopardize my whole dream.

Trace motioned toward the table. "Anywhere over there is fine."

Gemma blushed and quickly slid to the back side of the booth. "I was watching Sugar. She sure knows how to get up on that bed."

"I tacked a little stool to the end of the bed frame at my house so she could get up and down on it. She was driving me crazy at night wanting up on the bed and then down to go outside, so I came up with that idea and then made a second one for the trailer."

Gemma nodded, but her thoughts weren't on the dog or the steps.

Trace went on. "On the ranch, she has a doggy door in the kitchen that opens out onto a screened porch, and there's another one that goes down a ramp and outside to the yard which she owns. Even the big dogs let her think she's queen." He busied himself pouring coffee and reheating a stack of pancakes and bacon in the microwave as he talked. When they were done he set the plate before her and added a glass of orange juice and a cup of coffee.

"You sure don't look like a Chihuahua man," she said.

He chuckled.

Hell's bells! He even chuckled in a sexy Southern drawl that made little goose bumps rise up on her arms.

"You want to know the story about how I bought a Chihuahua?" he asked.

She poured warmed syrup on the pancakes. "I would love to hear that story. Did she stow away in your suitcase after a trip to Mexico?"

"Butter is in the syrup, by the way. I melt it and then add syrup and warm them together. Now, about Sugar? You aren't even close with the Mexico story. It's like this. Not last Christmas but the one before that, about eighteen months ago, I was dating a woman from Goodnight, Texas."

"My sister lives close to there in the wintertime. I've heard her mention Goodnight. She lives between Claude and Amarillo. She and her husband are part of a carnival that winters there," Gemma said between bites.

"Blaze McIntire?"

Gemma nodded.

"Colleen is your sister?"

Another nod.

Trace chuckled again. "Small world! I know Blaze well. Only met your sister once, but I can see the resemblance."

"Really?"

"Oh, yeah. Blaze and I've—" He chuckled again. "Guess I'd best hush or I'll get in trouble. Colleen doesn't need to know about all the things in Blaze's past."

"And your past?" Gemma asked.

"Colorful. We'll leave it at that. Now back to Sugar." He changed the subject. "The woman I was dating was tall, blonde, pretty. And sometime in the fall, must've been about the middle of October, we started talking about taking a Christmas trip together." He carried his plate to the table and sat down at the far end away from Gemma.

"To Mexico?"

Trace's brows knit together and he tilted his head to one side. "Why would you say that? Oh! Sugar is a Chihuahua. But no, we were thinking about Florida to the beach. I asked her what she wanted for Christmas and she said something that would fit inside a stocking this big," he held up his hands and measured about six inches, "and nothing bigger. So I figured she meant plane tickets to Florida and a long weekend in a fancy condo. I got them and they looked pretty small inside the red stocking and then I remembered that she'd thrown a fit over a Chihuahua in the pet store when we were in Amarillo at the mall. So I bought a six-week-old puppy and on Christmas Eve when we exchanged presents I stuffed the dog down into the stocking with the tickets."

Gemma finished her pancakes and sipped at the still hot coffee. "And?"

"She was allergic to dogs. She hated the beach and she wanted an engagement ring. I asked her why she let me think she wanted to go to the beach with me and she said she thought I was joking to throw her off base with the engagement ring."

"Wow!"

"Yep, I didn't do too hot that Christmas. I got a refund on the plane tickets and only lost the price of one night on the condo, but the dog was not returnable."

"And the name?"

Trace swallowed a gulp of coffee. "I took one look at the critter as she stormed out the door and sped out of my driveway and said, 'I guess visions of sugar plums weren't what was dancing in her head.'"

Gemma giggled. "And Sugar Plum stuck? What happened to the woman?"

"The dog's name on the registration papers is Sugar Plum Ziva."

"After Ziva David on *NCIS*?"

"You got it. Sugar might be small, but she's a force just like Ziva," Trace said.

"And the woman?"

"Oh, I run into the lady now and then at the café or in the grocery store. She's engaged to a CEO of some company out of Amarillo these days. Guess he understands her a lot better than I did."

Gemma clamped her hand over her mouth to keep the giggle from growing, but it was useless. She could just see the woman peeling out of a driveway in her fancy car, all mad as hell because she got a dog instead of a ring. One bitch sure didn't want another bitch in her house. The more she visualized the whole scene the funnier it got, and the giggle grew into a guffaw and that went to an infectious roar with Trace joining in.

Finally, Trace wiped at his eyes with a paper napkin. "It *is* funny, isn't it? I haven't laughed that hard in years, but the look on your face was hilarious. What would you have done if it had been you?"

"I bet it wasn't funny then. Did you love her? I would have taken you to court for custody of the dog. I love all animals except spiders and mice. Dogs. Cats. Horses. Even donkeys."

"No, it wasn't funny then, and I don't know if I loved her. I doubt it. She wasn't ranch material so there wasn't going to be a long-term relationship. I'm a rancher and have no intentions of being anything else."

"And what makes a woman ranch material?" Gemma asked.

"Not snarling her nose at a new baby calf or colt goes a long way," Trace answered.

Gemma understood perfectly. Her last relationship had ended in a hell of a bigger mess than what a Chihuahua dog could bring about. He'd been one of those pretty, spoiled rotten rich kids who didn't know the south end of a northbound broodmare from a hole in the ground. The only thing they had in common was a couple of friends and a few months of wild sex. The friends fell by the wayside and the sex couldn't hold the relationship together. She slid out of the booth and carried her dirty dishes to the sink where she washed them and set them in the trailer-sized drainer.

She picked up her bag and opened the door and Sugar bounded off the bed. "Thanks for breakfast. See you in St. Paul. Grab Sugar. I wouldn't want to have to chase her down."

He picked the dog up and held the door for Gemma. "Thanks for the conversation and for saving me from public humiliation. It could have been a mess if I'd been caught in the women's bathroom. See you later and you are so welcome to breakfast. We'll have to do it again."

—⁓—

Gemma was barely back out on I-90 when her cell phone rang. She put it on speakerphone and laid it beside her on the console before she even answered Liz's call.

Liz had been born and raised in a traveling carnival. The same one that Colleen and Blaze helped take care of nowadays. Liz had been the belly dancer and fortune-teller for the carnival, but when her Uncle Haskell left her a house and twenty acres she'd changed her lifestyle drastically. Every Christmas she'd asked Santa Claus for a house with no wheels and a sexy cowboy. Her Uncle Haskell took care of the house with no wheels and Gemma's brother, Raylen, turned out to be the sexy cowboy. They'd been married for eighteen months and Liz had told Gemma's fortune twice now. Once before she and Raylen married and once after. Both times there was a cowboy in her future and he was going to be hers by Christmas. But Christmas had come and gone the year before and no cowboy had dropped down on one knee to propose.

"Hey, Liz, what are you doing up so early?" Gemma asked.

"Early? We all don't get to sleep until ten o'clock and only work eight seconds a day," Liz teased.

"Ten o'clock my naturally born cowgirl ass! I rode that demon of a horse last night and didn't even stick around for the after-party and drove until two this morning, so don't be giving me any sass at this time of day," Gemma said.

Liz giggled. "Woke you up, didn't I? Congratulations on another win. Met a blond-haired cowboy yet?"

"Hell, no! I'm going to buy one of those signs to hang on my wall that says 'I believe' and write *don't* in big red letters between the two words. I think you used up all your magic chasing my brother down and roping him for your own. All the rest of the cowboys worth their salt are done gone."

"How about Trace Coleman? I hear he's giving you a run for your money."

"He's got dark hair, dark eyes, and a damn Chihuahua dog. What cowboy rides into a rodeo with a Chihuahua dog? There's something wrong with the picture even if he does make fantastic pancakes and—" She paused for a breath.

"Whoa!" Liz interrupted. "Back up and talk to me. When did you have breakfast with him? Did you do more than eat pancakes with him and his dog? And FYI, I think those little critters are precious."

"Hell no, I didn't do more than eat pancakes with him. And I will not. It would be a definite conflict of interest. He's giving me the stiffest ..."

Liz giggled before Gemma could complete the sentence.

"Okay, get your mind out of the gutter and let me finish. He's giving me the *stiffest* competition I've ever been up against. I swear it's going to take all my energy and concentration to beat him out enough for a place in the playoffs, Liz."

"Okay, then tell me more about the pretty eyes and the dog," Liz asked.

By the time Gemma had finished the story of the dog and perching on the vanity like an owl, Liz was giggling. When she could catch a breath she said, "Now tell me what happens when that cowboy touches you?"

That caught Gemma off guard and she almost told her about the heat and the vibes, but she stopped before she spoke and said, "What in the hell makes you think he's touched me?"

"I can hear agitation in your voice. He's kissed you, hasn't he? But you haven't had sex or you'd be all dreamy voiced instead of pissy," Liz answered.

"Don't be getting your hopes up that your fortune-telling mojo is saved by this cowboy, lady! You are a scam. I'm not going to find a cowboy and I'm damn sure not going to have a baby by then. Last year you promised that I'd have my very own cowboy by Christmas and it would be a forever thing. When it didn't happen, you said that the cards said Christmas and you assumed it was the next one coming around, but it must be this next one coming up. Are you fixing to tell me that it means the one next year and not this one again?"

"The cards said that you'd have a cowboy and a baby by this Christmas, not just a Christmas but this next one. But you've got to work with them, Gemma. You haven't done your part or you'd be pregnant by now," Liz told her.

"It's less than six months now until Christmas. I've been too damn busy even to have sex," Gemma countered.

"Never say never. If just kissing you has got you all worked up, just think about all that wonderful sex you could be having. And you could be pregnant by Christmas and that could be the baby I saw in the cards. It just showed a baby. It didn't say it was already born. The cards are never wrong. Don't lose hope, and you could help the cards out instead of working against them. You've got to have positive energy and think about falling in love. All that negativity is hindering

the outcome of my reading," Liz said. "Gotta go. Your
brother is waiting in the truck for me."

She hung up before Gemma could even say good-
bye. And homesickness set in just as quickly. Gemma
had only been gone a week, but she missed Ringgold.
She missed her little beauty shop where she caught
up on all the gossip from Tuesday through Saturdays.
She missed the Resistol Rodeo down by Dallas every
weekend in the summer where there were plenty of sexy
cowboys to flirt with her. She missed her brothers and
Liz and Austin, her sisters-in-law. She didn't want to
be driving through Montana. She wanted to be at home.
What in the hell was she thinking leaving it all behind
to chase a stupid dream?

When she had left Wichita Falls after the breakup
with her boyfriend, she had moved right back into her
old bedroom at the ranch. But then Raylen offered to
let her move in with him. When he married she moved
again, this time in with her older brother, Dewar, who
would be making coffee right about then. She could see
him fussing about in the kitchen getting the day started
and griping at her to wake up. He was next to the oldest child in the O'Donnell family with Rye holding the
firstborn place, then Raylen came along after Dewar,
and Colleen followed him. Gemma was the baby of the
family and she had learned early on to be tough or get
left out.

She had a special place in her heart for Dewar and
wondered what his future would be. Liz had read his
palm and the cards for him and said she could see into
the past and a woman was there but it was foggy. Liz
had trouble deciphering the cards that day and admitted

she couldn't get a handle on it. Liz said that she wished she could confer with an older fortune-teller because it appeared that she was seeing Dewar in another life, one back when covered wagons came across Texas. She'd said that Dewar must be an old soul. Was Trace Coleman an old soul, or was he just a cowboy living in the modern day?

Gemma slapped the steering wheel. Liz had lost her touch when she married Raylen. When she talked to her again, she intended to tell her that marriage had ended her fortune-telling. Liz and her tarot cards were crazy if they thought Dewar had lived in another life or that she'd have a baby by Christmas.

Gemma thought about all the women who were there when she had her fortune told and slapped the steering wheel again. "Jasmine was there when she told my fortune and I bet the cards saw her instead of me."

Jasmine had run the Chicken Fried Café in Ringgold up until the year before when she and Ace got married. And last month just before Gemma leased her beauty shop to Noreen and went on the rodeo rounds, Jasmine and Ace had announced that there was a baby on the way.

"That's what happened! Dammit!" Gemma swore and slapped the steering wheel one more time. "She was reading Jasmine's future, not mine. Jasmine got the blond-haired cowboy and now she's getting the baby for Christmas. If that ain't the luck? Where's my Irish when I need it?"

Chapter 3

THE NURSE WEIGHED THE LADY AND SHOWED HER TO A room, checked her blood pressure, and listened to the fetal heartbeat. "The baby is growing at a perfect rate. Any questions for the doctor this month?"

The lady shook her head.

"Well, Dr. Joyce will be in shortly. We will begin seeing you every two weeks until the last month and then it will be once a week that final four weeks if everything continues to progress so well."

The lady nodded.

She sat on the end of an exam table and read a book that she pulled out of her purse. The baby kicked, but she didn't put a hand on her rounded belly to feel it.

"Well, everything looks great," Dr. Joyce said as she came into the room. "You still feeling good?"

The lady nodded again. "I feel fine. I just want this to be over with and finished. I'm tired of putting my life on hold."

"You've got a while yet. You might change your mind."

"I won't," the woman said.

The jingle of Gemma's spurs as she climbed to the top of the chute sounded like church bells in her ears. She'd be glad when the whole tour was done because then she'd be back into her old comfortable rut. With the money from the final win, she'd buy a few acres, build a house, and start her own cattle herd. Ranching was in her blood, was what she knew, and she was ready to settle into it. But before she could do that she had to win enough to place in the semifinals and then the finals.

She'd drawn a wild bronc, new to the circuit, that hadn't been ridden more than half a dozen times. She had no idea if he could buck or if he'd come out of the chute like a dud firecracker, all fizz and no pop. She hoped he bucked like a possessed demon and she racked up enough points to glue another shamrock on her paper horseshoe.

Trace was the first rider of the evening and he had a high score of eighty-two points. The rider after him, a tall lanky cowboy she'd never heard about, got eighty, and Coby Taylor racked up seventy-nine. Competition got stiffer with every rodeo.

She measured the rein, jammed her boots down into the stirrups, and prepared for the mark out. She cleared her mind, lifted up on the rein, and nodded. And that's when she remembered that she hadn't touched her lucky horseshoe hat pin. The chute opened before she could even think about putting a finger on the pin, and she found out that she was definitely not riding a dud. The horse was all over the place trying to throw her off his back. The next eight seconds lasted two eternities and somewhere in the middle she stiffened her neck for just a moment and got a minor whiplash. She managed to stay on the big piebald critter, but when the buzzer sounded, she knew that she hadn't come close to winning the round. Her body felt as if it had barely survived a car crash.

When she was on the ground she could hear the announcer shouting into the microphone and the people in the stands were whooping and hollering for her. She removed her hat and did a graceful bow and that set off even louder catcalls and whoops.

"And that, ladies and gentlemen, was the last ride of the night in the bronc busting category. Gemma O'Donnell. Let's give it up for the lady! She came to us from Ringgold, Texas, and she's whipping her way toward the finals. Judges' scores are in and Miss Gemma has just racked up eighty big points. Not enough to take the purse from Trace Coleman, but a good healthy second place here tonight. Next we have bull riding and our first contestant is Landry Winters from Cheyenne, Wyoming. He's going to be coming out of chute eight riding Old Devil Bones."

Gemma waved at the crowd and threw out kisses as she made her way back to the chute to claim her saddle as soon as they got the bronc settled down enough to remove it. She might have lost the battle, but that didn't mean she should hang up her spurs and go home.

Next up on the circuit was the rodeo in Colorado Springs, thirteen hundred miles of long, lonesome highway from St. Paul. At least she had five days between the two rodeos and didn't have to drive night and day.

Even so, the next day was Independence Day, a really big family holiday at home in Ringgold. They had an enormous dinner, singing under the shade trees with everyone who could play an instrument participating, and their friends in and out all day. At dark they'd all load up in pickup trucks and drive across the river to watch the fireworks over in Terral. That had been the O'Donnell traditional holiday since she was a little girl.

She sighed as she sat down on a bale of hay.

Trace sat down beside her. "Do you always pout when you lose? Most people are ready to celebrate at a second-place winning."

"If you don't know a pout from homesickness then I don't expect you'd understand how I feel."

Trace sat down beside her. "Too far to drive?"

"You got it."

"Too much money to fly?"

"Congratulations," she said.

"Because I came up with that profound observation?"

"No, because you won. Groupies will be surrounding you at the dance after the rodeo," she said.

"That didn't sound very heartfelt to me, and I don't do the groupie scene, darlin'," he said.

"Life is what it is, and don't call me darlin'," she told him.

"Stings to be behind, don't it? I was where you are yesterday, remember? Might be there again after Colorado Springs. Save the congratulations until I win the title and money in Las Vegas," he said.

"Kudos will go to me in that final ride, cowboy, so I won't have to congratulate you," she said.

"Don't be countin' your chickens before they're hatched, *darlin'*. What are you doing for the holiday since you aren't going home?"

She shot him her very best drop-dead-and-go-to-hell look. "I'm not your darlin'. I don't count chickens before they're hatched. That was a promise, not a threat, and I'm driving to Colorado Springs for the next rodeo. Are you going home?"

"No, ma'am. It's too far and I've got to be in Colorado Springs in five days to whip you again," he taunted.

She bristled. "Keep dreaming right up to the end, cowboy."

"It's the gospel truth, not a dream. You really are going to pout for days because you can't be home for apple pie and fireworks, aren't you?"

She stood up too quick and the ground looked as if it was coming up to meet her. That's what she got for not eating supper, but hell's bells, she'd been too nervous to eat. And that was another thing she'd done wrong that evening. In addition to not touching her hat pin, she hadn't eaten a rodeo hamburger before she rode her bronc.

"You okay?" Trace asked.

"I'm fine!"

"You looked a little pale there for a minute and your eyes didn't focus. I saw you stiffen up out there and your neck didn't roll with the punches. You sure you ain't hurt?"

"I said I'm fine." To prove it she took off in a fast walk toward her trailer. There was nothing wrong with her that orange juice and a peanut butter and jelly sandwich wouldn't fix. She was not fragile and she would whip his sorry butt at the next rodeo.

"Hey, would you walk a little slower, darlin'? I like the way those chaps frame that cute little butt," Trace yelled.

She threw a go-to-hell look over her shoulder and kept going toward her trailer. Her chance at the ultimate bronc riding glory did not need to be complicated by a cowboy with a stupid pickup line like that. She slung the door open to her tiny trailer and then remembered that she hadn't retrieved her saddle yet and that made her mad all over again. She turned to go back and ran right into Trace. He dropped his saddle and grabbed her to stop the momentum that would have knocked both of them flat on their hind ends.

Her palms went to his broad, muscular chest. His hands landed at the chaps buckle near the small of her back. Her heart thumped in unison with his. She felt as if she'd been wrapped up in his arms for an hour, but it was only seconds before she pushed back and looked up into his dark eyes. For a moment she thought he might kiss her again, but he cleared his throat and stepped away from her.

"You trying to knock me down and break my arm to put me out of the competition? It won't work, darlin'. I could whip you with one arm in a cast. Don't be thinkin' because I let you win a couple to keep the crowds coming that I'll let you win the big one," he said.

"I wouldn't think of harming a bone on your egotistical body, cowboy. I'll beat you and there'll be no doubt that I did it fair and square. I could do it with an arm tied behind my back and eating a hamburger with the other hand while I ride, so don't be letting your quarter horse mouth get ahead of your stubborn mule ass. And you didn't let me win jack shit! I whipped you and all those other cowboys fair and square."

He chuckled, picked up his saddle, and headed toward his trailer. "I'll see you at the KOA campground in Meridian tomorrow evening."

"How did you know that's where I planned to stop?" she stuttered.

"Hey, darlin', I've got a laptop. I mapped out my route too. And that's the best place to stop at the end of the first day."

She stomped off one more time. She'd only gone a few steps when she remembered what he'd said about her chaps and looked back over her shoulder. He winked and she deliberately put an extra wiggle in her walk. Let him take that to bed with him tonight if he liked what chaps did for her butt. Let him have miserable dreams like she did and hopefully it would throw him off his ride in Colorado Springs.

She found her saddle, lugged it back to the trailer, stowed it, and removed her chaps, spurs, vest, boots, and the rest of her riding outfit. Standing beside the sink, she downed a whole glass of orange juice and then made a peanut butter and jelly sandwich. The dust that had boiled up from the arena as the horse had kicked and bucked had settled into the sweaty crevices in her neck. Her scalp tingled from a combination of dirt and sweat accumulating under the hatband. Even her toes felt gritty from the dirt that had filtered over the tops of her boots and inside her socks.

She couldn't go to a rodeo dance in that shape, so she took a fast shower in her tiny bathroom, getting wet, turning off the water, soaping up, rinsing quickly, and turning it off again. If she didn't need to refill her water tank and dump the holding tank, she would cancel her reservations in Meridian and stay in a Walmart parking lot. But other than campgrounds, it wasn't easy to find a place to take care of the plumbing in a travel trailer.

Sitting cross-legged in the middle of her bed, she dried her hair and ran a curling brush through the ends.

The extension cord she'd run from the plug behind the microwave kept getting twisted so the job took longer than it would have if she'd been in her beauty shop at home. She propped up a round mirror between her feet and tilted her head from one side to the other. Makeup or no makeup? Dancing would sweat it all off, but she would look better for a little while if she did. She finally opted to leave off the foundation and only do her eyes and apply a bit of red lipstick.

"Wonder how Trace would like it if I kissed all this lipstick off on his sexy lips?" she said to the reflection in the mirror.

"Oh, no! Don't even go there, Gemma O'Donnell," she fussed at herself.

Kissing him again would tangle things up so badly that she'd never get them unraveled. But that didn't stop her from yearning for him, dreaming about him, and wishing to hell he didn't ride broncs.

Landry rode bulls. She could flirt with him at the dance, but not Coby and definitely not Trace. Even that would mean she was playing with hot coals if she let him distract her. But an attraction to another bronc rider? Lord, that could cause an emotional wreck that would be far worse than anything she'd get on the back of a bronc.

"And that is a fact," she declared.

She stood up, dropped the towel, and stepped into red lace bikinis and a matching bra. She tugged on jeans that hung low on her hips and pulled a rhinestone-studded belt though the loops. Before she zipped the jeans or buckled the belt she flipped through the hangers in the closet until she found a sleeveless red shirt with a lace yoke and rhinestone buttons and put it on. Once she had it tucked into her jeans, she zipped and buckled up and sat down on the edge of the bed to put on socks and her bright red boots. She shoved her jean legs down into the tops of her boots and checked her reflection in the full mirror on the back of the closet door.

"I'll drink with the best of them and dance the leather off every old cowboy's boots. Pout because I can't go home, my ass!" she exclaimed.

She sprayed a mist of perfume on her wrists, on her neck, and a touch in her hair before settling a red cowboy hat with a rhinestone horseshoe on the upturned brim. She laid a palm on the horseshoe on her way out the door. A woman could never be too thin, too rich, or have too damn much luck.

Music was already blasting through the speakers when she reached the arena. Couples were out in the middle of the floor dancing to the band's lead singer belting out Travis Tritt's old song "T.R.O.U.B.L.E." She stepped out of the shadows near the chutes and suddenly a beer so cold that the outside of the bottle was sweating was thrust toward her. She took it, and a cowboy wearing all black grabbed the other hand and led her out to the middle of the arena.

"You looked like a hot pink blaze tonight. Old Travis is right. Trouble just walked through the door when you got here tonight," he whispered seductively in her ear as they danced. "I'd love to be your own personal trouble until daylight, darlin'. Just say the word and I'll be at your trailer door when the party is over."

She had one hand on his shoulder and the other one wrapped around the cold beer. She brought it to her lips and downed a quarter of it before she came up for air. Landry Winter's blue eyes danced as he flirted with her. He had blond hair and he was all cowboy. He was definitely interested, at least for one night, and that could easily turn into several on the rodeo trip. It might even lead to a beautiful wedding when Landry won the bull riding event and she took home the bronc riding money and glory.

But she didn't feel a blasted thing. Not one little sizzle! Hell, not even a tiny urge to kiss him. It wasn't fair! He was giving her his best lines and his best smile and she felt nada, nothing, zilch. He spun her out and brought her back to hug her close to him again. "What do you say, darlin'? I been watchin' you ever since spring and I sure like what I'm seein'."

"Got a long way to go tomorrow so I'll have to pass this time around. But hey, congratulations on that win tonight. You really did well."

The song ended and he dipped her low. "My offer will still be good after the Colorado Springs rodeo. Hell, it'll be good until hell freezes plumb over and the angels are ice skating on it."

"Now that's an original line if I ever heard one," she laughed.

"It's the God's gospel truth according to Landry Winters. And Landry would not lie to a pretty cowgirl like you, sweetheart," he said.

The song ended and Landry thanked her for the dance before he disappeared in a sea of hungry women looking for a handsome cowboy. She scanned the arena to see if Trace was at the dance. She found him leaning against a chute, beer in hand, women gathered around him like piglets hugged up to a trough of fresh corn mash. Her green eyes locked with his and one eyelid slid shut in a sexy wink.

His mouth turned up into a roguish grin that sent delicious little warm waves from her lips to her toes. Why in the hell couldn't she get that reaction with Landry? She tipped up the beer and finished it, tossed the bottle into the nearest trash can, and looked back at Trace. A redhead in tight Daisy Mae shorts, a top with only a bit more material than a Band-Aid, and hot pink boots must've thought he was smiling at her because she ran her hand down his bicep and snuggled in close to his side.

The band kicked into the old Mel Street song "Don't Be Angry," and the redhead led Trace out into the middle of the arena.

"Dammit!" Gemma fussed at herself for being jealous. The redhead was a hussy deluxe, but maybe that's what Trace really liked. And that song and dance about not getting tangled up with groupies might have been one big old bald-faced lie!

"Hello, Miz Gemma O'Donnell," a deep drawl said at her elbow. Half expecting to turn around and find Landry with another saddlebag full of pick-up lines or maybe Coby with his own brand of get-the-lady-to-fall-over-backward lines, she was amazed to see an older cowboy. He handed her a longneck of Coors and nodded toward the center of the arena.

"Want to make this old man the envy of all the young bucks in this place?" he asked.

Gemma sipped the beer, set it on a bale of hay, and put her hand in his. He put one arm around her waist and the other clasped her hand. His movements were so smooth that she felt like she was dancing with her father back in Ringgold.

"You did right good tonight on that ride, little lady. Cash would be mighty proud of you. I called him and told him that you might not have won first place but you damn sure did a fine job," he said.

"Thank you. You know my daddy and momma?"

"Yes, I do. They raise some of the prettiest horses in the world. Me and Cash have stuck many a boot up on a rail at the rodeos. I watched you grow up. Guess you don't recognize me, do you?"

She shook her head.

"I'm just an old bull rider who can't seem to stay away from a rowdy rodeo, especially the dancin' part. I was retired from ridin' long before you was big enough to talk Cash into lettin' you ride a bull or a bronc."

"Well, if you ride like you dance, honey, I'd say you do a fine job. I'm sorry, but I can't place you." She smiled.

"Did all right. I'd be Chopper McBride by name."

Gemma stopped breathing. Chopper was the best bull rider ever to hit the rodeos. He had trophies that the young generation could only dream about and was a legend whose name was whispered in reverence. She stared, slack jawed, like a teenager who'd just been kissed on the cheek by Justin Bieber. Words wouldn't come out of her mouth and she was amazed that she didn't step all over Chopper's toes. Her dad talked about him all the time, but she couldn't ever remember actually meeting the man.

"I saw Trace Coleman doing some flirting from across the arena," Chopper said.

"We're both antagonizing each other in hopes that we make the other one mess up so bad they'll go home," she said.

She'd barely gotten the last word out when Trace's arm brushed against hers as he twirled the redhead away in another direction. Her flesh tingled and a fresh flash of desire flared.

"You are both playing a dangerous game, honey. The vibes, as you young people call them, were dancin' around like water on a hot grill when he breezed past us," Chopper said.

"Dangerous?" Gemma asked seriously.

"Take it from an old wise man. When a butterfly flits too close to the flame, there's bound to be some smoke damage on its little wings. You're playin' with fire when it comes to Trace and he's doin' the same thing. There's a spark there that any fool could see even with his eyes closed. You are two strong people full of spit and vinegar. You remind me of two wildfires comin' at each other. Know what happens when they collide?"

"They hit with a force and burn each other out," she said.

"That's right. You think about that, darlin'. And that's enough advice from an old bull rider. You just be careful and tell Cash and Maddie hello for me," he said when the song ended.

He blended into the shadows before Gemma could tell him that she wasn't a butterfly. She was a tough woman and she knew what she was doing. She scanned the dance area for Trace. He caught her eye, pulled away from the group of women surrounding him, and started toward Gemma. Before he'd gone three steps, a blonde wrapped her arms around his neck and plastered herself against his body as the singer belted out "All Over Me" by Blake Shelton.

The woman was definitely working the song for all it was worth as she wiggled and squirmed right up next to Trace. Her visible panting probably had little to do with dancing and everything to do with all that sexy talk she was putting into his ear.

Gemma picked up the beer she'd set on the hay bale and finished it off while Trace danced with the blonde. Chopper was right. She was playing with red-hot fire and yet she couldn't help herself. He caught her eye again and rolled his eyes. She imagined resting her cheek on his broad chest and another blistering bout of heat dried up her mouth and made her wish for another beer.

When she looked at him again he mouthed, "Help me."

She shook her head. He'd gotten himself into the virtual vertical sex; he could damn well get himself out of it without her help.

The singer went right into "She Doesn't Know She's Got It," a faster, spicier song, also by Blake.

Gemma started dancing and was soon joined by a bunch of other girls. She kept an eye on Trace the whole time. The woman said something and he shook his head so she blew him a kiss and went on to Landry. When the next woman approached Trace he shook his head again, sipped his beer, and leaned against a chute.

Gemma slipped in seductive moves to torment him, but it worked in reverse because every time she looked at him, it was as if he took off another item of clothing with his eyes. She figured if he could heat up the dust around her, then she'd give him a dose of his own medicine. She put her hands over her head and clapped them together, swaying her hips to the beat of the drum. She shut her eyes and let the music, especially the fiddle, become a part of her as Blake sang about a girl who didn't know she had it or how bad he wanted it.

Did Trace really want what she had?

Suddenly the whole arena was blurring and swaying. The stars in the sky were blending together and the moon was getting smaller and smaller. Good Lord, she'd never gotten drunk on two beers in her entire life. And she wasn't even drinking on an empty stomach. The song finished and Trace made his way through the people to her side. His jeans bunched up over the toes of black dusty boots. His plaid shirt stuck to his body like glue, and the night breeze carried the scent of his shaving lotion ahead of him. She rolled her neck. Maybe she had gotten whiplash and it was bearing down on a nerve supplying oxygen to her brain.

"May I have this dance, ma'am?" Trace asked.

She took a step forward and the world did a forty-five-degree tilt to one side. She'd read about swooning in romance books, but there'd never been a cowboy in her past who'd given her a dose of the vapors. The band geared up for a Billy Currington song, one of Gemma's favorites because he said that beer was good, God was great, and people were crazy. Those three things were a given no matter where she was, whether it was at a big family gathering in Ringgold, Texas, or dancing with a tall dark-haired cowboy at a rodeo dance in Colorado.

She wrapped both arms around Trace's neck and laid her cheek on his chest. His heart pounded louder than the drums on the stage.

She'd only had two beers; she could not be drunk,

but she could not focus on anything but the beating of his heart. She'd been drunk before and suffered from hangovers. She'd cried in her beer, she'd giggled in her whiskey, but she'd never felt like she was floating.

She looked up at Trace and his eyes began to blur. His lips looked so delicious and his dark hair so soft. And then everything started slipping away. She opened her eyes wide and tried to get her legs to support her, but nothing worked. Everything went black and she sank into a deep black hole.

Chapter 4

TRACE HAD NEVER SEEN ANYONE PASS OUT AS COLD AS Gemma. He scooped her up and her face lolled against his chest, her arms flailed out limply, and her legs hung as if she had no bones in her body. He wasn't totally sure what to do next. Call the rodeo doctor? Take her to her trailer to sleep it off?

The song ended and another one started. Dancers changed partners quickly or else kept the one they had and the crowd began to sway and move again. No one noticed him carrying Gemma away from the arena lights and into the darkness. And she damn sure didn't wake up.

He sniffed the night air as he headed toward his trailer. Her exotic perfume covered up the smell of alcohol. She must've started knocking them back right after her ride because there was no way she could have gotten to the pass-out drunk stage on just two beers.

He shooed Sugar back away from the door and carried Gemma straight to his bed. She mumbled something when he carefully laid her down, but he couldn't understand a word. He pushed her hair back away from her face to fan out like a halo on the pillow. But to think that she looked like an angel lying there would be stretching the imagination. Gemma was hard as nails, spicier than Cajun cooking, and was by far the sassiest woman he'd ever met.

He sat down on the edge of the bed and leaned over to whisper in her ear, "Hey, Gemma, wake up!"

Nothing. Not even a rolling flicker behind her eyelids.

If she hadn't been stone cold drunk, she would have risen up off that pillow and scorched the hair off his chest with a fiery hissy fit. And then she'd do that sexy little wiggle stomp dance out of his trailer, slam the door hard enough to rattle Sugar's teeth, and throw looks off her shoulder that would blister the paint off his trailer.

He tried another angle. "Sweetheart, you were damn good in bed, but it's time to go home now. I don't let women sleep in my bed after sex no matter how good it is."

Nada. Not even a break in her breathing.

He looked down at the Chihuahua sitting beside the bed. "Sugar, I can't believe a woman who can ride a bronc like she does would pass out after two beers. I figured with her Irish blood, she could drink all of us cowboys under the table and then dance on the bar to celebrate."

Sugar whimpered and climbed the steps at the end of the bed. She eased up to the pillow and sniffed Gemma's face. Then she started at her chin and slurped all the way to her hairline in one big lick. Still Gemma didn't move a muscle.

"She's out, Sugar. Dropped like a light. Never seen anything quite like it, and it's a good thing that I was there or she'd be stretched out in the dirt. Whoa! Hold the hosses! She's not drunk. She'd be holding her head over a toilet if she was that drunk. She's drugged."

He lifted her hand and dropped it. It fell back on the bed with a thud. He did the same with her leg and got the same result.

"Somebody drugged her beer while she was dancing with Chopper. I saw her set it down on a bale of hay. That's why she's out so deep. I'm glad I was the one dancing with her. No tellin' where she'd be if I hadn't been. You mind sharing your pillows with her tonight?" he asked Sugar.

The tiny dog curled up next to Gemma, and Trace eased off the bed. He looked back over his shoulder at her before he kicked his boots off and stepped into the shower for the second time that evening. He left the door open just in case she roused and started kicking and screaming.

Afterwards he put on a pair of cotton knit lounging pants, and then stretched out on the bed next to her and Sugar. He laced his hands behind his head and thought about everything that had happened since he started the trip. It had already been an experience of firsts: his first time competing against a woman, first time seeing someone drugged, first time having his socks knocked off by a kiss.

He was thirty-two years old and had been dating since he was sixteen. He'd had relationships and almost married a couple of times. But there was something different about what was going on with him and Gemma. And there was damn sure something different in the way her kisses affected him.

This was his third rodeo circuit, and he hoped that old adage about the third time around being the charm was the gospel truth. Two years before he'd made his first attempt at winning enough money to buy the ranch and he'd steered clear of the rodeo groupies. He didn't even make the final cut that year, but he did find out the groupies had bets going about which one would get into his trailer first and how long she'd keep his attention. Ava hadn't done any betting, but she'd made it past the front door of his trailer in Lovington, New Mexico. That was less than a year ago, but looking back, it seemed like it never happened at all. She'd appeared out of nowhere at the dance after the rodeo. Her tight jeans and boots were brand spanking new and she didn't know how to two-step, but she was willing to learn. She hadn't known how to drink whiskey, but she'd learned to do that, too, that weekend. And when the band sang Conway Twitty's old song called "Tight Fittin' Jeans," she'd hugged up to him like a real cowgirl.

"This is the story of my life. I'm used to wearing pearls and riding in limos, but this weekend I'm out to see what it is about you cowboys that turns a woman into a hormonal fool. Got to admit, it wouldn't take a lot to turn me right now," she'd said.

He'd told her that that was the craziest come-on line he'd ever heard. The next morning he had awakened to those new jeans and boots lying beside his bed. One wild night had stretched into a weekend.

On Monday morning after breakfast she had dressed in her jeans and boots and told him, "It was fun, cowboy. I guess the fuss about you cowboys is well earned. I'm not disappointed, but it was just for one weekend. Now like that singer said the other night, I'm goin' back to my own world and you can stay in yours." She had shut the door behind her and he'd never seen her again.

He hadn't loved Ava; hell, he didn't even know her last name. He didn't have her phone number and he didn't want to see her again. He wished it had never happened. There should be something between a man and woman other than a bottle of expensive whiskey and too many beers to count before they went to bed.

He'd made it to the finals that year but wrecked in the Las Vegas ride. So one year he had stayed away from rodeo sex. The next year he'd had one weekend of it. Neither year had been a good one.

He looked over at Gemma again and wondered what this year, the third one and supposedly the charm, would bring. Neither Ava, nor the two women he'd fancied himself in love with, made his mouth go dry and his heart do double time like Gemma O'Donnell. She couldn't begin to understand how important it was to him to win that title and the money that went with it. He'd worked for his Uncle Teamer for the better part of ten years, and Teamer had offered to sign the ranch over to him lock, stock, and barrel.

"I haven't got kids and you've been like a son to me, Trace. Let me give you this land and cattle. Your grandpa left it to me so it's rightfully yours," he'd said.

"There are three more male cousins who deserve this as much as I do. I'll buy it, but I won't take it free of charge," Trace had told him.

Winning the bronc riding event in Vegas would give him the rest of the money he needed to make that happen. Gemma O'Donnell just wanted the glory and she could get that another year. He'd even sit in the crowd and cheer for her the next year, but this year belonged to Trace Coleman.

Sugar roused and looked at the woman lying on her pillow.

Trace shook his head slowly. "Wild horses couldn't

wake her up. But I will guaran-damn-tee that come morning that Irish beauty is going to wake up cussin' mad."

Gemma's arms were still beside her, her hair fanned out on the pillow, and her boot toes pointed straight up. She looked so much like a corpse that he checked her pulse to make sure she was alive.

"Hey!" he yelled again, but she didn't move.

"Gemma!" he yelled louder, and Sugar growled at him.

He tucked a strand of hair behind her ear so he could see her face. He liked her better when her pretty green eyes were wide open. If she was happy, they dazzled. If she was mad, dark storm clouds brewed in them.

He fell asleep pondering over what he'd see in those green eyes if they suddenly snapped open and saw him lying beside her. Would they go all soft and dreamy, or would a class five tornado come streaming out of them?

Gemma awoke to the aroma of coffee and bacon. Bless her brother Dewar's heart; he'd gotten up early and cooked. It must be Sunday morning because that was the only day of the week he'd even consider making breakfast. Her eyes snapped open and she sat straight up, grabbed her aching head, and fell backwards on the bed. Good God Almighty, what in the hell had she done the night before? She remembered a rodeo, so she and Dewar must have gone down to Mesquite, Texas. She could remember hearing the crowd whooping and hollering.

She drew her brows together in a deep frown and groaned. Her head throbbed like a son of a bitch. What in the hell had she drunk? She felt like she'd fallen into a vat of pure white lightning and sucked half of it down while trying to get out. She remembered riding. Was it the mechanical bull or a bronc? There was a beer when she first got to the dance and one after that, but when did she start drinking the hard stuff?

She distinctly remembered settling into the saddle and nodding at the clowns to open the gate. So she rode a bronc and then what? Why didn't Dewar stop her from getting so drunk that she'd pass plumb out? Some brother he was.

She eased one eye open, then realized she was not in her bed at home, and she wasn't even at Liz and Raylen's house, either.

What in the hell had she done? And worse yet, who did she do it with?

She snapped her eyelid shut and took a deep breath. Just that much effort shot an extra bolt of pain into her head. She reached up to grab it, but her arms felt like they were encased in concrete.

Shit! That must've been some raw liquor, she thought.

She remembered Trace Coleman having more points than she did and how disappointed she had been. She had taken a shower and changed for the rodeo dance. Someone had put a beer in her hands and she'd finished it quickly, then there had been dancing and another beer and that's where everything came to a screeching halt.

There's no way two beers put me on my butt. I can hold my own against three older brothers and I can out-drink my sister Colleen. How did I get home and into bed? Did I die and is this eternity? If I did, it has to be hell. But I can't be dead. My head hurts too bad for me to be dead.

She wiggled her toes to find them still restricted in

boots. She ran a hand down her side. She was still fully dressed. She opened both eyes even though the light hurt. Nothing. She was not at home in her trailer, so where was she? She didn't recognize a single thing. A soft whimper on the pillow beside her caused her to turn her head just in time for a doggy tongue to lick her face from chin to eyelid.

Where did Sugar fit into the picture? Nothing made a bit of sense. She shut her eyes again against the harsh bright light coming through the window and tried to think. Doggy breath. The aroma of bacon and coffee. Someone humming an old George Strait tune "Famous Last Words."

Holy Mother of God! She was in Trace's trailer. He was happy and cooking breakfast and she was in his bed. What in the hell had she done?

And he's humming about the famous last words of a fool? What did I say? Am I the fool?

She forced her eyes open one more time and looked down the length of the bed. He was putting plates on the table. He was every bit as sexy in those knit pajama bottoms as he was in tight-fitting jeans and chaps.

Shut up thinking like that! Try to think about what happened after that second beer.

He turned around and waved. "Good morning. I thought the smell of food might wake you up. I tried everything else but nothing worked."

What all did "everything else" cover anyway?

Gemma eased to a sitting position and checked one more time. Yep, she was fully dressed, complete with her boots still on her feet.

Trace carried a cup of coffee to the bed and put two

aspirin in her hand. "Something for the headache and to wake you. We've got more than four hundred miles to go before the end of the day."

She popped the pills in her mouth and washed them down with stout coffee. "What happened?" she whispered hoarsely.

"Two beers." He chuckled.

"Impossible."

He sat down on the edge of the bed. "I think someone drugged your beer. You left it sitting on a hay bale while you were dancing and when you finished it off, you passed out while we were dancing."

She handed him the coffee and held her head with both hands. "Well, that was stupid. I know better."

But you were watching me dance and your eyes made me all hot. Did I tell you that before I passed out?

"God, it even hurts to think. Who did it?"

"The last person I saw you dancing with was Chopper, but he wouldn't drug you. I wouldn't put it past Coby. He's pretty wild and he's had his eye on you."

"I can't remember anything after dancing to a fast song in a group of cowgirls. If that sumbitch doped me, he's in big trouble," she said.

Trace sat down on the edge of the bed. "You remember that much?"

"I remember dancing and waking up right here. What did I say or, worse yet, do?"

Trace chuckled. "You slept. I'd like to hold it over your head that you said something terrible or did something sexy, but you didn't. You just slept like you were drugged. You finished that dance in the group and downed your beer. I asked you to dance with me and you barely made it past the end of the song before you were out. I would have put you to bed in your trailer, but it I didn't know what might happen if I did, so I brought you here."

She mumbled, "Thank you."

He handed her the coffee and she sipped it. It did help erase the bitter, nasty taste in her mouth. If she ever figured out what sorry bastard drugged her beer, she fully well intended to repay the favor. Only he wouldn't wake up fully dressed in a bed with a Chihuahua licking his face. He'd wake up staked out spread eagle and naked on a fire ant bed. If he wanted a hot bed, then by damn she'd give him one.

She slung her legs over the side of the bed. The room did a couple of fast spins before it slowed down.

"Need some help there?"

"No, I can do it," she declared. She set the coffee on the end table and held on to the wall. Her legs were rubbery at first but they finally supported her and she took a couple of feeble steps toward the table.

Trace slung his legs over the bed toward the other side and followed her. Knowing he was back there to catch her if she fell gave her confidence and determination to make it to the table without help. She slid into the booth and sighed.

"This is miserable," she said.

"Think you can drive? We could stay right here until tomorrow," Trace said.

We could stay here? she thought. *Where did that "we" business come from?*

"This coffee and aspirin are helping. Once I eat something I'll be fine," she said.

"Your eyes still look dazed," he said.

"It's a crazy feeling not knowing what in the devil happened. I keep trying to remember something past the dance and I can't," she said.

He put a plate in front of her with three fried eggs, bacon, and two pieces of toast on the side and refilled her coffee cup before he carried a second plate to the table and joined her.

She picked up a piece of bacon with her fingers and ate it. It was crispy enough to crackle when she bit a piece off and it had been smoked to just the right flavor.

"I love breakfast food," she said.

"Me too. Good breakfast starts the day out right. Good supper ends it. Dinner can be a quick sandwich or leftovers from the night before," he said.

She cut up the eggs. "Just right. Over easy, whites done."

"Thank you, ma'am." He grinned. "That proves it, Gemma. You were drugged for sure. If you had a hangover, you damn sure wouldn't be eating greasy fried eggs."

She looked across the table at Trace but didn't nod in agreement. Moving her head still hurt. "You got that right. First time I ever got drunk enough to have a hangover, I didn't even want to eat a piece of dry toast."

Trace smiled again. He had a killer smile and dreamy eyes, and words could not begin to describe his body or his slow Texas drawl. He could ride a bronc and talk about horses, ranching, and rodeos, and could cook too. Why in the hell wasn't he married?

"What time is it?" she asked.

He glanced toward the clock on the microwave and her gaze followed his. It was seven thirty. If they were on the road at eight, they'd pull into the campground at five that afternoon. That should give her plenty of time to cook the traditional holiday supper before the fireworks show started at dark.

"I'll follow you today," he said. "And I need your cell phone number so we can keep in touch about stopping for food and potty breaks."

"You don't have to. I can take care of myself."

He chuckled.

She gave him the meanest look she could conjure up with a headache.

He raised both palms. "Hey, you want to go it on your own just say the word, darlin'. I'm just offering since you're not runnin' on all eight cylinders today."

"It's getting better," she grumbled. "But I'll take you up on the offer. And I'll even make supper to pay you back for protection and breakfast."

He raised an eyebrow. "You cook?"

She met his gaze without blinking. "You think I can't?"

"You want a fight? I can deliver it." He growled but his eyes were teasing instead of angry.

"No, I'm too messed up to fight. You'd win and then I'd hate myself. Yes, I cook," she answered between bites.

"What are you planning?"

"It's the Fourth of July. We'll have steaks on the grill at the campground, corn on the cob, and maybe summer goulash if I can find a fruit stand along the way."

"Summer goulash?" he asked.

"That would be potatoes, squash, onions, and tomatoes or whatever fresh vegetables I can find at a stand all put together in some foil and grilled with the steaks. And watermelon for dessert."

He polished off the rest of his omelet and smeared

grape jelly on the last piece of his toast. "Sounds like a meal fit for a king who just rescued the princess."

"Darlin', I'm not the princess. I'm the queen and I intend to have the crown in Vegas," she told him.

He leaned across the table until their noses were only inches apart. "Miss O'Donnell, to get that crown you are going to have to get past me."

"I can do it." Her green eyes locked with his brown ones.

He slowly straightened his back and picked up his coffee cup.

She was disappointed. She was so sure that he would kiss her that she could already taste the coffee on his lips. She felt cheated and then she was angry at herself for wanting him to kiss her at all.

"I believe that *you think* you can beat me," he said.

"I believe that *you think* I can't." She slid out of the booth. The room didn't sway and her feet were on solid ground once again.

"I guess we'll see what happens in the next five months."

"And like I told you before, one of us is going to be very happy. Thank you for breakfast. I'll be ready to leave in thirty minutes," she said.

The room seemed smaller when he slid out of the booth. Six feet two inches of a bronc rider took up a lot of real estate, especially in a small trailer. "I'll follow you. If you start feeling light-headed or sick just pull over and we'll stop earlier than the campground. We've got five days to get to Colorado Springs. We don't have to hurry."

He opened the door for her and followed her out into the bright sunlight. "Going to be another hot one. Thank goodness for air-conditioning."

She turned around and smiled up at him. "Amen."

His arms gathered her close to him and she barely had time to close her eyes before his lips had found hers in a searing kiss that came close to frying her underpants.

Tongue met tongue in a fiery mating dance, and their bodies pressed tightly together as if closeness would ease the aching pain brought on by steaming hot kisses. One kiss grew to two with the last one lingering on and on. Yet it ended too soon, and when he stepped back she had to get her bearings quickly or she would have fallen forward into his arms again.

"See you when we stop for lunch." He picked up her hand and wrote his phone number on her palm. "That's in case you need to call me."

He quickly disappeared back into his trailer.

Words would not come out of her swollen and hot mouth. And her hand was every bit as warm as her lips. So that first impromptu kiss hadn't created an oozy feeling down deep in her gut because of an adrenaline rush; she really was attracted to the cowboy.

"Dammit to hell on a rusty poker," she exclaimed.

With shaking hands, she fished her key from the pocket of her tight jeans and unlocked the door into her own trailer. Once inside, she threw herself backwards on the bed and stared at the ceiling.

She could not be involved with Trace. She couldn't let him kiss her again. It would be like sleeping with the enemy, and she'd never know if he was playing her or if he was seducing her with those blistering kisses just to mess up her head so she'd wreck at every rodeo. Or was he as attracted to her as she was to him? Either way, she'd never know the absolute truth.

She'd leased her beauty shop and given up a year of her life for this circuit round. No matter how much her heart whined for more kisses and a taste of what Trace would be like in bed, the answer was no. Her heart could get over it. It could not have both, and there'd be lots of cowboys in her future. The glory of the Vegas win was a one-time shot.

"I mean it!" she mumbled as she reached down and undid her belt. Then she sat up, undressed completely, padded to the tiny bathroom, took a quick shower, and washed her hair. She slipped into panties and a bra, a pair of jean shorts with frayed edges, sandals, and a yellow cotton top with spaghetti straps.

She'd locked the door securely and was on her way to get inside her truck when she saw Trace bringing Sugar back from a walk. She'd never get used to seeing a big tough cowboy with a little bitty dog prancing along beside him.

"Ready?" Trace asked.

"Are you?"

"Soon as I get in the truck. You go on first and I'll follow you," he said.

She nodded and settled into the pickup seat, belted up, and started the engine.

How could he act as if nothing had happened between them? It must be a man thing. Her insides were a pile of mush and her brain was barely functioning. She wanted to follow him back into the trailer and finish what they'd started with that kiss and be done with it. Maybe a good romp in the sheets *would* put an end to the fire.

Trace settled Sugar on her pillow in the passenger's seat of his black pickup truck, fired up the engine, and waited until he saw Gemma expertly back her trailer up and slowly pull away from the rodeo grounds. He fell in behind her and wished she was right there in the truck with him instead of looking at her license plate.

"Damn woman, anyway!" he said to Sugar. "Her lips are even softer than I thought they'd be, and the way she fit into my arms was like she belonged there. But I can't do it, Sugar. We can be friends and traveling buddies, but no more of those hot kisses. Besides, she might be trying to mess me up so she can have her glory ride and be the second woman to win the title. She's got two strikes against her. She's way out of my league and I could never trust her."

He was still arguing like a prosecution lawyer going after a guilty conviction when she signaled that she was getting off at the next exit. He was surprised to see that the whole morning had passed and it was lunchtime. He'd give her credit for one thing: she didn't piddle around when it came to getting from one place to the next. They'd put in two hundred and fifty miles since they left the rodeo grounds.

She was out of her vehicle and jogging toward the door before he could get Sugar's leash snapped and take her to the doggy section of the truck parking area. By the time Sugar had sniffed every blade of grass and chased a grasshopper out from under a rock, Gemma was back.

"Tell me what you want and I'll order for both of us. We can eat while we drive."

"Slave driver."

"Yep, I am. Now give me your order. I only allow thirty minutes for eating and then it's back on the road."

"You really are a slave driver," he said.

"Keep up or stay out of my way," she teased.

"I want two cheeseburgers with everything on them, a double order of fries, a chocolate shake, and a cup of coffee," he said.

She looked at her watch. "I'll take care of the orders and then watch Sugar while you have a potty break."

"Bossy as hell, ain't you?"

"I prefer to think of it as highly acute organizational skills."

"That's just fancy talk for bossy," he argued.

"Words are words. I'll order and be right back."

He watched her trot back inside. She looked just as good in those cutoff shorts as she did in tight jeans. It was going to be a long, long five months.

Chapter 5

THE SERIES OF SIGNS HUNG ON THE BARBED WIRE FENCE like the old Burma Shave signs years before. Fruit Stand Ahead. Watermelon. Okra. Peaches. Squash. Tomatoes. Souvenirs. One mile. Don't miss it. Exit now.

Gemma slapped on the signal for the exit, slowed down, and checked the rearview to be sure Trace was aware that she was turning off. It was bigger than the roadside stands in Texas where someone threw a tarp over a couple of folding tables or else over the bed of their pickup truck. It was a permanent pavilion with rows and rows of fresh fruit plus souvenirs and home-made furniture.

Trace pointed as they walked toward the building. "Hey, look at that picnic table."

"Howdy, folks," the man behind the counter said.

"Hello. You mind if we bring the dog in?" Trace asked.

"Long as it stays on that leash or you carry it. Them little ones is meaner and faster than the big ones most of the time," he said.

Trace held up the leash and the man nodded.

"Make you a good deal on one of them picnic tables. I'm trying to sell them before the new stuff gets here," the man said.

"They are beautiful, but I'm too far from home to buy one now," Trace said.

The man nodded.

Trace looked over his shoulder at Gemma. "I see a Coke machine over there. Want something to drink?" Trace asked.

"Cold root beer sounds pretty good."

He started for the machine and Sugar pulled against the leash to go outside. "I'll have to get it later. She's getting desperate. I'll let her run in the grass out by the trucks and then come help you carry your bags out."

Gemma understood Sugar's desperation. She looked around, saw a ladies room sign at the back of the place, and headed straight for it. It didn't have a bit of air-conditioning and felt like a sweatbox inside, so she didn't tarry to check her hair roots or her lipstick. When she went back out she found a small cart and pushed it straight to the watermelons. She thumped the ends of four before she found one that sounded right. Then she went on to the peaches, cantaloupe, green beans, onions, potatoes, and yellow squash. She was on her way to the counter when she looked up and saw a swinging sign advertising wind chimes at fifty percent off, so she made a turn and headed toward the back of the store.

She picked up one made of old silver spoons and shook it to hear the tinkling sound as they brushed against each other. She felt a presence and, expecting it to be Trace, she turned slowly. But it was a woman wearing a bright orange and turquoise caftan, sandals, and a turquoise turban on her head.

"I didn't mean to startle you. You were so engrossed that you didn't hear me."

Gemma held it up higher. "It is pretty, isn't it?"

"Yes, it is. I love wind chimes—and hair." She touched the turban.

Gemma raised an eyebrow.

"Cancer, but I'm in remission so they've promised I'll get it all back. I do like that wind chime. Are you buying it?" she said.

"I don't know. It reminds me of one that Momma has on the back porch, but the chimes are horseshoes. I have a construction paper horseshoe in my trailer out there. When I win at a rodeo bronc rider event I get to put a paper shamrock on it." Gemma didn't normally share personal things with strangers and suddenly wished she could take it all back.

The woman smiled brightly. "I bought a horseshoe and hung it above my door. My ancestors were Irish. We're a tough lot and I'm going to beat this cancer."

Gemma smiled. "Can I grow up and have your courage?"

The lady patted her on the arm. "Sure you can, darlin'. Now which one of us is going home with that wind chime?"

Gemma handed it to her. "You are. I'm going to buy that one with the shells because when I win the title in December, I'm taking a vacation to the beach."

"Now that is determination, planning, and ambition," she said. "Is that your husband out there with the little dog?"

"No, ma'am."

"Your feller then?"

"I'm not sure what he is," Gemma said honestly.

"You know him, though, and you are traveling together, right?"

"Yes, ma'am."

"You got to be from Texas. Folks up here aren't so quick to say ma'am."

"I'm from Ringgold, Texas. Little place right across

the Red River from Oklahoma. I'm on the rodeo circuit and I'm bound, damned, and determined to be the next woman to win the bronc riding event in the Vegas finals."

"Well, you go get it! Looks like maybe I need to have your courage," the lady said.

Gemma picked up her wind chime and headed for the front counter with the woman right behind her. "A word of advice from an old woman who should keep her mouth shut. Don't shut a door before you look to see what's behind it. And I'll mark it on my calendar to watch that Vegas rodeo."

"Thank you," Gemma said.

The woman paid for her items and they walked out of the fruit stand together. The lady got into a Cadillac and drove away.

"You buy out the whole place?" Trace looked at her cart.

She held up the wind chime. "Almost. Look at what I bought. It's going to remind me that I get a vacation when I win the title. You want me to take care of Sugar while you make a pit stop? I made a dash through the ladies room while I was in there. Got to warn you, though. There's no air-conditioning in the bathrooms and it's like a sweat lodge," she said.

He handed her the leash and she leaned against the truck to wait. Sugar chased a grasshopper, growled at a bee, and kicked dirt behind her to teach those bugs not to mess with a mean ferocious Chihuahua.

He brought back two bottles of ice-cold root beer and handed one to Gemma.

"Thank you," she said.

"You're welcome. See you in Boise."

He pushed the cart out to her truck, unloaded all her fruit and vegetables into the backseat, and opened her door, picked up Sugar, and then slammed her door shut.

"With those manners, my daddy would really, really like you," she mumbled.

They pulled into the Boise/Meridian KOA at four forty-five. The thermometer inside her truck said the outside temperature was ninety-six degrees, but it felt like it was only six degrees hotter than the devil's pitchfork when she stepped out of the air-conditioning into the blistering heat.

She hurried inside the small log cabin that served as an office with Trace right behind her, Sugar in his arms.

"Cute dog. Y'all got reservations?" an elderly gentleman with white hair and a white moustache asked.

"Yes, sir. Gemma O'Donnell."

"And Trace Coleman," Trace said.

"Oh, I thought you was a newly married couple. I seen it a million times. Folks get married and get a dog instead of a baby. I must have been wrong this time."

Gemma blushed crimson. "Guess so, sir."

He poked a few keys on the computer and looked up, "Okay, that was Gemma, Emma with a *G*?"

"That's right."

"Right here. And Trace Coleman. You'd be the bronc rider I been readin' so much about, right? I hear you done earned a spot at the big one this winter. I saw you ride last year in Cody."

"Not yet, but I'm workin' on it," Trace said.

"Well, I got y'all hooked up beside each other at the end of the park under a big shade tree. You want to give me that dog and I won't charge you for the night." His dark brown eyes twinkled in a chiseled face full of wrinkles.

Trace reached for his wallet. "No, thank you. I'll just pay."

"Oh! A sale table!" Gemma's eyes widened and she headed for a table near the back of the room.

"Things left from last year's stock. I got them marked real cheap, missy," the manager said.

She picked up a tiny dream catcher with a shell no bigger than her thumbnail embedded in the web. She held it up and the peacock feathers twirled in the breeze from the ceiling fan.

"I'll take this. Add it in with my bill for the night," she said.

When they had paid and were outside, Trace asked, "Why did you buy that?"

"Because I wanted it. See the shell in the middle? It's an omen that I'm going to win and vacation somewhere on a beach."

"Okay," Trace drew out the word to four syllables long. "I bet you still believe in Santa Claus if you believe that fairy tale."

She cocked her head to one side. "You don't? Didn't you ever sit on his knee?"

"Every year, and Mother has the pictures to prove it. What'd you ask for when you sat on his knee?"

She flashed him a brilliant smile. "Depends on what year."

"How old were you the last time you sat on his knee?"

"You mean last year?"

Trace smiled. "You really did?"

"Momma has the picture to prove it, but I'm not

telling you what I wished for. It's between me and Santa. He said he couldn't get it on such short notice, but he'd work on it for this year. We'll see if he's really magic or just a man in a suit."

"Come on, what was it?" Trace asked.

"Wild horses couldn't drag it out of me. Let's go make supper. I've been thinking about that watermelon all afternoon," she changed the subject. There was no way she'd tell him that she'd really asked Santa for her very own cowboy and a baby by the next Christmas.

They parked their trucks in the last two lots with a big shade tree between them. Trace climbed out of his truck, shook faded jean legs down over the tops of his scuffed-up boots, and clamped a retracting leash on Sugar's collar. He hitched it up to the leg of a picnic table and let her go twenty feet in any direction she chose. He sat down at the table and stretched his legs out in front of him.

"What can I do to help with supper?" he asked.

"You any good at grilling a steak?"

"You got a good steak?"

"Angus from my brother's ranch in Terral, Oklahoma, and there's a bottle of watermelon wine in there," she nodded back toward the trailer, "from my sister-in-law's cellar."

"Then you'd best let me cook it. It'd be a pure sin if you burned a good Angus T-bone," he said.

"Who said anything about a T-bone? I've got sirloins as big as a dinner plate. I brought half a dozen of them in my little freezer. I thawed two out for supper tonight, and they've been marinating in my secret sauce all day."

Trace wiggled his eyebrows. "Sounds sexy."

She air-slapped him on the arm and said, "Get your mind out of the gutter."

"Where should it be? We slept together last night."

Gemma clamped a hand over her mouth. "We did not!"

"Oh yes we did, darlin'! I don't mind sharing my bed, but a woman has never put me out of it altogether. Sugar and I were glad to let you sleep on the other side, but we did indeed sleep together," he said.

She sat down on the picnic table, propped her feet on the bench attached to it, and stared right into Trace's brown eyes.

"Okay, Trace, what is this?"

He grinned. "I thought you were smarter than that, woman. We talked about the picnic bench at the fruit stand and this one isn't that much different."

"What?" she asked.

"You asked me what this is. It is a picnic bench."

"You know what I'm talking about." Her tone was pure exasperation.

"A KOA with a grill so we can enjoy supper and fireworks," he continued to tease.

"I'm serious."

"Okay, then serious is what you get. Seems like we kinda fell into a friendship of sorts. We are going to the same places, doing the same things, talking the same language, and it's nice."

She nodded. "Okay, ground rules then. Whatever this is does not interfere in any way with our bronc riding. Agreed?"

"Absolutely. I'm not about to feel sorry for you and let you win just because you want your name in the marquee lights for being the second woman to get the title.

And I sure don't give a damn about you wearing that glory crown."

Her green eyes were daring when she caught his gaze. "And I'm not about to feel sorry for you because you want a ranch. I'm going to have that title, Trace Coleman. So now do you want to be my friend?"

"All's fair in love, war, and on the rodeo grounds, right?" he asked.

"Oh, yeah, it is! I'll do anything to break your concentration. I won't play fair, so be forewarned."

He grinned. "And I will do the same thing, so ground rules are accepted. Now let's get supper going. By the time it gets done I'm going to be half starved."

Trace walked into the trailer and suddenly her tiny trailer was jam-packed full of muscles and dreamy brown eyes and it was twenty degrees hotter. He took one look at the paper horseshoe on the back of the door and raised an eyebrow.

"Look closely and you'll understand," she said.

He looked at the shamrocks with the names of the towns where they'd ridden and realized that only the ones where she had won were glued to the paper horseshoe.

She tapped the top of the horseshoe. "And that's where I will hang the big one."

"Or not!"

"No doubts in my mind."

"Or mine!"

His eyes strayed to her bed where the table used to be. "I vote that we take the food into my trailer to eat. What can I do to help?"

"Soon as I get this done you can put it on the grill for a few minutes before we put the steaks on," she said.

She cut tiny newly harvested red potatoes in half and piled them on top of fresh green onions then topped them with yellow squash circles and a slice of tomato before pulling the edges of foil up to form a pocket. He husked and silked four ears of corn, slathered them with butter, and wrapped them in foil and bumped against her at least a dozen times, creating so much electricity between them that every touch felt like a blast from a policeman's Taser gun.

"All done! I'll get the charcoal going now," he said as he carried the steaks and corn outside.

Gemma heaved a sigh of relief. Good Lord, if she bumped against him one more time she was sure the whole trailer was going to ignite into a raging fire that would leave nothing but ashes and a metal framework in its wake. And he didn't act like it affected him one damn bit. Was the cowboy made of pure ice?

She wet a washcloth with cold water and held it on her face for a few seconds, but it didn't help the high color in her cheeks. She threw it into the sink and toted the vegetable pockets and a plastic tablecloth out to the table.

Trace looked up from the grill and said, "Aha, we're eating out here with the flies and mosquitoes, are we? I told you we could eat in my place since you don't have a table."

She stretched the tablecloth over the wooden table and secured it with half a dozen thumbtacks. "You are supposed to swat flies and cuss mosquitoes on July Fourth. They belong to the atmosphere."

"Reckon one of them will tell me what it was that you wished for when you sat on Santa's knee last Christmas?

I betcha that's why that fly keeps buzzing around my ears," he said.

"I'll bring a flyswat out next and you better hope he doesn't land on your ear, cowboy."

"Bring two. Maybe he'll land on your cute little fanny," Trace teased.

"That's a lame pickup line."

"It's not a line. It's a prayer," he said.

"I'm not into kinky stuff," she said and blushed again. They didn't sound nearly so ridiculous in her head as they did when they hit his ears.

"Oh? What are you into?"

"What are you into?" She turned the question back on him.

"You show me yours and I'll show you mine."

She started back into the trailer. "It's not show-and-tell day at the trailer park."

"So how do you like your steak?" he raised his voice when she shut the door.

She poked her head back out of the trailer and said, "Wipe the slobbers off his nose, slap his sorry ass on the grill for five minutes, and bring him to me."

"Rare it is, and you got that line from Pepper in *Cowboy Way*." Trace laughed. "I brought that movie with me. Want to watch it in my trailer after fireworks?"

"Sounds good to me," she agreed.

If her attention was on a movie, she wouldn't think about how much she'd like to kiss him again. Would his lips on hers always conjure up visions of tangled sheets and sweaty bodies, or were those first couple of times plain old beginner's luck?

She remembered Pepper in *Cowboy Way* with

his cowboy hat hanging just below his belly button. Suddenly, Trace Coleman was the cowboy and the hat was the one with the gold hat pin on the brim.

Dammit! Dammit! I need to cool down, not think naughty things that heat me up even more.

She grabbed the wet washcloth, added an ice cube to one corner, and went to work on her face again. It didn't do a hell of a lot to cool her down because she kept stealing glances out the kitchen window at him turning the steaks and talking to Sugar. She tried lip reading, but she couldn't understand a word of what he was saying so she imagined kissing those lips rather than listening to them talk.

She tossed the washcloth into the sink again and gave herself a stern lecture. She opened a drawer and took out a long butcher knife, cut the watermelon in half, and started cutting chunks from the heart into bite-sized pieces.

What would it be like to stretch him out on satin sheets and pile little bits of watermelon on his sexy body? He could handcuff my hands behind my back with those pink furry cuffs I saw at Christie's, and that way I could only use my lips and tongue to get at the watermelon. Dear God, I've got to stop this before it causes me to combust right here in the trailer.

The lecture worked until she started peeling fresh peaches.

These would look pretty damn good lined up from his belly button down, and I could pick them up with my teeth and put them in his mouth.

Fruit was not supposed to turn a woman on, and cutting it up was not supposed to produce pictures so hot they'd melt the devil's cute little forked tail. She cut up cantaloupe and shook her head every time another vision started.

"Hey, can you get this please?" she yelled from the doorway.

He jumped like he'd been shot and turned so quick that he was a blur. "You startled me."

"I can see that. What were you thinking about?"

He smiled. "That, darlin', is my business. Steaks will be done in about three minutes. Vegetables are tender. Are we eating caveman style?"

"No, I've got plates, forks, and even real knives, although if you did it right, the steaks will be tender enough to cut with a fork. Put this on the table for dessert and I'll bring them out," she said.

She'd give up her next shamrock to know what he was thinking.

Hell, no! I would not!

She argued with herself as she gathered up sturdy red plastic disposable plates, plastic forks, two real steak knives, along with a couple of paper napkins, a loaf of sliced Italian bread, and a tub of butter. Her hands were full, but she managed to make it from trailer to table without dropping anything, or drooling when he looked around at her with those damn sexy brown eyes.

Using tongs, he placed a foil package and a sirloin on her plate and turned back to the grill. "Drinks?" he asked.

"Beer or sweet tea?" she asked.

"Beer," he said.

She went back inside the trailer, got two longneck bottles from the tiny refrigerator, and yelled from the door before she took them out, "Coors?"

"Best there is if it's good and cold."

She handed him a bottle across the table and their hands barely brushed, but after the thoughts she'd been having, it was the same as red-hot coals landing in her palms.

"You'd better eat your food before you drink."

"Why?"

"If last night was any indication of your drinking ability, you'll pass out and I'd hate to waste your steak. Sugar might eat some of it, but those are big bruisers. I don't think I could eat two, and Uncle Teamer would shoot me if I wasted a single bite of a good beef steak."

She cut off a piece of steak, put it in her mouth, and chewed. It was absolutely perfect: rare, hot through the middle, and seasoned just right. When she swallowed she pointed her knife at him. "You got this steak done perfect, but darlin', I can outdrink any cowboy, including you, on the face of the earth. You want a match, just call the time and place."

"You are smiling. What's so funny?"

"I'm Irish and we can hold our liquor, and besides, my boobs are big." Gemma giggled.

"What's that got to do with anything?"

"Well, according to Irish legend, it has to do with the boobs. Liquor all goes there before it hits the brain. I've got enough to handle a lot when you add it to my Irish heritage."

Trace's chuckle turned into a guffaw. "Cute story, but don't ever think for a minute that you can outdrink or outride me, Gemma O'Donnell."

"I don't think anything. I know I can do both," she said.

A whole string of popping firecrackers sounded in the distance.

Gemma jumped and dropped a piece of steak on the ground.

Sugar hugged up to Trace's leg under the table and whimpered.

Trace chuckled again.

"What's so funny?"

"You could outdrink and outride me, but a firecracker spooks you. I think that's funny," he said.

"Laugh now. Cry later," she smarted off and changed the subject. "Guess some folks are gettin' an early start on the evening show."

"When I was a kid, my father let me start popping firecrackers before dark. Probably so I'd shut up begging him about when we could put off the fireworks he had bought for the evening. How about you and your brothers?"

"Oh, yeah! We'd do firecrackers all afternoon and then ride over to Terral to watch the fireworks. They rope off the street in front of the school and it's a big show. Ringgold is too small to have its own display."

"Houston has a show that goes on for hours. But I always liked the one we had in the backyard just as well. You mentioned watermelon wine?" he said.

"It is chilling to have with dessert. It's too sweet to eat with a good steak," she said.

Another round of firecrackers went off and Sugar yelped.

Trace unfastened the leash and carried the tiny dog into his trailer.

"Poor baby," Gemma said when he returned.

"She'll be all right. She was already snuggled down in the pillows. This is a very good steak. Mostly I don't like marinades. I like the flavor of a good steak just like it is, but this isn't overpowering. Want to share your secret?"

She shook her head. "Old family secret, darlin', and I could tell you, but then… well, you know what those Navy SEALs say."

"Would I get to pick the way I die?"

She looked across the table to find him staring right into her eyes. "Maybe. What have you got in mind?"

His voice had dropped an octave and caressed her skin as surely as if he'd been touching her with his big rough hands. "It has to do with a whole night in my bed, lots of watermelon wine, and long slow kisses."

"Are you trying to seduce me with words?" she asked.

"I don't know. Is it working?"

Call his bluff! Don't let him get into your head and get ahead of you!

"And what if I said that sounded like a fine idea?" she asked.

"Then I'd go get the wine and carry you inside the trailer to my bed," he said.

"Sounds nice, but poor little Sugar has been traumatized enough. We can't throw her out of her pillows. It wouldn't be right," she teased.

Gemma had had relationships in her twenty-eight years. But the past couple of years nothing had crossed her path that even looked interesting. After that last fiasco she was gun-shy and didn't trust her own judgment when it came to men, but it didn't stop her from wanting a family—not one bit.

Trace gave her another one of his killer smiles. It was almost as heady as the kiss.

"I'll get the wine," she blurted out and escaped again into her tiny trailer where she cooled her face one more time with the wet cloth.

"At this rate I'll wash all my skin off before the night is over!" she whispered.

She stacked everything she needed and picked up the bottle with Austin's label on the front. He reached for the wine and glasses. With very little effort he uncorked the bottle and poured while she set out fruit and bowls. He filled a bowl with fruit, tasted it first, and then sipped the wine.

She shut her eyes tightly. She'd look at the sky, her food, hell, even the ants making a beeline for the edge of the trash can before she let her eyes wander to his lips again.

Trace nodded in appreciation. "Very good together. I usually don't like wine or mixed drinks. I'm a cold beer man most of the time, but occasionally I like a double shot of Jack Daniel's with one cube of ice. What about you?"

"The same. Cold beer on a hot night. Jack Daniel's, neat though, on special occasions. But I do like Austin's watermelon wine, and when we girls get together things can get pretty funny after we polish off a few bottles of it," she said.

"Your smile says that there are stories to be heard. Talk, lady," Trace said.

"Darlin', husbands or wild horses couldn't drag it out of us about what happens on girls' night out."

"Like coon huntin'," he said.

"What?"

"Coon huntin'. When us menfolk go coon huntin' we don't tell anyone what we talk about either," Trace said.

Gemma frowned. Just what did all the menfolk in her family and their friends talk about when they went coon hunting? Damn that Trace anyway for the hundredth time that day. Raising a question like that. She'd never thought about what the guys talked about.

"Gotcha!" He laughed.

"You are a snake in the grass," she said.

"It's not against the rules."

"I'll get even," she declared.

"I look forward to it. It's at least two hours before dark. Let's take our wine inside and watch a movie before they start. We can be cool until it's time to come back out and see all the pretty colors." He picked up the bottle of wine and led the way to his trailer.

She followed and hoped the air-conditioning in his trailer would cool her thoughts as well as her skin. She stepped inside and stopped in the kitchen area. Where was the television, anyway?

Trace was halfway to the bed when he turned to see where she was.

"It's in here," he said.

But her feet wouldn't move. Sitting on the bed with Trace after all the sexy thoughts she'd entertained all day and evening was begging for danger.

His gaze started at her toes and moved up her legs to the hem of her cutoff jean shorts and farther, taking a moment at chest level to get even softer, and then to her lips. Hot liquid want was in his eyes when they locked with hers, something that would not be denied. Or if it was the same degree of heat she felt, maybe it could not be denied.

He set the wine on the cabinet, took a step toward her, and she took one toward him. He picked up her hands and held them.

"You are a very beautiful woman, Gemma," he whispered seductively.

His thumbs grazed the tender part of her palms. His eyes searched hers as if asking permission to kiss her. Pure fire radiated between them. And his lips came closer and closer.

She couldn't look at anything else. She couldn't think about anything else but his mouth and the way his lips parted ever so gently. The kiss was both sweet and spicy hot, sending delicious ripples of pent-up desire shooting through her veins like scalding hot lava.

She wiggled her hands free, snaked them around his neck, and tangled her fingers in his hair. He backed up and sat down on the bed and drew her onto his lap. She thought with every kiss that she'd explode. She tried to slow the process down by thinking about riding broncs, but a picture of him in his chaps came to mind and sparks danced around the bedroom like lightning streaks. If he could control the bedroom scene like he did a bronc, they were in for a long, long evening of amazing sex.

His hands rested on her slim waist, but she wanted them to travel. Up! Down! It didn't matter as long as they went somewhere. She moved back enough that she could tug at the top snap on his shirt and little popping sounds opened it up. She ran her fingertips down the soft hair on his chest and he groaned.

Good! I'm glad my touch makes you as hot as yours does me.

He eased a hand up her back, unfastened her bra, and gently massaged her back from neck to waist. His rough hands felt so good on her skin that she didn't want him to quit the gentle massage on her back, and yet she wanted his hands to move on to touch more and more, to see how many blazes he could start all at once on her body.

It had been months since Gemma had had sex. It was as if the whole scene was being played out in slow motion and she loved every moment of the foreplay. Tracc tensed and pulled back, asking with his eyes if he should stop or go on. She pulled his shirttail from his jeans and unbuckled his belt.

He moved his hands around to touch her breasts. She unzipped his jeans and slipped a hand down inside them. She bit back the gasp when she realized the size and readiness of his erection.

Damn! That old wives tale about foot size is true.

"Are you sure about this?" he whispered softly in her ear.

His hot breath mixed with the deep drawl of his voice added gasoline to the raging fire inside her.

"Yes, I'm sure," she whispered back.

He picked her up and laid her on the bed, carried Sugar into the other part of the trailer, and pulled the door shut. He removed his clothing and boots while she watched. His eyes never left hers, and she couldn't have blinked if it had meant going blind for the rest of her life. He was even more magnificent without all the trappings of clothing than he was in those tight jeans. His chest was broad with fine hair traveling down the V of his body to an erection all ready and willing. His thigh muscles were taut and chiseled, his calves were muscled, and his biceps looked like those of a weight lifter. The whole package was even more than she'd wished for when she'd sat on Santa's lap and asked him for a cowboy. Evidently, Santa or fate, or maybe both, had a really big sense of humor.

When he stretched out fully naked beside her, she ran her hands down his chest.

"God, your cool hands feel like silk," he mumbled.

"And yours feel like coals of fire on my skin," she said.

"It's been a while, darlin'. I won't be running a marathon this first time," he whispered.

"It's been a helluva long time in my world too. I was thinking a nice sprint."

He tugged her shorts down over her hips, removed her silk panties in one long sweep, and then flipped her shirt up over her head. The shirt and bra landed somewhere near the door when he tossed them over his shoulder.

"Ready?"

She gulped and nodded.

The first thrust made her gasp, but he leaned close, nibbled on her ear as he began a slow, steady rhythm, and said, "You are delicious."

She couldn't argue with that line because he was just as tasty. She tangled her fingers in his hair and brought his mouth to hers in a series of sizzling hot kisses as she rocked with him, urging him to increase the rhythm. He slipped his hands under her and cupped her hips.

She'd never experienced such raw deep need nor never known such depths of want. When she couldn't take anymore, she pleaded with him to join her in the climax. He covered her mouth in deep, passionate kisses and she forgot all about wanting it to end. And then he muttered her name and she could feel the tension draining from his body.

"Oh!" she said.

"Yes!" he answered.

Trace buried his face in her hair and all the sun rays in the world were trapped in the bedroom. The romance books lying around her beauty shop talked about sex like that, but she'd thought it was fiction right up until that moment. She'd experienced afterglow, but she'd never experienced it in living Technicolor like what was surrounding her right then.

She nuzzled her lips into his neck. "Is that real or is it the aftereffects?"

"Both!"

"Fan-damn-tastic," she said.

"No, darlin'. It was magic," he stammered.

She put a finger over his lips. "If that was a sprint, I'm not sure we could stand a marathon."

Gemma ran her hand down his muscular back and the scalding hot feeling was still there wanting another round.

Dear Lord, she'd opened Pandora's box. What did she do now?

Chapter 6

TRACE REACHED ACROSS GEMMA'S NAKED BODY AND pulled the cord to raise the mini blinds. She turned over, used his arm for a pillow, and pulled the sheet up over them. A burst of color filled the whole window in dazzling sparkles. Before it had time to fall to the earth in slow motion, the next shower came with a loud pop and an array of red, white, and blue. It wasn't completely dissolved when another crack brought about a purple, pink, and lime green display even bigger than the one before.

"This is the way to watch the fireworks. Lying in bed with a beautiful woman in my arms," Trace whispered.

Gemma looked over her shoulder into his eyes. "Fireworks inside the trailer and now fireworks outside."

A loud sizzling noise took her attention back to the window. "Oh! Look at that one. It filled the whole window."

"I'd rather look at you," he said huskily.

She giggled.

"What's so funny?"

"Do you tell that to all the girls who watch fireworks naked with you?" she asked.

Trace removed his arm and sat up. "It was not a line, and I meant it. And for your information, smart-ass, I've never watched fireworks with another naked woman. You are the first one."

She popped up and drew the sheet tighter around her body. "Hey, don't go all pouty."

"I do not pout, and FYI, I meant what I said."

"Well, on that note, I'm going home. Thank you."

It had been wonderful, even better than wonderful, but now she was angry at herself for allowing it to happen. Having sex with him had not put out the desire but made it even more acute and it simply could not go on another minute.

"Don't thank me for the sex," he said.

"I didn't. I was thanking you for everything else today. And FYI, I don't thank men for sex," she said.

She slung her legs over the side of the bed and gathered up her clothing. Trace propped up on an elbow with the bedsheet covering the lower half of his body and watched her. She was a spitfire when she wasn't mad; angry, she was a force resembling a pissed off tornado.

Her butt wiggled into cute little black underpants that weren't even an inch wide on the side. Watching her slide them up her legs caused a stirring that he didn't think was possible after that bout of sex. She reached around behind her back and fastened her bra and then bent over to shake her breasts down into the black lace cups. His fingers itched to touch them one more time before she put them away. Then she pulled on jean shorts and a shirt.

He sighed.

His toys were all put away and suddenly he wanted to get them out again and play until morning.

"Stay with me, Gemma. The fireworks aren't even over and you could spend the night right here," he said.

"I've had all the fireworks I'd better have for one night," she said.

"Then just snuggle with me," he said.

She bent over the bed and kissed him on the forehead. "Good night, Trace. I'll see you tomorrow."

"Breakfast is at seven in my kitchen. Wagon train leaves at eight," he said.

"My wagon might leave earlier than that."

"And you called me pouty?"

She turned quickly and shot him a drop-graveyard-dead look. "I do not pout and I'll be here for breakfast. What can I bring?"

"A healthy appetite for food and for anything else you might have in mind."

"In your dreams! Good night."

When she opened the door Sugar bounded into the room, up her special stairs, and landed on Gemma's pillow where she turned around several times and then plopped down to sleep.

Trace turned over and watched out the other bedroom window until he saw her lights come on. In a few minutes they went off again. There she was no more than twenty feet from him and yet she might as well be across the whole state. He turned over to see another bright flash of sparkles in the other window and hugged a pillow.

"Sugar, I should put an end to this, but I can't."

The Chihuahua's tail thumped against the pillow.

"Nothing permanent can ever come of it."

Sugar shut her eyes and sighed.

"That's just the way I feel too, girl," Trace said.

He dreamed of Gemma again that night. She'd wrecked in the final ride in Vegas and he'd won the prize. Then he dropped down on one knee and proposed to her. She looked at him the same way she had when they were arguing and walked off with a foggy mist closing around her. When he awoke the next morning, he was hugging a pillow and frantically calling out her name.

Sugar was standing on her pillow staring at him as if he'd lost his mind.

He kicked the sheet off and slung his legs over the side of the bed. "She's going to be the death of me and I've only known her a few weeks."

Sugar meandered down the bed and onto the floor.

"She might be playing me yet, even after last night. She might just be messing with me until I can't ride for thinking about her and then laugh when I lose everything."

Sugar barked at the front door.

"Okay, I'll stop thinking about her and take you out for a walk. And I don't think she's that kind of woman either, Sugar. I'm just damn confused and I hate this feeling."

Trace pulled on his jeans and a shirt, slipped his feet into flip-flops, and took down the dog leash from the hook beside the door.

The dog danced around so much he had trouble getting the leash hooked.

"Dammit! Stand still. I swear all women are trouble, no matter what the species. Can't live with them and it's against the law to shoot 'em," he groused.

He finally clasped the leash on her collar and slung the door open to find Gemma standing there with her hand up, ready to knock.

"Good morning," she said cheerfully.

As if she hadn't been surly the night before. As if she hadn't accused him of pouting. Point proven about his tirade against all females, no matter what the species.

She wore a white sundress and matching white sandals. The sun peeking over the horizon behind her parked a halolike aura above her head, and big white fluffy clouds in the sky behind her looked like angel wings. But the night before Gemma had proven that she was not an angel. She was all hot, desirable woman in bed and hot, mad woman when she was angry.

"You are beautiful this morning," he said.

"Thank you. You just getting up?" she asked.

He wiggled his eyebrows. "Time-wise or otherwise."

"You know what I mean," she stammered.

"Time-wise, yes. But otherwise, it could be arranged."

"Your mind is in the gutter again!"

He held the door open for her, but she didn't come inside. "You bring out the worst in me. Come on in. We'll have breakfast in a few minutes."

"We could do fast food," she suggested.

He shook his head. "We have time to cook. I'll start coffee if you'll take Sugar out for her walk."

Dreams of Trace had haunted Gemma all night. In the last one he had fallen off a bronc, and the way he was going from horse to ground in slow motion, she was sure he would break his neck. Before he hit the earth, she awoke with start and sat straight up in bed. The whole thing with him had to end or she'd be crazy by the time the circuit was finished. The best way to do it was cut it off cold turkey so she would simply back her rig out and be on her way. She'd be sure not to stop at the same campgrounds and double sure not to park beside him at the rodeos.

But if the tables were turned and he was about to leave

with no explanation... well, she had to talk to him just to be able to live with herself. She owed him more than just running away, for the friendship on the road and all they'd shared—and especially since he'd saved her from the sorry bastard who drugged her. She didn't like having to explain, but she couldn't leave without talking to him. So she marched right up to his door and knocked.

She planned to tell him that any kind of relationship complicated matters too much and that this was good-bye. Then he opened the door and his dark hair was all mussed up and he said she was beautiful. She sucked up the drool and opened her mouth to tell him what she had to say and it wouldn't come out.

Sugar stopped to squat in a bed of clover, and Gemma looked out toward the horizon. The sun was an orange and yellow ball sitting more than halfway up on the horizon. She should be seeing it in her rearview mirror, not holding onto a leash with a Chihuahua at the other end smelling every single blade of grass.

After breakfast she was determined to have a heart-to-heart with Trace Coleman, even if she had to shut her eyes so she couldn't see him. No matter who won, this wasn't something that could last. Like Chopper said, it was like two wild grass fires that sent shooting flames halfway to heaven when they collide, but soon they burn themselves out and there's nothing left but dead grass, dead trees, and lots of black ash. If she won she could take a huge belt buckle, enough money to buy her own place, and get out of Dewar's house, get the title she wanted, and take a broken heart with her back to Ringgold. If she didn't, she could take home a broken heart. It was a lose-lose situation.

Sugar chased a grasshopper, checked out a spider, made another wet spot on the grass, and ran back to Gemma with her tongue hanging out. Gemma started back toward Trace's trailer, but Sugar didn't move. She tugged on the leash and the dog still didn't budge.

"You lazy girl. You want me to carry you home, don't you?"

It was the word *home* that finally lit up the lightbulb in her head.

Gemma needed to go home. She couldn't make a sensible decision as long as Trace Coleman was right in front of her, but she could figure things out in Ringgold, Texas. And she could easily be on her way in just a few days. There was a whole week between the next two rodeos, plenty of time for a trip to Ringgold where she could put Trace out of her mind and heart.

She picked Sugar up and carried her toward the smell of sausage and coffee. The mixed aromas made her even more homesick. Her Granny O'Malley would be bustling around in her kitchen that morning and there would be coffee brewing, and possibly sausage since Grandpa liked it so well. Gemma often stopped in when she was exercising the horses in the early morning. If she went home to her regular routine, everything would be just fine; she just knew it!

She opened the trailer door and Sugar bounded inside. "Smells good in here," she said.

She bent down on one knee to undo the leash and when she stood up, Trace was in front of her. He extended a hand and she took it. His eyes locked on hers and he drew her close to his chest. She had intended to use that moment to explain to him what was on her mind, but she could not force herself to move. The back of his hand inched its way down her cheek and her breath caught. His eyes were soft and unfocused, and he brushed sweet kisses on her eyelids.

Her whole body hummed. The night before his kisses had been fervent, passionate, and hot enough to scald the hair out of the devil's ears. That morning they were soft, gentle, and left her aching for more. Finally, he worked his way to her mouth and ran his tongue around her lips, teasing them open for a kiss so full of passion that it made her gasp.

"Good morning. I wanted to do that before, but watermelon wine does not make for decent morning breath," he whispered.

She was breathless, but she managed to say, "Good morning to you."

Dammit anyway! He was everything she'd always wanted. Why did fate have to put him in her pathway at the wrong time?

He took a step back and motioned toward the table. "Have a seat. Breakfast is almost ready. Sausage gravy and canned biscuits. I can't get the hang of biscuits. I can do toast real good, but biscuits in my house come out of a can. The only time I ever made them Uncle Teamer said that I'd best put them in the trash because the government men might come haul me away for making weapons of mass destruction."

She swallowed a giggle. Trace was a weapon of mass destruction. He could destroy a heart and paralyze a brain with his long, slow kisses.

"I'll get the juice and coffee." She busied herself.

The way the air crackled around her and Trace every

time they touched, they needed a kitchen the size of a football field. If the kiss hadn't solidified her decision to go home for a week, preparing breakfast in a trailer dang sure finalized her plans. He definitely was a WMD!

Yes, sir, she was going home between the Colorado Springs and Cheyenne rodeos and nothing could change her mind. Maybe her sister-in-law, Liz, would read the tarot cards for her again and tell her that Trace Coleman was evil and she should stay away from him. Or maybe Austin, her other sister-in-law, who had a famous gut that always got in a twist when something wasn't right, would have some words of wisdom for her. Something or someone at home would put her back on the right track, one in which she was in total and complete control. Of that, she was sure.

Trace put the food on the table and sat down. "Did you sleep well?"

"Just fine," she lied. "How about you?"

"Like a baby," he answered.

She giggled.

"What's so funny?"

"People say that, but a baby doesn't sleep well," Gemma told him.

"Then, yes, ma'am, Sugar and I slept very well. You got plans between the Colorado Springs and Cheyenne rodeos?"

"Why?" she asked and wanted to bite her tongue. It was the perfect opportunity to tell him that she was going home, and then with a week's distance between them, it would be much easier to rearrange her plans so that they weren't constantly thrown together.

"My cousin in Colorado Springs called this morning

while you were out with Sugar. There's a week between that rodeo and the one in Cheyenne. He wants me to help him with kid week on his dude ranch. There's a bunch of city kids coming to the ranch They'll learn all about ranching and spend a lot of time outdoors. I'll be the boys' cabin sponsor, but he needs a lady to be in the girls' cabin. He pays really well for the week. Want a job?"

She really meant to say that she was going home for a few days, but what came out of her mouth was, "Sure! That sounds like fun."

The words were out.

Trace was grinning like he'd won the lottery.

Those damn drugs must still be in her system from the beer two days ago. Never in her entire life had her mind said one thing, her heart another, and her mouth a third. Now she understood multiple personalities. She'd always figured that only one at a time came out to play. The personalities in Gemma all wanted center stage and fought like siblings.

"What do I do? Just supervise?"

"You'll be in a cabin with ten girls. There's an itinerary, but part of the time you're on your own. Like for the craft things and keeping peace between them. That's your decision and no one gets in your way. It's kind of like you are the teacher and principal both for a week. You ever heard of a leadership conference?"

She shook her head.

"My folks are big on them. They even sponsor one in Houston. It's a learning experience that teaches teamwork and to lean on your team members in times of stress or need."

"That's what family is for," she said.

"These kids come from broken homes or no homes. Some of them have a mother. Some a father. Few have both. There might even be a couple from an orphanage and you can bet there will be some from foster homes. They'll be wary, but you'll be amazed what friendships get formed in a week. Lester's been doing this for several years now. Some of his first kids are graduating high school and they write him these awesome notes about how that week turned their life around."

Her heart melted at the softness in his voice. "Sounds like a pretty big responsibility."

"You can do it. They'll love you," he said.

"Have you done this before?" she asked.

"A few times. My cousins make a lot of money with the dude ranch, but kid's week is their way of giving back. Not one of the kids has to pay a dime for their week. The rest of the summer and fall is for adults. This is the only week that he takes in kids. Adults don't need supervision, but he's always scrambling to find someone to help out on kid week."

"I have ten girls? You have ten boys, right? Where are they from? All the same place or different towns?"

"Ten boys. Ten girls. All from inner cities. Dallas. Chicago. New York City. Detroit. Los Angeles. Cities like that. They learn about horses, cows, gardening, ranching, and making new friends. It's a working ranch so you'll be right at home."

She swallowed hard. How in the devil would she chaperone ten city girls? She'd lived in Ringgold, Texas, population less than a hundred, her whole life. Country girls she could take care of without a problem. They spoke the same language, listened to the same music, but inner-city kids. Lord, they'd have her running circles like a dog chasing its tail. What in the hell was she thinking? Thinking—evidently her brain lost the ability to do that basic function when Trace was in the room.

He reached across the tiny table and laid his hand on hers. "They'll love someone like you."

"And why is that?"

"You are independent as hell. Sassy as the devil. And beautiful as a model."

"Thank you."

She slid her hand out in the pretense of needing both of them to slather butter on a biscuit. She could bluff her way through anything, but not while his touch was sending up dazzling sparks that rivaled the fireworks show the night before.

It was one week, for goodness sakes. She wasn't signing her life away in blood forever amen. It would last seven days, and when it was over, she'd ride in the Cheyenne rodeo and go home where she'd sort everything out once and for all.

Trace reached for the coffee pot and refilled their cups. "My three cousins run the ranch. Lester, Hill, and Harper. They are all older than I am but not much. We were like stair steps—Lester was born one year, the twins, Hill and Harper, the next, and then me the next. We're the only the grandkids on my dad's side of the family. On Mother's side, I'm the only grandchild and she's an only child."

"Okay." Gemma wondered why he was telling her that.

"They all three live on the ranch."

"Wives?"

"None of us are married or have ever been married. You have cousins?"

"A lot more than three. Momma is the baby of a big family, and Daddy is the oldest of a big family. The Irish like babies." She laughed.

"So do I," Trace said and then changed the subject. "Your girls will be in the nine- to eleven-year-old range. They arrive in time to throw down their bags, eat supper in the dining cabin, and load up in the two ranch vans to go to the rodeo. After we get through with the rodeo, we'll drive out to their place and start to work right then. You are going to love it."

According to Trace, the kids would love her. She would love the ranch. She would love the kids. There was a hell of a lot of love going on in the trailer kitchen that morning, and the L word terrified Gemma. Just thinking it made her want to run back to Ringgold and hide behind her scissors and hair dye.

Trace pointed to the clock. "Five minutes until eight. The wagon train leaves at eight every morning according to the wagon master."

She slid out of the booth, carried her paper plate and disposable cutlery, and tossed it in the trash can. "What else do I need to do to help with cleanup?"

Trace shook his head. "I've already washed the gravy pan and the biscuit pan. So it's done. Just one more thing."

He wrapped his arms around her and kissed her with more hunger than before. "That's to hold me until tonight."

She wrapped her arms around his neck, drawing his lips to hers for a second kiss. She tasted the remnants of sausage and coffee mixed with just a touch of orange juice.

"That's to hold me until tonight," she whispered.

"God, Gemma, I could forget about a rodeo and just hold you all day."

"God, Trace, there's no woman in the world that would make you forget about the rodeo," she said.

He glared at her, his eyes hard and brittle. "You sure know how to wreck the hell out of a good mood, woman."

"Now if I could just figure out a way to wreck the hell out of your bronc riding, I'd have it made." She smiled.

"You are a witch in a cowgirl hat!"

"You are a warlock in spurs!"

His eyes twinkled. "Go get your damn broom and let's move out."

"I'll be right ahead of you."

They were on the road less than an hour when her phone rang. She glanced down to see that it was Trace and pushed the speaker button. "Yes?"

"Does the witch mind if we make a pit stop? Sugar is about to explode."

"You need to teach her to go before you leave."

"Pulling off at the next exit whether you do or not."

"Oh, okay, but don't make a habit of it. We've got a lot of miles to put in before the day is done."

He chuckled and the light went out on the phone.

If she and Trace had met under different circumstances, they would have still had obstacles to overcome. He was bullheaded and she was stubborn. Not two good qualities to throw in a burlap bag and tie the end shut. But they hadn't met in another world, they'd met in this one at the worst possible time in her life and career. Sex hadn't done a thing to put out the raging desire she had for him, not like she'd hoped it would. If anything it had just made it all the hotter. She mulled over the whole thing all day, but everything was still unsettled when the sun began to set and they reached their destination that evening.

Dusk was just settling when they reached the campground in Rawlins, Wyoming. The small log cabin office just inside the grounds didn't offer trinkets for sale so she paid for her parking space and followed Trace out to the front porch.

Sugar chased a butterfly and Trace leaned against the side of the porch post. "Penny for your thoughts," he said.

"I was thinking that someday my granddaughter will ask me about this trip and how much fun I'd have telling her all about Sugar."

"You going to tell her about the hot sex we had last night?" he asked.

She blushed scarlet. "Trace Coleman! Of course not. A granny doesn't tell her granddaughters such things. Besides, by then she wouldn't believe me anyway. In her eyes, I'll be an old gray-haired woman with wrinkles who never had or even wanted sex."

He held up a palm. "You'll still be hot and sexy when you are old and gray. And don't be givin' me no shit about that being a line, either."

She pointed and changed the subject. "Look at that view. Isn't it gorgeous? But I do miss the trees and rolling hills back home."

"There aren't many trees in Goodnight, Texas. It's mainly land and sky," he said.

"Like Claude," Gemma said.

Trace nodded. "It looks like another trailer is turning this way. Guess we'd better get out of the way."

She stepped off the porch. "Grilled cheese sand-wiches and the rest of the fruit salad for supper?"

"Sounds good to me. You bring the fruit and I'll make the sandwiches soon as I get electricity hooked up. Trailer will cool down pretty quick when the air conditioner gets going, or we can eat out on the picnic table. It's a fairly nice night and I don't hear too many mosquitoes buzzing around."

"Sounds good to me. I've been inside that truck all day. I could look at this view until it gets too dark to see anything."

She crawled into the driver's seat of her club cab truck and drove slowly toward the lot at the back of the campground. They were falling into a routine and there didn't seem to be a dang thing she could do about it. If she opened her mouth, the wrong thing came out. If she tried to walk away from a kiss, her legs wouldn't move. The only thing she could do was let fate have its way and see where it led. Maybe it would grow tired of their bickering eventually and just let the relationship or friendship, or whatever the hell it was, die in its sleep.

She parked in her assigned lot, hooked up to the elec-tricity, and picked up the bowl of fruit. She knocked on Trace's trailer door and he opened it wearing nothing but boots, a cowboy hat held right below his belly but-ton, and a smile.

"Holy shit, Trace!"

"You don't like my outfit, Miz Wagon Master? I styled it after Pepper on your favorite movie. He was skinnier than me, though."

She stepped inside the trailer and shut the door with her foot. He reached out a hand and took the fruit from her, set it on the counter, and tossed the cowboy hat on the table.

She looked down. "I didn't ever see what was behind Pepper's cowboy hat, but it probably wasn't nearly that nice."

Trace chuckled. "Thank you, ma'am. I've thought about this all day, and believe me, it made for a hard day in every sense of the word. And that, darlin', is not a line either. It's the truth as you can well see."

He pulled her close and his hands were everywhere, unzipping the white sundress, slipping it down over her hips and draping it across a chair in the corner, kissing her breasts, sliding her silky bikini underpants down to her ankles, and then working his way up her legs with his lips and tongue until he reached her mouth where he kissed her so long and hard that her knees went weak.

She hopped up into his arms and wrapped her legs around his hips. Urgent, demanding kisses swept her away in their need, and she arched against him, feeling every bit of his muscular body touching her bare skin. He pushed the fruit salad to one side, set her on the cabinet top, and slid into her with a powerful thrust that brought out a throaty groan from her.

"That… feels… so… good," she said in short raspy words.

"Every bit as good as I imagined all day." His drawl was even deeper than usual.

The cool cabinet was against her warm butt. His breath was hot on the soft spot of her neck. The contrast was sexy enough to send her into hormone heaven, but then he pushed inside and the heat was so intense that she thought of hell's flames. His thrusts made her dig her heels in and hang on to his shoulders with her finger-nails. Nothing else mattered but satisfying the want and need engulfing her whole being.

Not rodeos.

Not the whoosh in her ears.

Nothing but satisfaction.

Her legs gripped his hips tighter than they'd ever gripped a bronc. The exhilaration when he groaned something that sounded like her name, or it might have been something about a witch in a cowgirl hat bedazzling him, beat the hell out of hearing the buzzer at the end of an eight-second ride.

Trace carried her still wrapped around his body to the bedroom and fell back on the bed with her beside him.

"Was that a marathon?" she asked.

"It was an eight-second ride that lasted ten minutes. A marathon is longer," he panted.

"Mmmm," she mumbled.

He adjusted their positions, nestling her in the crook of his arm so he could see her face. "Open your eyes, Gemma."

They popped open even though she tried to keep them shut. "Why?"

"I love the color. They are the color of moss on the back side of a tree in the fall of the year," he continued.

She started to say something, but he put a finger over her lips.

"It might not sound romantic, but I'm thinking of a big oak tree right beside my house in Goodnight and that is home. So it is romantic because I'd love to take you there sometime, Gemma."

"That is the most romantic thing anyone has ever said to me." She sighed.

"Sleep or food?" He nuzzled down into her luxurious long red hair.

"Food. Sleep. More sex."

"Your wish is my command. We'll have sandwiches and fruit in bed. Take a nap and dream about sex in fields of clover or maybe in a hayloft and then wake up and make it come true."

"Now that's definitely romantic."

His eyes sparkled and then he smiled. He pulled her into a sitting position and removed a brush from the bedside table.

Her eyes widened. "What are you going to do with that?"

"I'm not into kinky stuff. Plain old foreplay and sex is fantastic enough. I'm going to brush your hair and braid it. It's sticking to your neck."

When all the tangles were out, he deftly French braided her hair into a long rope down her back, secured it with a rubber band, and kissed her right below the ear.

Forget afterglow. Hair brushing and braiding pushed it out of the picture.

"Now you can feel the air on your neck," he said. "I love long hair and I'm a sucker for redheads."

"Trace," she stammered. "To begin with, my hair is dyed. It's really dark brown. And next, I've never fallen into bed with a man I've only known a few weeks before. I just want you to know that."

"Well, I'm sure I'd like your hair any color you want to make it. And I didn't think you were that type of woman, darlin'," he whispered as he massaged her back and neck. "I didn't plan on this either."

Her tense muscles relaxed under his fingertips. "That is heaven," she said.

"*You* are heaven," he said.

So that's what was in Pandora's box. She'd wondered ever since she was a little girl and now she'd figured it out.

Heaven on one side, hell on the other. Which one would still be standing in December?

Chapter 7

SEVERAL OTHER TRAILERS WERE ALREADY PARKED when Gemma crawled out of the truck on the rodeo grounds at sundown. Excitement floated in the mountain air like smoke in a cheap honky-tonk. The smell of dust, animals, and beer and the summer weather brought on what Gemma tagged "rodeo weather." Since she'd been a little girl, she couldn't wait for winter to end and spring to arrive so they could start going to the rodeo on weekends. She loved the whole scene: cowboys, bulls, horses, hats, boots, trailers, long rides, noise—all of it. And she loved getting to the grounds a whole day before she had to ride the next night.

She'd barely gotten the electricity hooked up and was back inside the trailer when Trace knocked on the door and then opened it a crack. A hand slithered through the small opening and held out a beer.

Gemma grabbed it and slung the door open all the way.

He stepped into the trailer. "It ain't Coors but it's cold."

She shut the door. "Where's your buddies? I saw them headed toward your trailer the minute you parked."

"Jealous?"

"No, I am not. I just figured you'd be off checking the bulls and broncs and seeing what mean critter you drew for the ride tomorrow night." She guzzled down several long gulps of the beer.

"I told them we were claiming a spot but leaving soon

as we did. We are headed on out to Lester's dude ranch and let you get the lay of the land before you take on ten girls."

She looked him right in the eye and didn't blink. "Did it ever occur to you that I want to be here tonight, that maybe I don't want to go out to the dude ranch right now?"

"Well, pardon me." His head did a bobble with each word.

You are letting a little jealousy ruin things, girl. Back up and settle down, her inner voice advised.

I'm not jealous, she argued.

Of course you are. You thought he'd come running to open the door for you like the gentleman he is and instead he talked to his rodeo buddies.

Oh, hush!

"You are doing that again," he said.

"Doing what?"

"Arguing with yourself."

"How do you know?"

"Because I do the same thing. Let's start all over," he said. "Would you like to spend tonight at the ranch to get acquainted with the place before the kids come? You can do laundry, unpack, take a bath in a big claw-foot tub, and relax."

"I'd kill for a bath in a big, deep tub. My granny has one like that, so yes, I would like to spend the night at the ranch. And what will you be doing while I do all those things?" she asked.

He shot her his best killer smile. "That's up to you, darlin'."

"And if I want something kinky?"

"I told you I don't do kinky," he said.

"Not even black fur handcuffs and maybe a little watermelon on your body if I promise not to bite?" she teased.

"That's not kinky. That's plain old cowboy sex." He chuckled. "Want to practice right now?"

She shook her head. "Not after that drive we just did. Let's take my truck. It's got a club cab and we can throw the laundry bags in the backseat. In yours we'd have to put them in the back and they might blow away."

"You are changing the subject," he said.

"Yes, I am. Much more of that kind of sexy talk will burn down my trailer and I need it to get from rodeo to rodeo."

His arms slipped around her waist and pulled her back against him. "I missed you today. Short phone conversations don't let me touch you or smell your hair or kiss you."

She turned and he pinned her against the doorjamb with a hand on either side of her shoulders. She rolled up on her toes and his lips met hers in a scorching kiss that sent shock waves to her toes.

He broke the kiss and stepped back. "I'll go get my stuff ready and unhitch the trailer for you then."

Gemma barely nodded. To get her mind off what she wanted to do, she did what she should do and filled a long tubular bag made of oatmeal-colored canvas with sheets, towels, clothing, and the rest of her laundry. Then she packed a small duffel bag with clothing and was crossing the floor when Trace stuck his head in the door again.

His eyes slowly undressed her—an item at a time. A wide grin split his handsome face and he said, "Well, shucks, I was hoping you'd meet me in nothing but your boots and a smile."

She giggled. "And a hat?"

"That does sound sexy. Hold that thought for a few hours. Here, I'll take those to the truck for you."

She locked the trailer door and turned to see Trace with his hand in the air. "Toss me the keys."

"I'm driving," she said.

His eyes narrowed and his lips almost disappeared when he clamped them together. "I'll drive. I know the way," he said.

"You can tell me where to make the turns," she answered.

He rounded the front end of the truck and held the driver's door open for her, waited until she was buckled in, and then slammed the door shut with enough force to rattle the windows.

Sugar whimpered from her perch on the console.

Gemma scratched her ears and crooned to her. "Men are like that, Sugar. They get mad if they don't get their way. Be glad that you don't have to deal with little Chihuahua boys who think they are God."

When Trace was in the truck, Sugar crawled over into his lap. He folded his arms over his chest and ignored the dog, which made Gemma even madder.

Gemma put the key in the ignition and started the engine. "Sugar didn't cross you. I did, so don't take it out on her."

"I'm not," Trace growled.

"Which way?" Her tone was cold.

"When you get out of the grounds go south for six miles then turn back to the west." His was just as chilly.

"So you don't like to sit in that seat?" she asked.

He kept his eyes straight ahead. "Not when there's a lady in the vehicle."

"Why? Do you have to be in control?"

"When I'm in the vehicle with a woman, I should drive. It's respect, not control."

"Are we fighting?" she asked.

"No, ma'am. We are having a discussion. When we fight you won't have to ask."

Five miles south of Colorado Springs she saw a sign advertising Coleman's Dude Ranch. She quickly read the directions that said to turn right in one mile and checked the speedometer. At the end of a mile she turned and passed under a metal arch with Coleman welded across the top in big letters. The road was wide enough for two vehicles but narrow enough that she was glad she didn't have to pass a semi or even another pickup truck. Still Trace sat on his side of the truck like a puffed up toad frog. She fought the urge to stop the truck, kick him out on the side of the lane, and put it in reverse.

"Okay, macho man," she said when she reached the end of the lane, "which way now?"

He pointed straight ahead. She passed horse corrals, several barns, and three long shotgun-style cabins near the white two-story house with a wide front porch. Two hounds were sleeping on the steps of a wide front porch. Rocking chairs beckoned from deep shadows, and light flowed in golden splendor from the windows onto the lawn.

"Which cabin is mine?" she asked.

"Menfolk are next to the house, then the dining cabin, and finally the ladies."

"Okay, this is enough, Trace. If you are going to be a jackass because I drove, then get out and go have fun with your cousins because I'm going back the rodeo grounds. I don't have to put up with your pouting shit."

He chuckled.

Gemma didn't see a damn thing funny. Her green eyes flashed anger and she raised both eyebrows halfway to her hairline.

"You are a pistol when you are angry," he said.

"You are a jackass when you are angry," she shot right back.

He held out his hand. "I've been told that before. Guess it could be true. Truce?"

She ignored it. "Do you realize that as long as you call the shots and I play along everything is all fine and dandy? But the minute I cross you, you act like a grizzly bear with an abscessed tooth?"

He folded his arms over his chest.

She did the same.

"Now we are fighting. Want to have makeup sex later tonight?"

The tension in the truck was thick enough that a sharp machete couldn't have cut through it, and suddenly the whole scene was hilarious. They were fighting over who drove her truck six miles. She burst into laughter so loud that it bounced around in the truck like marbles in a tin can.

"Dammit, cowboy! It's not funny," she wiped at her eyes.

"I didn't say anything funny. I just asked if you wanted to have makeup sex."

"I know, but why in the hell are we fighting about

driving? That's a piss-poor thing to fight about when we've got bigger things we could really put to the test."

He unfastened both seat belts and pulled her across the wide bench seat to his side. He cupped her cheeks with his hands and lowered his lips to hers.

"It'll take more than that to be called makeup sex," she whispered.

"Oh, darlin', that was just a teaser. We'll get around to the real thing later tonight. Lester said supper is at eight so rather than having pickup sex we'd best go on inside. Most of the time supper is at six, but he and the twins were making hay all day."

Gemma sputtered. "You did not tell me we were invited to dinner. I didn't even change clothes."

He kissed her again. "You look like a million bucks. Hungry?"

She looked down at her shirt and jeans. At least she hadn't spilled anything on them that day, even if they were wrinkled. She pulled her hair loose from the braid and pulled the sides up with a clamp from her purse leaving the rest to fall in soft waves down her back. She checked her reflection in the rearview mirror and applied a bit of lipstick and mist of perfume.

"Best I can do on short notice. You could have told me this morning," she said grumpily.

"I didn't know it until an hour ago when Lester called and invited us. Then you got all huffy and had to drive." Trace slid out of the passenger's seat and held the door for her. "You look beautiful, as always. Just don't let those cousins of mine take you away from me."

"Hmmph," she said. "You'd have to own me first and that ain't damned likely, cowboy."

Lester met them at the door and motioned them in-side. He was as tall as Trace but his hair was blond and his eyes clear blue. They definitely shared DNA from the shape of their faces and their muscular bodies, but Gemma thought Trace was by far the more handsome of the two.

"Lester, meet the woman I told you about. This is Gemma O'Donnell. Gemma, this is the oldest one of my cousins."

"Right pleased to meet you, ma'am, and thank you for agreeing to sponsor in our girls' cabin this week. Supper will be ready in a few minutes. Y'all come on in and make yourselves at home," Lester said.

"I'm looking forward to meeting the girls, and it's nice to meet you," Gemma said.

"I need to put Sugar in the boys' cabin," Trace said.

"Still travelin' with that glorified rat." Lester laughed.

"Shhh, you'll hurt her feelings," Gemma told him.

Lester smiled. "Take her on down there and turn her loose. Hill has supper just about ready to set on the table."

"Come with me, Gemma?" Trace asked.

"You've got about five minutes." Lester disappeared through a doorway off the foyer.

Trace snapped the leash on Sugar and let her make a couple of stops on the way from the house to the first cabin. He turned on the lights and put her inside and then laced his fingers with Gemma's.

"You do look beautiful, Gemma. I'm not shootin' you a line," he said when they reached the house again.

"Yeah, well, it's dark out here so you can't see what I really look like," she told him.

"Honey, all I have to do is shut my eyes and I can see

what you look like clothed, half-dressed, or naked," he whispered as he opened the door and stood to one side to let her go into the house first.

She poked him on the arm. "Shhh, Lester will hear you."

"Did I hear my name?" Lester appeared from a room with delicious food smells following him.

"You did," Trace answered.

"But you don't want to know what it was about," Gemma said.

"I know Trace, so I'll listen to the lady. We've heard all about your folks up in these parts. Any time you want to sell Glorious Danny Boy, me and the boys will hock the ranch and sell Trace on the auction block as a slave to buy him." His voice wasn't as deep as Trace's, and it didn't have that slow Texas drawl.

"Momma would sell me before she would that horse." The door opened right into the living room, which looked masculine with its soft leather furniture, plasma television, and hefty oak coffee table.

"How much?" Trace whispered low enough for her ears only.

Stairs went up off to her right and doors opened to her left. Another tall blond cowboy came out of the nearest door wiping his hands. "Hi, Trace, and you have to be Gemma. I'm Hill Coleman. Trace told us you were beautiful, but he didn't do you justice. Come on in and set up to the table. Harper will be down in a minute. He had to go wash up a bit."

Like part of a country song on a continuous loop, Gemma kept replaying what Hill had said: "Trace told us you were beautiful."

Harper yelled from the top of the stairs, "I'm on my

way. Don't be startin' without me. Trace will get all the best parts."

Boots made a rat-a-tat noise on the steps as he hurried down.

Gemma looked up at still another handsome blue eyed, blond-haired cowboy and then back at Hill. They were so much alike that she couldn't tell them apart.

"Twins, remember?" Trace said. "Hill is an inch taller and Harper has longer hair."

"I do not, and he's only half an inch taller."

"And there's the way you tell them apart." Trace chuckled. "Harper will always argue that point. I've known them since they were born and sometimes I can't even tell who is who, but if I mention their height then Harper argues and I can tell them apart that way."

"It's on the table," Hill said. "And if you really want to tell us apart, then remember I cooked tonight. Harper does a pretty good job of simple things, but you won't ever get yeast bread when he cooks. He and Trace, neither one could make a pan of biscuits that couldn't be used for skeet shootin'."

Harper led the way to the country kitchen. "Come on now. Stop telling tales."

"So you all cook?" Gemma asked after Trace held her chair for her.

Harper answered, "We take turns. Momma said boys had to learn to cook just like girls."

"You have sisters?"

"No, ma'am," Harper said. "Momma said after she had three boys she was afraid to try for a girl because she might get another mean boy. You got sisters?"

"One sister, Colleen. Three brothers."

"Bless your momma's heart," Hill said.

"She's pretty tough and she believed in boys being able to cook and girls being able to ride a bronc or pull a calf," Gemma said.

"Wise woman," Lester said.

"Pardon me for changing the subject here, but how is Uncle Teamer?" Hill asked Trace.

"Doin' good. He's ready to retire and I'm ready to buy him out soon as I get the money together."

"He's been ready for a couple of years," Hill said.

"Little bit of history, Gemma." Hill smiled. "There are three brothers in the Coleman family. Teamer, our father, and Trace's dad are brothers. Trace's dad didn't take to ranchin'. He's a lawyer in Houston and Trace is the only chicken in that nest. Teamer never married and didn't have any kids, so he wants to give Trace the ranch, but Trace has a stubborn streak a mile wide and won't take it without paying for it. My daddy and momma retired about five years ago and turned this place over to the three of us."

There Gemma sat with three blond cowboys that fit the fortune Liz told just fine and yet not a one of them made her heart do double time.

"I can believe that about a stubborn streak." She smiled.

"Oh, yeah! He's got the worst one of all of us," Hill said.

"Hey, now." Trace smiled.

"Okay, change of subject. We want to make another offer now that we got you here. How about staying on two weeks? Kids one week and senior citizens the next?"

"Senior citizens?" Gemma asked.

"I like the kids, but I love the old folks when they are here a week. The same ones have been coming the past five years. Youngest one is about seventy and they are a hoot," Lester said.

"You could drive up to Cheyenne for the rodeo and come back the next day. That's when they arrive and they'll stay a week. You'd have three days to go from here to Dodge City for the next one, and it's only six hundred and fifty miles," Hill said.

Trace looked at Gemma and she shook her head. She'd had more than one major brain malfunction since she met Trace, but she wasn't going to succumb to any more.

"I'm going home between Cheyenne and Dodge City. I'm homesick and I got to tell you, this supper is delicious, but it's not helping cure my homesickness. Every bite tastes just like my granny's cookin', and I swear these hot rolls are as good as Momma's. Sorry, guys. Why would you need counselors for senior citizens anyway? Aren't they considered adults?" she asked.

Hill chuckled. "Well, thank you for the compliments. It don't get no better than that, darlin'. We were just hoping to hang on to Trace another week. We don't get together nearly often enough."

"Thanks, but no thanks," Gemma said. "Can't stay away from Ringgold, Texas, too long or I get all melancholy, but you can keep Trace if you want. He doesn't have to go where I go or even take me to the airport. I'm a big girl."

Trace snorted. "You? Melancholy? More like another *M* word."

"And what would that be?" she asked.

"Mean. Don't let her fool you, guys. She's meaner than a junkyard dog."

"Are you calling me a bitch?" She accentuated every word with a poke of her fork.

"No, ma'am. I'm not nearly that brave," he said.

Hill laughed. "Man, you done backed yourself up in a corner. You'd best do some sweet-talkin' or we'll have to call the undertaker when she kills you with that fork."

Gemma laid her fork down. "Darlin', you'd best never get that brave or I won't need a fork. I'll take care of you with my bare hands. And I am homesick. I like getting away from Ringgold, but that's where my roots are. I love traveling and the excitement of the rodeo, but what I really like is my chunk of north Texas dirt."

Trace felt the same way about Goodnight, Texas. He'd never want to leave there permanently. But hearing her say those words put a whole new spin on their relationship. She wouldn't ever leave Ringgold. He'd never leave Goodnight, and there was two hundred miles between the two small towns.

After supper the brothers shooed them out of the house.

"Y'all got unpacking and settlin' in to do. We'll take care of cleanup," Hill said.

"He means I'll take care of cleanup," Harper teased. "But you do both need to check the agenda for next week to see if you want anything changed, so get on out of here."

"Thank you for supper, for the cleanup, and for everything else," Gemma said.

Trace nodded in agreement. "We don't mind helping."

Lester shook his head. "You go on and get your beauty rest even though you don't need it."

"Be careful, she'll be accusing you of shootin' her a line," Trace said.

"Darlin', that's the gospel truth. Ain't no bullshit to it." Lester grinned.

"Thank you," Gemma said.

Trace looped her arm into his. "And now we are going."

Once they were out on the porch, he removed her arm and said, "I'll walk down to your cabin. You can drive and then I'll unload your baggage."

"Hey," she called out when he'd gone three steps.

He turned in time to see something flying toward him. He reached up and grabbed the keys before they hit him in the face.

"You drive. I'll walk. I need it after that meal."

By the time she arrived, he'd unlocked the door and her bags were sitting inside the door. She stepped inside to find a long rectangular room lined with bunk beds on either side. An open door at the very end showed a bedroom with a king-sized bed. She headed straight for it. Trace followed her into the enormous room with a recliner, television, private bathroom with the big claw-foot tub that Trace had promised, and a stacked washer and dryer combination.

"This is great," she said. "And this bathroom is all mine? I don't have to share with the girls?"

"All yours," Trace said. He laced his fingers in hers. "Come with me and I'll show you the one that they use."

It was enormous with several stalls and five divided showers with pink shower curtains. Vanities had plenty of outlets for hair driers and mirrors above that stretched the length of the whole wall for primping.

Trace led her back out into the main room where the walls were rough-hewn logs, and area rugs separated the living area from the bedroom space. Two deep leather sofas in a dark brown color, a plasma television, and a computer station took up space on one side. Comfortable chairs and a wall filled with books were on the other side. She wondered which area would entice her girls the most: books or entertainment.

Between the sofa area and the beds there was a small kitchen area with a stove, cabinets, and a refrigerator. She pointed at it and asked, "Do we cook some of our meals here?"

"No, three meals a day are served in the dining cabin. The kitchen is for night snacks or whatever you want to do with the girls, like craft projects or popcorn."

He picked up her laundry bag and carried it to the bedroom at the end, came back, and got her duffel bag and set it on the bed. "What do you want to do first?"

She raised a dark eyebrow. "You're asking and not telling?"

"I am," he said.

"Then I'd like to take a bath in that tub over there. I'd like to lie back in it and not get out until I look like a prune."

Trace smiled. "Your wish is my command, darlin'."

"You've got a wicked look in your eyes."

"You think that big old tub would hold both of us?"

She smiled. "Oh, yeah."

He slipped his shirt over his head and reached out to help her remove hers. "You ever had sex in an old-fashioned bathtub?"

She shook her head. "Not any kind of bathtub. You?"

"No. That makes us both bathtub virgins, but I betcha we can figure it out."

She kicked off her boots and peeled her jeans down

over her hips while he started running the water. When he turned around she was wearing only bright red lacy underpants.

"Nice outfit there, Miz O'Donnell," he said.

"Thank you, Mr. Coleman. I wore it just for you," she flirted.

He started humming "Your Man" by Josh Turner as he pulled his shirt over his head and kicked his boots over next to the vanity. Her blood pressure shot up when the lyrics came to mind. It went up another ten points when he removed his jeans and wasn't wearing underwear. One of those huge Mexican sombreros could have hung on what was behind his zipper.

After three nights of glorious sex, it would be a miracle if she could even stay on a horse eight seconds at the rodeo. Was that what Trace was attempting to do—wear her out and give her too much to think about to win the purse in Colorado Springs?

He dropped down on his knees and ran his hands up her legs from ankles to waist. She expected him to peel her lacy underwear in one long sliding swoop, but he kissed her belly button and then moved around to her hip where he latched on to the edge of the lace with his teeth and tugged them down a quarter of an inch at a time.

Ripples of goose bumps rose up on her body and she shivered.

"I thought you didn't like kinky."

"Honey, this ain't kinky. It's just plain old foreplay. You like it?" he mumbled.

"Mmmm," was the only sound that would come out of her mouth.

When she was totally naked, he picked her up and put

her into the water and then crawled in the tub with her. She straddled him and picked up the washcloth from the chair beside the tub.

"My turn." She nibbled on his earlobe. "You have to sit perfectly still and let me give you a bath before the sex starts."

"You are killing me, Gemma."

"But what a way to go, right?"

He reached up to wrap his arms around her and she shook her head. "It's like a lap dance. You can't touch, but I can."

He stretched an arm out on either side of the tub and gave himself over to her. She lathered his body with soap and then slowly rinsed it by squeezing the washcloth over him until the soap was gone. Then she rose up on her knees and washed his hair, massaging his scalp with her fingertips until he groaned.

"You are so damn sexy," she said.

"Is that a line you use on all your boyfriends?"

"Darlin', I don't shoot lines of bullshit. I state the gospel truth."

But the word *boyfriend* did not escape her. Was that what Trace was at this point? If so, how did she deal with it?

"God, woman, I'm not going to even be up for a dash. Forget the sprint and the marathon," he growled.

"I'm so damn hot that I was thinking about an eight-second ride to start with," she said.

"That I think I can manage," he said.

She wrapped her legs around his body and lowered herself onto his wet erection. She measured the washcloth like a rein and then nodded as if the chute was about to open and they started the ride. He was the bronc and she only had to stay on for eight seconds. The buzzer should've sounded long before it did. Eight seconds soon grew to eight minutes with her meeting him thrust for thrust until it ended in a blast that came close to blowing her eardrums out.

He wrapped his arms tightly around her and buried his face in her shoulder. "Many more nights like these past three and I'll be dead."

"I'll wear black to your funeral and take home the prize in Vegas," she said breathlessly.

"You are heartless," he said. "But remember, after tomorrow night we'll have separate cabins and a whole week of babysitting. Then a day of rodeo and a two-day trip to Dodge City and you are going home."

"Then we'd better make hay while the sun is shining. You ever had bunk bed sex?" she asked.

"No and I don't intend to lose my bunk bed virginity tonight when there's a big old king-sized bed right in there waiting on us," he declared.

Chapter 8

GEMMA FELT THE HORSE'S MUSCLES RIPPLE IN PROTEST when she eased into the saddle and shoved the heels of her boots down into the stirrups. He was ready for action, but then so was she. She needed to win because Trace was ahead of her. Not that it was a given fact that one of them would win that night. Coby Taylor was a cowboy with a drive that could easily whip both of them if they didn't keep on their toes, and Billy Washington was moving up the ranks pretty danged fast. She measured the rein, inhaled deeply, let it all out slowly, and motioned for the gate to be opened.

It was a toss-up as to whether the announcer or the crowd was more excited when Dancer put both hind feet toward the sky and tried to send her into a long greasy slide into the dirt or when he bowed up in the middle and tried a new tactic. It was when he was doing another kick that a fat wasp lit on the knuckles of her rein hand. The stinging pain began and Gemma had to fight off the instinct to let go and slap at it with her free hand. Eight seconds became eight years as she tried to live through the pain tattooing her knuckle. She managed to stay with Dancer all the way to the end, but before the buzzer went off she knew her rhythm had been off and her scores would be low.

"And that, cowboys and cowgirls, was Gemma O'Donnell, our only woman contestant in today's bronc riding event. Give it up for a spunky lady from Ringgold, Texas, who just held on for the full eight seconds," he said.

She removed her signature pink hat and bowed for the screaming crowd in spite of the stinging, swollen knuckle where the wasp had worked his evil magic. Damn the bug anyway. She hoped a wild bull stomped the hell out of it in the next round.

"Judges' scores are in for Gemma."

She held her breath and waited.

"Seventy-eight points. Not bad for the lady beating Coby Taylor by one point! And she came in second behind Billy Washington who had seventy-nine points. Give it up for Gemma one more time," the announcer said.

She waved to the cheering crowd with her hat and disappeared back into the shadows. Granny O'Malley had taught her to make a paste of baking soda and water for bee stings and burns, and she had both in her trailer. She had started off in a jog when she heard the announcer telling everyone that Trace Coleman was up next. She stopped in her tracks and climbed up the side of a chute for a better view. No way was a damned wasp sting getting in the way of her watching Trace's ride.

~~~

Trace checked his spurs and climbed up the side of the chute. He slid into the saddle and shoved his boots down into the stirrups. He tested the rein and measured it to just the right length, lifted up on it, and nodded to open the gates. From the moment they swung open he was one with the bronc: legs right for the mark out, legs back and then forward like a dance until the buzzer sounded.

Had it really been eight seconds? He felt as if he could have ridden the horse into total submission. He slid off the side with the help of the rescue rider to see a standing crowd whistling, screaming, and waving.

"Now that was a ride!" The announcer's voice was more excited than it had been all evening. "I can see why Trace Coleman from Goodnight, Texas, is the number one choice for this year's bronc riding title. And the judges are already done with their tally sheets. That will be eighty-two points for Trace Coleman in the best ride of the night. Give it up again for Trace Coleman, who walks away from the rodeo tonight with an even closer shot at the finals in December."

He waved to the crowd and then headed to the chutes to claim his saddle. He'd barely made it out of the arena when he saw Gemma running, spurs jingling toward her trailer. He took off after her in a long-legged lope and found her standing in front of the small kitchen sink in a hot travel trailer with tears streaming down her face.

"Did you do that on purpose?" he asked gruffly. "Dammit, Gemma, tell me you didn't let me win."

"Hell, no! I gave it my best."

"Then what is the matter with you? You get mad, cuss, and kick, but I've never seen you cry because you lost," he said.

She held up her hand covered in a white paste. "It hurts."

He grabbed it and held it steady. "Is it broken? I'll call the rodeo doctor and we'll go right to the hospital. Shit, Gemma, I didn't know you'd gotten hurt. I thought you were having trouble out there. You weren't as smooth as usual, but I didn't know you'd broken your arm."

"Wasp stung my rein hand while I was riding," she said.

He dropped her hand and wrapped her up in his arms. "How in the hell did you stay on the horse for the full eight seconds?"

"I'm meaner than the wasp." She hiccupped.

Trace chuckled. "Is he dead?"

"I hope so."

"What's on your hand? Baking soda?"

She nodded. "Granny uses it."

"So does Uncle Teamer. It'll take the sting out and tomorrow you won't even know you got bit."

She raised her head and looked at him. "You had a good ride. Congratulations."

He lowered his lips to hers and kissed her gently. "Considering that you came in pretty damn close with a wasp biting the shit out of your hand, I'd say you had a better one." He scooped her up into his arms and carried her to the bed where he sat down with her in his lap. He removed her vest and tossed it on the pillows.

Being there with Trace felt right, and that terrified her worse than a wasp sting ever could.

―――

They stayed until the end of the rodeo and Gemma didn't even argue with Trace about who was driving back to the dude ranch. She had barely gotten inside the cabin when the front door opened and Hill pushed inside with ten girls behind him. Ten sets of eyes scanned the big room, some stopping at the bunk beds, some going to the kitchen area, and one looking right at her.

"Hello, ladies. I'm Gemma O'Donnell. I'm your counselor for this week, and since there is one of me and ten of you, you will find name tags on your pillows."

Hill tipped his hat and disappeared out the door.

"House rule number one is that you put them on first thing in the morning and pin them to the side of your bed at night. That's for me as much as it is for your roommates because I have trouble remembering names. House rule number two is if you have a problem, you bring it to me and we'll do our best to solve it. Now I know you are probably tired so first thing is showers, second is bedtime snacks, and third is sleep. Tomorrow we'll get up at seven. Breakfast is at seven thirty, and the only thing you have to do before we go to the dining cabin is make your bed and put on your name tag. If you want to primp or need extra time in the morning, it's up to you to get up earlier than that. Any questions?"

The smallest girl raised her hand. "How did you stay on that horse for that long?"

"It wasn't easy tonight. A wasp decided to ride with me and stung my knuckle the whole time I was riding." Gemma held up her hand with the red mark still visible on her middle knuckle.

"Ouch! I bet that hurt. I would've got off that horse and cried," the girl said.

"Sometimes you got to work through the pain and get on with it," Gemma said.

"Who gets first in the bathroom?" she asked.

"Lower bunks get first showers tonight. Upper ones tomorrow night. That sound fair?"

Everyone nodded.

"Then find your bunks and your footlockers and get unpacked. Afterwards go take a shower and wash the rodeo dust out of your hair," Gemma said.

Finding their name tags created a flurry and soon the

showers were going full blast. The five waiting their turn sat on their beds and watched Gemma as she arranged chocolate chip cookies on a platter, set out ten glasses for milk and/or apple juice, and started making bags of popcorn in the microwave.

When the first five came from the shower with white fluffy towels turban-style around their heads and dressed in a variety of nightshirts or pajamas, the second bunch bailed off the top bunks and headed for the bathroom.

"I like popcorn," the youngest said.

"So do I. My momma makes caramel corn," Gemma said.

"Is caramel corn kind of like Cracker Jacks?" she said.

"Yes, it is, and you are Carly, right?" Gemma remembered putting that name on the first bunk.

The girl nodded.

"Well, Carly, why don't you five come on over here and get started? We're going to be pretty informal at this dude ranch so we can get to know each other while the others are getting finished."

The girls paraded to the table and sat down.

"Can we sing like they did at the camp in the movies?" Carly asked.

Gemma smiled. "Well, that's a possibility. Why don't you all be thinking of your favorite song?"

In a few minutes ten girls were around the table and Gemma poured out sacks of popcorn into a big plastic bowl. She set it in the middle of the table and said, "Okay, starting with Carly, everyone is going to introduce themselves. Tell all of us your name, your age, where you are from, and what kind of music you like while we are snacking."

"I'm Carly and I'm from Dallas. And I'm ten years old and I like Maroon 5."

"Deanna from Chicago. I'm eleven and I like gospel music."

"Fiona from Albuquerque. I'm eleven and I like rap."

"Kelsey from Los Angeles. I'm eleven and I like alternative rock."

Gemma filled a small bowl with popcorn and tried her best to remember a bit about each girl. Carly could be clingy. Fiona was defensive. Kelsey was shy.

"April from Washington, D.C. I'm ten and I like country music."

"Beth and I'm ten and I like Stevie Nicks."

"Chantelle from Omaha. I'm ten and I love rap."

"Jessie from Nashville and I'm country. I'm eleven but I'll be twelve in a month and I'm going to be a country music star someday."

"Angie from New Orleans and I like jazz. Oh, and I'm eleven too."

"Katy from Atlanta and I like jazz and I'm eleven."

"Now can we sing?" Carly persisted.

"Do you sing?" Fiona asked Gemma.

Their accents were all as different as their looks. Carly had red curly hair like Annie from the play. Deanna and Fiona were blondes. Kelsey and Katy had light brown hair, and Angie and Jessie had jet-black hair and brown eyes. Chantelle and Beth were brunettes. Angie's hair was what Gemma's granny referred to as dishwater blonde and was cut in a short straight page boy at chin level.

"Yes, I do, and I have a Dobro in my room if you want me to play it while you sing," Gemma said.

"Country?" Jessie asked with a new gleam in her eyes.

"That's what I sing. That and folk music, but you all like different things so let's sing silly old songs. That sound all right?" Gemma asked.

All ten girls smiled and nodded. "Starting tomorrow night we will have an hour in the evening for crafts. I've got a great idea for you girls to work on and we can start making them tomorrow evening," Gemma said. "Finish your snacks and crawl up in your beds and we'll sing just before lights out time. Tonight you get an extra hour because of the rodeo, but the rest of the week it goes dark at ten thirty."

That night Jessie and April put a country spin on "Apples and Bananas."

Fiona and Chantelle worked in some rap on "Take Me Out to the Ballgame."

Gemma turned out the lights and slipped out the front door. The ice had been broken and they were whispering and giggling when she left the room. That alone was covering a lot of ground with ten young girls who were so very different. Thank goodness she'd been a Girl Scout and knew a bunch of silly campfire songs or she'd have been out in the cold about what songs to sing with them.

"So how did it go?" Trace asked from the deep shadows beside the porch.

She turned quickly. "Where did you come from?"

"Been waitin' right here for you. So?"

"It went well. They're whispering and not fighting."

"I heard you singing and laughing. My boys are still circling each other like banty roosters or maybe seasoned tomcats." Trace chuckled.

"Make them sing," Gemma said. "It's common ground, cowboy. We're going to start on a craft project tomorrow night and that will get them to talking to each other even more," Gemma said.

"How's the hand?" He reached across the distance and brought it to his lips.

Gemma gasped. "It's fine. I'd forgotten all about it."

He picked her up and with her feet dangling off the ground, his lips met hers in a clash of passion.

Crickets sang.

Frogs chirped.

Cows bawled.

But Gemma didn't hear anything but a whoosh in her ears like when she blocked everything out before a ride.

"I already miss you," he said.

"We are on the same dude ranch. We'll see each other every day," she said.

"It's not the same as the past four nights. Good night, darlin'."

He brushed another quick kiss across her lips and strolled back to his cabin. She watched him go. The cowboy strut, the way his jeans fit, the way the moonlight lit up his dark hair, and the set of his head all sent little electric shocks of want through her body.

She sighed and went back inside the cabin.

Chapter 9

GEMMA'S CELL PHONE ALARM WENT OFF AT EXACTLY six thirty the next morning. She rolled over and whined when she realized she was hugged up to a pillow instead of Trace. She threw her legs over the side, then put her elbows on her knees and her face in her palms. She didn't want to be awake. She didn't want to be responsible for ten girls. She wanted to be in Ringgold visiting all her friends, helping out in her beauty shop, or else she wanted to be tangled up in the sheets with Trace after a hot bout of sex. Neither one was going to happen.

"I don't like you!" A high-pitched Southern voice cut the silence from the front room of the cabin.

"Well, I hate you. You are nothing but a baby and you'll never make it a whole week without your mommy." Deanna's Chicago accent came through strong.

Gemma wasted no time getting from her quarters to the other room before the hair pulling began. When she opened the door, Carly and Deanna were squared off in the middle of the floor. Deanna was the biggest, but Carly looked like a scrapper who could hold her own in any catfight.

Gemma got between them and said, "Okay, ladies. What's the problem this early in the morning?"

Deanna pointed. "She woke up early and started singing stupid songs and woke us all up with her dumb voice. She couldn't sing if her life depended on it."

Carly piped up before Deanna could say another word. "Well, I'm not a baby and she called me a baby and she's the one who was whimpering after we went to bed last night. I hate her."

"I did not whimper and I hate you too!"

Gemma crossed her arms. "Okay, settle down, both of you. Any of the rest of you don't like some member of the group?"

No one said a word. "Are you sure? Speak up right now because this is your last chance. Either tell me now or else you can't say a word later on."

Fiona raised one hand and pointed at Jessie with the other one. "I don't like her."

"What'd I do?" Jessie asked.

"You snore."

"I do not!" Jessie declared.

"Yes you do, and it sounds like a dying frog."

"How would you know what a frog sounds like? And I do not snore."

Gemma held up her hand. "Enough. So Jessie and Fiona don't like each other either. Anyone else?"

Kelsey raised her hand and pointed at April. "She thinks she's all hoity-toity and better than the rest of us. She was humming after we went to sleep and I asked her to hush and she said that she was the best singer here and you like her better so you wouldn't make her stop."

"Anyone else?" Gemma asked.

No one raised their hand.

"Okay, this helps me a lot. I'm assigning partners this morning so now I know what to do. Y'all ever watch any cop shows on television?"

All ten heads nodded.

"Then you understand partners, right? That means you've got your partner's back at all times. If a bobcat or a coyote comes down from the mountains and is about to eat your partner, you fight that critter and don't even think of leaving her there to get hurt. If she falls in a gopher hole and sprains her ankle, you don't laugh at her, but you become her crutch to get back to the cabin. Understand? It means that you will stick to your partner like glue this whole week and if I catch you more than five feet away from your partner then there will be a reckoning."

"What about going to the bathroom?" Carly asked.

"You stand by the door until your partner comes out."

"What's a reckoning?" Deanna asked.

"It's a decision that I make if it happens, and believe me, you don't want a reckoning," Gemma said.

More nods.

"Okay, partners for this whole week are Angie and Katy and Beth and Chantelle."

Partners looked each other over and back at her.

"Carly and Deanna," Gemma said.

"But I hate her," Deanna said.

"You'd better learn to like her a little bit because if the wild critters come, she's the one who might save your sorry butt," Gemma said.

"Next is Fiona and Jessie."

"I'll go home before I partner with her," Jessie said.

"We can make that happen before lunch," Gemma said.

"Okay, I'll do it," Jessie recanted.

"Good. By the end of the week you'll be friends," Gemma said.

"Yeah, right!" Fiona said.

"That means I've got to partner with her." Kelsey pointed at April.

"Looks that way," Gemma said.

"I won't do it. I'll call my momma," April said.

"Darlin', you won't have to call your momma. I'll do it for you," Gemma said.

April crossed her arms over her chest and pouted. "I don't like it."

"You don't have to like it. You just have to do it and do it well. It's bed-making time and then I want you all dressed for a morning in the hay field. Right after breakfast we're having a contest to see who can bring in the most bales and get them stacked in the barn. Boys against girls. You goin' to let those boys whup your butts this morning?" Gemma asked.

"What is the prize?" Deanna asked.

"Knowing that you won," Gemma told her.

She tossed back her shoulder-length blond hair and shot Gemma a go-to-hell look.

"And," Gemma went on. "It's just a suggestion, but if I was you all, I'd get my partner to braid my hair this morning because hauling hay is hot work. And if the boys win on the first day, they're going to rub it in your faces at supper tonight and probably all week long. You know how they act when they win. All cocky and smarty-britches, struttin' around and crowing like roosters. You want to listen to that all week, then just let them get ahead of you this morning in the hay field. I'll be out in fifteen minutes. I want you ready and your beds made and we'll go to breakfast together."

When Gemma returned, the two sets of partners who didn't despise each other were setting at the table, their heads together plotting about how they'd whip the boys. The other six were sulking on their beds.

"We've got a full day ahead of us and tonight we start working on our craft. It'll take all week to finish it. So are you three sets of partners going to sulk and pout all week?" Gemma asked.

"Five feet? Really?" Jessie asked.

"That's the rule," Gemma said.

Jessie hopped down off the bed and looked back at Fiona. "Come on. I can't get more than five feet ahead of you and I'm hungry, and them dumb old boys ain't about to beat me."

Gemma smiled and led the way to the door. "Eat hearty. You'll need the energy, and believe me, the boys' counselor is going to tell them that they can beat you with one hand tied behind their backs. They think they are dealing with sissies, I'm sure."

Carly hopped off her bed and squared her shoulders. "I'm not a sissy."

"You've got all day to prove it." Gemma said.

The boys were already in the dining hall. Bacon, coffee, eggs, hash browns, grits, and gravy were on the buffet along with piles of hot biscuits, juice, and milk. Trace rolled his eyes at Gemma when she came in with her girls.

"Busy morning?" she asked.

"What have I gotten myself into? I believe this is the worst bunch of young'uns I've ever seen. They're just a step up from hooligans and two steps down from gangsters," he whispered.

"I've already settled catfights," she said out of the corner of her mouth.

The breakfast bell dinged and all the kids looked at the counselors and one another. The girls were huddled together against one wall shooting daggers at the pimply faced boys. The guys were grouped up together behind Trace looking at everything in the dining cabin but the girls.

"That means you can eat now," Trace said.

"Ladies first," one of the boys said and looked straight at Trace.

He smiled at the pimple-faced kid and nodded.

"Very gentlemanly," Trace said.

Deanna left the group but was careful not to go more than five steps from her partner. She bowed up to the boy and said, "Today we'll go first. But we don't need your charity. We're goin' to show you how to haul hay after breakfast and pick more apples than you do this afternoon. We are meaner and we can work as hard as any of you old boys."

The kid bowed up to her. "You wanna bet?"

"Sure. If we do better than you today then we get to go first again tomorrow morning even though it's your day. Right, girls?" Deanna said.

All nine of the remaining girls lined up beside her and nodded.

"And if we beat you, what do we get?" the kid asked.

Carly stepped up beside Deanna. "You get to go first for breakfast."

"But we already get that."

"Okay, then you can come over to our porch and sing with us tonight. But if we win, and we will, buster, then you don't get to."

"Deal!"

Trace chuckled. "How'd you get them whipped into shape so soon?"

"I called their bluff."

"Breakfast is getting cold and we're burnin' daylight, kids," Lester yelled from the table where the buffet was laid out.

The race was on as soon as Trace showed them how to load and stack hay. The boys finished the first pickup load and taunted the girls as they sat on top of it for the ride back to the barn.

"We're better than you are. When we get back we'll show you how it's done," the oldest boy yelled.

The girls huddled up heads down, butts stuck out, and reminded Gemma of a football team. They joined hands, whispered and pointed, and then did a yell that sounded like, "Beat boys."

Evidently they'd worked out a system because they had two pickup trucks loaded and ready to go to the barn by the time the boys got back with one truck.

"You guys cheated. Miz O'Donnell and Mr. Coleman helped you, didn't they?"

"No, they did not! We just let y'all get ahead so you'd get all cocky and lazy. And you did. Now we'll show you how it's done. We're going to get our two hundred bales in the barn and have time to sit on the porch and drink sweet tea while y'all are still working," Jessie said.

Two more trucks rolled into the field and six girls stayed behind to load while four went with the trucks to unload them. And at the end of the day the girls loaded and stacked two hundred small bales of hay half an hour faster than the boys. The guys grumbled around all during lunch but they'd learned their lesson. When it came time to go to the apple orchard they'd worked out their plan to unite and conquer.

When Trace rang the cowbell to give them the green light, the smaller boys climbed the ladders like monkeys and tossed apples down to the bigger boys who put them in baskets and then handed them off to Damian and Tyrelle to carry to the flatbed trailers.

"Guess they learned to stop boasting and get their butts to work," Trace said when the competition was finished and the boys won by three bushels.

"Momma says the hardest lesson a kid ever learns is when to shut their mouths and get to work. They did good learning that the first day," Gemma said.

The boys won the apple-picking contest and had a whole new swagger to their walk as they followed Trace back to their cabin. At supper they came into the dining tent with their hair combed, their hands washed, and smiles on their faces.

"We beat you!" Damian told Jessie.

"That was just plain old apples. We beat you at the hard job. We can haul hay better than you can and that's supposed to be a boy job. You're going to have to work hard to overcome that," Jessie answered.

"Oh, yeah, well, we just let you win so you wouldn't cry like little babies," Marty declared.

"And we let you win at the apples so you wouldn't pout around the rest of the week like you did at lunchtime," Fiona put in her two cents worth.

"Don't it just make you itch for a big family?" Gemma whispered to Trace.

"Oh, yeah! I'd send the boys to military school and the girls off to a convent," he answered.

"If y'all can stop bickering long enough to eat, supper is ready." Lester grinned.

"Do we get to sing?" Marty asked.

"Sure you do. It was an even tic today. Girls won in the hay field. Boys won in the orchard, so everyone gets to sing right after supper," Gemma said. "But the girls get to choose the songs."

"Well, shit! I mean sugar." Damian blushed.

"You already calling me sweet names." Jessie giggled.

"No, I am not. I wouldn't call you anything sweet as sugar. You are a bitch." He clamped his hand over his mouth and looked at Trace.

"That's two. On three you get to go back to the cabin and think about cleaning up your speech," Trace said.

"I am not a bitch, anyway," Jessie said.

Gemma stepped between them. "You want to be each other's partner the rest of the night?"

"No, ma'am," Jessie said seriously.

"Huh-uh!" Damian shook his head.

"Lester has called supper. Let's get with it. Boys first tonight," Gemma said.

"Thank you for coming up with the idea of name tags. I swear it's the only way I can remember their names," Trace said.

"We do that at Bible school at the Ringgold church. It works," Gemma told him.

Fiona and Jessie got the job of choosing the songs that evening. They argued. They fussed, but they worked together and twenty voices blended together as they sang the banana song again.

Trace had followed Gemma's lead and assigned partners with his guys. Damian griped that his partner, Marty, couldn't sing and he wanted a new partner, and Marty declared that Damian's voice was changing and he couldn't sing either.

"You sound like your momma callin' in the hogs," Marty said.

"Don't you be dissin' my momma, boy. You don't know nothing about my momma," Damian told him.

"Well, then your sister," Marty said.

"You are asking for a bruising, boy."

"Bring it right on. I'm not a boy, man, and I could beat your skinny"—he paused and looked at Trace—"hind end with one hand tied behind my back and a"—he looked at Trace again—"Big Mac in the other one."

"You got the five-foot rule yet?" Gemma asked.

Trace raised an eyebrow.

"Jessie, darlin', come tell Mr. Coleman about the five-foot rule."

Jessie raised her voice over the boys and began to explain it. By the time she was finished, all twenty kids were as quiet as if they'd been sitting on the front row in a church during a funeral.

"You guys hear that?" Trace asked.

Damian barely nodded.

"As of right now, it's in effect for all of you. I'd suggest you learn to get along or it's going to be a real long week." He grinned.

Marty grimaced and kicked at the dirt. "Man, that's cold."

"Yep, it is."

Gemma spoke up, "We are making a project in our

cabin and tomorrow each one of the girls is to be on the lookout for something small and unique on their trip. You boys might look for something too."

"Are we making something?" Marty asked.

"Of course. Wouldn't be camp without a project. We will be making a dream catcher, so think of that while you are out tomorrow." Trace slipped an arm around Gemma and chuckled. "If they find a horse apple, they'll think they found a fossil."

"The trick is to make each one of them think they've found a gold nugget no matter what it is," Gemma said.

Lester touched her on the shoulder. "This week is all about building confidence and character. You're already doing a fantastic job."

She shrugged. "I'm just using some of the tricks Momma used on us kids. It ain't nothing special, but thank you," Gemma said. "Look at them. They're actually talking to each other and not fighting. Did you tell those boys that we're having a dance on Thursday night?"

"God, no!" Trace gasped. "They'd worry themselves to death. Let them get to know the ladies and then they'll be ready for a dance."

At eight o'clock Trace took his tribe home and Gemma took her girls inside where she had ten small wooden boxes sitting on a long folding table with chairs lined up around it. Bottles of paint were scattered down the middle of the table along with paintbrushes.

"What's that?" April asked.

"Projects," Gemma said. Part of the agenda involved an hour of crafts each evening and she'd come up with the idea of making the boxes as their craft project. She'd sent Hill to town that morning with a list of what she needed and he'd brought it back while the kids were in the apple orchard.

"Don't look like much to me," April said.

"That's because they aren't finished. We'll paint them tonight. Any color you want or any combination of colors," Gemma said.

"Who are they for? I'm not making a present for a boy," Carly declared.

"You are to do your best artistic work. And while you are on field trips this week, if you find a special rock or leaf or maybe an arrowhead, you could bring it back to go on your project. Make it as if you were going to take it home with you to remember this week," Gemma answered. "And on Friday morning just before you leave I'll tell you who it is for."

"Mine is going to be yellow," Katy said. "With a hot pink lid that has swirls of yellow."

"Have fun," Gemma said and sat down at the head of the table to referee in case one of them started slinging paint like they did barbs. Girls! How did her mother ever survive raising two girls? Trace couldn't be having as much trouble with his boys. It wasn't possible.

At the end of an hour the table looked like a tornado hit a Sherwin-Williams paint store, but they were talking and laughing. At nine o'clock Gemma told them to get their brushes washed in the kitchen sink and put the lids on the paint bottles tightly.

"It can't be time for bed yet," Angie argued.

Gemma pointed at the clock. "We've got an hour every night to work on our craft and it really is bedtime. Top bunkers hit the showers first and bottom bunkers help me set up night snacks."

At ten thirty when she turned out the lights, Carly was already snoring and Deanna had a pillow crammed over her ears. Gemma slipped out the door to find Trace sitting in a rocking chair on the porch. He patted his leg and she sat down on his lap.

He cupped her chin and turned her face so he could kiss her lips, sweetly at first then harder and more demanding. "So do you want ten daughters?"

"Bite your tongue." She gasped between kisses.

He nuzzled his face into the soft part of her neck. "You are very good with them."

"I'm good with horses. That don't mean I want ten of them right next to my bedroom," she told him.

"Let's sneak off to the hayloft," he said.

"Not on your life, cowboy. Sure as I did, they'd get into an all-out catfight with claws bared and gnashing teeth."

"Honeymoon is over then?" he asked.

She giggled. "Four nights of wild sex does not make a marriage."

"How many does it take?"

"A helluva lot more than four. Now kiss me good night. Six thirty comes early."

He bookcased her cheeks with his palms and gave her a kiss that made her wish she'd gone to the hayloft with him and be damned to the possible catfights.

Chapter 10

GEMMA AWOKE EARLY THE NEXT MORNING AND TIPTOED to the kitchen area to make a pot of coffee. While it brewed she studied her sleeping girls one at a time. Carly was tall and lanky for a ten-year-old girl, kind of like a three-month-old colt that was still all gangly legs. She really did snore, but Deanna, bless her heart, had shoved cotton balls in her ears and had turned around in the bunk with her feet toward Carly and her head where her feet should have been. Deanna was one of those blondes with dark brown eyes, heavy lashes that rested like a fan on her cheeks, and high cheekbones. Her face was triangular and her mouth wide.

Fiona was also a blonde, but where Deanna was a diva, Fiona looked like she could take down an offensive linebacker and enjoy doing it. She was a big girl, not overweight by any means, but taller than the rest of the girls and big-boned.

Kelsey was the quiet one of the group, but Gemma didn't think for a minute that the short girl couldn't hold her own against even Fiona. It was in her eyes. She didn't have to smart off to anyone and there wouldn't be a day when Kelsey threatened. She'd just step up to the plate and deliver.

April, who was partnered with Kelsey, sat back and waited to see what everyone else did before she started. When they were painting boxes she was the last one to pick a color, but she was meticulous in her job. Gemma pegged her for an artist who would enjoy the solitary life if she ever had the opportunity.

Beth and Chantelle, both brunettes, one from Detroit and one from Omaha, fit right into their partnership. They sat together at mealtime and whispered while they were working on their boxes. Neither of them had as much artistic ability as April, but Gemma would lay dollars to grasshoppers that together they could take on the world.

Jessie was the mouthy one. Black hair, blue eyes, loud, and brassy. She'd push her way into whatever she wanted. Being partners with Carly would teach them both a lot.

Angie from New Orleans had a Cajun look about her with her black hair and dark eyes. She and Katy made perfect partners with their love for jazz music and Southern accents.

The coffee gurgled one last time and Gemma left her sleeping beauties to pour a cup. She carried it outside to the porch and watched the sun rise over the mountains. The crickets and tree frogs sounded the same as they did back home in Ringgold and suddenly a whole new bout of homesickness set in.

"Dammit!" she swore under her breath. That's what she got for even thinking about home and family.

"Dammit, what?" Trace said from the shadows.

She jumped and spilled coffee all over her nightshirt. "You scared the shit out of me. Now I've got coffee stains all down my front."

"Take it off," he teased.

"I don't think so, cowboy," she said.

"I have a name. Why don't you use it?" he asked tersely.

Until that moment Gemma hadn't realized that most of the time she called him *cowboy*. In the same moment she realized why she did, but there was no way she was telling him.

"Who pissed in your coffee this morning?" she snapped.

He ignored her question. "As long as you call me cowboy and not Trace, I'm just competition and a romp in the sheets. I'm not a real person who might get in the way of your glory win in Vegas, right?"

She didn't answer and he pushed on.

"So I'm your one-man groupie for the tour? Is that what I am, Miz O'Donnell? Do you always pick out one lucky cowboy to be your plaything for the circuit?"

She stood up slowly. "If that's what you think then you haven't learned much about me at all."

He held up both palms. "Hey, I'm just asking. You can agree or deny, but be honest and call it what it is."

She bowed up to him, her nose so close to his that she could see the pupils in his eyes and they were downright angry.

"Don't you dare put me in a corner and expect me not to fight my way out. I don't have to explain jack shit to you. But I will tell you one thing, and that is you will not get in my way when it comes to winning."

"Anyone tell you that you are cute when you are mad?"

"Flattery means less than shit to me right now, and don't you dare laugh at me. I'm mad and I may not be over it for days. You just made some pretty mean accusations there… cowboy."

The beginnings of the smile faded. "The truth hurts, don't it? See you at breakfast." He took two steps back and the shadow of the cabin swallowed him up as he disappeared around the corner.

Her girls grumbled when they rolled out of their bunks, but when it was time to go to the dining cabin they were wide-eyed and ready for the day.

"We'll be picking green beans this morning and right after that we're taking a sack lunch on a long hike up toward those mountains in the distance, so you might want to braid your hair or put it in a ponytail," she said.

It wasn't easy keeping her voice calm when she wanted to yell and kick something, but she managed with lots of effort.

Deanna picked up Curly's brush and began to work the tangles from her long, red, kinky curly hair.

"Ouch. You pull on purpose. You are worse than my granny," Carly said.

"Well, sit still and stop trying to squeeze your neck down into your backbone," Deanna said.

"Enough bickering this morning." Gemma took the brush from her hands and deftly braided Carly's hair while the rest of the girls looked on.

"Who are you mad at?" Deanna asked.

"None of you," Gemma answered.

"That cowboy, Mr. Coleman, been mean to you?" Angie asked.

"No, he hasn't. We just had a little disagreement this morning."

"He throw his coffee on you?" Jessie asked.

"No, I spilled my coffee," Gemma explained.

"I'll put a Cajun curse on him if he's not nice to you," Angie said.

"It's just fine. Really. Now let's go to breakfast and

then go show the boys we can work a garden better than they can," Gemma said.

The minute she walked into the dining room she spotted Trace talking to Hill, who was on cooking duty that day. He said something to Hill who turned around and waved and motioned toward the buffet.

"Breakfast is ready. Help yourselves. Don't be shy. I'll be flipping pancakes in the kitchen as long as you kids want to eat them. Remember you are gathering your supper right after you get done with breakfast. I checked the vegetable garden this morning and there's more than green beans, so your counselors will divide you up into partners. One will pick ripe tomatoes. One will pick cucumbers, but only those that are at least six inches long. Others will pick the green beans, and then there is squash and okra."

"And we get to eat all that for supper?" Carly asked.

"Along with fried chicken and hot biscuits," Hill said.

"We have to kill the chicken and pick the feathers too?" Damian asked.

"No, we wouldn't expect you boys do that," Jessie yelled across the rectangular dining cabin. "We did it last night before we went to bed so you wouldn't get all sick and upchuck at the sight of blood."

Damian glared at her.

Fiona threw up a hand and high-fived her partner.

Gemma smiled.

Trace looked the other way.

Gemma sat with her girls at breakfast and listened to Jessie and Fiona plot about how to get ahead of the boys even more. Little did they realize that on Friday night they'd want those same boys, even Damian, to dance

with them—but then, maybe not! Jessie and Fiona were
a force when they walked into a room. They might just
form a big circle like Gemma and all those rodeo ladies
did after the St. Paul rodeo and dance by themselves.

*But who will I dance with if Trace is still acting like a
jackass over me calling him cowboy instead of his name?*

"Why are you having breakfast with us? You and
Mister Sexy Cowboy fightin'?" Jessie whispered across
the table.

"He is a sexy hunk, ain't he?" Fiona said out of the
corner of her mouth.

"Oh, yeah, if he wasn't so old I'd kiss him," Angie
said in her deep Southern drawl.

Katy poked her on the arm. "Angie!"

"Don't be actin' all high and mighty. You were the
one who said he was sexy last night, and besides, I know
he's too old for me. But if he had a son that looked like
him then I'd kiss him for sure, *chérie*," Angie said.

"My name is Angie, not Sherry."

"I didn't say Sherry, I said *chérie*. That's what we
say in New Orleans instead of darlin'," Angie told her.

Gemma caught Trace's movement from the corner
of her eye. He'd loaded his plate with sausage and pancakes and was headed toward her, but then he made an
abrupt turn to the right and went into the kitchen.

"See, he's avoidin' you. What happened? Yesterday
he couldn't keep his eyes off you," Jessie whispered.

"We had an argument," Gemma said. These were
street-savvy girls who'd smell a lie a mile away and call
her on it. If she wanted their trust she had to be honest.

*And you have to be honest with Trace if you want his
trust too.*

"What about?" Jessie pried.

"I'm not a counselor all the time. I'm a hairdresser in Ringgold, Texas, and I grew up on a horse ranch, not totally unlike this one. But I also ride broncs in the rodeos and I'm on the rodeo circuit right now. So is Trace and we are in competition with each other for the right to ride in the finals in Las Vegas in December," she explained.

Jessie nodded. "And you can't let him get under your skin or you might let him win."

Gemma nodded.

"But he wants to get under your skin, don't he? He was lookin' at you yesterday morning like he could kiss you," Angie said.

"That's tough," Katy whispered.

"Well, I say forget the sorry sucker. There's lots more cowboys in the world. Come on to Nashville if you want to find one even sexier than him," Jessie told her.

Hill appeared at the end of the room and shook a cowbell to get everyone's attention. "Hey, listen up. Here are the picking chores."

Trace joined Hill at the end of a long table and looked over his boys. "For the contest, Damian, you are with Tyrelle." And he went on to pair them into five different groups.

"Ahh, man! I don't like the idea of a new partner," Tyrelle said in a heavy Boston accent.

"I'll trade with him," Chipper, a kid from Texas, said.

"No trading," Trace said sternly.

"But—" Damian started to argue.

A look from Trace ended the whole thing before it went one word further.

Gemma bit the inside of her lip to keep from smiling. He was teaching the guys to accept change. She thought about that, but her girls were doing so well that she didn't want to upset the apple cart. Trace would make an excellent father someday. A pang of jealousy flared up hotter than pure acid at the idea of another woman bearing his children.

She looked at Hill with his blond hair and sparkling blue eyes. Not one hormone even wiggled. She looked back at Trace and her whole body hummed.

"Okay," Hill said. "I've got the chores in this hat. Each team picks one and then they can decide how they're going to go about gathering supper. My suggestion is that one partner picks vegetables and the other one carries the harvest bucket to fill up, but you can figure out how to get them from the garden to my kitchen. Be sure and put your slip of paper on the top of your bucket when you bring them in. Points will be taken off for unripe vegetables or for broken plants when Harper takes a walk through the garden. Be gentle, kids. That's your supper out there."

Carly and Deanna drew out a paper that had beans on it and Deanna looked at Gemma. "Do they grow on trees or what?"

"They grow on low vines. You pick the ones about the size of your index finger or larger," Gemma said quietly.

"Do we measure every one of them?" Carly asked.

"No, just do a guesstimate," Gemma answered.

Beth touched Gemma on the arm. "We've got tomatoes. Will you show us what to do?"

Gemma nodded.

"Okra! What is okra?" Fiona's eyes widened.

"It's this stuff that is wonderful fried, but I never saw it in anything but a plastic bag from the freezer at the grocery store," Carly explained.

"I'll show you how to harvest it," Gemma said. She hated cutting okra. It made her hands itch and there were always bugs around the plants. Big old flat ones that hung on the leaves and wanted to crawl up her arms.

"Is it horrible? You are snarling your nose," Fiona said.

"We'll have a huddle-up after breakfast and I'll explain," Gemma said.

"Like in football?" April asked.

Gemma nodded.

All ten girls finished their food, carried their disposable plates to the trash can, and headed for the front porch. Gemma followed right behind them and stopped on the front porch of the girls' cabin. The boys were still polishing off pancakes so she didn't have to whisper, but she did huddle them all together just like a football team right outside the dining room door.

"Okay, here's the deal," she said.

"Blue forty-two?" Carly whispered.

"No, bugs eight million," Gemma said. "Gardens have bugs. They try to keep them under control, but they are still there. If you scream and stomp around like you are afraid, those boys will be in heaven. They'll catch them and throw them at you and they'll act all superior and macho. So if you see a bug, kill it and be quiet about it."

"How?" April's eyes widened.

"There is no wrong way to kill a bug," Gemma said.

"Stomp the sumbitch like a cockroach," Carly said.

Gemma started to fuss at Carly for using foul

language, but it was the same thing that she was thinking so she held her tongue and nodded. "And there could be a little snake or spider."

"Wow, this is more dangerous than gang territory," Kelsey said.

"In its own way, it is. Now are we ready to show those boys we're not afraid of anything?" Gemma asked.

They all put their hands in a pile and Jessie yelled, "Pick beans!"

As the luck of the draw would have it, Damian and his partner, Tyrelle, had drawn the job of cutting okra and Trace set them to work on the row right beside Jessie and Fiona. Once Gemma showed them what size pods to harvest and how to use the knife to make a clean cut, she went to check on her other four teams, but the arguments over in the okra rows could be heard halfway to Ringgold, Texas.

"Boy, I'm holding a knife. You don't want to be givin' me no smack," Fiona told Damian.

"You think I ain't got a knife too?" Tyrelle asked. "Oh, oh! There's a bug. Jessie, I swear it's big as a dollar bill. You girls better run. It's goin' to jump right down your shirt."

"Where?" Jessie asked.

"Right here." Damian held up the leaf.

Jessie took a step over to his row, flipped the bug off, and ground it into the dust. "There, boys. Just call me if you see another one."

"She's tough as my momma," Tyrelle said.

Jessie pointed a long slender finger at him. "And don't you forget it."

Gemma was proud of her girls. Jessie might be the head she-coon in the mix, but they were standing their own ground. She'd even bet that after a couple of lessons Jessie and Fiona both would be able to manhandle a bronc.

Then the air split wide open when Chantelle set up a screaming howl over near the squash plants. "It's a rat!"

Gemma's blood ran cold. She hated spiders and bugs, but she really hated rats and mice. Damian took off in a dead run and grabbed up the varmint by the tail, holding it out at arm's length.

"Funniest rat I ever saw. It's blind." He cocked his head to one side and his straight black hair fell over his eyes. "Look, Tyrelle. I ain't never seen no blind rat."

"It's a mole," Trace said from the end of the garden. "Bring it on down here and we'll take care of it. They can damage the roots of the garden plants."

Damian nodded. "I didn't think it was no rat. You girls need saving again just call me and Tyrelle. We ain't afraid of no rats. Heck, I've seen bigger ones than that on my way to school."

"Thank you." Chantelle shivered. "I hate rats."

Damian puffed out his chest. "Any time."

Score one for the girls and one for the boys, Gemma thought. She looked up and caught Trace looking her way, but he deftly slid his gaze toward the boys and walked away.

She'd looked forward to the hike toward the mountains ever since they'd seen the schedule for the week. But in her imagination she and Trace would bring up the rear, letting the twenty kids run on ahead to discover all kinds of nature items, some for the girls to take back to put in their treasure boxes. They'd have a whole afternoon together, but it didn't work that way. Trace made sure he took the lead in the hike, saying that he was the tracker and he'd scare away the snakes and other varmints that might harm the hikers. And she brought up the rear all alone.

Less than half an hour into the hike the girls and boys were mixed up together like a passel of newborn puppies. They didn't need much supervision and the sheer noise of their laughing, bantering, and stomping around would put any kind of wild animal on the run so she had plenty of time to mull over all that had happened since she pulled into the Cody rodeo two weeks before.

Looking back, it had been a hormonal roller-coaster ride from the time Trace reached out a hand to help her. From there it was all downhill with one coincidence after another throwing them together. She'd been around sexy cowboys her whole life, so why did this one make her juices boil? Maybe it wasn't all coincidence but fate tossing them together time after time. And Liz said that you couldn't fight fate.

Well, Liz was wrong just like she was on the bit about her having a cowboy and a baby of her own by the end of the year. It wasn't happening. She'd proven that she could fight with fate that morning when she spilled coffee on her favorite nightshirt. She'd damn sure fought with Trace, hadn't she? And he was fate spelled with all capital letters.

She kicked a pinecone out of the way and reached down to pick it up. A white feather was stuck in the scales of the cones. She turned it over several times and looked around the area for the tree it might have fallen from, but the only pine trees were far out in the distance.

"Wonder if one of the guys want it for their dream catcher?" she whispered.

"Did you say something?" Carly turned around and asked.

"I was just talking to myself. Did you find something to go on your box?"

Carly shook her head. "I'm still looking. Did you? I saw you pick something up."

"I found something," Jessie yelled and held up a long slender feather. It glistened in the sunlight. "What's it from?"

"Looks like alien's hair to me," Tyrelle teased.

Damian crossed his arms over his chest. "It's a feather out of an Indian's headdress."

Trace turned and walked back a few feet to where the kids had all gathered around Jessie. "It's a hawk's feather. It'll look very nice on whatever your craft project is. Good eyes, Jessie."

At that point, Gemma thought he might stroll on back to where she was, but he didn't. He completely ignored her. If he wanted to play that way then she could oblige him. And the truth of the matter, hurt or not, was that she knew why she called him cowboy and it didn't have a damn thing to do with his name. It was because she really wanted him to be *the* cowboy and if she kept calling him that maybe Liz would read the cards again and tell her that there was a dark-haired cowboy in her future.

Damn his sorry old hide anyway! A stubborn Missouri mule didn't have a thing on him. Why she even wanted him in her future was a mystery.

They returned at five o'clock with twenty kids still hyped up over their finds. The aroma of cooking food wafting out from the dining tent hit their noses. It was thirty minutes until suppertime and the kids were tired, cranky, and starting to bicker. She looked at Trace who just shrugged. Some father he would be in a crisis. He'd probably leave all the discipline to her. High color filled her cheeks at the notion of having his children. She turned around to face the kids so he couldn't see the blush.

"Okay, we've got a few minutes. Everyone gather up on our porch and let us all see what you found today," Gemma said.

That brought the boys back to attention and stopped the girls' whining. When they'd each had a turn at show-and-tell, Trace stepped forward with a small rock and held out his hand.

"Is it an arrowhead?" Damian asked.

"No, but the shape reminded me of one that I found down in the Palo Duro Canyon back when I was about your age," he said.

"What's a palo whatever you said?" Damian asked.

"I'll tell you about it while we get cleaned up for supper. We'll see you ladies later." Trace tipped his straw hat toward the girls but didn't look at Gemma.

"Did you find something, Gemma?" Carly asked.

She held out her pinecone with the white feather in it.

"Wow! A white feather," Angie said.

"So what?" Jessie smarted off.

"A white feather means good luck in Cajun. If you find one something wonderful will happen to you."

"That's bull," Jessie said.

"Might be to you but I'm Cajun and it's magic to me. Miss Gemma is going to find out that today was a lucky day. That it's stuck down in a pinecone is even better. A pinecone means that love is coming her way."

Gemma looked at the pinecone. She might be weaving a tale, but Gemma liked it.

"I hope she's right," she mumbled.

"I am right. When you are an old lady you will remember today and your white feather and it will make you smile."

"Well, I don't want to talk about love and feathers. I'm starving to death," Jessie declared. "Let's go get ready for supper."

They all took off for the bathrooms. Gemma made a mad dash through the fastest shower she'd ever taken, slipped into a white sundress, jammed her feet down into her lucky pink cowboy boots, brushed out her hair, and applied a little perfume. She'd show that stubborn cowboy what he was missing.

"Wow! You look all fancy," Fiona exclaimed when Gemma came out of her bedroom.

"Thank you. Are we all ready?"

"Two hours past ready," Carly said. "My stomach was growling a long time ago."

"So you are going to make him sorry for being mean this morning," Jessie whispered to Gemma on the way out the door.

Not much got past a twelve-year-old kid from Nashville who evidently watched entirely too many chick flicks.

"You bet I am," Gemma said and changed the subject. "So tell me, do you like fried okra?"

"Oh, yeah, and sliced tomatoes with it and fried chicken. My granny cooks like that when we go see her down south of Nashville. She buys it from the farmer's market and it tastes so good. You think Hill can make it taste like Granny does?" Jessie asked.

"I wouldn't be a bit surprised."

The boys had clean hands, shining faces, and their hair was combed. Even Damian's long dark hair was tamed back into a short ponytail at the nape of his neck. They quickly met the girls at the door and the dining hall was no longer segregated. The hike that afternoon had created friendships, and boys and girls sat together in groups around the table, waiting for Hill to call supper.

Finally, he came out of the kitchen and rang the dinner bell, but there was no food on the buffet table. Carly moaned and rolled her eyes.

"Tonight we'll be having a big family dinner. Two tables with the food down the middle. Don't matter which table you sit at because the same kind of food will be on both tables. So all you kids are responsible for coming to the kitchen and carrying a bowl to your table. You are to pick up whatever it was that you harvested this morning and take it to your table. We'll be sitting at the table over in the corner with the counselors. When it's all down the middle then you can sit down and commence to passing it."

"This is great," Gemma said.

"By the second night they are beginning to mingle and talk more. This gets them to visiting about what they harvested, how good it tastes or how much they hate it if they've never tried it and don't like it," Harper explained. "See how gently they are carrying bowls and platters."

Gemma smiled at him. "It's sure not your first rodeo, is it?"

Harper's eyes twinkled. "No, ma'am, it is not."

"And I bet by Friday they are all exchanging phone numbers and email addresses," she said.

"Those who have such things. The others will be giving out snail mail addresses. At the dance we give each of them a small notebook with our logo on the front. They can put whatever they want inside. Most of them use it for phone numbers and addresses."

Hill carried out a platter of fried chicken and set it on the table he'd designated for the adults. "Y'all either carry or starve." He looked at Gemma and Trace. "You don't help, you don't eat."

They headed for the kitchen at the same time, but they both were careful not to touch or even look at the other one. She reached for a bowl of squash with her left hand and a plate of steaming hot biscuits with her right. Her right hand brushed against Harper's arm and not one single little fizzle of a spark danced across the floor. The fingertips on her left hand barely touched Trace's as he reached for the same bowl of squash and something akin to lightning bolts lit up the whole kitchen.

He jerked his hand back and asked, "You ready to talk?"

"Are you?"

"I'm not sure."

"Then we'll wait another day," she said.

"Putting it off so you don't have to own up to the truth?" he asked.

"I'll talk anytime you want to. I'm not putting off anything. But I wouldn't even want to talk to St. Peter right now. I'm hungry and when I get hungry I get real cranky. Granny calls it my Jesus mood. She says even Jesus couldn't live with me when I'm hungry. So it would not be a good time to test my mettle, cowboy."

"My name is Trace," he growled.

"Cowboy. Trace. It doesn't matter if it's Donald

Duck. You better let me eat before we get into this talk," she said.

"Tomorrow is early enough."

"Are you playing games with me?" she asked on the way to the table with him so close to her side that she could smell his cologne.

"I could ask you the same question," he answered.

"If you two don't stop talking and get that food over here, we're starting without you," Harper singsonged.

Gemma heard Jessie giggle, but she didn't look toward the table.

Chapter 11

CARLY TOSSED AN OLD MAGAZINE IN FRONT OF GEMMA and pointed to a picture of a movie star wearing a fancy ball gown. Her hair was swept up in a slick twist with a riot of curls on the top of her head.

"Where'd this come from?" Gemma asked.

"I got it out of the trash last year and I brought it with me. That's what I want to look like tonight," she said.

"Honey, I don't sew and if I did I couldn't make a dress like that in five hours," Gemma said.

"I'm not talking about the dress. I want my hair to do that and I want to borrow some of your makeup. I'll wear my green sundress for the dance, but I want to be pretty and you *are* a hairdresser. You said so. And I bet you know how to put on makeup, too."

The other nine girls gathered round to see what Carly wanted to look like.

Deanna held up her hands. "And fingernails. Can you do a French manicure? I always wanted one of them, but do you know how much they charge at the mall to do your nails like that?"

"Please!" Jessie begged. "We'll help. Just tell us what to do."

"Okay," Gemma agreed. "The end of the craft table will be our beauty shop. First we'll do nails, then hair, and finally makeup."

"What do we do first?" Katy asked.

"You will all take a shower and wash your hair. Pay attention to dirt under your nails and toenails. We might as well do both while we're at it. Princesses or cowgirls, neither one go to the ranch dance with nasty toenails. Carly, Deanna, Katy, Angie, and Jessie, you all go to the showers first. The rest of you clear off the craft table. Move all the excess paint and decorations onto the cabinet. I'll get out the curling iron, nail polish, and hair spray while you do that."

She checked the clock. Ten girls in five hours would be pushing the time frame, but she could do it if they all pitched in and helped.

Fiona jumped off her bunk and started to work. "What do you want me to do with our craft boxes?"

"Put them on the kitchen table. We won't be needing night snacks since we'll be coming home from the party late. Beth, you come with me and help me carry stuff," Gemma called over her shoulder.

She handed Beth the cosmetic case and looked seriously at the big tub. Five girls at a time could soak their feet in bath salts in that thing if the sides were flat enough for them to sit on, but they weren't.

"What are you thinking about? You got this weird look on your face," Beth said.

"I'm trying to figure out something to use as a foot bath. Before we do toes we need to soak your feet and lotion them up so they'll be all pretty," Gemma answered.

Beth opened the cabinets under the sink and pointed. "We got one of them in our bathroom too. Carly says that it's a puke bucket, but Jessie said it's for mopping up the floors. We could use them both and do two at a time."

Gemma hugged her.

"You are a genius," she said.

Beth blushed. "Will you tell my momma that?"

"Anytime, darlin'." Gemma grabbed the bucket and turned on the water in her bathtub. She adjusted the temperature, threw a handful of bath salts into the bucket, and filled it with warm water.

"Want me to bring the other one in here?"

"Did you see what I just did?" Gemma asked.

Beth nodded.

"I want you to do the same thing. Set that case in my bedroom and your next job is to fix another bucket of water."

Gemma carried the bucket to the table and met Carly coming out of the bathroom. Her head was wrapped in a towel and another one was tucked around her body. "What do I put on? My nightshirt?"

Gemma nodded. "That's fine until it's time for hair and then you will wear one of my snap-front Western shirts so that your hair doesn't get messed up when you pull the shirt off."

Carly looked at the bucket of water. "What is that for?"

"To soak your feet. I told you that we're doing pedicures too. Put your feet in it while I do your nails and then we'll work on your toes," Gemma explained.

Carly sat down, stuck her feet into the bucket, and splayed her fingers out on the table in front of Gemma.

"That water feels soft on my feet," Carly said.

"It's bath salts," Gemma explained.

"Who gets this one?" Beth asked.

"Angie," Gemma said. "When Carly is done, Angie will be next. Someone will take Carly's bucket to my bathroom and dump the water in the tub. Beth will show you how to do the next one. When it's her turn then someone else can take over."

Gemma was filing Carly's broken uneven nails when Fiona led the last five out of the bathroom and they all settled into their chairs.

"While I do this you can pick out your polish. Whatever you pick out for your nails goes on your toenails too. And I do have a few jewels so you can each choose some for your big toenails," Gemma said.

"Pink, red, blue, or purple." Carly touched each bottle. "I want blue because my green dress has big blue flowers and I want diamonds on my toenails."

"You other girls be deciding," Gemma said. "We don't have time for hum-hawing around."

"What's hum-hawing?" Jessie asked.

"That's like not being able to make up your mind," Angie told her.

"Well, there ain't none of that hum-crap for me. I want pink and I want them red stars on my toes," Jessie said.

Gemma had made a trip into town on Wednesday to pick up a few more supplies for their craft project and on the way back she'd passed a dollar store. She needed a package of emery boards and hair spray and while she was in the cosmetic aisle she noticed the fingernail polish. She'd bought each of her girls a small bottle of fingernail polish, a tube of flavored lip gloss, and a fingernail file. After a whole week of making the boxes it seemed only fitting that they find a surprise when they opened them up on their way home the next day.

"Hey, girls, before I forget. When you come home from the dance tonight you are going to be too hyped up to sleep so you have one more project to finish," Gemma said.

"What?" Jessie asked.

"There will be some stationary, a pen, and an envelope on your pillow. I want you to write a letter to your partner. Tell them anything you want, but remember someone is writing about you while you are writing about them. When you get done, put your note in the envelope, seal it, and put it on the table. I'll take care of them in the morning."

"Oh, man! I'm not good at that stuff," Fiona said.

"Then it will be a good lesson," Gemma told her.

Carly was so mesmerized by her pretty nails that she couldn't look at anything else until her toenails were done and then they took center stage. "Look, Deanna. Ain't they pretty? And look at the sparkle on my toenail. Man, I'm going to be a princess tonight."

Deanna smiled and patted her on the shoulder. Gemma's heart almost burst with pride. But by the time she finished the last little girl's makeup, she felt like she'd been put through an old wringer washing machine. "And now it's my turn. Can you all sit right here and wait for me? And if any of you get into a catfight and mess up one of my hairdos or chip a single fingernail, I swear, I'll make you stay in this cabin all night and no one will see how pretty you are."

"Yes, Momma Gemma." Jessie giggled.

──◆◆◆──

"Just one more time," Tyrelle begged Trace. "I ain't got that last part down just right yet."

"Okay, Damian, come on over here. You are ready and Tyrelle needs a partner," Trace said.

"Ah, man! I don't like bein' the girl. I like to lead and I'm goin' to show Jessie how it's done tonight. I bet them girls ain't been practicing like we have," Damian said.

"Well, you're going to help Tyrelle one more time," Trace said. "That's what partners are for."

"Okay, but man, you better not wig out on me and stand over in the corner after I teach you all about this dancing stuff," Damian said.

Trace was proud of his boys. They'd come a long way from that wary passel that had stumbled into his cabin that first night. Their hair was slicked back, their faces clean, and their shoes or boots shined. They'd brushed their teeth and even used some of his aftershave as cologne.

Trace pushed a button on the CD machine and George Strait sang "I Cross My Heart." It was a good beat for two-stepping and they'd practiced two nights on the dance. Trace just hoped that when they got to the dining cabin that they all didn't "wig out" as Damian said.

"Hey, guys, remember this will be a country dance," he reminded them.

"We could do this to rap, man! We are that good!" Tyrelle told him. "Okay, Damian, my bro, I got it now. And then I'm going to tip her back like they do in the movies and she's goin' to know that us boys are the winners for the whole week."

The song ended and the boys all lined up for one more inspection before they walked out the door. Trace checked each of them, straightening a collar here and dusting off a shoe there.

"Okay, boys. You've worked hard all week. Go make me proud tonight. Show those girls you aren't afraid to dance, but most of all go have a good time," Trace said.

Even their walk changed as they went to the dining hall where the dance music was already playing loudly. Their backs were straight and their strut pronounced. They were ready to show the girls they were real cowboys and real cowboys could two-step.

—∿—

Hill and Harper had decorated the dining cabin, making it into a ranch house dance. Country music played on the CD machine. Hay bales were stacked up in the corner, and oil lamps sat in the windows.

The punch bowl was ready, and cookies in the shape of horseshoes, Stetson hats, and cowboy boots filled platters.

"Oh, my," Gemma exclaimed when she led her girls into the dance. "You guys did a great job. How on earth did you transform it to this since suppertime?"

Hill grinned. "Thank you, ma'am. We had to work fast, but Harper had it all designed on paper and we just did what he said."

Carly gasped. "It's like a cowboy movie."

Deanna whispered. "It's beautiful."

Damian boldly crossed the room and held out his hand to Jessie. "May I have this dance, ma'am?"

She looked at Gemma and for a fleeting moment Gemma thought she might bolt and run like a coyote on a hot summer night. But when Gemma smiled, Jessie took his hand and nodded. He led her to the middle of the dance floor and with at least a foot of space between their bodies, they two-stepped to a George Strait tune.

"Your girls are lookin' good," Trace said.

She'd never get used to the oozy feeling his warm

breath on her neck caused. She wanted to kiss him right there under the mistletoe and then sneak off to the nearest hayloft or blanket under the stars to do more than kiss. But there was still the cold war to deal with before there would be any more kisses.

"Yes, they are, and so are your boys. Look at them dancin' with the girls. How'd you get them to do that? Most boys are too shy to dance," she said.

"Thank you, ma'am. It took as much work for me to put enough confidence in them to dance as it did for you to make all those girls look like princesses tonight."

"And I can see what you and those boys have been doing in the evenings the past two nights. How many of them had even heard of two-stepping?"

He put a hand over his heart. "Guilty as charged. I couldn't teach them what I didn't know, so two-steppin' and a little swing is going to be it for the night. Damian could do some fancy footwork to rap, but it wouldn't work with country music songs. He caught on faster than any of them."

She looped her arm through his. "Are you going to ask me to dance or do I have to wait for Tyrelle? Or are we still fighting?"

"He's got his eye on Fiona, but Miz Gemma, may I have this dance? And we still have a talk to do, but I don't think we're fighting."

Hill punched a couple of buttons and Travis Tritt's song blared from the machinery.

"Swing it is," Trace said.

On one twirl Gemma noticed Hill and a brunette doing some fancy footwork and Harper and a short blonde wearing cowboy boots like hers, only in pink, weren't doing such a shabby job either.

"Who are those ladies?" she asked.

"Current girlfriends. Lester has gone to pick up his woman. There he is coming in the door right now. She owns a Western wear shop in town," he answered just before he swung her out again in a series of twirls.

When the song ended Gemma was panting.

"Is it me, the dancing, or are you out of shape?" Trace asked.

"All of the above," she gasped.

Trace smiled. "Now that's a good answer, darlin'. Want to sit out the next one? Looks like the kids are doing fine out on the floor so find a chair and I'll bring you a cup of punch."

She nodded and melted into the nearest chair. Jessie and Damian were dancing again, this time a little closer. Tyrelle was teaching Fiona a two-step with an extra kick thrown in the mix. The rest of the kids were dancing all in a pile like kids did these days, but when the song ended and a slow one began, they chose up partners and the two-stepping began all over again.

Trace put a cup of punch in her hands and sat down beside her. "Gemma, I didn't mean to let this go on this long, but I was busy in the evenings teaching the boys to dance so I didn't get over to your cabin. Want to take a walk right now? I'd say there are plenty of chaperones at this dance."

Gemma shook her head. "No. It can wait. I don't want to miss a single minute of all this fun. I worked five hours on those girls this afternoon."

Trace leaned over and kissed her on the earlobe. "I'd let you work five hours on me."

It took all her willpower to sit still, but she managed. "Be careful about making me all hot, darlin'. Remember what they say about paybacks."

Trace chuckled and sat up straight. "At least I've graduated from cowboy to darlin'. That's enough for one night anyway, Miz O'Donnell. We can talk after the rodeo tomorrow night when I show you who is boss one more time."

"How the mighty are fallen," she quipped.

"Hemingway?" he asked.

Lester walked up beside them and said, "David in the Bible when Jonathan and Saul were slain. I want you two to meet Georgia. She's from Colorado Springs and owns a Western wear store over there."

Gemma nodded up at the tall blonde wearing jeans and boots. "Pleased to meet you."

"We're on our way to the punch bowl. Can we bring you something?"

Gemma shook her head. "I'm fine right now."

When they'd gone, Trace picked up her hand and teased the palm with his thumb. "So you think you are mean as David? You got a sling and a couple of rocks in your back pocket?"

"I got a determination to win in my back pocket," she said.

His thumb was driving her completely crazy. How could one rough old cowboy thumb create so many naughty thoughts in a room full of kids, anyway?

"So do I, darlin'," he whispered.

She wasn't sure when Hill and his girlfriend crossed the dance floor, but suddenly there they were, right in front of her and Trace. The girl wore a cute little red sundress and a silver bead necklace.

"Gemma, meet Chris Smith," Hill said.

Gemma pulled her hand free and stuck it out. "Pleasure to meet you."

CAROLYN BROWN

Chris shook with her and then slipped her hand back into Hill's. "The kids seem to be having a good time. I teach this age group. It's hard to get them on the dance floor together even when they've known each other for years. You really have done a lot in just one week."

"They've come a long way," Trace said. "If you'll excuse us, Gemma promised me the next slow dance."

He held out his hand and she stood up.

"What was that all about?" she asked.

He slipped his arms around her waist. "Tonight I don't play well with others. I don't want to share. I missed you, Gemma," he said.

His heart was beating loudly in her ear. The steady rhythm seemed to be telling her that he was as solid as his heartbeat, that he'd never hurt her.

"I've been right here all week," she said.

"Yes, and that was even harder than you being a hundred miles away."

"What are we going to do about us?" She looked up into his eyes.

"I guess that's what we need to talk about after the ride tomorrow night."

―――

Everything was a flurry on Saturday morning. Last-minute checks to make sure everyone had all their things in the right suitcases. One more look under the bunk beds and in the bathroom for anything that might have been left behind. Breakfast was finished. Good-byes and hugs to Hill, Harper, Lester, and Trace.

The bus rumbled up to the front of the cabin and Gemma panicked. She couldn't let them go back to the

big city life. What if they got tangled up in gangs or
started doing drugs? Her chest felt like an elephant was
sitting on it when Carly wrapped her arms around her
waist and hugged her one more time.

She wanted to gather all ten of them up like a
mother hen with her peeps and carry them to Ringgold
where they'd have a makeover every weekend and
a dance at least once a month. They should live in
a town so small that if they did anything that they
shouldn't, she'd know about it before they even got
home from school.

Carly's lip quivered when she handed Gemma a
folded piece of paper. "We wrote a letter to our partners
last night, but then we decided to write something to
you. It's all right here in the envelope."

Gemma swallowed a baseball-sized lump and hugged
the child one more time. "I'll read them all later. I've got
your addresses and you have mine. Write me and tell me
what's going on in your life."

"Can we take our boxes home with us now?"
Deanna asked.

"No, you can't take your box, but each one of you
can give your box to your partner. No peeking inside
until you are on the airplane going home. There's a little
surprise for you and the note that your partner wrote to
you inside the box. It will give you something to read on
the ride," Gemma said.

Carly handed Deanna her bright-colored box. "You
made a pretty good partner. If you are ever in Dallas,
come and stay with me."

"If you'll quit snoring I might do that. And if you
ever get to Chicago, you come see me," Deanna said

with tears rolling down her cheeks as she gave her pretty trinket box to Carly.

Lester poked his head in the door. "Time to go, ladies. Boys are on the bus and you've got to be at the airport in just a little while."

Gemma followed them out, helped get them settled, and waved from the porch until the bus was out of sight.

Trace stepped up behind her and slipped his arm around her waist. "Can you imagine watching your own kids leave for camp or even their first day of school?"

She buried her head in his shoulder. "I'm never having children. I couldn't stand the pain of kindergarten."

The doctor listened to the baby's heartbeat and looked at the lady's chart. "Why are you having this child if you don't want it?"

"That is personal, and I really don't even want to talk about it. I'm treating this like a disease that I will be cured of when it is removed from my body."

"Adoption? I've got several people on a list who would love to give the baby a good home," Dr. Joyce said.

"That could be a possibility. I'll get in touch with you if it becomes necessary. Not long until the C-section, right?"

"That's right, but there is no reason why you couldn't have this child naturally. You might even change your mind about motherhood if you went through childbirth."

The lady smiled. "It's a tumor that will be removed surgically, and I have no interest in motherhood. Not now or ever. I'll see you in two weeks."

Chapter 12

THE WHITE LINES IN THE MIDDLE OF THE HIGHWAY whipped past at seventy five miles per hour and Gemma's thought pattern spun around in her head at the same speed. She had to remember to touch her lucky horseshoe. She had to eat a hamburger from the rodeo grounds even if they didn't get there until time to ride. Tomorrow morning she was flying home. She'd be there in time for Sunday dinner, and they were having music out on the lawn afterwards.

She and Trace still needed to talk, but that might have to wait until they got to the Dodge City rodeo at the end of the month. By then she'd have things sorted out and finalized. And once Gemma reached that point, not even wild horses could make her change her mind.

Josh Turner's "Your Man," the ringtone she'd set up for Trace's calls, started playing on her cell phone. She reached over to the console and touched the speakerphone button.

"Ready to pull off for lunch?" she asked.

"Only if you are. We're only about an hour from the rodeo grounds. I can wait for a rodeo hot dog or maybe they'll have gyros," Trace said.

"I was looking forward to a rodeo hamburger."

"Does that bring you good luck?"

She hesitated.

"It does, doesn't it? You have to eat a burger from

the rodeo grounds before the ride to get your mojo," he teased.

"And yours is a hot dog, right? Would that be with or without a beer?" she shot right back at him.

"No beer, darlin'. Can't drink a drop before a ride," he admitted.

"And that's part of your mojo too, isn't it?"

"I'm a better poker player than that. I'm not giving up my tell, darlin'. Speakin' of poker, how about a game after the rodeo? In my trailer?"

"What's the stakes?" she asked.

"I was thinkin' one item of clothing at a time," he said in a husky voice.

Gemma's overactive imagination gave her a flash of Trace losing his last sock when she laid out a full house. "I'm a damn good poker player. You sure you want to go there?" she asked.

"Oh, yeah, I'm real sure. And every time I win a piece of your getup, I get to take it off however I want. You have to lie still and let me take my time," he teased.

"Lie?" she asked.

"Sure. We'll play right in the middle of my bed."

She lowered her voice. "And when you lose an item of clothing do I get the same privilege?"

He chuckled. "Yes, ma'am, and I'll look forward to it. But there is no way you will beat me."

"I'll bring a brand-new deck of cards. That way we'll both know they haven't been marked. Right after the rodeo dance is over, we'll meet at your trailer, and honey, you ain't played with a pro until you play with me," Gemma said.

"Why wait until after the rodeo dance?"

"Because I'm going to celebrate my win and you are going to dance with me. Besides, the Cheyenne rodeo is my favorite of all of them. I would have liked to have been here the whole week."

"You are on, darlin'. Now tell me, are you dead serious about going home tomorrow morning?" he asked.

"Yes, I am. I can't wait to get there. I didn't realize how homesick I'd be after only a month. Are you going back to help on the dude ranch?"

"No, I'm flying home too. Thought I'd drive my trailer down to Dodge City and park it and fly in and out of there. That what you got in mind?" he asked.

She nodded and then realized he wasn't sitting right beside her.

"Yes, it is," she answered. "Two days to Dodge City, park, and be home before nightfall. On Sunday my family is all gathering and we're having music under the shade trees. Colleen and Blaze will even be there for the afternoon. The carnival is traveling from one place to another and they said they'd make a forty-mile detour and spend the afternoon with us."

"You *sound* homesick." He laughed.

"I am, and I'm glad we've got some time between Cheyenne and Dodge City. Where's Sugar? I don't hear her."

"Sleeping like a baby on her pillow over in the passenger's seat. Those boys about wore her out. Looks like I've got a call from my father. Talk to you later," Trace said.

———∿∿∿———

Trace had a short conversation with his father and then turned on the radio and kept time with his thumbs on the steering wheel as Josh Turner sang "Would You Go with Me" on the station out of Cheyenne. The lyrics asked if she'd go with him if they rolled down streets of fire, and if he gave her his hand would she take it and make him the happiest man in the world.

"What do you think, Sugar—would Gemma take my hand or would she bite it?" Trace asked.

Sugar looked up and yipped.

"Yep, that's what I figured. She'd bite it for sure."

Ava had said that he looked like Josh Turner. She said that's why she picked him out of a sea of cowboys that night. He remembered playing Josh's new CD over and over that weekend and Ava telling him that his voice was almost that deep but not quite.

"Lord, what was I thinkin'?" he said aloud.

The DJ was talking again, saying, "And we've got another request for a Josh Turner. Amber from Denver wants to hear 'No Rush.' So here it is, folks. I wonder if Amber is making a statement to someone in Denver."

The piano music started off slow and then the violins joined in as Josh talked through the first few lines. He said they had something special and were right on the edge of falling in love. He talked about walkin', talkin', and dreamin' with her. Then he said that he'd been wonderin' if she'd been feelin' it too, but there was no rush.

He kept a steady beat on the steering wheel, but the words spoke right to his own heart as Josh sang them. Gemma was the kind of woman he could walk, talk, and dream with through the whole journey of life, not just a hot, wicked weekend. But he didn't have a damn thing to offer her unless he walked away the winner in Vegas. She deserved better than a ranch foreman and he might not even be that if his Uncle Teamer sold the ranch to someone else and the new owner brought in his own crew.

"Shit!" He slapped the steering wheel so hard that Sugar jerked awake with a yip.

She looked at him with a question in her big eyes.

"Okay, I know you like her and you hated Ava, but dammit! Why am I even comparing the two of them? I don't compare her to the woman I bought you for, so why do I group her and Ava together?"

Because it's been a year since I had a woman in my bed and Ava was the last one. And because Gemma makes me crazy.

"And I don't even know where I stand with her," Trace told Sugar.

—⁓—

Gemma felt the energy of the rodeo before she even opened the door. The entire town of Cheyenne was geared up for a whole week, culminating with the big rodeo that night. They had a cattle roundup and brought them into town, carnivals, and all kinds of excitement before the rodeo.

But tonight belonged to her, and she'd glue the shamrock to the horseshoe and then go home for a week. She was humming when she stepped out into the bright sunlight.

She rounded the end of her truck at the same time Trace opened his door and stepped out. He stretched his arms over his head and rolled the driving kinks from his neck. Then he opened his arms and she walked into them.

He buried his face in her hair and inhaled. The remnants

of coconut shampoo blended with the exotic perfume that she wore and stirred his pulse into a racing mode.

"Want to play a little poker right now?" he whispered huskily.

She giggled. "No, I do not."

He leaned back and looked into her dark green dreamy eyes. "Afraid it might mess with your mojo?"

"Hell, yeah! I don't meddle with the mojo, cowboy. After I win tonight then there'll be time for poker and you can get ready to lose everything you are wearing. I've got a hankering for that shirt you will be wearing after the rides. It will be your lucky one, right?"

"I don't think so, darlin'. I'll change before we start because you sure ain't winnin' that shirt. But if we aren't going to play then let's go find some food. I'm starving," he said.

"Look." Gemma pointed to the passenger window where Sugar was staring at them. Her little pink tongue lolled out and the look on her face said she needed a place to squat.

Trace opened the door, picked her up, and quickly fastened the leash to her collar. When he set her down she made a beeline for a spot under the trailer and didn't even bother to sniff out the best place. When she finished she came back and barked at Trace who handed her off to Gemma.

"Hold her please while I get hooked up to electricity and get the cooler going. She'll suffocate if the air isn't going," he said.

Sugar wiggled in Gemma's arms and licked at her face.

"Hey, did you miss me? I bet those old boys in that cabin weren't nearly as nice to you as my girls would have been. And your mean old master was mad at me so he didn't even bring you to visit. I missed you too, pretty girl, and if he does that again, we'll both bite him, won't we?" Gemma talked baby talk as she scratched Sugar's ears.

"Do I get to pick the spot?" Trace yelled from the doorway.

"Hey, hey, so you made it. I didn't know you had a dog," a voice said right behind Gemma.

She turned so quickly that she almost dropped Sugar. Landry Winter's nose wasn't a foot from hers and he was smiling like he'd just won the bull riding event of the year.

"I thought maybe you'd given up and gone home. Some of us been parked here all week," he said.

"Not until I win in Vegas. I'm in it for the long haul," she told him.

"You going to be at the dance tonight?" he asked.

"Of course. I'll be celebrating."

"Save me a dance and I'll buy you a beer and maybe afterwards we'll have our own party," he whispered.

"I don't think so," she said. "I've already got plans."

"So it's true that you and Trace Coleman hooked up for the circuit? Well, honey, you just remember that you can change horses in the middle of the stream and this old bull rider will be ready any time you are." He kissed his fingertips and touched her forehead before he turned and swaggered away.

Landry had a rugged, chiseled look about him and mischief danced in his eyes, but his touch on her forehead did nothing. Trace could create more heat in her body with a glance across the arena than Landry did with his come-on line and fingertip kiss.

The air conditioner in the trailer started to hum and Trace yelled out the door, "Bring her on inside. It won't take long to cool down now."

Gemma stepped inside and the ceiling vents were already spewing cold air. She set Sugar down on the floor, and the little dog hurried over to her food and water dishes.

"She's happy. You ready to go get that hamburger now?" Trace asked.

Gemma rolled up on her tiptoes and brushed a kiss across his lips. Yep, the fire was still there and her body tingled in anticipation of the party after the rodeo dance. She might even let him win the poker game. It would be a consolation prize after she won the bronc busting contest that evening.

Chapter 13

GEMMA SETTLED INTO THE SADDLE, TOUCHED HER lucky horseshoe hat pin, and measured the reins. She wiggled in the saddle to make sure it was exactly right, shoved her boot heels down into the stirrups, got her legs in the right position for the mark out, and cleared her mind of everything.

Eight seconds after she motioned for the gates to open the ride was over. Thirty seconds afterwards she was already on the ground waiting for the announcer to give the score and holding her breath. Trace had drawn a meaner-than-hell bronc that had a buck like she'd never seen before. The damned horse's hooves barely hit the ground in the whole eight seconds and Trace had come away with a seventy-nine, tying it up with Coby Taylor who also had a seventy-nine.

"And here they are, cowboys and cowgirls. Scores for the last ride of the evening, and Miz Gemma O'Donnell beats the guys by one point with an eighty. So put your hands together and let's hear it for the lady rider tonight from Ringgold, Texas, who is headed for the playoffs if she keeps riding like she just did."

Gemma took a bow and headed back behind the chutes to collect her saddle. She'd done it! By golly, she'd won and she could take that news home to Ringgold. She was now the top money winner in the bronc busting competition. Eight seconds could change it in Dodge City at the end of July, but right that minute she was on top of the pile.

"Good ride," Coby said from the shadows.

"Thanks," Gemma said.

He stepped out and grabbed her arm, spun her around, and landed a hard kiss right on her lips. She was so stunned that she couldn't move for a few seconds, and when she could regain her senses she pushed him hard and took a step back.

"You sorry sumbitch; what did you do that for?" she asked.

"You didn't mind when Trace Coleman did it. You fussed at him, but I hear you two have hooked up quite a bit," Coby said.

"That still didn't give you the right and it's none of your business." She wiped her mouth. Her lips felt like they'd been raped, not loved.

"Aww, come on, Gemma, don't wipe it away. You deserved that kiss. You beat out me and Trace to get it," Coby said.

"I don't like your way of thinking. Do you kiss Trace when he wins?"

Coby's laugh was brittle. "You're playing in a field where you don't belong. Get ready for some backlash, woman."

"Don't call me woman!" She gave Coby her meanest go-to-hell look and walked away from him. In a few long, easy strides he was beside her.

"Darlin', don't be like that. We could be good together. I've had my eye on you since St. Paul and I felt the vibes when we danced together," he said.

She stopped and jabbed a finger in his chest. "But I

didn't. I'm not interested, and don't ever try that stunt again or you'll be picking yourself up out of the dust."

"And who is going to put me there? Trace Coleman?"

"I fight my own fights, Coby. Just don't touch me again and stay away from me," she said.

"He said you were a hellcat." Coby laughed.

"He must know me real well." Gemma took her saddle from a tall, middle-aged cowboy. Dust shot up around her boots with every step on the way to her trailer. She set the saddle on the steps, opened the door, and picked it back up. When it had been put away, she took her shoebox out and opened it. The Cheyenne shamrock was right on top and the glue stick at her fingertips on the counter. She covered the back of the four-leaf clover and smacked it on the horseshoe, stood back, and wiped her mouth one more time.

A hard knock on the door made her jump. If it was Coby, she fully well intended to kick him off the step and out into the dirt. Damn him, anyway, for taking all the joy out of the win. She slung open the door to find Trace standing there with a grin on his face.

"Good ride," he said. "I expected to see you dancing around, not looking like you just sucked all the juice out of a lemon."

"I'm sorry. That damned Coby made me mad."

Trace stepped inside and his expression went stone cold serious. "What did he do?"

"Nothing that I didn't take care of."

"Don't be getting too happy with your place. It's a long way from here to there." He pointed to the top of the horseshoe.

Gemma smiled. "Oh, yeah, cowboy! Well, I intend to make the journey and be the winner."

He pulled her into his arms. Every nerve ending in her body purred. She actually felt her back arching like a cat.

"I missed this all last week."

"Me too, but you were being a stubborn ass and wouldn't talk to me. Which reminds me, we still haven't had that talk yet." She quickly turned around. No way was he kissing her in her trailer.

"Want to blow off the dance and fall into bed?"

"I want to go to the dance and then…" She let the sentence drag.

"As long as there is a then, I can wait. And we'll have that talk later," he said.

"Give me two minutes to get out of these chaps and get my spurs off," she said.

He sat down on the edge of her bed and unbuckled her chaps. "Anything else I can remove for you, darlin'?"

"Later, maybe. Right now I want to dance and I don't want to see Coby again," she said.

"If he comes around I'll take care of him," Trace said.

"No, if he comes around, I'll take care of him again. He doesn't think I belong in the competition and he's just mad because he's getting his ass whipped." She brushed out her hair and reapplied lipstick. "You ready?"

"Sure I am," he said.

When they reached the arena, Trace led her out into the center and drew her into his arms for a slow dance. The lead singer of the band was doing a number by Josh Turner called "Angels Fall Sometimes."

It seemed like everywhere he turned lately Josh was singing. Was it an omen?

The lyrics talked about her being out of his league and

that she'd found out he wasn't a saint. It said he woke up
every morning surprised to find that she was still around
and said that every now and then angels fall sometimes.

Trace swallowed a lump in his throat. He felt the song
rather than heard it, and he would give his kingdom if
the angel in his arms would fall in love with him.

They danced through six or seven dances. During
the slow songs she melted into his arms so close to his
body that air couldn't get between them. During the fast
ones, he swung her out from him until she was giggling
and breathless.

And then a redhead tapped her on the shoulder and
said, "Mind if I cut in?"

Gemma stepped back and laughed when Trace rolled
his eyes toward the star-studded sky. It was all part of the
dance and she'd had him to herself for half an hour. She
turned to walk away and Landry Winters grabbed her
arm and spun her around. She came to a screeching halt
right at his chest and he tipped her chin up with his fist.

"Rumor has it that you and Trace are getting awful
close. Is that really true?" he asked.

Gemma backed up. "I'd say that's our business. You
said something like that this afternoon when we drove
up on the grounds, remember?"

"Yes, but I heard some more. I hear you are living
with him now."

"That's none of your business, Landry. But even if
I was, is there something wrong with that?" she asked.

"Be careful, darlin'. He'll break your heart."

Landry was a good dancer, but other than the hot
July night, there wasn't a bit of heat between them. She
looked up into his pretty face and smiled.

"Would you break my heart?"

Landry's dimples deepened when he smiled. "Of course not. I'd be right up-front and say that it was a fling, but that Trace, he'll promise you the moon and deliver a heartache."

"That's a helluva pick-up line." She laughed.

"It's my best one. Is it working?" Landry asked.

She shook her head and took a step back when the song ended. "You'd best try it on one of those girls over there staring right at you. I bet they'll be willing for a rodeo fling."

"You get tired of him, come on around to my trailer. I'll kick them all out for a night with you." Landry tipped his hat and in a few long strides he was shooting a line of bullshit to the women who'd been eyeballing him.

"You ready for that game of poker?" Trace whispered right behind her as he slipped both arms around her waist.

"I'm ready to go, but I forgot to buy cards and I bet your deck is marked, isn't it?" she teased.

"Forget the cards." He laced his fingers in hers and led her out of the light into the shadows.

They'd only gone a few yards toward the trailers when he scooped her up into his arms and carried her tightly against his chest the rest of the way. He unlocked the trailer door and set her down on the steps, stood back, and let her go in ahead of him. When he was inside, he shut the door, locked it, and wrapped his arms around her tightly. His lips found hers in a clash of passion, and he backed her up toward the bedroom. His big hands splayed out on her bare flesh under her shirt, and every sane thought left her mind as a tsunami of raging desire took over her body. With one tug she undid the pearl snaps on his shirt and ran her hands across the hard muscles on his chest and abs.

"You are getting pretty good at undoing my shirt," he whispered.

"Yes, I am. I love the way those snaps pop and reveal that big broad chest," she said.

Sugar whimpered when they landed on the bed and took off in a trot into the kitchen. Trace pulled the door shut with one hand without stopping the steaming hot kisses. Suddenly, she was undoing his belt buckle and he was removing her clothing as fast as his hands could move.

She didn't even think about a long hour of foreplay or about him taking off her bikini underpants with his teeth. She just wanted him. The foreplay had happened on the dance floor when he dropped his hat over the small of her back as they danced, when he'd sang along with Josh Turner about angels falling out of heaven and how lucky he was, and when he'd picked her up and carried her to the trailer.

Clothing flew into every corner of the room and she wasn't even aware when she lost her boots, but when he rolled on top of her on the bed, his lips still on hers and his tongue doing wicked things inside her mouth, she realized she was still wearing socks. She wrapped her legs tightly around his body and he found his way into her with a firm thrust. Trace's lips felt like fire on her mouth and she didn't want his hands to ever stop playing all over her body.

She arched against him and called out his name, "Trace!"

"What did you say?" he groaned.

"I said, Trace!" she repeated.

It was over in a flash.

"God, I'm so sorry, darlin'. I wanted it to be so good tonight. I wanted to take you to the top a dozen times, but you said my name," he growled.

He eased to one side and she cuddled up next to him, her face buried in his shoulder. Landry had been wrong because something that felt so right couldn't produce a heartache.

"Who gives a damn about a dozen times when the first one knocks your socks off?" She panted.

He buried his face into her hair. "You really are an angel."

"I've got you fooled. All this hair isn't covering up a halo. It's hiding horns," she said.

"Gemma, you said my name. You didn't call me cowboy!"

"Well, I'll be damned. I did, didn't I?" She laughed. "Rolls off the tongue right well."

"Say it again."

"Trace... Coleman," she whispered seductively into his ear.

"God, that's so sexy."

"And that's a corny line," she said.

"Well, try this one on for size. You are sexy even in your socks, and you are beautiful even with your hair all mussed up," he said.

"You are sexy with one sock on and one off and all sweaty in tangled up sheets," she whispered.

He sucked in air to say something, but a hard knock on the trailer door brought him to a sudden sitting position. "What the hell?"

He threw his legs over the side of the bed and grabbed a pair of plaid pajama bottoms, jerked them on, and opened the door. Sugar bounded up the stairs and into the bed, turned around three times on his pillow, and laid down, her big eyes staring right at Gemma.

Moonlight silhouetted Trace in the doorway. Gemma sat up for a better view of him standing there, shirtless and his pajama bottoms riding low on his hips. But she couldn't see well enough so she grabbed the top sheet, wrapped it around her, and tucked the ends under her arm. She stepped around the corner out into the kitchen to see three young women circling the steps below him like coyotes after a roadkill possum, all giggling and pointing one to the other.

Trace shook his head and one woman stepped out away from the others. "I drew the long straw so I get to be the one since you don't want a group party. But I'm telling you we could have a hell of a foursome if you're willing."

Her voice was tinny and slightly slurred. Her hair was that brassy red that comes from a bottle. She wore skin-tight shorts, a skimpy halter, and cowboy boots. Her face looked like she'd been ridden hard too many times.

Trace shook his head and chuckled. "No thanks, ladies."

"You sure, honey? We promise to give you a ride even wilder than that bronc did tonight," the redhead said.

"Good night, ladies." He started to shut the door.

The redhead stuck her foot in it. "I got a message for you since you don't want to play ride 'em cowboy with us tonight. Ava says hello and she's got a surprise for you. Says she'll definitely have it for you at Lovington, New Mexico."

"And what is this big surprise?" Trace asked.

"Can't tell you now, but it's goin' to blow your world apart." The redhead laughed and backed away from the door. "Okay, girls, we've bombed out. Let's go back to the bar and see who is left."

Trace shut the door and leaned on the backside. "Guess you heard that?"

"I did."

"Ava was my one big journey into the groupie world. It happened last year and it lasted one weekend. And she wasn't even a groupie. She just came to a rodeo to see if cowboys were all she'd heard they could be. After one weekend, she went on her way and I've not heard a word from her since."

"Thank you, Trace. You don't owe me explanations about your past, but I appreciate that. Come on back to bed and let's get some sleep."

He drew her into his arms and shut his eyes. Any other woman would have thrown a fit and left him to sleep alone. He really had an angel in his arms just like Josh sang about.

———⁓———

Trace and Sugar were gone when she awoke at seven o'clock the next morning, but he'd left a pot of coffee on the counter. She wanted to be mad about the Ava woman, but she couldn't. Gemma had a past too. She'd lived with her last boyfriend before they'd had the fight of the century and she'd moved out. So what right did she have to be mad because Trace had a past?

"But jealousy is a different matter. I can be bullfrog green with jealousy if I want to and it can even make me cranky," she said.

She poured a cup and drank it as she pulled her cell phone from her purse. She dialed the beauty shop number in Ringgold and Noreen picked up on the first ring. "Hi, Gemma! You ready to sell me this shop yet?"

"Hell, no! I can't wait to get home and back into the business. I don't know whatever made me think I was cut out to be a rambler. I miss my roots," Gemma said.

Noreen laughed. "Maybe when you start winning money hand over fist you'll change your mind. I can only hope. I heard that you whupped the boys last night."

"I did, but that don't mean I'll change my mind about home," Gemma said.

"Suppose you want all the gossip?"

"I'm withering up and dying from lack of it."

"Okay, Lucy and Tyson went to the courthouse and got married Monday morning."

"What!" Gemma gasped. "And she didn't even call me. Did she wear a pretty dress and have flowers and a cake afterwards?"

"Jasmine and Ace went with them. Guess Tyson is moving into her trailer out on the ranch and they're going to keep working there as usual. I love that woman. She's my savior. And yes, she wore a pretty blue sundress and Jasmine made sure she had white roses in her bouquet and Tyson was real handsome in his Sunday suit. And you knew that Jasmine and Ace are expecting a baby?"

"I got that news already and I'm still mad at Liz for getting my cards and hers all mixed up."

"Here comes Slade's aunt and granny, so I've got to go. You think real hard about selling me this business. I'm happier than I've ever been in my life, and I think

I could get a banker to float me a loan," Noreen said before she hung up.

Noreen Featherstone was another of Lucy's stray puppies. Lucy had appeared at the Longhorn Inn a couple of years before, right after Pearl inherited it. She was on the run from an abusive husband and Pearl hired her to work at the Inn. Before long Lucy had formed a group somewhat like AA, only for abused women, and she was still running it. Lucy worked like an employment agency as well as a counselor to the women. When Gemma first started talking about doing the rodeo rounds, Lucy knew about a hairdresser looking for a job. So she and Noreen decided on a deal and now she was fixing hair and hearing all the local gossip in Ringgold while Gemma busted broncs.

"I don't want to wait years and years. I want a baby now and I want a husband to hold me. I want one who'll think I'm the queen of the universe. I want my cowboy and I want a baby and it ain't happenin' by Christmas this year because it ain't possible. Hells bells, I'm out here busting my butt for a title when I should be back home chasing cowboys," Gemma grumbled.

Her phone rang and she pushed the answer button.

"Gemma, guess what? Me and Tyson got married. I would have called you sooner but he planned a little three-day honeymoon. We flew to South Padre and had a cabin right on the water and it was fantastic," Lucy said.

"Noreen just told me," Gemma answered.

"Oops!" Lucy giggled.

"So tell me all about it," Gemma said.

"I'm in love. I mean I'm really in love. I was married before but I didn't even know this kind of thing existed. If you ever find it, grab hold with both hands and don't let go. Words don't even describe what I've got with Tyson. We are so happy and we've decided to stay right here on the ranch in my trailer for now, but later on Jasmine and Ace said we could build a small house anywhere we want. We've been looking around trying to decide where to put it."

Gemma sighed. "I'm happy for you, Lucy. I really am. You aren't going to stop your abused women meetings, are you?"

"There will always be abused women who need a helping hand. It's helped me as much or more than it helps them, and Tyson doesn't want me to quit my work. Got to go now. I'm making chocolate cakes for lunch today."

Gemma groaned as the phone went dead. "Home cooking! I'd do murder for a chunk of Lucy's chocolate cake."

"Mornin', sunshine," Trace drawled as he and Sugar came inside. "What's that about doing murder? Am I in trouble?"

"No, you aren't in trouble. I just talked to the lady who's leasing my beauty shop and found out my good friend Lucy got married. And then I talked to Lucy and I'm really, really homesick," she said.

Trace sat down on the edge of the bed. "Are any of your friends and family coming to the finals in Vegas?"

Gemma's eyes twinkled. "Every one of them, I'm sure. I have three older brothers and I'm the baby sister of the family. Plus there's Ace and Wil, who are like brothers since they're my oldest brother Rye's best friends. You sure you want to meet them?"

—⁓—

The nurse wheeled the baby into room 312 and the woman pointed at the door. "Take it away. I do not want to see it."

"But she is so cute. She's got dark hair and…"

The woman raised her voice. "I said to take it away. I don't care what it looks like and I will not touch it. I told the doctor to advise the whole staff not to bring that into my room and I want no visitors allowed in my room either. So go!"

The nurse wheeled the clear bassinet out into the hall-way and eased the door shut. They'd said at the desk that she didn't want to see the baby, but sometimes mothers did change their minds. It was instinct to love your child, wasn't it?

"Still isn't interested?" Dr. Joyce asked right behind her.

The nurse shook her head. "Help me to understand, Doc. How can a mother carry a baby nine months and not want it? This isn't a rape case, is it?"

"No, but it was like a one-night stand from what I gather. She didn't ever want children and her contraceptive failed."

"We going to keep her here and put her up for adoption?"

Dr. Joyce shook her head. "She has hired a nanny who will take the baby home with her. Who knows? Maybe the nanny can help her change her mind."

"I don't think so. She looks pretty determined. Who is she?"

"A very determined woman who does not want children."

Chapter 14

THEY WERE BARELY FIVE MILES OUT OF CHEYENNE heading south when Gemma's phone rang. She hit the speaker button and Trace's voice came through.

"I just talked to my Uncle Teamer. He is so excited about me coming home that he's made me homesick. I know how you feel now."

"Call me back in half an hour. That's Austin beeping in and she'll talk thirty minutes."

"BFF instead of phone sex. I'm hurt," he said.

She started to say something but the line was dead. She pushed a button and said, "Hello, Austin."

"Hello, yourself. Maddie just called and said you're coming home for a few days. Is that true? And congratulations on winning last night, before we get started on the scoop on Trace."

"Thank you, and there is no scoop on Trace. We're both going home for the week between the Dodge City and Cheyenne rodeos. How is Rachel? I miss her so much."

"She's in love with that colt of Liz's at the horse ranch. He comes straight to her when she gets into the pasture and she leads him all over the place. They have a language of their own. He'll neigh and she'll fuss at him in her baby talk, and Maddie says she's going to grow up to be a horse whisperer," Austin said.

"I'm missing too much of her growing up. Star lets her lead him without balking? Maybe she'll be a jockey. Momma must be bustin' her buttons with pride," Gemma said.

"Oh, yeah, Maddie takes her lawn chair out there and plenty of water bottles. I think she and Rachel could pitch a tent and live in the corral with Star. But Rachel was in this week for her checkup and the pediatrician says she'll probably be close to six feet tall, so forget about her being a jockey. She might be a trainer, but she won't be riding in competition. Unless she decides to do bronc busting like her Aunt Gemma."

"Nothing wrong with that either," Gemma said.

"Okay, enough evasion. You are trying to skirt the issue of Trace Coleman. We've already looked him up on the Internet and seen a couple videos of him riding. He's damn good. You've got some competition in that one. Now your turn. Tell me about him."

"I'd rather talk all morning about Rachel. I can't believe she's two already. When are you having a baby sister or brother for her?"

"In eight months, but we haven't told anyone else yet. And if you do, I'll douse you with poisoned watermelon wine. I just peed on a stick yesterday and I've been busting at the seams to tell, but we're waiting until Sunday when everyone is together. Baby is due in March."

"Oh! Oh!" Gemma was speechless.

"Now about this bronc riding cowboy. Everything else has been said," Austin told her. "So talk!"

"Shit!"

"What?"

"Jasmine got my blond-haired cowboy and my baby by Christmas. And I bet you got my next fortune. I can't have a baby by Christmas, but I thought that I just might get one by spring and now you laid claim to that. I just can't win. Someone is always too close to me when Liz tells my fortune and they wind up with my babies and my cowboys."

"When did you sleep with him?" Austin asked.

"Who?"

"Trace Coleman, I guess. Or is there another cowboy that's making spring babies with you?"

"I'm not pregnant. I told you, everyone else keeps stepping in front of me and getting my fortune. Is Rye ecstatic?"

"Oh, yes! He wants a dozen kids."

"And what do you want, Austin?"

"To make him happy. I love kids. Didn't realize it until we had Rachel, but she is so much fun. A dozen sounds like a good round number to me, especially since you won't get on the ball."

"Me? Liz and Colleen both are married. Talk to them. And Dewar could find a wife and help out there too," Gemma argued.

"Trace Coleman?" Austin said.

"Is a bronc rider. Was ahead of me until last night. Might be ahead of me again. Looks like we'll both make the playoffs if our luck holds. He's sexy and a damn good rider. And you can meet him at the finals if we both make it that far and then tell me what you think of him," Gemma said.

"Friend and foe?" Austin asked. "How do you handle that?"

"Friend outside of the arena. Foe inside it."

"Sounds very complicated. Which one is best?"

"Pretty equal right now. Now let's talk about Lucy and her getting married."

"Liz has a girls' night out planned for Tuesday. It's a wedding shower for Lucy with no guys. It's at her house, but believe me, we're going to want a full report about what is going on with this new cowboy. Is Trace good in bed?"

"Good Lord!"

Austin laughed. "That good, huh?"

"On that note I'm telling you good-bye. I'll see you real soon."

"And Tuesday you are going to answer a bunch of questions, so get ready for it," Austin said and hung up.

Gemma stared at the long stretch of highway in front of her and let her mind wander. The more she thought, the more complicated the situation became. Trace was hard as nails. She'd never have to worry about him letting her win a competition. He'd always give the ride a hundred and ten percent and when she did beat him, there would be no doubt that she did it on her own merits.

But then he had a soft side like when he sang that song as they were dancing. And the way he picked her up and carried her to the trailer and didn't even balk at the threshold. The way he just seemed to know if she wanted to be touched and sweet-talked for a long time before sex or if she was ready and wanted it right then.

"Good grief! I think I'm actually falling for this cowboy."

The miles ticked off slowly in Trace's truck. Miles, all six hundred plus that they'd make before pulling into Dodge City, went by at a snail's pace even though he was driving seventy-five miles an hour.

He wished that he was going home with her. He would have gladly changed his plans if she'd invited him, but she didn't.

"I'd get along fine with her family and friends. We're all ranchin' and rodeo people, and I do like her a lot. Wonder if she was waiting on me to invite her to go to Goodnight with me?" he said aloud.

Sugar chose that moment to lick his hand as if she agreed with him.

"Well, I do like her. She's independent as hell and speaks her mind. I betcha if she wanted an engagement ring for Christmas she'd step right up to the jewelry store window and point at the one she wanted," Trace told the dog.

Sugar yipped once, shut her eyes, and put a paw over her nose.

"Some friend you are," Trace said. "I thought we were going to visit to put in a few miles."

Trace opened the console between them and rifled through the CDs until he came to a Rascal Flatts. When the second song, "This Everyday Love," played, he chuckled out loud. The singer said that every afternoon he made a phone call to listen to the voice that warmed his heart.

"Hell, she don't warm it," he said aloud. "She sets it ablaze like an out-of-control Texas wildfire, but you are right, partner; I wouldn't change a thing about her. Not even her fierce determination."

Every song on the CD reminded him of Gemma in some crazy way. One song said that if he ever wrote the story of his life it would begin where she came into his life. And that he was born the day she kissed him and died the day she left him, but that he'd lived the time that she loved him.

"Does she love me?" Trace wondered aloud.

He had no idea what the answer to that question was, but down deep in his heart he knew that something would definitely die when the rodeo circuit was over and she went home to Ringgold. That's where her family, her beauty shop, and her life were all located. His life was over two hundred miles away in west Texas on a ranch outside of Goodnight, and he was too invested in it to make a change.

"Love won't conquer all, not even if Rascal Flatts thinks it will," he said. "Things are so sizzling hot between us right now that it couldn't last without burning up every emotion we have. Okay, okay, I'm analyzing out loud."

—⁓—

It was almost dark when they reached the rodeo grounds at Dodge City and made arrangements to leave their trailers and Gemma's truck there for a week. The place was empty and hollow sounding with none of the frantic energy that went on when a rodeo was set up on the grounds.

Every muscle in Gemma's body ached from riding and driving for the past nine hours. What she'd give for a long soaking bath couldn't be measured in dollars, but she'd have to make do that night with a shower in the trailer.

She bent forward and touched her nose to her knees when she crawled out of her truck. When it felt as if her backbone was as long as it was supposed to be and not scrunched up into six inches of space, she slowly straightened up. She raised both her hands in the air and leaned to the right as far as her tired muscles would let her and then to the left.

Trace watched the whole process from his truck as he fastened the leash to Sugar's collar. Gemma moved like an exotic cat. No wonder she could sit a bucking bronc for eight seconds and then stand in the arena like a ballerina while she waited for the scores. His couldn't blink for fear he'd miss her next move.

Finally, she caught him staring and said, "What?"

"Hungry?" he asked hoarsely.

"Starving, but there are no vendors. It's kind of spooky to be here without all the sparkle and fizz, isn't it?" she answered.

He nodded. "Pack a bag and let's go get a motel room for the night. We'll get pizza delivery or room service or whatever you want."

Her eyes lit up. "With a Jacuzzi in the room?"

He nodded. "If we can find a room with one."

"I'd eat bologna and cheese sandwiches if I could have a Jacuzzi tonight," she declared.

"We'll have to bring Sugar with us, but I'll take her pillow and she'll be happy in the bathroom," he said.

"She can sleep with us for all I care. I just want to soak the soreness out of my body."

"Then La Quinta it is," Trace said with a brilliant smile.

Half an hour later they were checked into a Jacuzzi suite. The door opened into a sitting room with a sofa, two chairs, and a plasma television the wall. And right there to the right of the cozy seating arrangement was an enormous Jacuzzi.

"Yes, yes, yes!" Gemma said. "I'm not even going to be nice and say you can get in first."

"That's right sweet of you," Trace said. "Only this ride is going to be a tie, my lady. That thing is plenty big enough for both of us."

She raised an eyebrow and hurried through an archway in the bedroom area. The king-sized bed looked softer than clouds, but it would have to wait until later. She cocked an ear toward the living area and couldn't hear water running so maybe Trace had changed his mind about sharing the tub. She heard him plop down on the sofa and start talking to Sugar.

"Dammit!" she swore under her breath.

Snippets of how they'd spend the last night they'd have together had flashed though her mind all day. None of them involved him sitting on the sofa watching television while she lazed in a Jacuzzi all alone.

She dropped her purse and duffel bag on the floor beside the bed, stripped out of all her clothing, and padded naked and barefoot to the tub. She turned on the water, adjusted it, twisted her ponytail into a messy bun, and secured it with a clamp she'd dug out of her purse.

The water was barely ankle deep when she sat down in it and leaned her head back on a rolled towel, but the faucet was spitting it out with such force that it wouldn't take long to fill completely.

"Comfortable?" Trace asked from the sofa where he and Sugar had collapsed.

"It will be when it's full. Shuck out of those clothes and come on in," she said.

When she heard a boot thump she slid one eye open to watch the show. Trace kicked off the other boot and caught her staring, flashed his most brilliant smile ever, and opened up his laptop.

"Dammit, Trace! You can check your emails any- where. Jacuzzi suites are not free. I know you paid high dollar for this room," she grouched.

His grin got even bigger when he hit a few keys and suddenly music came floating out of the tinny speakers on the computer. Blake Shelton was singing "Hillbilly Bone," and Trace turned it into the sexiest damn strip song in the whole world.

He undid his belt buckle to the beat of the drums, and Gemma couldn't even blink for fear she'd miss some- thing. It took so long to unzip his jeans that she thought she'd die before he finally got them undone. And dur- ing the whole process, his dark eyes never left hers. He peeled his britches down to his ankles and kicked them to one side and then pulled his shirt up to reveal abs that a weight lifter would commit homicide for. The song ended at the same time he was totally naked, wearing nothing but a smile.

She crooked a finger, motioning him to get in with her. Still staring right into her eyes, he leaned forward and kissed her hard without touching her anywhere else. Her whole body begged for more, more touching, more kisses.

"Honey Bee" by Blake was playing when he finally slid into the water. His toes came to rest against her thigh and he wiggled them in a gentle massage. How in the hell toes against her leg could turn her on was a mystery, but not as great a one as how the water kept from boiling.

He pushed the button and the water began to bubble,

sending massaging jets against her back. The sensation of his foot against her skin, the bursting bubbles on her back, and the vision of the fine dark hair on his chest matted down with water sent delicious warmth through her body.

"I really will be your honeybee." He grinned.

"We never had our talk."

"We've got weeks and weeks to figure this out," he answered.

She nodded. "New game rules."

"You're going to let me win at Vegas?" he asked.

"Hell no!"

"Then I get to call the game rules for this Jacuzzi. Only one body part can touch the other one. My foot on your thigh for two whole minutes, moving any way I want it to move and then it's your turn," he said.

She grinned. "I can live with those rules. Your two minutes are up, so it's my turn."

She rose up in the water just as "Angels Fall Sometimes" began to play. She started a very slow dance, bending at the waist to brush a kiss across his lips without touching another part of his body. When Josh sang about her bringing pieces of heaven every day to his life, Gemma kissed Trace again—with more passion and lingering all the way through the lyrics about him not being afraid to dream high with her by his side.

"Your turn," she said when the song ended.

"Lord Have Mercy on a Country Boy" started playing, and the mischievous look in his eyes said that he was going to make her pay dearly for her sexy dance.

"I choose one finger and your beautiful face."

How in the hell could a finger on her face be sexy,

she wondered. But in less than fifteen seconds she was panting. He made love to her face using only the forefinger on his right hand. His finger moved down her jawline so softly that it felt like butterfly wings brushing against her skin.

His lips moved so close to hers that she could taste the kiss, and then he traced the outline of her full lips with his finger. She had to tense her body to keep from reaching out and pulling his lips to hers for a kiss. His touch on her eyelids shot sensations all the way to her toenails, and the bridge of her nose became an erogenous zone when he drew a line to her chin and then down her neck. He stopped before he reached her breasts.

"Just the neck up this time. Next time I'll choose another area of your gorgeous body," he said.

"Game over. I can't take anymore," she whispered hoarsely and straddled his lap.

"I really will be your honeybee," he mumbled as she guided him into her.

"I know. We are hotter'n hell together, Trace."

They moved as if they were meant to make love underwater, the sensation of the jets making them both hotter with every thrust.

"This is even better than bathtub sex," she gasped

"More room and the bubbles are sin in a bucket," he said.

He brought her to the edge of satisfaction several times before she tangled her hands in his hair and whispered his name. "Trace, please, darlin'."

"Right now?" he asked.

"Yes!"

One more hard thrust and she leaned backwards so far

that her hair touched the water behind her. She hadn't even realized that he'd removed the clamp and taken out the ponytail holder until she snuggled back into the crook of his neck and her hair fell around her face.

That's some hot damn sex when I don't even know when he takes my hair down.

Chapter 15

MADDIE NODDED AT GRANDPA. QUIETNESS FELL OVER the house as everyone bowed their heads. Grandpa said a short grace and immediately the noise level went from dead silent to raising-the-roof clamor in two seconds.

Maddie nudged Gemma with her elbow.

"Come on over here. We'll let the noisy bunch have the table and you and I'll sit at this card table right here. I need to hear more about this cowboy you've been keeping company with. I looked him up and found out that his father is a lawyer and his mother is a judge. How in the world did he ever get into ranching and rodeo?"

"His Uncle Teamer is a rancher and all three of his cousins are ranchers."

Gemma's father, Cash, yelled from the end of the big dining room table, "How do the cowboys take a cowgirl giving them such rugged competition?"

"They don't like it a bit," Gemma answered.

"Well, you keep showin' them who's boss." Cash chuckled.

Gemma nodded. "Momma, this is wonderful chicken and dressing."

Maddie buttered a hot roll and asked, "Do those cowboys treat you with respect?"

"If they don't, they don't live to ride the next time." Gemma laughed.

Cash yelled across the din again, "That's my girl. She's right, Maddie. This is damn fine dressin'."

Dalton, one of Ace's younger brothers, joined Maddie and Gemma at their table. "I hear you are giving Trace Coleman a run for his money. Did he think he could just waltz into the rodeo scene and steal the whole show?"

Gemma smiled. "He's not all that egotistical, but I'm going to win."

"That sounds pretty egotistical to me." Dalton grinned.

Gemma slapped him on the arm and kept eating.

He grabbed his bicep and pretended to grimace. "She hit me. She's mean, Maddie."

Maddie smiled. "Children, you are supposed to behave at Sunday dinner. After dinner you can go out to the horse barn and duke it out, but be nice at the dinner table. I'm finished, so I'm going to go cut the pies and get out the ice cream for the cobbler."

"Need some help?" Dalton asked.

Maddie stood up and laid a hand on Dalton's shoulder. "Thank you, but Ace came over before church this morning and helped get the ice cream ready. We made it by his momma's recipe using peaches instead of bananas since they're in season right now."

"Does Trace Coleman raise horses or just cattle out there in the Panhandle?" Dalton turned back to look at Gemma.

"I have no idea and I'm tired of hearing about, talking about, or listening to people discuss Trace Coleman. I'm the one who is home."

"Yes, ma'am. Guess you got a soft spot where that rough old bronc rider is concerned."

"He's just a cowboy like all of you," she said.

Maddie sat back down in her chair. "When she wins the title and the money in Vegas she's going to buy her own piece of land. I've got one picked out between us and Henrietta that she's going to fall in love with the minute she sees it."

"I'll pick out my own land when I win!" Gemma exclaimed.

"Well, it just now went on the market and I told Willard Dean that you might be interested so he's holding it until you win. I haven't got a problem with you fallin' for that cowboy, Gemma, but you will live around here when you settle down."

"And if I don't?" Gemma asked.

"Marry Dalton," Maddie said.

"That could be arranged." Dalton grinned. "I've always had a thing for older women."

"Ouch!" Gemma grabbed her heart as if he'd stabbed her.

"Want me to drop down on my knee right now? That way I'd get the woman and the ranch I've been wanting to buy for over a year. I went out to Willard's yesterday and gave him a bid, but he said he was under a verbal contract until December. You win. You buy the ranch and marry me and we'll live happily ever after."

"You are crazy." Gemma laughed.

"Hey, Dewar, how long are you going to let your sister live in your house?" Dalton yelled above the noise.

"Until I find a wife. They say no house is big enough for two women." Dewar laughed.

"That settles it." Gemma laughed. "I can be there until hell freezes over because Dewar is one of those bad boys. He's not husband material."

"Oh, finish your dinner," Maddie grumbled. "Granny's been talking about you coming home all week so we can play and sing. But put this in your pipe, young lady: you are not getting married to a cowboy who lives that far away. I'll sabotage the whole thing if I have to. Dalton, don't take your offer of marriage off the table before December."

"Ain't got a woman in mind right now and I'll gladly marry Gemma to get Willard's place. Then when she dies I'll still be young enough to get me a trophy wife to strut around Montague County with." He laughed.

"Good Lord! You are planning my marriage and my funeral all at one time." Gemma groaned.

"Well, you are the older woman. You are at least five or six years older than me so you should die before me," Dalton said. "Maddie, did you say there was peach cobbler to go with that ice cream? I was thinking of another helping of chicken and dressin', but if there is cobbler, I'm holding out for dessert."

"There's pecan pie and peach cobbler. And when is Colleen getting here anyway? I know you made that cobbler and ice cream special for her, Momma." Gemma pointed to the bowl in front of Maddie.

"Colleen called at midmorning and said they were running late. Something about packing up the carnival this morning. Anyway, she'll be here in a few more minutes. She said twelve thirty at the latest but not to hold dinner for her," Maddie answered and held a spoonful of ice cream toward Gemma. "Taste this. It's always better after it sets up. Just think, you could have this every summer if you marry Dalton, because his momma has the recipe."

Gemma had no choice but to open her mouth. "Y'all are crazy. I'm not engaged to Trace Coleman. He hasn't even mentioned marriage, so wiggle around in that seat, Momma, and get your panties out of that wad they're in."

Before Maddie could scold her, Colleen and Blaze rushed inside the house.

"We're here! And Dewar, if you ate all my ice cream, I'm going to whip you all over this yard," Colleen said.

"Can I sell tickets to the show?" Austin asked.

Colleen stopped long enough to hug her and headed straight for the kitchen.

Gemma pushed back her chair and followed Colleen into the kitchen. "You look good, girl."

Colleen gave her a quick hug on the run. "So do you! I'm starving. I'll catch the rest of you later, but if I don't eat I'll faint plumb away. That man out there didn't give me anything but cold funnel cakes for breakfast this morning."

"She's not telling the whole truth and nothing but the truth. And where is Trace Coleman? I heard he might be here," Blaze called out.

"He's not here and Gemma is going to marry Dalton and buy Willard Dean's ranch," Maddie said.

The whole dining room went silent.

"Maddie is teasing," Dalton said. "I couldn't marry Gemma. Lord, that would be like marryin' up with my older sister."

"I can see I've missed something." Blaze headed for the kitchen. "Hey, don't you eat all that dressin', woman. I've been waitin' a whole week to get at your momma's chicken and dressin'."

Colleen slung her natural burgundy-colored hair over

her shoulder and grinned at her husband. "You'd better hurry up then. And if any of the rest of you want some more dressin', you'd best shove your way to the buffet because when this man gets started, there won't be anything left."

Gemma went back to the dining room and touched her sister-in-law, Liz, on the shoulder. "You done eating?"

Liz stood up. "Sure am."

"Let's go on outside and tune up the Dobro and fiddle, then," Gemma said.

"I'm ready." She pushed back an empty ice cream bowl.

Leaving the air-conditioning for outside was like stepping from a freezer into a bake oven. By the time she and Liz reached the shade tree where the chairs were set up with the instruments, Gemma's thin cotton blouse hung limp and stuck to her sweaty body.

"It's too hot to play out here. The instruments shouldn't even be sitting in this heat. We need to take this inside," Gemma said.

"Maddie says we're playing outside and Granny has looked forward to it all week. And we only brought the instruments out just before you drove up. It's hot, but it's coming out of the cool into it that is a bitch. You'll adjust. Besides, you can't tell me you haven't been hot this month, but I got to tell you, Maddie is going to be cussin' mad if there's something serious going on with that Trace Coleman. She's working an angle to get you to buy a ranch close to Ringgold so you'll be tied to the area. She says she's not losing you."

Gemma sighed.

"Pretty obvious, wasn't she, with all that talk about marrying Dalton? If he was any other cowboy but

Dalton Riley, he would have been embarrassed to the bone, but he played along with the joke pretty damn good." Liz laughed.

Gemma picked up the Dobro and sat down. Her thighs stuck to the metal chair with a fine layer of sweat as she strummed down across the strings, made adjustments to tune the instrument, and strummed again.

Liz positioned her fiddle on her shoulder and ran the bow down the strings, made an adjustment, and tried again. "She's been like a cat in hot water ever since you told her about being drugged and sleeping in Trace's trailer. He's got a reputation like Blaze had, you know?"

"For what? Being a good bronc buster and bull rider?"

Liz sat down beside Gemma. "No, for womanizing. How is he in bed?"

Gemma blushed. "Reputation don't always tell the truth."

"You aren't going to answer me, are you?"

"Y'all girls gettin' it all ready?" Granny joined them.

"Saved by the bell." Liz laughed.

Granny chose the mandolin that afternoon and ran through a few chords on it with Liz and Gemma following her lead. Raylen joined them next and picked up a second violin.

"Okay, before they all get here give me some 'The Devil Went Down to Georgia,'" Granny said.

"You always ask for that." Liz grinned.

"And I always will. Someday one of you is going to make a mistake and I'll declare one of you the best fiddler in the state, but I got to hear it every time so I can be sure it's still a tie."

Granny pointed at Gemma. "And you come sit by me while they're fiddlin'."

Gemma moved down two chairs and fast fiddling music drifted out across the whole ranch.

Granny patted her on the shoulder. "I told Maddie to let you make your own decisions about where you might settle down and who you will marry or else she'll regret the whole thing in years to come."

"It's not serious, Granny," Gemma said. "Momma doesn't need to be trying to buy a ranch for me or worrying about me getting married. I swear, she's got wedding bells on the brain."

"Honey, she's been scared out of her mind about this new feller. She says she hears it in your voice and she ain't wantin' both of her daughters to run off to the Panhandle. I ain't never seen her act like this neither."

"I don't know what she thinks she's hearing, but all I've got on my mind is winning this bronc busting event in Vegas," Gemma said.

Before the song ended the yard had filled up with folks—some picking up instruments, some sitting on quilts. Some leaning against the trees.

Granny yelled out, "Bill Bailey," and they all started playing at the same time.

When they finished she handed off the mandolin to Raylen who laid his fiddle to one side and fell in behind the rest of the musicians as they played "Red River Valley." Gemma handed the Dobro to Colleen and sat down on the quilt. Rachel backed up and sat down in her lap. She hugged the little dark-haired girl, loving the smell of baby shampoo and sweaty kid all mixed up together.

"Hey, everyone, we're here. Don't start gossip without me." Pearl waved from the truck. She and Wil each carried a wiggling toddler son with dark hair and more energy than a class-five tornado. They set them down on the edge of the quilt and both boys made a beeline for Rachel, grabbed her by the hands, and pulled.

She left Gemma's lap and led them to Austin.

"Star?" she said.

"After a while. You and the boys go play in the sandbox." Austin pointed toward the play area with a sandbox and swing set under the shade of a big pecan tree.

The three kids scampered off to the sandbox and the bright-colored toys sitting along the side.

Liz laid down her fiddle and joined the group on the quilt. She poked Gemma on the leg. "Confession time. Pretend I'm your priest and we're in two little dark rooms. Now tell me all about Trace Coleman. Has Maddie got something to really worry about?"

"I'm not Catholic, and if you're a priest, I'm St. Peter." Gemma laughed.

"I don't care who is what!" Pearl exclaimed. "What are y'all talkin' about? What'd I miss? I knew we should've told Momma that we couldn't meet her for Sunday dinner in Bowie. I missed something good, didn't I?"

"Oh, yeah, you did," Colleen joined them. "They can play without me. I wouldn't miss this gossip session for the world. Momma is ready to crucify you."

"I thought you weren't going to let any cowboys ruin your game," Pearl said.

Colleen smiled. "Looks like one is about to do just that, and he lives right out by Claude, so if she hooks up with him she'll be close to me in the winters. Momma might hate the idea, but I love it."

"Talk!" Pearl pointed at Gemma.

Liz pointed at Gemma. "Maddie is going to put a chastity belt on you and send you to a convent on a deserted island."

Gemma put up both palms defensively. "Y'all stop it! He's my biggest competition. So Liz, your fortune-telling is still in question, and Colleen, don't get your hopes up that I'll be living in Goodnight, Texas, when the dust settles in Vegas. Don't you think if this was really all that serious that he would have invited me to go home with him?"

A short burst of laughter came from Austin's corner. "Honey, you aren't fooling me! I'd bet dollars to fool's gold that it is serious as hell. Why didn't you invite him here?"

"Because Momma would have a heart attack."

Maddie laid the Dobro on the chair and started out across the lawn.

"Huh-oh," Liz muttered.

Maddie settled down right in the middle of all six young women, and Granny drug up a chair at the edge.

"I heard my name," Maddie said.

"I said that you'd have had a heart attack if I invited Trace Coleman home with me for a week," Gemma said honestly.

Maddie pointed her finger. "Gemma Irene O'Donnell!"

"I don't know why everyone keeps pointing at me today," Gemma said. "I couldn't wait to get home, but now I wish I would've stayed on the dude ranch this week."

Liz spread her arms out. "Move back, everyone. I've

been in this family a whole year and I didn't even know Gemma had a second name. Hell is about to rain brimstone down upon us all."

"Why did you tell Willard I might buy his ranch? And why were you going on about me marrying Dalton?" Gemma asked.

"She's right, Maddie. You want her to settle right here in Ringgold and you're going about it all wrong," Granny said.

"You don't get a vote in this," Maddie told her mother.

Granny laughed. "Hey, I might have done some manipulation in my day, but it didn't involve buying a damned ranch. Besides, I knew Cash O'Donnell was the man for you. I was right, too. You love Cash and you've got five beautiful children. He's a damn good father."

Maddie started to point but dropped her hand. "I don't want you to move away from Ringgold."

"Momma, don't be looking at wedding dresses just yet. I think there's something about a proposal and there ain't been one yet," Gemma said.

"Hmmmph!" Maddie snorted. "Your lips are saying one thing. Your eyes say another."

Granny touched her daughter on the shoulder. "Maddie, don't worry about how many chickens you got to feed until they hatch."

The music stopped and Rye smiled at Austin. She stood up and he slipped an arm around her waist. "Hey, everyone, gather around. We've got some news."

Gemma could have kissed her older brother for choosing that moment to make his announcement.

Rye took a deep breath. "Rachel will have a baby sister or brother next March. Right now she says she wants a brother like Jesse and John, but we'll be real happy with whatever we get."

It went from quiet to full-blown noise in less than two seconds. Everyone, including Maddie, was busy hugging Rye and Austin when Gemma's phone buzzed in her hip pocket. *Trace Calling* showed up on the screen, so she carried it away from the noise and sat down in Grandpa's rocking chair on the front porch.

Trace's voice was even deeper over the phone, and she wished she was lying beside him in his bed.

"I miss you. Are you okay?"

"I keep tellin' you I'm tough, but my momma is trying to force me into buying a ranch in Ringgold. I wish I'd stayed on at the dude ranch."

Trace chuckled. "I don't hear music. I thought y'all were playing music this afternoon."

"Austin and Rye just announced that they are having another baby in March so they're getting all the attention, thank God!"

"Call me if things get too hot and we'll go to Dodge City early."

"Will do," she said.

───※───

Trace pulled into the yard in front of his house on the Coleman ranch just as Teamer came out onto the porch. He shaded his eyes with his hand and then waved at Trace. "Come on in out of the heat, son. Sunday Supper is near to bein' ready, and the boys are washin' up. Thought I was going to have to come get you."

Trace turned Sugar loose and she took off like a streak toward Teamer. He scooped her up while her legs were still churning and got a face full of doggy licks for his welcome.

"That old cowboy ought to leave you here with me when he goes off on his trips. Goodness only knows he don't take care of you right while you're out there on the road," Teamer crooned.

"She's spoiled rotten." Trace laid a hand on his uncle's shoulder and squeezed.

"Trace, I got something to say but not tonight. We are goin' to talk about this ranch while you are home, so you might as well get ready for it, son."

Trace chuckled. It was good to be home, and his uncle could talk and he'd listen. That didn't mean he'd obey.

"I'm hungry. I missed Louis's cookin'."

Teamer was tall and lanky, sinewy but strong-looking, had a mop of gray hair that always needed trimming, and clear blue eyes that could cut steel when he was angry. "Hey, boys, he's here. Time to put it on the table."

Trace smelled grilled steaks when he followed Teamer into the house. "Louis did do the cooking tonight, huh?"

Louis carried a platter piled high with steaks into the dining room and set them on the table. He was a short, stocky cowboy with bowed legs and a spare tire around his middle right above his belt. His face was as round as his body and his thick gray hair cut close to his head.

Louis clapped Trace on the shoulder. "Of course I grilled the steaks. Teamer would char them so black that the hound dogs out in the yard would be gnawin' on them when the winter snow comes. And I made the chocolate pies for dessert, and the rest of the meal. I keep tellin' that old fart that we need a woman on the place. One that can cook. Then I could go on back out in the fields and do some real work. I'm gettin' fat stayin' in the kitchen so much."

Teamer sat down at the end of the table and pointed at Louis. "And I keep tellin' that old fart that a woman would mess up our way of doin' things. Hell, she'd probably want to put doilies all over everything and start collectin' ugly ceramic ducks and elephants. And besides, he's old so he's got a right to get fat."

Gage and Kevlin both came through the kitchen door at the same time. Gage was eighteen and starting college that fall. He was six inches shorter than Trace but square built and strong as an ox. It was his fourth year working for Teamer in the summer months. His young brother, Kevlin, would be a junior in high school come fall, and it was his second summer on the Coleman ranch.

"Thank God you are here for a few days!" Gage said. "Those two need some discipline, and me and Kevlin, well, they don't listen to a thing we have to say."

"Y'all had to put up with this ever since I left?" Trace asked.

Gage nodded, but his face split into a wide grin. "They're like an old married couple. Bitchin' and snappin' at each other all the time. But let me or Kevlin say a word and they stick together like Siamese twins. You need to straighten 'em both out while you are home."

Trace looked at Kevlin.

The younger boy just shook his head. "Never a dull minute. We missed you, and what's this about you foolin' around and lettin' a girl whip your scrawny ass?

We need to give you some more lessons on stayin' in the saddle?"

Trace shook his head slowly. "That's one piece of sassy baggage that's been whippin' me. And if you got any magic tricks about how to get more points, I'm all for learning. How about right now we dive into those steaks before Louis throws it all out for the dogs in a fit of anger."

Teamer passed the platter of steaks, followed by bowls of steaming fried potatoes, fried squash, and black-eyed peas. Then he started a platter of sliced cucumber, tomatoes, and peppers around. The finale was a big plate of hot biscuits.

They set into their food like hungry hounds after a long night of coon hunting. Teamer was the first one to break the silence and only after he'd finished half his food.

"So talk to us and tell us why that woman is beating your ass," he said.

"Because she's that good. We're both linin' up pretty solid to be finalists. I just hope that she'll have a big wreck then and I can come home with the win at the end," Trace said.

"And maybe she won't," Louis said.

"Guess we'll know soon enough."

"What does she look like? We saw her on television, but mostly all we saw was a blur of hot pink when she come out of the chute. Is she all mannish lookin', and does she dip snuff?" Kevlin said.

Trace thought before he spoke. "She's about five feet three inches tall and has to put rocks in her pockets to hold her down in a hard windstorm. She's got red hair, but she tells me it's out of a bottle and she is a natural brunette, the most amazing green eyes, and she's meaner than a rattlesnake when it comes to riding and soft as an angel when she's not riding."

"I'd let someone like that win for sure. You kissed her yet?" Kevlin said.

"You better watch that hussy. She'll be throwing you off your ride, and when the dust settles she'll have the prize and you'll have a busted ego," Louis said.

Trace looked at Teamer.

"She as good as they say?"

Trace nodded.

"She know anything about ranchin'?"

Another nod.

"Now answer Kevlin's question, son," Teamer said.

"Which one?" Trace asked.

"That one about kissin' her."

Trace shook his head. "Good cowboys don't kiss and tell. You taught me that yourself, remember?"

Teamer chuckled. "I'd say she'd do to ride the river with, son. Now eat the rest of your dinner. Potatoes and squash ain't worth shit when they're cold. Besides, we got chocolate pies in the icebox, and Louis will whine like a little girl if you boys don't brag on them."

Lucy looked around the room at the decorations, the cake, the presents, and all her friends.

"Hey, you aren't supposed to cry," Wilma said.

"But you all did this just for me." Lucy sniffled.

"And look what all you've done for us," Wilma told her. "I work for Liz, and Noreen is picking up her life at the beauty shop, and look around, Lucy, at all the women you've helped get their lives back on track."

Gemma patted her on the back. "And those like me who still need you to get theirs on track."

"Come on and sit down. You are going to open presents first and then eat cake and talk until we run out of things to talk about," Liz said.

Lucy dabbed her eyes. "Then I reckon I'd better call Tyson and tell him I won't be home for two days because it'll take us that long to catch up on gossip, and let me tell you right now, I've never opened this many presents in my whole life, total, not just at one sittin', and I'm going to enjoy every moment, so don't rush me."

Lucy was a small woman with nondescript brown hair, big soulful eyes, and a heart as big as the whole state of Texas, especially when it came to those in her abused women's program.

She'd barely gotten started opening presents when Gemma's phone vibrated in her back pocket. She slipped off to the bathroom, put the potty lid down, and sat down before she answered Trace's tenth call that day.

"Party over?" he asked.

"Just beginning. Lucy is opening presents, but she's slow as molasses in Alaska in December. She even keeps the paper and the ribbons. So we can talk for a few minutes," she whispered.

"Where are you? I don't hear squealing and lots of woman oohing and ahhing over presents."

"I'm in the bathroom."

Trace chuckled in his deep drawl. "Lock the door, take off all your clothes, and send me a naked picture of you in the mirror."

"Trace Coleman!"

"I will if you will," he teased.

"I don't need a picture. All I have to do is shut my eyes to see you are doing a strip to 'Hillbilly Bone.'"

A long pregnant pause made her hold the phone out to see if she'd lost connection.

"Trace?"

"I'm lying here on the bed looking out at the stars. I'm naked and the cold air from the ceiling fan is making the hair on my arms stand straight up. I'm thinking about you all wet and slick doing that little dance for me in the Jacuzzi," he whispered.

Crimson crept up her neck and into her cheeks. "I will get even."

"Turned you on, did I?"

"Let's just say I'll have to wash my face in cold water and stay in here until I stop panting before I go back out there."

"Hey, Gemma. I… miss… you," he said seductively.

"You are in big trouble."

She'd barely gotten back to her chair when her phone vibrated again. She slipped it out and laid it on the chair seat beside her. Trace had sent her a text: *Does being in big trouble mean you're going to let me win in Dodge City?*

She carefully sent back a message: *Dream on!*

She turned off her phone and shoved it in her hip pocket.

"Okay, Lucy, now tell us all about this wedding and why it was so sudden," Gemma teased.

"Sudden!" Lucy exclaimed. "I thought I never was going to get that man out of his shell enough to propose to me. And when he finally did I got him to the altar as fast as I could so he wouldn't change his mind."

Gemma wondered what she'd do if Trace proposed. Would she rush him to the church the very next day or would she want the big wedding that Colleen had? Could they live together more than a week without the wildfire burning itself out? She loved everything about Ringgold, but she also wanted to be back at the rodeo with Trace. She already missed bickering with him, his kisses, and the way her body felt when he touched her. The week was going to last forever.

———✦———

Trace was in the hay field when his phone rang. He drug it out of a sweaty shirt pocket and answered, "Hello, darlin'," in his best Conway Twitty impression.

"Is it really only Thursday? I feel like I've been home a month."

"Momma still mad?" Trace asked.

"No, she's over that. Momma don't stay mad long. But I'm ready to bust broncs and smell rodeo dust."

"It's addictive, isn't it?"

"Tomorrow won't never get here, will it?"

"Want me to put down these hay hooks and come get you right now?" he asked.

"What I want and what I'll get are two different things. Since I'm home and there's an extra rider to exercise the horses, Raylen and Liz went off on a three-day holiday to spend time with her grandpa and uncle. They're over in your part of the world and I'm in Ringgold."

"Seems to me that not long ago you couldn't wait to get home to Ringgold where your roots are. Why aren't you fixing hair this week?"

"I'm going to fix hair this afternoon," Gemma said.

"I need a haircut. If I wait until next week, will you cut it for me? Naked?" he asked.

She moaned at the picture that produced. "Which one of us?"

"Both," he said.

"One naked haircut after I win in Dodge City."

"You will never get to me say yes to that," he said.

She laughed. "I'll give you a haircut no matter who wins and we can both be naked. You sure you'll trust me with scissors when I win? I'll be pretty giddy."

"Well, I sure wouldn't trust you with them when you lose and I win," he said. "You'll cut my ear off just for spite."

"Long as I don't harm your hands, I reckon you could give up one ear," she teased.

"What are you wearing right now?"

"Nothing, darlin'. I'm riding bareback as naked as the day I was born. My hair is flowing down my back, and the wind is in my face."

"You are a witch, Gemma O'Donnell. Now I'll have that picture in my mind all day."

"I told you paybacks are a bitch, didn't I? Now we are even."

He slid the phone back in his pocket, picked up the hooks, and slung another bale of hay off the back of the truck into the barn. Kevlin grabbed it, stacked it, and turned for the next one.

"Was that the hottie you been moonin' around about all week?" he asked Trace.

"It was Gemma, but I haven't been moonin' around," Trace answered.

"Yeah, man, you have. You better be careful or that hussy will use all that moonin' to make you feel sorry for her and let her win. Then she'll run off with some other rich cowboy and you'll be left with nothin' but a pair of spurs and a gold hat pin."

"You sure are wise for a sixteen-year-old kid," Trace said sarcastically.

Kevlin smiled and wiped sweat from his forehead with a red bandana. "Out of the mouths of babes. I been around the rodeo arena a few times. Them women can sure mess you up, no matter how old you are or how pretty they are."

It was noon when Gemma opened the door to her beauty shop and got a whiff of hair spray, dye, and fingernail polish all mixed together. It was almost as intoxicating as the dust in the arena while she rode a bronc.

"I was wondering if you'd come around or if you'd call and tell me you had something else going today, what with Liz and Raylen gone." Noreen's Native American blood showed in her high cheekbones, her long dark hair, and brown eyes. She was tall and rail thin, wore jeans, a knit shirt, and sneakers.

"Oh, no! I had to see how things were going. Looks like you are keeping the place up in fine style," Gemma said.

"Here comes Nellie Luckadeau and her sister. Which one do you want?"

"I'll take Ellen. I need to get my hands in the dye and do some ratting. The higher I can get that red hair for Ellen, the better she likes it," Gemma answered.

Ellen's eyes lit up when she saw Gemma. "Well,

lookee here—who has come home just to fix my hair today? I swear Noreen is good, but darlin', she don't know how to rat like you do. No offence, Noreen. And you are keeping your hair red. That's what's bringing you good luck with that cowboy that has Maddie in a mood. I told you that red hair was the best good luck token you could take with you on this trip."

"This girl has been ratting hair so long it's second nature to her. Get in a chair and let her take them pins out before she goes to washin' and settin'," Noreen said.

Gemma fell into the work just as easily as she rode the broncs. Both were second nature like Noreen said. She removed the pins from Ellen's hair and brushed it out, then fastened a cape around her shoulders and led her back to the sinks.

"So what's been going on since I left?" she asked.

"Slade and Jane are expecting their third baby. This one is a boy, and them two girls they've already got is going to make him toe the line. Two older sisters need a little brother. Me and Nellie needed a brother, but all we got was each other. If we'd have had a brother he would make her not be so grumpy in her old age. I tell you, she's got so cranky that I can't hardly even live with her. Do you know she still won't let me drive?" Ellen tattled.

Nellie piped up from the sink right next to her sister. "She hasn't driven in years because she's got lead feet and thinks she's a teenager. Hell, Gemma, I don't even drive anymore except for the old work trucks and tractors out on the property. Jane just dropped us off for our hair fixin's while she runs into Bowie for her doctor's appointment."

Ellen shut her eyes while Gemma scrubbed her

scalp. "She's not lyin'. I do like speed and hot men and hard liquor."

"She's been wild her whole life." Nellie sighed.

"And I've lived every minute of it."

"If you want to drive so damn bad then you can drive the work truck, but you can't drive the tractor because they are too damned expensive to fix and you'd break something for sure."

Ellen giggled like a schoolgirl. "Can I drive the truck to the dance tomorrow night?"

Nellie almost came up out of the chair but checked herself. "Hell, no! You can't drive it off the property. It's not even tagged."

"Well, I could drive it so fast that the policeman couldn't even tell that it didn't have a tag," Ellen said.

"No! And that is final," Nellie said.

"Shit! What's the use of gettin' my hair all done and not even be able to cruise over to Wichita Falls for a dance?"

Gemma giggled.

"Don't laugh at her," Nellie said. "It makes her worse."

"Oh, hush. Just because you got old don't mean I intend to," Ellen said.

Gemma rinsed and conditioned Ellen's over-dyed, over-ratted, and over-sprayed hair. Then she wrapped a towel around her head and pushed the lever to raise the chair up.

"Let's go get your dye mixed and on. Nellie, has she always been a redhead?" Gemma asked, knowing that question would set them off again.

"Ever since she was born, and she's had the temper to go with it. I swear I didn't think that attitude came in a box of hair dye, but it does." Nellie laughed.

She loved listening to them bicker and argue and hoped when she and Colleen were old that they were just like them. If she lived in the Panhandle they'd be close enough as old women that they might even end up living on the same property in their old age, like Nellie and Ellen.

"Okay, enough bitchin' from us two old women," Nellie said bluntly. "We want to hear about this cowboy who is makin' Maddie close to havin' a heart attack."

It was on the end of Gemma's tongue to say, "I miss him like crazy."

But Ellen took off before she could say a word. "I know menfolk real well. How is he in bed?"

"Ellen!" Noreen said.

"Well, I got to know if he's any good in bed before I pass judgment. Does he make you go all oozy when he kisses you?" Ellen asked.

"Ellen, for God's sake!" Nellie slapped her arm.

"I'll call the cops and sue you for elderly abuse if you do that again." Ellen glared at her. "Does he?" She looked in the mirror at Gemma's reflection.

"Yes, he does," Gemma said.

Ellen stuck her tongue out at Nellie. "Then I expect he's worth whatever it takes to get him roped down."

"Maddie is going to be a handful," Nellie said.

"Yes, she is," Noreen agreed.

Gemma listened with one ear to them go from one gossip topic to another. The other ear stayed focused on the cell phone in the back pocket of her jeans. Maybe Trace would call when he took a break. She missed him so damn much that it hurt, and her mother could get over it. If he appeared at the door of her beauty shop right then and asked her to run away with him, she'd drop the hair dye and be gone before Nellie could roll her eyes at Ellen one more time.

———※———

Gemma awoke on Friday morning at the crack of dawn. She couldn't sleep so she went to the stables and saddled up a mare. When the sun peeked over the horizon she was exercising her third horse of the morning and heading out over the rolling hills toward her Granny's house. The door opened before she could rap on it, and Granny motioned her inside.

"We seen you ridin' out over the rise and hoped you'd come for breakfast. Your grandpa made pancakes and sausage this morning. Never cooked a meal in his life until he retired, and now I gotta fight him to get in the kitchen."

Grandpa poured pancake batter on a cast-iron griddle and talked as he cooked. "Sit right down there, sweet baby girl. How's it been goin' this week? Maddie over that snit?"

Gemma picked up a sausage patty from the plate in the middle of the table and nibbled at the corners. "She's gettin' over it. I called Willard and told him not to hang on to the ranch in hopes that I'd buy it. Dalton Riley has made him a pretty good offer on it and I think he'll sell to him."

"She wanted you to have Creed Riley, but he up and married that painter from out in the Panhandle last winter. Until then his eyes were still wanderin'. He just couldn't get settled on one woman," Grandpa said. "When a man's eyes stop wanderin' and he can't see nothin' except the pretty little gal right in front of him, then he's ready to settle down."

"So, Great and Noble Wise Man, what if I did get tangled up with Trace Coleman?" Gemma asked.

Granny popped her hands on her hips. "Don't call him no wise man. Lord, child, that was the men who came to bring presents to baby Jesus. Your grandpa ain't that smart. Coffee or juice?"

"Coffee, and I believe Grandpa might be that smart, Granny."

"Y'all two stop your bickerin' and I'll tell you my opinion. Soon as I serve up some breakfast."

The pancakes were browned perfectly, so Gemma held her plate out and Grandpa stacked three huge ones up on it.

"Grandpa, I love Ringgold and my roots are deep here, but…" she said.

"But you might like that cowboy enough to dig them roots up and plant them somewhere else?" Grandpa asked.

"I wanted to come home and find answers, but all I got was more questions," she said.

"Darlin', you got one ass. You can't ride two broncs with it at one time. Make a choice and don't never look back, just forward. It's your choice to make. Not mine or Granny's or your momma's or daddy's. It's your ass and you decide which one of them broncs is going to give you the best ride for the rest of your life. And that's my opinion," Grandpa told her.

"See, he is wise," Gemma said.

Granny kissed him on the cheek. "I know it, but it's not good to tell him. Now, let's talk about the new baby that Austin is having. I hope it's another girl. Rachel needs a playmate and they can have boys the next couple of times around."

Grandpa shrugged. "I hope she has triplet boys and they're all just as ornery as Maddie's first three was. Remember when they was little and we couldn't keep up with them?"

Granny smiled. "Lord, they was a handful."

"Why would you wish that on Rye and Austin?" Gemma asked.

"Ask your grandmother about the time that Rye and Dewar come to stay with us and we caught them about to jump off the house. Rye was about four and Dewar wasn't but two. Lord, I thought your granny would die before I could get up that ladder and get them boys off the roof."

Gemma mulled over and over that remark about Trace having eyes only for her as she listened to her grandmother tell the age-old story one more time.

Chapter 16

WOMEN CAME AND WENT IN THE AIRPORT BATHROOM while Gemma checked her reflection in the mirror and reapplied lipstick. The constant buzz of hundreds of conversations filtered into the restroom like smoke in a dusty old honky-tonk. She looked at her watch, picked up her purse, and walked out—and there was Trace leaning against the wall. She blinked, but he didn't disappear. She blinked again, holding her eyes shut longer, but he was still there when she opened them. She squealed, did a little hop, and wrapped her legs around his waist and her arms around his neck.

"I missed you," she said.

He cupped her butt with his hands and kissed her so hard and passionately that she felt the hunger. When the kiss finally ended, she put her feet on the floor but kept her arms around his neck.

"I missed you too. Was that kiss the prelude to an invitation?" he asked hoarsely.

"Not right here, but it is for later. How did you get here?"

"My flight connects through here. I just made sure I was on the same one you are for the rest of the trip." He brushed another kiss across her lips.

Gemma looked around. "Where is Sugar?"

"Teamer talked me into leaving her with him for the month. Little traitor ran into his house and hid under his bed when it was time to leave."

"His house? You don't live in the same house?"

Trace laced his fingers in hers and led her to the boarding gate. "It's a big operation. Started out as one cotton farm, and then the farm next to it came up for sale, so Teamer bought it. It was a cattle ranch. Angus and Longhorns. When I came into the picture, right out of college, he settled me into the little house on the cattle part of the operation. It's not anything fancy. Just a two-bedroom frame house that needs painting right now, but I haven't had time to do it. It's a mile back down a dirt road from Teamer's place. The bunkhouse is on the original cotton farm and Louis lives there."

"Louis?"

"He was the foreman until he retired. Now he cooks, and he and Uncle Teamer act like an old married couple. They fight and bicker all the time and even argue over who'll get the prettiest lady at the Saturday night dance down at their favorite bar."

Gemma thought of Nellie and Ellen. What kind of sparks would fly if Teamer and Louis ever went to a dance where those two sassy old gals were? She was still thinking about that when they boarded.

"How'd you get a seat next to me?" She put her purse in the overhead compartment and sat down beside him.

"That, darlin', was pure luck."

He rested his hand on her thigh. "I really missed you. Did you see your old boyfriends?"

"Did you see Ava?"

Trace's jaw clamped shut.

"Aha!" Gemma said.

"What?" he barked.

"You show me yours or I don't show you mine. We

can leave the past in the past or we can discuss it, cowboy. Your choice," she said.

"Ava was the one-weekend stand experience, like I told you. I haven't heard from her since. Your turn," he said.

"I did not see any old boyfriends in Ringgold. A couple of years ago, I lived with a very rich, very spoiled guy for a few months. We split almost two years ago. Haven't heard from or seen him since. Just as soon not ever. 'Nuff said, or do you want to elaborate on that weekend with Ava?"

"'Nuff said as far as I'm concerned. On to the future," Trace said.

"Agreed."

"Good. By the way, you look pretty damn sexy in those cutoff jeans," he teased.

"Well, thank you, sir. I didn't get dressed up because I figured I'd just be on a plane all day. I didn't know you were going to surprise me."

"We do have that layover in Oklahoma City for three hours. We'll have lunch at the seafood place in the airport. You'll knock them all dead in those shorts, boots, and whatever you call that shirt."

"That sounds delicious, and this is called a halter top." She giggled.

"Well, I like it. Looks like it would come off right easy," he said.

"Want to meet me in the bathroom and see if that mile-high stuff is as good as they say it is?"

He shook his head. "I told you I don't do kinky stuff."

"Darlin', it can't get kinky in a tiny bathroom."

"I'd rather wait for a big bed and lots of foreplay," he whispered.

"To tell the truth, the whole truth, and all that shit, I'd rather wait too." She snuggled in close to his side, air-conditioning blowing cool air on her warm skin, and Trace planting an occasional kiss on the top of her head or forehead. It seemed like she'd just shut her eyes when the plane landed with a little bump. She awoke with a start. "Where are we?"

"In Oklahoma City. Hungry?" He tipped her chin up and kissed her eyelids. "You slept hard, darlin'. You mumbled in your sleep, but I couldn't understand a word of what you were saying."

His lips settled on hers in the sweetest kiss she'd ever had in her life. Then he started humming.

She recognized the tune immediately. It was an old Stonewall Jackson song titled "Don't Be Angry."

"What would I have to be mad at you about?"

"I hope not a single thing." He retrieved her purse from the overhead and handed it to her. "I'm surprised that you recognize that song," he said.

"It's one of Grandpa's requests when we play on Sunday afternoon. Sometimes Rye sings the words and Grandpa and Granny two-step to it. How did you know it?"

"Uncle Teamer has it on an old vinyl record and I've heard it a million times," Trace said.

With his hand on the small of her back, he ushered her down the corridor, out into the airport, and down a couple of doors to the seafood restaurant.

The waitress appeared and asked, "Reservations?"

"Yes, Coleman, table for four."

Four? Did Trace say four? He'd made a mistake. They only needed a table for two.

"Your party is already here. Follow me."

Gemma set her heels. "What is going on, Trace?"

"Don't be angry with me, darlin'," he singsonged.

He grabbed her hand and she went with him, but her dark brows were knit together in wrinkled furrows.

A man in a three-piece suit, expensive as hell and tailor made from the looks of it, stood up and waved from a table. The lady seated beside him wore a gorgeous dress, a little lacy shrug, and high-heeled shoes, all white and all silk. Her dark hair was pulled into a sleek bun at the nape of her neck, and her blue eyes looked troubled as she watched Trace near the table.

"Gemma, this is my mother, Judge Mary Coleman, and my father, Thomas Coleman, who is a lawyer. Gemma is the woman I've been telling y'all about, the one who is keeping me on my toes and who is my stiffest competition in the bronc riding competition," Trace said smoothly.

Thomas shook hands with Gemma, and Judge Mary nodded. Trace slid a chair out and Gemma melted into it, careful to sit up straight and not keep sliding until she was under the table. Damn Trace's soul to hell for all eternity. He was in so much trouble that he didn't have enough days left in his life to get out of it.

"I'm very pleased to meet both of you," Gemma said. "When we were in Colorado Springs, Lester, Hill, and Harper told me about you. I understand you live in Houston?"

"We do. Thomas has a law practice and I'm a judge there. Thomas was raised on a ranch out in the Panhandle, but he never liked it like his two brothers. So you ride broncs?"

Gemma put on her best smile, but it felt fake. "Yes,

ma'am, and I also ride bulls. I was raised on a horse ranch and have three older brothers and an older sister."

"And you are giving my son a run for his money?" Thomas asked.

"I hope so." Gemma's pulse raced and her ears rang like she'd been too close to a shotgun when it went off. "But it works the other way too. He's giving me a run for my money. It's a tight contest, but things can change in eight seconds."

Judge Mary might be a judge and she might try all kinds of cases where she had a poker face, but what she thought of Gemma was etched into her face like writing on a tombstone. And it was not a pretty sight.

"Shall we order?" Thomas asked.

"I'll have shrimp scampi and a longneck Coors in the bottle," Gemma said.

"Me too," Trace said.

Thomas motioned for the waitress.

"Two scampi dinners and two bottles of Coors. Two lobster dinners and a bottle of whatever wine you suggest," he said.

The lady nodded and hurried off to the kitchen.

Judge Mary raised both eyebrows so high that they kissed her dark bangs. "Beer? Really, Trace!"

He shrugged. "It's hot. I like beer. Let's not fight, Mother."

Judge Mary smiled, but it didn't reach her eyes. "We should never have let him spend summers with Teamer. I swear that man put all kinds of crazy ideas in his head."

"He didn't have to put them there, Mother. They were always there. I'm not a city person. I love the wide open spaces and the smell of dirt. And if I win the Vegas ride, I'm using every single dime of the money and my savings to buy that ranch," Trace said.

"So what brings y'all to Oklahoma City?" Gemma changed the subject.

"Investments. Thomas wants to invest in some oil properties and I'm not sure with the economy the way it is that it's a good time to sink any money at all in the venture. So we came up here to look things over before we make a final decision. When Trace said he was flying through here and had a nice layover, we arranged to have lunch with him," Judge Mary answered.

"We'll be flying back to Houston on the two o'clock flight," Thomas said.

The waitress brought two beers, a bottle of white wine, and two stemmed glasses to the table. "Your salads will be here shortly. Anything else I can get you?"

Thomas shook his head and she departed. "We wanted Trace to go into law. I guess you've already figured that out, Gemma. But he loves ranchin' just like my brothers and my parents did."

Gemma turned up the bottle and swallowed several times before setting it back on the table. "I can understand what you are saying. My momma has five children. One left the area and she didn't like it a bit. She gives me fits about not settling around Ringgold."

Trace reached under the table and laid a hand on her leg. She picked it up and dropped it off to one side. He wasn't out of trouble yet. He could have told her that they were meeting his parents. She wouldn't have worn a halter top which was all mussed up from sleeping. She would have worn jeans or maybe a flowing skirt instead of cutoff denim shorts, and sandals instead of cowboy boots. She was afraid to even think about her makeup and hair.

Judge Mary wouldn't be a bit fooled by the fact that Gemma knew how to sit up straight, and use a napkin and a fork. No, sir! It was written in that woman's eyes that she knew her son was sleeping with Gemma and she did not approve. Had it been a case tried in her court, she would have sentenced Gemma to life at the North Pole.

Trace Coleman had fallen from grace, and a hand on her thigh was not going to put him back on his pedestal. Hell, he could forfeit the ride the next evening and she still wouldn't be in a forgiving mood.

Chapter 17

"I'M NOT SO SURE I WANT YOU COMING AT ME WITH scissors," Trace said.

"We are both fully clothed, and if you don't get a haircut your hair will fall in your eyes and then you'll use that as an excuse for losing." Gemma whipped a towel around his shoulders and picked up her scissors.

"But I wanted it naked," he said.

"You don't get it naked because you didn't tell me we were going to meet your parents so I could be presentable. God Almighty, Trace, what were you thinking, or were you?"

"Evidently I wasn't. My mother has already called and told me I was an idiot."

She held his hair up with one hand and cut it into a feathered back cut. "You could have told me earlier."

"I was going to tell you, but damn it, Gemma, I swear my brain went to mush when I saw you come out of that bathroom. And then you went to sleep. And besides, you looked damn fine to me."

Snip. Snip. Snip. She hoped he was scared to death that she'd take off an ear. "I looked like Daisy May Clampett after a hard night of hookin'."

"Well, that's sexy as hell," he argued.

"Sexy as hell is not the first impression I wanted your folks to have about me," she said.

"I'm sorry," he said.

"Do you mean it? Really, really mean it?"

"Yes, I do," he said.

"Okay then."

"You'll stop bitchin' at me?"

"Oh, honey, I'll do more than that."

She laid the scissors down and stripped out of her jeans and halter top, tossed her underpants in the corner, and removed her boots. "Now I'll cut your hair naked."

He stood up and unbuckled his belt. She put a hand on his shoulder.

"No! Just me. It's part of your punishment. You have to keep your hands on your knees the whole time."

"Gemma, you really are killing me this time!"

"I hope so. Keep your head still or there'll be gaps as wide as the Red River in your hair."

"But I can't see you," he groaned.

"I know, darlin'," she whispered softly in his ear.

"I want to touch you," he said.

"We'll take care of that later."

"How much later?"

"Maybe six seconds before your zipper breaks."

"You are a witch from hell, woman."

"Remember that if you ever think about not telling me your momma is going to be in the same room with me again."

He was almighty uncomfortable when she finally finished his hair, straddled his lap, and slowly undid his zipper.

"Poor baby. That was like penning up a pit bull in a shoebox." She laughed.

He grabbed her butt with both hands and carried her to his bed where he tossed her in the middle and quickly removed his clothing. When he landed on top of her, his lips latched onto hers in a long, lingering kiss that she didn't ever want to end. And then he was inside her moving fast.

"Don't stop," she said.

"I don't intend to."

He brought her right up the brink of a climax and then slowed down.

"You are driving me crazy," she said.

"Paybacks are a bitch."

She rocked against his thrusts until he speeded up and finally hit the top at the exact same second. She wrapped her legs around him, and he kissed her until she couldn't breathe.

"God, that was good," he said.

"God doesn't care if it's good or not," she said.

"Then Gemma, that was wonderful. Does she care?"

"Hell, yeah! Now let's sleep for an hour before we go see what's happening on the grounds."

"You really were beautiful in those shorts and shirt," he whispered.

She forgave him as she fell asleep in his arms. It was where she wanted to be, not in Ringgold, Texas, but right there in Trace's arms. Her ass had chosen which horse it wanted to ride. Now all she had to do was convince Trace and stay away from her mother until the dust settled.

—∽∽—

Gemma looked over the top of the chute at Pretty Baby, muscles tensing and a look in his eyes that said his full name was probably Lucifer's Pretty Baby. He had a

solid reputation with the rodeo crew as being one tough
son of a bitch to ride. His percentage of wrecks was
somewhere around eighty, but Gemma was determined
to lower his statistics in the next minute. She eased down
into her saddle, jammed her boot heels into the stirrups,
measured the rein, and touched her lucky horseshoe hat
pin. She'd eaten a rodeo hamburger and forgiven Trace
for not telling her about his parents. Nothing negative
was sitting on her shoulders.

She inhaled deeply and nodded. The gate opened
and Pretty Baby came out with gusto. The crowd roared
somewhere in a tunnel that was way far away. The announcer was yelling into the microphone something
about Gemma O'Donnell taming the wild bronc.

And then Pretty Baby did a dance step that she wasn't
expecting. It happened just as the buzzer sounded and
she started to roll to one side. Another two seconds
and she would have lasted the whole ride, but when the
horse flipped so far to one side that he almost kissed his
own butt, Gemma's foot came loose.

Her left foot left the stirrup and the right one hung,
leaving her shoulder to drag in the dirt as Pretty Baby
spun her around the arena for a full five seconds before her boot heel dislodged and sent her skittering. Her
mouth, nose, and eyes filled with arena sand, and she
came up spitting and sputtering to a crowd screaming
and yelling.

She stood up, bowed, and let a clown lead her back
to the chutes where she dunked her head into a watering
trough to get the dirt out of her eyes and ears. When
she came up for air, the announcer was yelling, "And
our next contestant is Trace Coleman from Goodnight,

Texas. He's riding Devil Dog tonight out of chute six. Our rodeo clown, Low Britches, just signaled that Gemma is all right, so while Trace is getting ready, let's give it up for our little lady from Ringgold, Texas, who almost showed Pretty Baby who was boss tonight."

The crowd's whoops and whistles were muffled as she stuck her head in the water again. That had been her worst wreck ever, and she'd be sore as hell the coming morning. There'd be bruises and aches in places she didn't even know about. Thank God it was six days until the Lovington, New Mexico, ride so she could heal up. Where in the hell had she gone wrong, anyway? She'd done all the right things to keep her mojo going and hadn't even thought about Trace except that one time to congratulate herself on forgiving him.

The announcer sounded like he was screaming into the microphone again, "And that was Trace Coleman, showing the rodeo world how it's done! Trace just racked up eighty-one points to beat out Coby by one point. Now that's some close bronc busters, folks. Let's hear it for all the contestants tonight before we go on to the bull riding with Landry Winters starting the competition right here in Dodge City!"

Gemma brushed her wet hair back from her face with her hands. The scrape down her jawline stung like wildfire, but it wasn't bleeding too badly. Her left boot felt tight, which meant her ankle was swelling. She started toward her trailer to check the damage more carefully and fell to her knees with the first step.

Strong arms scooped her up and she looked up into Trace's worried face.

"Hey, you," she whined.

"How bad is it? Is it broken? My God, Gemma, I thought I'd die before I could get off that damn bronc and see about you. You were limping and your face was covered with dirt."

He jogged toward her trailer. Chap fringe flared out in the hot night breeze. Spurs jingled. Boots heels sent up baby dust devils with every step.

"It's a sprain. I've had them before. Ice and prop it up. My cheek is just a scrape. It was the dirt in my eyes that scared me. For a second there I wondered if we could train Sugar to be a Seeing Eye dog," she said.

"Don't even tease about that," he growled.

He eased her down to stand on her right foot while she opened the trailer door, and then he carried her inside. When she was sitting on the side of her bed, he dropped to his knees and tugged at her boot.

"Ouch! Ouch! Let me do it," she said.

He stood up and stuck his hand deep into his pocket. "You can't. Your foot is swollen. It's not coming off."

"Hell, no! You will not cut my boot off, Trace! Not without a fight. These are my lucky boots. They've gone to every rodeo with me for the past ten years," she said.

With his thumbnail he pulled a long sharp blade out of the knife.

"They are not!" He pointed toward the floor.

She looked down and moaned. That's where she went wrong. She'd worn the wrong boots. Her lucky boots were standing beside her bed and she'd shoved her feet right back down into the old boots that she'd worn on the flight from Ringgold to Dodge City. What in the devil had she been thinking about anyway?

He looked at her.

She nodded.

He carefully slit the boot leather down the inner seam. "If I do it this way, you can take them to the boot shop and they might be able to repair them."

He removed the boot and her sock and gasped. "It's already turning purple. We need to get you into the shower, get all the dirt cleaned off you, and prop this thing up with ice. I'll be surprised if you can even ride in Lovington."

He removed her other boot and slipped his arms around her. "Hold on to me and stand on your right leg."

She grimaced when she stood up and put weight on it, but she'd had sprains before and she'd had a broken ankle once when she was a teenager. She knew the difference and he was right—it would be a miracle if she was able to ride in Lovington.

He removed her chaps, then the rest of her clothing, and carried her strip-stark naked to her tiny bathroom. He started the water and set her down under the shower.

"Get on out of here before you ruin those chaps and bitch about it until eternity dawns," she said. "And shut the door. I can hold on to the wall and take a shower standing on one leg."

"I'll get out of these chaps and be right here when you get done, but I'm not closing the door all the way shut. You might need me," he said.

Mud streamed down her body as the water washed away half a bushel of the arena dirt. When she was finally clean, she turned the faucet off and eased the door open. Trace was leaning against the doorjamb with a big white towel in his hands. He took one step forward, wrapped it around her, and swept her off her feet.

He sat down on the edge of the bed, picked up another towel, and rubbed the water from her hair before he brushed the tangles out. After that he gently dried the water droplets from her shoulders and the rest of her body and dressed her in underpants and an oversized nightshirt. Then he propped her leg up and opened the refrigerator. He found the flexible ice pack in the freezer and molded it around her ankle.

"Where's something for that scrape?"

"In the kit beside my bed." Every cowboy and cowgirl's traveling kit contained an ice pack, a heat pad, aspirin, Tylenol, antiseptic spray, antibiotic ointment, and ibuprofen.

He shook out a couple of Tylenol and handed her a bottle of water from the fridge. "No beer or dancing tonight, lady."

Then he squeezed ointment on his fingertip and applied it to the scrape on her jaw. When he finished, he settled her back against more pillows and stretched out beside her on the bed. He laced his fingers with hers and squeezed gently.

"Now what in the hell happened out there? You survived a damn bee, woman. Did some fool grease your saddle?" he asked gruffly.

She laid her head on his shoulder. "If I'd been drinking I could call it a hangover. Last time I wrecked this bad was when I tried to ride a bronc after proving I could best my sister at shots."

"But you weren't drinking. You haven't even had a beer since yesterday at lunch."

She giggled. "If it wasn't a hangover, then it might be the result of a bangover! From now on, no sex on the night before or the day of a rodeo. And absolutely no naked haircuts, even though your hair does look sexy."

"What about the night after a rodeo?" he asked.

"That is optional, but tonight ain't an option."

"Of course it's not, but I'm going to carry you over to my place where the bed is bigger and more comfortable. I won't leave you alone, Gemma. You ready?"

She yawned. "I'm not arguing."

He sat straight up and ran his fingers over her entire head, carefully probing and searching. "You shouldn't be sleepy this early, Gemma. Do you have a concussion? Look at me so I can see your pupils. Do you feel dizzy or bumfuzzled?"

She shook her head. "I got a mouthful of dirt and it got in my eyes, so they are probably bloodshot, but I didn't hit anything but soft dirt when I fell. The pills you gave me are making me sleepy. I'm very drug sensitive. Two Tylenol knock me on my ass for ten or twelve hours. That's probably why that drug in my beer hit me so hard."

He rolled off the side of the bed and gathered her into his arms. "I'll get you settled and come back to lock up."

"Anything you say." She was already drowsy.

He put her to bed, propped her ankle on a pillow, and wrapped the ice pack around it. "I'll lock the door. Don't move until I get back."

"I promise," she said.

Her eyes grew heavier while he went to claim their saddles and lock up her trailer. She was barely awake when he returned with his saddle, carefully stowed it away in the closet, and disappeared into the bathroom. When he got into bed with her, she snuggled up to his side and used his shoulder for a pillow.

Her neck was in a kink when she awoke the next morning, and the ice pack was a lukewarm lump next to her ankle. Trace's eyes were wide open and he reached over and touched the end of her nose.

"Good morning, beautiful," he said.

"I'm so sure I'm beautiful with my hair all tangled and a scrape on my face, not to mention my foot," she grumbled.

"Grumpy this morning, are we?" he asked.

"Yes, I am." She nodded.

"Does coffee tame the beast down?"

"It usually does."

He pushed the sheet back and threw his legs over the side of the bed.

"I need to go to the bathroom," she said.

He picked her up like he would a child and set her on the floor. "Use my arm like a crutch."

"I can use the wall to hobble to the bathroom. If we were in a house or even a hotel room, I would use you for a crutch, but I can make it four feet to the bathroom," she grumbled. She shut the bathroom door. Sitting on the potty wasn't a problem, but it took some maneuvering to get up.

"You going to be able to drive?" He raised his voice so she could hear through the closed door.

She opened the door, hopped to the edge of the bed, and sat down. "Of course I can drive. It's my left foot. I don't use it to drive."

"We can go halfway today and finish up tomorrow. We've got six days."

"Sounds good to me," she said.

He started coffee and then opened the cabinet doors. "What do you want for breakfast?"

"Cereal is fine."

"That's not breakfast. That barely qualifies as food. We haven't had time to shop so we'll stop at the first IHOP. Then we can call it a day at lunchtime and you can rest that foot all afternoon and night."

She nodded. "Okay. And I could polish my saddle, readjust the stirrups, and get my boots ready for the rodeo while I rest the foot, right?"

He slid a sideways look her way. "I had something else in mind."

She wiggled her dark eyebrows. "Something that would produce a bangover so I'll wreck in New Mexico?"

He chuckled. "It sounds like fun, but no, ma'am. I will not have you saying that I screwed your brains out so I could win the title. No sex until after the rodeo in New Mexico."

She sucked air for a whole five seconds. "That's six days, Trace!"

He laughed out loud. "Then no sex tonight and none the night before the Lovington rodeo. That sound better?"

She figured up the nights in her head. None that night. None the night of the rodeo. That left three nights free.

"I can live with that."

He carried a cup of steaming hot black coffee to the bedside and put it in her hands, poured himself a cup, and sat down beside her.

"I wish I had my crutches from back home," she said. "It would make getting around a lot easier."

Trace opened a closet door and brought out a set of aluminum crutches. "We'll have to adjust them, but there they are. I got a sprain last year and had to hobble around until I could buy them. Swore I'd never travel without them again."

With a few swift movements, he had them adjusted to the right height and handed them to her. "You going to try to prove that you can beat me in New Mexico even with a busted ankle? I'm telling you right now, that is my win."

"Spit in one hand and wish in the other, cowboy. We'll see which one fills up fastest."

"Oh, we're back to the cowboy stuff, are we?"

"When it comes to bronc riding, you'll always be cowboy to me."

"Well, then this cowboy is going to get everything ready to hit the road in fifteen minutes."

"I'll be ready," she said.

They stopped at the Corral RV Park in Dalhart, Texas, at noon. The campground had wide pull-through lots with shade trees spaced just right to give the campers some relief from the blistering hot August sun. Gemma unfastened her seat belt and opened the truck door. Cold air wasted no time rushing out. Hot air replaced it so fast that she was sweating before she swung her legs out and eased down on her right foot. She hobbled around to the pickup's back door and grabbed her crutches.

"Hey, I was coming around to help you," Trace yelled.

"I need to walk on this leg or it'll get lazy," she said. "You reckon we could get pizza delivered out here?"

"Probably. I'll see what I can do about getting a delivery when you are in my trailer. And we're having spaghetti for supper. I make a mean pot of spaghetti, and you, darlin', are going to spend the day with that ankle propped on a pillow. We'll ice it this afternoon and by tomorrow it should be better."

She didn't start to move. "Give me a minute to look around. We stayed right here every year when I was a little girl. Momma and Daddy would bring the big trailer and all five of us kids. It's not until next week and we'll be in Lovington. The whole town is probably gearing up this week for the XIT Rodeo and Reunion. Grandpa brought Momma when she was just a kid, and then Momma and Daddy always brought us kids."

Trace slipped an arm around her shoulders. "I came with Uncle Teamer two years. When I was twelve and again when I was thirteen. I loved it and Mother threatened to ban me to my room and make me read Hemingway or Faulkner if I didn't stop talking about the barbecue and the country music."

"Did Teamer take you to see the Empty Saddle Monument?" she asked.

"Oh, yeah! I kept the framed picture of me standing in front of it in my dresser drawer. I was afraid Mother would burn it." He chuckled.

"She hates ranchin' that bad?" Gemma asked.

"No, she doesn't hate it at all. She actually likes to go to Goodnight for a couple of days and relax. What she doesn't like is me likin' ranchin'. She wanted me to be a lawyer. Coleman and Coleman was her big dream. It was all right that I got a business degree, because afterward she'd see to it I got into prelaw. But I shattered her hopes when I moved to Goodnight. She hasn't forgiven me yet."

"She will," Gemma said.

"What makes you so sure?" Trace asked.

"Because she loves you," she said.

———◦∿◦———

The next day they drove all the way into Lovington, New Mexico, and parked on the rodeo grounds. Gemma's foot was looking better and she still had three days before she needed it to be well enough to get her boot on and make it into the saddle. Even if it hurt like a son of a bitch, she could endure it for eight seconds.

They pulled their trailers into a couple of lots back behind the rodeo and fair grounds. Vendors and the carnival crew were already setting up, and excitement was as thick as the dust. Lovington, New Mexico, wasn't a lot different than Dalhart, Texas: cotton, cattle, oil wells, cowboys and cowgirls, and rodeo fever everywhere she looked.

Lovington, like Dalhart, wasn't a big town. Nowhere near ten thousand people, it had a small-town feel to it. The rodeo with the carnival, the mutton bustin', and the music for four whole days was the highlight of the whole summer, and everyone couldn't wait for it to get started.

In just three days, everything would be in full swing. Then the excitement would turn into sheer frenzy as kids ran from one ride to another, one game booth to the next, and back and forth from snow cone stands to corn dog vendors. There'd be more fancy cowboy hats and boots than anywhere short of a Western-wear store. And cowboys would be everywhere, trying to win the favor of the cowgirls with big hair and tight-fitting jeans. It was rodeo time in Lovington, and life was good.

The rodeo motto was "Livin' Life in Eight Seconds,"

and Gemma couldn't get that line out of her head. When she started the circuit, she would have agreed whole-heartedly. Now she wasn't so sure. Those eight seconds were an important part of her life. Each one brought her closer and closer to her dream, but that wasn't all there was to life. Even when the dream became reality, it wasn't really, really life.

By the time she got the seat belt unfastened, Trace had opened the door and held out his hand to help her out of the truck. She put her hands on his shoulders and carefully slid out to land on one foot.

Slipping his hands under her arms, he picked her up and kissed her, letting his tongue tease her lips open and make promises for later that night.

When he set her down he said, "I missed you today. I wanted to call several times, but you've got the foot problem and I was afraid for you to talk and drive. But it's been the longest damn two hundred miles I've ever driven. I could stand right here and kiss you all afternoon."

"Sounds good to me, but I'd have energy to do more than kiss if we could find something to eat first."

She reached for her crutches, but he beat her to them. "Here you go. Have I told you that you are beautiful with those cute little braids?"

She smiled up at him. "I look like Laura Ingalls with them, and honey, she was not beautiful."

The hot dog and hamburger vendor was set up for business, so they ordered one of each and Trace carried them to the tables set up under an awning attached to the end of the wagon.

"Looks like it's going to be an exciting one," Trace said. "I hate to ride when the crowd is dull, don't you?"

"I don't ever know if they are happy or dull. I just block everything out and ride," she answered.

"Hey, Trace Coleman," a red-haired woman yelled from halfway across the grounds.

He waved and squinted. "Who is that? Is that your sister?"

The mention of her sister got Gemma's attention immediately. "No, hair is too carrot red. Colleen's is burgundy. But I've seen that woman before. She was one of that group who knocked on your door, who wanted to have a foursome with you, remember? She said that Ava had a surprise."

"Oh, yeah," Trace said coldly.

"Looks like she intends to try to seduce you again as fast as she's coming this way," Gemma said.

"Hey, I've been on the lookout for you since yesterday. I thought that was your trailer when you drove onto the grounds, but I waited until I saw you get out of it to call Ava. There she is. I was just supposed to keep you busy until she got here so she wouldn't have to hunt you down." The woman waved at a shiny black car driving toward them, and then headed off toward the funnel cake wagon.

"Damn!" Trace said.

"Might as well get it over with," Gemma told him.

The car came to a stop and a tall blonde wearing a spaghetti-strapped flowing sundress in a bright splash of color, designer high heels, and a killer smile got out of the driver's seat. She left the engine running and walked around the car.

"Hello, Trace," she said. She didn't have an accent at all. Not Southern. Not Northern. Her tone was as flat as the New Mexico landscape.

Gemma stood up.

"Don't you dare leave," Trace said.

She sat back down beside him.

He nodded toward the woman. "Hello, Ava. What brings you to Lovington? Last time I saw you, you said you'd had all the cowboys and rodeo business you ever wanted."

"I meant it. I'm not staying for the rodeo. I flew down here, rented a car, and came to see you. May I sit down?"

"Of course. This is Gemma O'Donnell."

"I know who she is," Ava said. "I've kept up with your every move these past months. Hello, Gemma. I'm Ava."

"Pleased to meet you," Gemma said.

Ava sat down gracefully and put her arms on the table. "We have a problem, Trace. Do you want to discuss it in front of Gemma?"

"Gemma is my friend. We can discuss anything in front of her."

Ava laughed. It had a crackling, humorless sound to it as if it came from her throat and not her heart. "I expect you are more than friends, but that's your business, none of mine. Okay, here goes. When we had our fling, I was engaged to an archeologist doing research in Africa. We'd had an argument and I was very angry. Why or what about isn't important. You just need to know that before I go on."

"Okay," Trace said.

"He'd been gone two months. So when I fell into the point one percent of women that get pregnant on the pill, I knew the baby wasn't his. And you were the only man I'd been with other than him. I could have gotten rid of it, but I'm a big contributor to the Pro-Life organization and if the tabloids got hold of that kind of news it wouldn't be such a good thing, especially for my fiancé, who is a very private person. So we decided I'd have the baby and put it up for adoption."

All the color drained from Trace's face.

Gemma reached across the space and laced her fingers into his.

Ava went on. "Then I found out that since I knew who the father was and even named you on the birth certificate that you had to sign the papers for me to adopt the baby out. I brought the papers for you to sign."

"But," Trace started.

Ava held up a hand. "I also brought the baby. It's your choice. Keep her or take her to the nearest hospital with all the legal documents and tell them to find her a suitable family. It certainly doesn't matter to me. I carried her. I gave birth to her. But I do not want children, now or ever."

"Where is she?" Gemma asked.

"She's sleeping in the backseat of the car in her car seat. That's why I left the engine running. She was born two weeks ago. Please take her out for me. I'm not supposed to lift anything that heavy yet. The papers are in a folder beside her, and there's a diaper bag with formula and diapers. The nanny I hired has a notebook among the papers that tells what she has done for the baby on a daily basis the past two weeks. I had her by Cesarean birth and I wasn't allowed to travel for two weeks."

Trace didn't move.

Ava tucked a strand of hair behind her ear. "I signed the documents giving up all my rights so you won't have any trouble when you give her up for adoption."

"I can't," Trace said.

"I don't expect you to. Never did. I don't want her either."

"I did not say that," Trace enunciated slowly in a growl. "I could never give up my child."

Ava shrugged. "It's up to you. I did what I had to. Now you can do whatever you want to. Anything else you want to know before I go?"

Gemma was stunned. "How can you do that? Carry a baby nine months and then just give her away?"

"I demanded that they take the baby by C-section so that I could think of it as a surgery. If you had a gallbladder removed, would you want to hold it and cuddle it up next to you? I hired a lady to take care of her so I didn't have to touch her. That same nanny traveled with me on the plane and will go home with me this afternoon. She put her into the rental car and I haven't even looked at her any more than absolutely necessary. Like I said, I don't want kids. Never did. I won't ever look back on this and get all warm and fuzzy."

"What if you change your mind in ten years? What makes it fair that you know all about Trace and he knows nothing about you?"

"Life is not fair. Good-bye, Gemma, and rest assured I will not come back in ten years for that child. The heart does not grieve what the eyes do not see."

Trace stood up slowly and headed for the car. He opened the back door and when he turned around to face Gemma, he had a baby seat in one hand, a diaper bag over his shoulder, and a folder full of papers tucked under his arm.

Ava stood up just as slowly and got into the car. "I

went ahead and named her, but it can be changed if you want to amend the birth certificate. I remembered looking at your driver's license and seeing that your name is Joseph Trace. There was snow on the holly bushes the day I found out I was pregnant. So I named her Holly Jo."

Gemma's ears rang with Liz's voice when she had told her fortune in the spring: "You will definitely have a cowboy of your very own and a baby by this Christmas."

She had not said a cowboy of your very own and *you two will have a baby together.*

Chapter 18

HE SET THE BABY ON THE TABLE AND SLUMPED INTO A chair. "Gemma, I don't know anything about this business, and you have every right to be angry. What am I going to do? She said she was on the pill and…"

She laid a finger over his lips. "Shhh. I'm angry at Ava, but why would I be angry at you? You had no idea about any of this. If you'd have said you were taking that child to an adoption agency, I would have walked away from you and never looked back. Look at her, Trace. She has your dark hair and lips. Take her out of that thing and hold her."

His face went pale. "I don't know how."

Gemma hobbled over to the car seat and unfastened the buckles. "See, it's easy once you get the hang of it. I learned with Rachel."

Trace shook his head. "I could have figured that out. That's not the problem. I've never held a baby in my whole life. They scare the hell out of me."

Gemma sat down in a chair nearest the car seat. She loved babies, and not picking up that poor little motherless child was the hardest thing she'd ever done.

She touched his cheek and said, "Slip a hand under her bottom and support her head with the other, then hold her close to your heart so she can hear the beat. Sugar was a hell of a lot smaller than that when you got her, wasn't she? And I bet she wiggled more than a two-week-old baby."

He did exactly what Gemma told him and held his daughter so close that he could feel her little heart beating next to his chest. His expression went from bewildered to amazed in a split second. He leaned back and looked down at Holly and she snuggled down in his arms.

"Oh, my!" he said.

"See, nothing to it," Gemma told him. "It's a lot easier than riding a bronc."

"But a bronc event is only eight seconds. This is a lifetime," he said softly.

"Yes, it is. Once a parent, always a parent. You can't go back, only forward."

"She's so tiny."

"And beautiful."

Trace's smile barely turned up the corners of his mouth. "Come and sit in my lap. I want to share this moment with you. You will help me, won't you?"

Tears dammed up behind Gemma's eyelashes when she sat down on Trace's knee. When she touched the baby's hand, Holly wrapped her fingers around Gemma's pinky.

"That woman is heartless. I could never give up something this precious. It'll take both of us to take care of her at the rodeos. I'll watch her while you ride and you can while I ride. And we'll take turns on the night feedings."

Trace cut his eyes around at her. "The what?"

"Night feedings. You can't just put a pan of water and a bowl of food beside her bed. Someone is going to be getting up every three to four hours to feed this little girl. Her tummy won't hold enough formula to last longer than that. Mind if I look into that folder and see how much she weighed?"

"Of course not. You need to know everything."

She moved into a chair right beside him and thumbed through legal documents and finally found the birth certificate. "Holly Jo Coleman was born July 15th. She was nineteen inches long and weighed six pounds and two ounces. She'll be eating every three to four hours for sure. Babies that weigh more than eight pounds eat more, so they sleep longer."

"How do you know all this?" Trace asked.

Gemma touched Holly's face. The baby opened her mouth and turned toward her hand.

"She's getting hungry. And I know all that because Austin was terrified about being a mother. She was an only child, and she was afraid she'd do something wrong, so she read baby books by the dozens and we heard about them all the time. Then Pearl got pregnant with the twins and it was the same thing all over again. And I used to keep the nursery at the church on Sunday mornings."

"Thank God!" Trace said. "What do we do now? Is there food in that bag?"

Gemma rummaged through it. "Six diapers. Two bottles of formula. One extra blanket and no more clothes. We can change her diaper and feed her, but we've got to go to the store pretty quick. And that means we have to unhitch my trailer."

"Why your trailer?"

"Because my truck has a backseat. It's against the law to put a baby in the front seat of a vehicle. She can't ride in your truck. Guess we've got some plans to make."

Worry etched into Trace's face like lines on a road map. "I don't feel anything. Shouldn't I be overwhelmed like those guys in the movies when they hold their babies? I bet Rye and Wil felt something when their babies were born. Is there something wrong with me? Is this really my child?"

Gemma patted his shoulder. "Nothing is wrong with you. Rye and Wil and now Ace all had nine months to get ready for a baby, and they had it with someone they were in love with. They didn't have a baby dropped out of heaven into their arms. Be patient. One day at a time, like the old song says. Right now, we go to the nearest store and buy necessities," she said.

He set the diaper bag and the folder in the car seat, carried it in one hand, and cradled the baby in the other. Gemma picked up her crutches and the three of them headed back to her truck.

"Eight seconds can change the world," she said.

"You talkin' about ridin' or this?"

"Both. Who would have thought that thirty minutes ago when we walked away from my truck we'd come back with a baby?"

"What is this going to do to our relationship?" he asked.

"We have a relationship?"

"Don't tease."

She braced her back against the truck. "I expect if what we have is strong enough to withstand the competition we are in, then one little bundle of smelly pooped diaper won't hurt it too much."

He took a deep breath and snarled. "Is that what that is? I thought we were downwind from a hog lot."

"Lay her on the backseat and put the diaper bag on the floor. I can take care of that in no time," she said.

Trace watched over her shoulder while she changed

Holly's diaper. "Maybe I should forget the rest of the circuit and go home."

"Why? She don't know if she's being raised up these first months in a trailer or a mansion. We can do this, Trace. Don't give up on your dream." Gemma picked up the baby and held her close to her chest. Holly started rooting around, hunting for food.

"What do I do now?" he asked.

"You put that car seat in the backseat and strap it down with the seat belts. Then we go to your trailer and heat up a bottle so I can feed her. After that we'll go to the store and buy supplies. Then we'll come back and figure out what we're doing after the ride tonight."

"You are fan-damn-tastic, woman."

"I can't carry her and use crutches, so help please," Gemma started.

Trace cut her off mid-sentence when he picked her up. She held the baby in her arms and Trace held her like a new bride. He carried both of them to his trailer and set them in the middle of his bed.

"I'll go back and get that diaper bag and papers now," he said.

She stretched Holly out on her knees and checked her toes and fingers: ten of each. Then she touched her little ears and traced the outline of her lips. "You are perfect, sweetheart. And you'll have the best daddy in the whole world when he settles down and realizes that a little angel just got dropped into his lap."

Holly had begun to whimper by the time Trace returned and he panicked.

"Is she all right? What do we do now? Should we take her to the hospital and have a doctor look at her?"

"She is hungry, Trace. Run hot water in a pan or a bowl in the sink and stick one of those bottles in it, then you can feed her," Gemma said.

He swished the bottle back and forth. "How will I know when it's ready?"

"Pick it up and let a drop fall on your wrist," she answered.

He followed her instructions and said, "I can't feel it."

"Then it's ready. Come on over here and sit down beside me."

When he sat down, his eyes reminded her of a scared rabbit. "Will you do it this time and let me watch? Like the diaper thing. If I see how to do it then I'll be able to take on the job."

Gemma cradled Holly in her arms, held the bottle to her mouth, and the baby latched right on to it. "See, it's not a lot different than feeding a calf."

"Except with a calf you put it in a bucket." Trace laughed nervously.

She looked up to find him staring into her eyes. "What?" she asked.

"You are beautiful holding that baby." He kissed her and sparks flew around the trailer just like always.

"Whew!" she said. "I wondered if a baby would change the fire power. It didn't."

He chuckled again. "I wondered the same thing, but I do believe that kiss was the hottest one yet."

"Burp time and you get to do it." She put the baby in his arms.

"How?"

"Put her on your shoulder and pat her gently on the back."

"Like this?"

Gemma leaned back and glared at him. "You rascal. You lied to me. You've done this before."

He shook his head. "I saw it on television."

Holly burped loud and clear, shoved her thumb in her mouth, and made sucking sounds.

Trace handed her back to Gemma. "Thumb sucker? Will that ruin her teeth or give her a speech problem?"

"We'll get her a pacifier at the store and that will take care of any problems. While I finish feeding her, can you get my trailer and truck unhitched? Why don't we use my truck from now on and your trailer?"

"Sounds good, but how?"

"Remember, Ace and his brothers are coming to the rodeo. Momma and Dewar were pouting, remember?"

"Lord, I barely remember my name," he said.

She went on, "We can send your truck and my trailer back with them. It'll be a tight squeeze to fit all my things plus Holly's in your place, but it can be done. My saddle can ride in the backseat beside her car seat, and if you'll put your tool chest over in the bed of my truck we can store things in it. We can share the gas and food expenses."

He was shaking his head before she got the last word out. "I can pay for those things. If you're going to help with this baby, it's the least I can do."

Gemma looked him in the eye. "Don't get defensive with me, cowboy."

He smiled. "I'm not. I just wanted you to know up front that I'll pay for everything if you'll just help me."

Gemma nodded. "Deal. She's about finished with this bottle. You want to burp her or go unhitch my trailer?"

"You can't unhitch a trailer with your foot like that."

"Then I'll do the burping and you do the unhitching," she said.

He waved at the door.

She groaned. "Dammit! And don't let me hear you repeating that, Miss Holly. I want hitching as in a permanent relationship, and that's a fact."

Half an hour later they were in her truck, baby in the car seat and Gemma looking through papers while Trace drove. They'd only driven a mile when they saw a Dollar General store with its big yellow sign.

"Is this all right?" Trace asked.

"Just fine. Oh, oh!"

He tapped the brakes. "What?"

"Don't stop. Go on and park. I just found a DNA paper. That redheaded groupie witch must have been helping her out all along."

Trace found a spot close to the door and turned to face Gemma. "What are you talking about?"

"Says here that the baby is yours. Ninety-nine point nine percent positive. Looks like they took your DNA from a beer bottle. I didn't know they could do that. I thought that was just something on television cop shows."

"I'd feel better if I had another one done," he said.

"Then do it, but I betcha she's yours. If Ava hadn't known she was, then she wouldn't have given her to you," Gemma said.

He pinched his nose between his thumb and forefinger. "Man! I never thought I'd be having a conversation like this when I woke up this morning. And I still have to call my parents."

"I have to call Momma and Ace," she said.

"Why Ace?"

"Remember, we are going to ask him to take our extra rig home. And Momma because I want to."

He held the door to the store for her, and the lady behind the checkout counter greeted them. "Hot enough for y'all?"

"Yes, ma'am," Gemma said.

She had blond hair cut in a neckline with a spiky top. Blue eyes were set deep in a bed of wrinkles that said she'd seen middle age come and go a while back. "My uncle said he saw a whole caravan of lizards last week headin' north. Guess even they've had all of this summer heat they can stand. Girl, it must be miserable to have crutches and a new baby both. But looks like your husband is a good man. Most men I know wouldn't be carryin' a baby around without one of them buckets. Can I help y'all with anything?"

"We need formula and diapers," Gemma said.

"Baby stuff is that way." The lady pointed. "Boy or girl?"

"Girl," Gemma answered.

"How old is she?"

"Two weeks."

"Man, you look damn fine to have just had a baby two weeks ago. Took me months to get back in my clothes. Y'all need any help, you just holler."

"Thank you." Gemma said.

Trace held Holly cradled in one arm and pushed a cart with the other. He stopped midway down the aisle and shook his head.

"Where do we even start?"

Gemma pointed to the second shelf down from the

top. "Three cans of that powdered formula. Two packages of those newborn diapers."

"Three?"

Gemma steadied a crutch and reached around him. "A can will last just about a week, but we don't want to run out in the middle of the night. Diapers won't last that long. We need three packages of these blankets."

"Just tell me what and how many and I'll put it in the cart. I'm afraid you are going to fall," he said.

She backed up a step. "Okay then, three packages of those undershirts and three of these gowns."

Trace picked up things and tossed them into the cart. "Why three?"

"That makes nine of each and she'll go through them in a hurry. Especially if she's a spitter, and if she's not, a diaper might leak or worse. And we'll have to do laundry more often too, so we might as well get a bottle of that baby laundry soap."

"Do we need bottles or are those two from the bag enough? Don't they have to be sterilized?" Trace asked.

She propped the crutch tightly under her arm and pointed. "Those are what we need. They are just shells that you put liners in. Get a couple of boxes of liners. That way we can toss the liners in the trash and only sterilize nipples in the microwave."

"I'm glad you're here," Trace said.

"You are welcome. Are you going to let me win this week?" she teased.

He shook his head. "I am not! You know the rules. When it comes to the competition, we aren't even friends."

Gemma smiled. "You got it! Oh, we've got to have that thing."

"What is it?" Trace asked.

"A fold-up stroller for when we take her to the rodeo. We can put it under your bed when we aren't using it, but we need it," she said. "And now for the pretty stuff. Five outfits should be enough right here at first, wouldn't you think?"

"For what?"

"Trace Coleman, this baby is not going out in public dressed in a nightgown or a knit undershirt. She's going to have some pretty things, and when I can get to a Western-wear store she'll have cute little cowgirl things. Look!"

He turned to see her flipping through a round rack of baby things. She quickly picked out half a dozen pink dresses with matching diaper covers and tossed them into the cart.

"And that should do it for this week," she said.

"You mean this is a once every week thing?"

"Oh, honey, at least that much, maybe more." She smiled.

"You are enjoying this way, way too much."

She nodded. "Yes, I am. Now let's go home and play with her. I swear she's such a good baby. She hasn't fussed a single bit."

~~~

The day went past in a blur. Holly ate. Holly slept. Holly had her diaper changed and her gown at least three times that day. Then it was time for bed and Trace stopped dead in his tracks.

"What now? I can't sleep with her, Gemma. I'm a big man. What if I rolled on her or my pillow got all tangled up in her face?"

Gemma exhaled in exasperation. "We forgot to buy a bassinet."

"A what?"

"It's a small baby bed. They can use them until they're about three months old."

"What does it look like?"

Gemma held her arms out. "About this long and this wide with legs on it and rollers so it can be moved around, and sometimes they have a little canopy thing with lace and frills for little girls."

Trace's brown eyes narrowed. "I got an idea. I'll be right back."

He was gone ten minutes and returned with a big wooden box about the size of a bassinet but without a hood, legs, or a fancy little mattress.

"Will this do?"

"I expect it would, but isn't that a feed box?"

"Yep, it is, but it's brand spanking new. Never had a single bit of feed or hay in it. Man I bought it from swears he was going to start using it tomorrow, but he'll go get another one."

Gemma cocked her head to one side. "We could fold a blanket several times for a mattress and put the box beside the bed."

"Then it will work?"

"Yes, and she can say she was a true cowgirl from the time she was two weeks old," Gemma said.

Trace grinned. "Maybe that will keep my mother from trying to turn her into a lawyer or a judge."

Chapter 19

BABY HOLLY WAS BATHED, FED, DRESSED IN A CLEAN pink nightgown, and her dark hair brushed, but Gemma continued to hold her. Sitting in the middle of Trace's big bed, she rocked the baby back and forth and hummed to her.

The sight put a catch in Trace's chest. He wished Gemma had been the one that had gotten pregnant with his child. He finished dumping the baby's bathwater down the sink, rinsed the big plastic bowl, and in a few easy strides was beside the bed. He leaned down and kissed Gemma on the forehead and then Holly on the cheek.

"Thank you, one more time. I wouldn't know what or how to do anything, but I'm learning fast," he said.

"You'll get the hang of it. Look at her sleeping. Isn't she beautiful?"

"Yes, she is," Trace said, but he was staring at Gemma, not at his new daughter. He cleared his throat and sat down beside her. "Hey, I need to call my dad to see about all this legal stuff. You okay while I step outside? How long do you think it's going to take us to get to Oregon after this rodeo?"

"We've got a week to get there. If we have a horrible night with her, then we'll only go a couple of hundred miles. If she sleeps good, we'll go more. Go call your folks. I think you are procrastinating," Gemma answered.

"Yes, I am, but before I make the call—" He paused.

Gemma looked up at him. "What?"

He took a deep breath and spit it all out without stopping. "From Hermiston it's only three hundred miles to Bremerton, Washington. That's just a day's trip, and then it is two weeks until the rodeo there. Would you fly to Goodnight with me and spend that two weeks at my house? We wouldn't be so cramped and I could help Uncle Teamer. We could fly back to Bremerton, ride that night, and then drive down to Ellensburg."

Gemma nodded. "Yes, I will."

Trace let out a lungful of air in a whoosh.

"You didn't think I'd say yes, did you?"

He kissed her on the cheek. "I was almost afraid to even ask."

"Go make your call now. I'm going to talk to Momma and then Ace while you visit with your folks."

Trace carried the folder with all the information in it outside with him. He held his breath again after he dialed his father's phone number. It rang four times before his dad picked up.

"Yes?"

"Dad, Trace here."

"I have caller ID, Son. I know who is calling. Your mother and I just finished dinner and we're in a taxi on our way home."

"I have a daughter," Trace blurted out.

"Is this a joke?"

"No, sir. Put it on speaker so Mother can hear. I need some legal advice, and I only want to tell this story once," he said.

He started at the beginning and told them exactly what documents were in the folder.

"Now what do I do?" he asked.

"Are you positive the child is yours, and that if it is, the mother has given up all rights?"

"Looks that way on paper, but I can fax them to you tomorrow morning for you to look at," Trace said.

There was a pause before his mother spoke. "First thing you do is drop down on your knees and promise Gemma O'Donnell half your kingdom for being so generous with her time. I'm still mad at you for bringing her to dinner with us and not even telling her or us. I was so stunned that she probably thinks I'm horrid, and nothing your father or I said came out right."

"What?" Trace said.

"I'm a grandmother now, Son. I can say whatever I want."

"You always have anyway," Trace said.

"Yes, I have, but it'll get worse now. I've got court and your father has cases in the next few days, but we will be in Bremerton for that rodeo. I want to see my granddaughter. And Gemma deserves better than meeting us without giving her a chance to refuse or even pretty up. Good Lord, Trace, I would have shot your father if he'd taken me to see your grandparents without a notice."

"And," his father chimed in, "now she's taking on a child you fathered with another woman from a weekend bender?"

"Okay, okay, I goofed. I wanted her to meet you all. And I thought it would be a nice surprise for both of you. All I hear from you, Mother, is how you wish I'd find a nice girl and settle down. Now about this legal stuff?" Trace asked.

"Sounds like it's pretty well taken care of, Son. I want another DNA just for absolute proof in case this woman ever comes back. And send all those documents to me first thing in the morning," his father said. "I'll file them all in the state of Texas. You want to change her names?"

Trace hesitated.

"Talk it over with Gemma," his mother said.

"She's agreed to go to Goodnight to spend the two weeks between Hermiston and Bremerton to help me with Holly."

"Good, then we will plan on seeing you at Teamer's rather than flying all the way to Washington. We'll be in touch, and you tell Gemma that we're coming," his mother said.

‑‑‑‑‑‑‑

Gemma laid Holly in her bed and dug her cell phone out of her purse.

She hit the speed dial for her mother and waited.

"Hi, kiddo. Where are you? How's the ankle? You really should forfeit your entry fee and not ride in this rodeo. You can win the next one with a good foot rather than hurting this one again and not winning either," Maddie said.

"I'd forgotten about my ankle. Trace still makes me use crutches, but it's healing pretty fast, and I hate to give up my entry fee. Are you sitting down, Momma?"

"You didn't marry that man, did you?"

Gemma sputtered. "What made you say that?"

"Your tone. There's something different about it."

"No, I did not marry him. But I'm sitting here looking

at his baby." Gemma went on to tell her the whole story before Maddie could butt in again.

"Oh my!" Maddie said when she finished.

"Is that all you've got to say?"

"For right now it is because I'm shocked speechless. Don't you dare fall in love with that baby and mistake it for real love for the man. That wouldn't be fair to either of you, and you better think twice about getting too attached to the baby because it'll just make it harder to leave her when the time comes."

"For someone who is stunned into silence you are doing a really good job of talking. Ace is here. I hadn't even called him and wasn't expecting to see him until the rodeo, but he just stuck his head in the trailer door so I'll call you later." She ended the call with a touch of a finger.

Blake and Dalton followed Ace into the small trailer with Trace behind them. The brothers stood around the feed box and stared down at the sleeping child.

"Well, I bet that was a big surprise!" Ace said.

Gemma slid off the bed. "Yes, it was. I thought y'all were coming for the rodeo."

"Bull was ready early," Creed said.

Ace bent down on one knee to get a better look at the baby. "We won't be staying for the rodeo. But we've worked out a plan with Trace. Blake is going to hitch up to your trailer and take it home with him. He had planned to go on west of here and check out a ranch, but it sold today. That's why he brought his own truck and can take your trailer home."

"I might look at a couple of places between here and home. You tell your momma about this?" Blake asked Gemma.

"Just did."

"Liz and Jasmine?" Ace asked.

"Not yet."

Ace stood up. "Then I call dibs on telling Jasmine, and you can tell Liz."

"I wish that was mine," Dalton said.

Gemma gulped. "You do?"

"I'm so ready for a wife and kids now that I have bought my own place," he said.

Blake touched the edge of the baby's bed. "I can't believe you've got her in a feed box. Throw a little hay in there and she'd look like the nativity scene down at the Ringgold church when we have the Christmas pageant. Remember when Rachel was the baby for it and she cooed and gooed at her momma the whole time the kings were there?"

"Those were her uncles and she knew them. She damn sure didn't coo at you three, did she? And besides, this is nearly August, not December," Gemma said.

"No, she set up a howl," Ace answered.

Trace looked at Gemma.

"Her uncles and father were the three kings, and these three were the shepherds. Maybe y'all should have brought her shiny presents instead of leading a baaing sheep up on the platform," Gemma explained to Trace.

"Gemma was the angel that night. She had a crooked wire hanger covered in silver tinsel on her head," Ace said.

Trace shook his head. "Angel? Y'all let her be an angel?"

Blake's booming laugh woke the baby. "I'm sorry, but that's exactly what I said when I saw her all draped in a bedsheet with that halo on her head."

Gemma picked Holly up. "Well, this is a real angel."

She suddenly realized that Holly would be in Goodnight, Texas, celebrating her first Christmas with her father and his family at the end of December. Gemma would be in Ringgold with her family.

Oh, no, I will not! I'm not leaving. Trace can get used to the idea one day at a time and even think it's his idea when he asks me to stay on forever.

"And come Christmas, she might even be teething and even Jesus won't be able to get along with her then," Blake said. "Remember those times with our nephews and our niece?" He looked at his brothers.

Ace's face went serious. "Come Christmas, I'll be a daddy! It just hit me. I'm going to have one of those."

"Maybe two if you want to stay up with Wil and Pearl," Blake said.

"Oh, no!" Ace said. "They did an ultrasound and I saw my daughter and there's just one of her."

"Okay, while my big brother is digesting the idea of fatherhood, let's go get these trailers changed over. We've got a bull in a trailer out there and a lot of miles to go," Blake said.

"Tell me again how you manage to take care of this," Gemma asked.

"Blake brought his truck, so he's going to take your trailer all the way home. Dalton is going to follow me in Trace's truck and we'll leave it at Goodnight, then he'll get in with me and we'll go on home," Ace said.

Gemma handed the baby to Trace. "I'll go get my things out of the trailer."

"Would you mind if I used your trailer on the way? It would save some hotel expenses while I'm looking around. There's a couple of pieces of property I want to look at around Vernon," Blake asked.

"Not one bit. It's not very big, but it works for one person just fine. You might even find a woman camped right next to you in a trailer park that will change your luck," Gemma teased.

"Ain't happenin'. My luck is plumb run out with the women. I'm going to be the old bachelor uncle who spoils his nephews and nieces."

An hour later she'd moved in with Trace. He'd better get used to it because she intended to be around forever.

Chapter 20

GEMMA FED HOLLY. TRACE BURPED HER, AND THEN they'd stared at her for several minutes after they put her into her makeshift bed.

"We'd better get some sleep. She'll be ready to eat again in four hours, max," Gemma said.

Trace pulled her down on the bed. She cuddled up next to his side and shut her eyes. When she opened them a minute later, nothing had changed. There was still a baby in a big wooden box next to her. She didn't have a trailer of her own anymore. And her saddle was in the backseat of her truck. And she'd made up her mind about her future and set it in solid stone.

"Did today really happen?" Trace asked.

Gemma kissed him on the jaw. "It didn't happen. That would mean it was over and an end had occurred. It is happening. No end in sight. Once a father, always a father, even when she's grown."

"That scares me," he said.

"It should terrify you. It's a big job."

He kissed her on the forehead. "I'm worn completely out both mentally and physically. How about you, Gemma?"

"Yes, on all counts. You go take a shower and then I'll get one and we'll get some sleep. It'll be a short four hours."

It seemed like she'd barely shut her eyes when Holly whimpered. She looked at the clock and only an hour had passed. The baby couldn't be hungry yet. She rolled out of Trace's arms and tucked the blanket back around Holly's feet. Then Gemma could not go back to sleep.

One thing after another kept her awake. She worried about her saddle in the truck. Would the heat tomorrow cause it to get out of the fit? Then she mulled over and over the fact that she was now officially living with Trace. If they had big fight, the only place she could go was outside.

She shivered when she realized how much trust they'd put in each other. It was her truck but it was his trailer. She could drive off and leave him stranded with a baby on the side of the road. But he could throw her and all her belongings out and she wouldn't have a home.

Home!

There was that word again.

Finally, she beat her pillow into submission and fell asleep only to be awakened by pitiful little cries two hours later. When she opened her eyes, Trace was sitting straight up in bed, his hair a mess, and his eyes wide open.

He dug his fists into his eyes. "I'll heat the bottle if you'll change her diaper."

"Okay," she said.

This time he fed her and Gemma did the burping. In thirty minutes Holly was fed and asleep again. Trace curled up to Gemma's back with his arm around her.

"We make a good team," he whispered.

"Yes, we do," she said groggily.

Gemma looked down at a bronc who would have been cussing a blue streak if he could've talked. He snorted and tried to shake the saddle off. Everything about Sugar Baby said there wasn't a sweet bone in his body and he couldn't wait to toss her into the dirt.

The first order of business was that she had to stop thinking about the eighty-one points Trace had just racked up, about the fact that he was watching Holly all by himself, and about the fact that her foot hurt like a son of a bitch in that boot. When she could get all that out of her mind she'd be fine.

"Well, shit!" she said.

"What?" the cowboy at the top of the chute asked.

"My lucky horseshoe and my shamrocks are headed toward Texas."

The cowboy frowned.

"You wouldn't understand."

"Don't reckon I would. You ready?"

She measured the rein again and touched her lucky hat pin.

Sugar Baby came out of the chute with all four feet off the ground and his back straight up in the air. She knew the crowd was putting out some noise, and the announcer's voice was full of excitement. Her feet went back, spurs raked, feet came forward, and ankle throbbed. It was like doing a line dance on a broken foot. She should've taken her mother's advice, but oh, no, she had to prove that she could ride with a sprained ankle.

The buzzer sounded and a rescue rider grabbed her around the waist. She slid off the horse and winced when both her feet hit the ground.

"And that, cowboys and cowgirls, was Gemma O'Donnell from Ringgold, Texas, who was tied with Trace Coleman for the top-seeded place in this year's

Million Dollar Pro Rodeo Tour right here at the Lovington Rodeo. Trace has racked up eight-one big points, and now the judges are handing me their scores for Gemma O'Donnell. And oh, my goodness, I don't believe this—" The announcer's booming voice held so much excitement that the crowd quieted.

Gemma held her breath. Had she beat him even with a busted ankle and very little sleep?

"They are still in a tie! They both have eighty-one points and will split tonight's purse at this silver event! Good luck to both of you in the next rodeo. We'll all be watching to see if you break this tie then. And now we've got barrel racing, starting with the queen herself of barrel racing, Katy McQueen, from Austin, Texas."

Gemma bowed to the crowd and limped off to the chutes where Trace and Holly waited. So they were still in a tie? That beat having to listen to him brag about whipping her butt for the next fifteen hundred miles as they drove to Oregon.

The days flew by with such speed that Gemma wondered at night where they'd gone. She and Trace had bought a baby monitor, but they were so worn out by evening that most of the time they didn't want to do anything but cuddle a few minutes and fall asleep.

August was almost half done when they parked in Oregon that evening, and after the rodeo the next night they'd fly to Amarillo. She wondered if they'd have time for sex at the ranch or if this was the way it was going to be. Maybe they'd had a wild, hot affair and now they'd slid back into nothing more than a deep friendship.

"Get all prettied up," Trace said when they went from the truck to the trailer that evening.

"Why?"

"Because this is date night. I'm taking my two pretty girls out to dinner and a movie and then we're going to put that monitor gizmo you bought to use. I've been thinking about you all day, and I want more than cuddling tonight, darlin'."

"And what if I'm too damn tired?" she smarted off.

"Then you go on to sleep and I'll wake you when it's over," he teased.

She giggled. "Where did you get that line? And you know damn well that a dozen of your kisses will heat me up until there won't be any sleeping until it is over, so don't tease me."

"Made it up on the spot. And darlin', your kisses do the same to me."

He set Holly's car seat on the table, turned on the air to cool the trailer down, and opened his arms to Gemma. She took a step and he pulled her so close that she could hear his heart beat. Not yet! They weren't anything more than friends yet!

"Do we have to wait for dinner, a movie, and ten o'clock feeding?" she whispered. "She's asleep right now."

Trace grasped her butt, and with one hop, her legs were around his waist. His lips met hers in a hard kiss that sent tsunami-sized waves of desire shooting from her lips to her lower gut. Tongue met tongue in enough fiery heat to burn down the whole state of Oregon. She didn't know when her shirt and bra left her body, but suddenly she was naked from the waist up, on the bed, and the door was shut. His mouth left her lips long enough to taste her breasts and then latched on to her lower lip again.

"God, I missed this," he moaned between kisses.

She reached between them, undid his belt buckle, and unzipped his jeans, then ran a hand down inside to tease an already rock-hard erection.

"Me too." She gasped.

Her jeans and underpants disappeared like magic, and he was naked and making love to her just as fast. She'd expected it to be a slam, bam, thank-you-ma'am bout, but after the first thrust, he slowed the rhythm so much that it was tender and sweet. His lips were everywhere. On her eyelids, her earlobes, her neck, and his hands wandered from her ribs to her breasts and to her face.

They'd had wild, wonderful sex.

They'd had sex on the cabinet top and in an old-fashioned claw-foot bathtub.

But Gemma felt like Trace was making love to her, not having sex. And in that moment she knew beyond the faintest shadow of a doubt that she'd chosen the right horse to ride the rest of her life.

She reached a climax long before he did and then another one, and then he collapsed on top of her with a growl that sounded faintly like, "love you." But she wasn't sure.

"Good idea there, sweetheart," he murmured when he could breathe again.

"Yes, sir, it damn sure was."

He rolled, taking her with him. "We've made it a whole week in a trailer with a baby. Honey, we're ready to take on the world."

Or Goodnight, Texas, she thought.

Chapter 21

GEMMA PICKED UP HOLLY'S CAR SEAT WITH ONE HAND, her diaper bag with the other, and followed Trace out of the house. He turned around at the bottom step and kissed her on the forehead. The horizon split the sun on the eastern horizon, making it look like half an orange lying out there toward the Atlantic Ocean. Goodnight, Texas, was flat country with nothing but dirt, cotton, cows, and lots of summer blue sky. When they'd arrived the day before, Gemma's soul felt as if it had come home. She loved the trees and rolling hills around Ringgold, but there was something majestic about nothing but land and sky.

"See you at noon. You sure you're all right with watching her while I get some work done?" Trace touched Holly's cheek.

"I'm fine with watching her, but I'm going with you," Gemma said.

Teamer chuckled from the far end of the porch where he was sitting in a rocking chair that needed paint as bad as the house.

They both looked his way.

He threw up a palm. "Don't mind me. Get on with the argument. Just don't take too long. We're wastin' time."

Trace jerked his eyes around to meet Gemma's. She wouldn't have let him win anyway, but she sure didn't intend to lose the battle with Teamer watching.

"The hay field is no place for a baby," he said.

"Momma raised all of us in a hay field, and darlin', we did not have an air-conditioned tractor in those days. I can drive a tractor and get a helluva lot more done than sitting on the front porch of this house and worrying about your momma coming tonight."

Trace started toward the pickup. "I said no!"

Teamer stood up and followed him.

Gemma stood still, but she raised her voice. "You don't get to say jack shit, cowboy! Holly and I outvoted you. She says if she's going to grow up on this place, then by damn, she's going to learn how to be a ranchin' woman. And does she need to remind you that her first days were spent in a feed box? So either we both go or you can stay home and I'll go help Teamer cut hay. Either way, I'm goin'. Your choice as to whether you are or not."

"You are some piece of work, Gemma O'Donnell," Trace growled.

"You knew that before you asked me to come to your ranch for two weeks. As John Wayne said, 'We're burnin' daylight.' You stayin' or are *we* goin'?"

Teamer chuckled.

"You are exasperating," he said.

"That would be the pot calling the kettle black, now wouldn't it?"

He exhaled loudly. "Okay, let's go. You got enough diapers and bottles?"

"Right here. She'll only need one feeding between now and noon. Should be just about break time." She smiled.

"I wish Louis would've been here. We would've bet on which one of you would win and I would've made a dollar." Teamer laughed again.

"Thank you for putting your money on me." Gemma smiled.

"Don't thank me. I know a good filly when I see one." Teamer got into his old work truck and led the way to the pasture.

Gemma drove the big John Deere tractor with Holly in her car seat right beside her. The baby cooed and gooed along with the country music radio station and really made a lot of noise when the DJ played "You Look So Good in Love," by George Strait. The cab was cool. George kept them entertained. And the tractor hummed right along, leaving mounds of alfalfa to cure in the hot sunshine.

They'd flown out of Washington still tied for the lead place in the finals. Billy Washington had come in from the bottom of the list to blow everyone out of the water at the Oregon rodeo with eighty-four points. Teamer had driven into Amarillo and picked them up at the airport the day before. She'd liked him from the minute she met him. He reminded her of her father, Cash. Slow talking, tall, lanky, and bright, twinkling eyes. The amazing thing was that thinking about her father did not make her homesick, and when she stepped foot on the ranch in Goodnight, looked at the little house and across the land to the sky on the far horizon, her soul had said that she was home.

"He's got rocks for brains if he thinks he can boss me around just because we're in his stomping territory, right, baby girl? Because it's not just his territory any-more; it's mine too. And the quicker he realizes it, the better off we'll all be," Gemma told Holly when they were in the tractor.

Holly smiled at Gemma's voice.

"That's right. He's funny as a two-dollar bill for entertainin' notions of leaving us in the house to stew and fret all day about his parents coming to visit. Thank God they're staying with Teamer. I'd be crazy as a loon in a hailstorm if they were right in the house with us all weekend," she talked to Holly. "And you'll be meeting Granny and Grandpa for the first time, ladybug. Wonder if they'll let you call them that or if they'll want some kind of cutesy names."

At six weeks Holly wasn't interested in anything but getting her hand to her mouth and gnawing on it. She didn't care that the second DNA had proven that she was indeed Trace's child or that her name was formally now Holly Mary-Jo Coleman on her new amended birth certificate.

"I'm glad those new papers said that there isn't a doubt in the world that you belong to your daddy. I wouldn't have trusted a beer bottle DNA either," she said as she whipped the big tractor around at the end of the hay field and started back across it, keeping the tires in the furrows.

The phone rang and she put it on speaker.

"Hello. Are you still mad at me?" she asked.

Trace's laugh answered her. "Teamer says you remind him of his mother."

"You didn't answer my question," Gemma said.

"No, I'm not mad at you."

"Good. How are you doin' in your field? Gonna get it cut by suppertime?"

"Probably."

"Betcha I cut more than you do today, and I've got a baby in the tractor," she teased.

"Is everything a contest with you?" Trace asked.

"Of course. I'm the baby of five kids. We'd bet on who could run from the house to the barn fastest or who could swat the most flies on the back porch before dinner."

"You are kidding me! You really counted dead flies?" Trace asked.

"Oh, yeah! I'm the queen. I got fifty-three one evening. But Raylen beat me when it came to catching fireflies and putting them in a jar."

Trace laughed again. "I want half a dozen kids so they can do those things."

Gemma was caught off guard and didn't know how to answer him.

"You there?" he asked.

"I'm here. Why do I remind Teamer of his mother?"

"Grandma was headstrong, opinionated, and nobody got ahead of her. She was a pistol. Could outride and out-plow Grandpa in her youth," Trace answered.

"That is a great compliment. I will have to thank him."

Trace chuckled. "How's Holly?"

"She says to tell you that her fist tastes real good and that she likes George Strait. She hasn't fussed about riding in the tractor, so I think she's going to be a good ranchin' girl. We'll have to let her decide for sure when she's older. She might want to be a ballerina on the New York City stage and wear high-heeled shoes and business suits. And we need to start looking for a pony. She needs to start riding early on."

"My daughter can wear high heels, but not in New York City. She's a Texan and she'll stay one," Trace said.

"She'll be whatever she wants to be," Gemma argued.

"If she decides she wants to be a woman astronaut, then by damn she can be one."

"Like you are a bronc rider in a man's world?" he asked.

"Don't go there, Trace."

"The main reason I called is to tell you that Mother and Dad are flying up in their plane instead of taking a commercial flight. They'll be here at noon. Louis is cooking dinner for all of us in the house. We'll be stopping for the day at about eleven so we can clean up a bit. I don't expect you want to meet them wearing jeans with holes in the knees and with your hair in dog ears? Now, personally, I think you look like an angel in that getup, and the fact that you can drive a tractor and cut hay puts a halo above your head in Teamer's eyes. But darlin', Mother already gave me one dressing down for not telling her about that first dinner, so I'm not about to make that same mistake twice."

"You better not ever do that again, Trace Coleman. I would like to stop at eleven so I can at least take a shower and get Holly all prettied up to meet them," Gemma said.

"Another thing." Trace paused again.

"Remember I'm bullheaded like your Granny Coleman," she said.

"Oh, I'm finding that out the hard way. What would it take to talk you into coming back to Goodnight with me after the Washington rodeo? Your beauty shop is leased until the end of the year and it's a helluva long way for me to go for a haircut. I could pay you," he said.

Her heart thumped and then raced.

"You don't have to pay me. I'll do it," she said. That gave him several more weeks to figure out that he couldn't live without an opinionated woman like his grandmother had been.

"Oh, one more thing, darlin'." His voice dropped down to a gravelly drawl.

"Trace, you're about out of one more things," she said.

"This is the last one. Are you wearing underpants?"

"Trace Coleman!"

"What color are they?"

"Holly is right here beside me."

"Are they those little lacy things I took off with my teeth?"

"I told you…"

"Or are you going commando today so when we get home I can peel those clothes off you and make wild passionate love to you before we go to lunch?"

"You better curb your imagination, cowboy."

"Can't. It keeps thinking about you in those cute little underbritches. If Holly is taking a nap we could at least get a quickie."

"You'd best start thinking about a dirty diaper or a shoulder full of sour milk to cool your jets down, because it's going to take the whole hour for me and Holly to get beautiful."

He laughed. "Darlin', you and Holly are beautiful just like you are."

Gemma unbuckled Holly, adjusted her bonnet, and handed her to Trace. "Here, you carry her inside, in your arms, not in the carrier."

"Why?"

"Because your mother is going to want to hold her

right now and you should be the one holding her the first time they see her," Gemma explained.

Trace adjusted the baby in the crook of his left arm and laced his fingers with Gemma's with his right hand. "Have I told you lately that you are an incredible woman?"

Gemma wore a white sundress, gold hoop earrings, and her lucky cowboy boots, the ones she usually reserved for bronc riding. Her dark hair had been washed, dried, and styled, and her makeup was flawless.

Trace had shaved, put on creased jeans and freshly shined boots, and a soft chambray shirt with pearl snaps, and Gemma had feathered his dark hair back with a handful of mousse.

Baby Holly was dolled up in a cute little white dress, a white lace bonnet with a wide brim, and white socks with lace ruffles. She smelled like baby lotion and looked like an angel with her dark hair and big eyes.

Not that it would matter anyway. Gemma and Trace could be wearing burlap feed bags tied at the waist with rope and their feet could be bare. The only thing Mary and Thomas Coleman were going to see was Holly.

"We are here," Trace yelled at the door.

Mary got up from the rocking chair in the living area and walked toward him with her hands held out. He handed Holly over and grabbed Gemma's hand tightly.

Thomas came from the kitchen and stood beside his wife as she looked down into the baby's face, wide-eyed at the new person holding her. To Gemma it was a slow-motion scene, and she wondered if any one of the three would ever blink. Then tears filled Mary's eyes and rolled down her cheeks. She didn't brush them away but let them drop on her light blue sweater.

"She's absolutely beautiful, Trace. She's the image of you as a baby except for her eyes. I think they're going to be dark green like your father's and Gemma's," she said.

Gemma looked up at Trace.

He smiled and smacked a kiss on her forehead. "Yep, I believe they are. At first I thought they were brown, but the older she gets the greener they turn. Maybe someday she'll be as pretty as Gemma."

"I don't mind being a grandpa, but it's kind of tough thinkin' that my trophy wife is a grandma," Thomas said.

"If she's lucky she'll be as pretty as Gemma, and I'm not a trophy wife, Thomas Coleman. I wish I had a dozen of these. Come sit beside me, Gemma. You men go on and help Louis finish up the dinner," Mary said.

Trace let go of Gemma's hand, hugged his mother, shook hands with his father, and followed Teamer and his father into the kitchen. Gemma sat down on the sofa beside the rocking chair.

"So how do you feel about this baby?" Mary asked.

"I love her. I don't have a child of my own, but I can't believe it would be any closer to me than Holly is," Gemma said honestly.

"I thought so. I could see it in your eyes. What are you going to do about it?"

Gemma was suddenly as nervous as a long-tailed cat in a room full of rocking chairs. "Well, to start with, Trace wants me to stay here until after the Vegas rodeo to help take care of her. I'm free to do that so I agreed. We'll cross the next bridge after I whip his butt in that rodeo."

"Teamer would give him this ranch or we'd buy it for him. What better place to raise my grandchild than in wide open spaces with plenty of room for her to grow?"

Mary removed Holly's bonnet and touched her hair. "We didn't need to do that second DNA test. She looks just like Trace did when he was this age."

Gemma pulled Holly's socks off so Mary could count her toes. "He's a proud man. He wants to know that he bought this ranch with his own money. And it made everyone more comfortable to have a real DNA swab and not one off a beer bottle."

"They are all there, pretty and pink," Mary said. "He should have told you that he was bringing you to meet us at the restaurant. Men don't think sometimes."

"He learned his lesson. He told me today." Gemma smiled.

"I see that. You look lovely."

"Thank you. Do you really want a dozen grandchildren?"

"Yes, I do. I wanted more children but had a problem after Trace was born and they had to do a hysterectomy. I'm glad you talked him into naming her after me," Mary said.

"She looked like a Holly Mary-Jo to me." Gemma reached over and Holly grasped her finger.

"She's going to be very smart," Mary said.

"Maybe even a judge."

"Or maybe a cowgirl who rides wild horses?"

"Dinner is ready," Louis announced.

"I can hold her and eat with one hand," Mary said.

"We've got her carrier in the truck."

"If you don't mind, I'd just as soon hold her."

"Not at all," Gemma said.

"I'm glad we had this time alone," Mary whispered on the way to the dining room.

Gemma touched her shoulder. "Me too."

———

Later that night after they'd put Holly to bed in an old rocking cradle that Teamer had hauled down off the attic, Gemma curled up next to Trace. He hugged her tightly to his side and kissed her on the top of the head.

"Momma likes you. So did Dad."

"And you?"

"Honey, I love you."

The room went as still as the arena just before the gates opened. Gemma thought she'd heard him wrong and that he said, "I like you." Surely he hadn't really said the *L* word, or had he?

"Well?" Trace finally said.

"Are you sure?" she asked.

Trace laughed. "Very."

"How do you know?"

"Easy. It didn't pain me to say the words and it feels right."

She sat straight up, flipped around, threw a leg over him, and sat on him like he was a wild bronc. "Look me in the eyes and say it again."

"I love you, Gemma." His eyes did not leave hers.

She leaned forward, propped her hands on the pillow beside his head, and kissed him. And it did feel right.

"I love you too," she whispered.

He tangled his hands in her long hair and drew her lips back to his and rolled over until he was on top of her. "Promise?"

"Kiss me again and I'll promise."

He sealed the deal with a sweet, lingering kiss. He

tasted her lips slowly and moved his hands under her nightshirt, touching all the places that made her shiver.

"Make love to me," she whispered.

"That's exactly what I'm doing, and I'm starting with long, slow kisses just like the song says."

"What if I want fast and furious?"

"Then you'll have to wait until tomorrow night. I bet Mother would gladly babysit and let us go out to dinner."

"No! I'm not leaving that baby alone with anyone, not yet," she said.

"Then it will be long slow kisses and…" He let the sentence trail off as he started down her body, taking off clothing and throwing it on the floor and kissing every inch of her skin.

"Whew!" she panted.

"You are so beautiful and I love you so much," he said.

"This isn't sex. This is…" She panted.

"…making love," he finished for her. "Got to admit, I like it just as well, and darlin', I plan to do it often."

"Trace," she gasped, "I do love you. I really, really do."

Chapter 22

GEMMA'S SPURS JINGLED AGAINST THE CHUTE AS SHE climbed up the side. Not far away, Holly was busy pitching a real hissy fit in her stroller. She didn't even stop crying when Trace picked her up and held her close to his vest. He'd ridden just minutes before and beat both Billy's and Coby's tie of eighty points by one point. Now all she had to do was put the baby's cries out of her mind, do her eight seconds, and beat them all.

She felt the horse tense against her knees. She cleared her mind, got prepared for the mark out, then nodded.

The announcer screamed above the Omaha fans and said more in eight seconds than Gemma could have thought in eight hours. "Look at her ride, cowboys and cowgirls. She's got that bronc under control. The only woman in the contest this year, Miss Gemma O'Donnell, and she's showing the boys how it's done, let me tell you." He went on and on, but the only thing Gemma heard was, "And there's the buzzer. She's stayed with him the whole time. Let's see what the judges have to say about that ride from Gemma from Ringgold, Texas."

She was on the ground with her hat in her hand when she heard the news. "Well, darlin', that was one helluva ride, and you taught that big black bruiser who was boss, but it looks like Trace Coleman wins this round. You racked up eighty points to make it a three-way tie for second place. You didn't win this round, honey, but we'll see all four of you again in Vegas in December where it's anybody's game and the stakes are high. And now we'll go right into the bull riding."

Gemma bowed to a noisy crowed and walked out of the arena. The tie had finally been broken that started back in Lovington. Trace was ahead by ten thousand dollars, but they were both going to the finals.

A cold breeze kicked up, and Gemma hurried to the place where she'd left Trace and Holly. Her cell phone rang and she answered it without missing a step.

"So do I put the next shamrock on that has playoffs written in silver glitter on the lucky horseshoe hanging on the side of the refrigerator?" Maddie asked.

"No, Momma. I missed it. Second place with a three-way tie, but I'm going to Vegas. So is Billy Washington, Coby Taylor, and Trace."

"I'm sorry, darlin'. I know you wanted to go as the number one contestant, but the important thing is that you'll be going to the finals. We'll all be there. Whole bunch of us are flying in. Except for Jasmine and Ace. She says she can have a baby in the plane, at the rodeo, or in a Vegas hospital, but Ace says she is not flying when she's that close to her due date. Done got a whole suite of rooms reserved so don't be making any hotel plans. How's that baby girl?"

"I'm surprised you can't hear her. I'm heading right toward her and she's screaming her head off. Here, Trace, take this phone and give me that child," Gemma said.

"Hello?" Trace said.

Gemma crooned to Holly. "It's okay, sweetheart. I'm

here. I should've taken you with me. I could've held you in my rein hand and still got a high score."

"Congratulations, Trace," Maddie said.

"Thank you. Will we see you in Vegas?"

"Oh, yes, but we will see you and the baby a couple of weeks before that. My rule is that all my kids come home for Thanksgiving."

"Is that an invitation?" Trace asked.

"No, that is an order. Now give the phone back to Gemma. If she could ride a bronc and hold a baby at the same time like I just now heard her say, then she can damn sure hold a baby and talk to me," Maddie said.

Trace handed the phone to Gemma.

"Yes, ma'am. We will. I promise. Call everyone for me."

She jammed it into her vest pocket and looked at him.

"What?" she asked.

He grabbed her around the waist and hugged both her and Holly at the same time. "We made it, Gemma. We're going to the finals."

"Was there ever a doubt? I'm still going to whip your sorry old ass even though I'm in love with you, cowboy."

"We'll see about that, darlin'."

"What now?"

"Now we go home to Goodnight and live until the second weekend in December." He kept an arm around her shoulders and pushed the stroller with the other hand as they started toward the stands.

"Hey, you two—good rides!" Coby yelled from the shadows.

"Same back atcha," Gemma hollered.

"See you in Vegas where neither one of you is going home with the cash or the glory," Coby said.

"Bring it on, big boy," Gemma taunted.

"You should've left that rodeo with me the night you passed out and you wouldn't be strapped down with a baby," he smarted off.

Gemma handed Holly to Trace and covered the ground between them in long strides. "What did you say? Were you the one who put that shit in my beer that night?"

"Figure it out for yourself. But remember, I could've offered you a helluva lot more than Trace Coleman has given you," he whispered.

Gemma moved up to within an inch of Coby's nose. "Thank you. If you hadn't put that in my drink, I'd have never fallen in love with Trace."

Coby blushed so crimson that Gemma could've lit a cigarette off the end of his nose. He opened his mouth, but nothing would come out.

"When you get on the bronc in Vegas, you remember that losers seldom win a damn thing and only a loser would dope a woman's drink to get her into bed. A real man doesn't have to use anything but charm," Gemma threw over her shoulder.

"What was that all about?" Trace asked.

"He's the one who drugged my beer that night. I was thanking him because I got you out of the deal."

"Okay, let's take Holly up in the stands and watch the rest of the rodeo."

"I figured I'd have to fight you when you found that out," she said.

"Darlin', you told me way back there that you fought your own battles. And besides, I agree with Teamer. You are as big a force as Grandma Coleman."

Chopper McBride swaggered over to them and stuck out his hand. "Congratulations, son. I was on my way to buy a beer. Can I get you kids one?"

Trace shook with the old rodeo legend. "Thank you, sir. We're on our way to the stands. We'll get one on the way. Appreciate the offer, though."

"Y'all both gave us a run for our money all season." He chuckled. "Truth is I made a few hundred bettin' on one or the other of you all summer. And now I don't know where to put my bet for the finals. I reckon you could tame the devil, Trace, but Gemma, she's going to make you work your ass off for it. She might even whip your sorry old butt when the time comes. So who do I put my money on?" he asked with a gleam in his eyes.

"On me," Gemma said. "I'm going to win."

"What you got to say about that?" Chopper asked Trace.

"I'd say that she is full of hot air," Trace answered.

Chopper guffawed. "Okay, then, I'm going to put half my money on Trace and the other half on Gemma. That way I win no matter what. Now turn that baby around here and let me look at her. Y'all look like a regular family, but you got to get her some chaps and boots. Can't never start 'em too early."

Chapter 23

September ended.

October flew by like it had wings, and every day Gemma wondered what would happen after the final rodeo. Trace had said that he loved her two months before, and every night those three magic words came out of his mouth just before he went to sleep. They'd fallen into a working relationship that involved ranching, which she knew as well as he did, hot heavy sex some nights and sweet lovemaking others, raising a baby, and sharing life. Some days they made it all the way from daylight to dark without hitting a speed bump; others they didn't get finished with breakfast before they hit the first one.

November came in with a blast of cold wind that said winter was on the way. By the middle of the month they'd already had freezing weather, but the sun was out on Thanksgiving morning when they loaded Holly into Gemma's truck and headed east to Ringgold for the day and night. Teamer and Louis planned a big Thanksgiving supper on Friday night with Trace's parents flying in from Houston.

They made it in record time and parked in the yard beside several other trucks. Holly had slept most of the way and woke up hungry just a mile from the house. She fussed and fumed and chewed on her hands.

"Bottle?" Trace asked.

"Time for baby food. I brought sweet potatoes

because that's her favorite and it's Thanksgiving," Gemma said. "We'll be there in five more minutes and I can heat them up."

Trace looked in the rearview mirror. "You hear that, baby girl? Just a little bit more and you won't have to chew all the hide off your knuckles." He looked over at Gemma. "Excited to be home?"

Home.

There it was again. Home. But it wasn't in Ringgold anymore. It was in Goodnight where she'd settled into a two-bedroom frame house.

"I'm always excited to see Momma and Daddy and all my friends and family. A couple of years ago about this time we had a big party over at Liz and Raylen's place. It was before they got married and her carnie family had a gig in Bowie. So they parked at Liz's place and she had Christmas right before Thanksgiving."

"And?"

"And I wish it was Christmas, Trace. I wish this was all over and we didn't have it hanging over our heads."

"Why?"

The smile that broke out of a serious face was devilish. "So Momma could put my biggest shamrock on the lucky horseshoe, and me and Holly could dance around a real Christmas tree."

He parked the truck. "But what if you don't win?"

"Honey, there is not a doubt in my mind that I'm going to be a winner that night," she said.

"I wish to hell I had that kind of confidence."

She reached over and kissed him on the cheek. And then the passenger door flew open and Raylen gave her a big bear hug.

"You did it, Sister. You made the finals and we're all coming and Momma is throwing a fit so you'd best get in the house. Is this the new baby? She's so pretty. Can I carry her inside? Liz swears she's going to be the first one to hold her and that she'll put a spell on her so she'll like her Aunt Liz better than anyone else. But if you let me hold her first, she'll like me best. And you must be Trace. I'm glad to meet you, but I want to hold this baby more than I want to shake your hand."

Trace chuckled.

Gemma nodded.

Raylen unfastened the baby seat and picked Holly up. "Look at that. She likes me. I tell you, I've got a way with babies. Remember how Rachel liked me better than Dewar?"

"Hey, now!" Dewar said right behind his younger brother. "She did not. She's always liked me better, but she didn't want to hurt your feelings. Let me look at this girl. Trace, you'd best polish up the shotgun when she's sixteen."

"Why's that? She's not dating until she's twenty-five and then only if I'm with her. Maybe she can go on car or pickup dates alone when she's thirty." Trace laughed.

Raylen did not get into the house before the door opened and he was surrounded with women: Liz, Colleen, Maddie, Granny, Jasmine, Pearl, and Austin.

"Oh my Lord, Jasmine!" Gemma gasped. "Are you going to have that baby today?"

"I wish I could. I'm ready for her to be here, but doc says a couple more weeks at least. She's going to come out big enough to drive a tractor, I swear." Jasmine laughed. "Look at what you done brought home. She's gorgeous. I hope my daughter has hair like that, but with Ace for a daddy, she'll probably be bald as a cue ball."

"Hey, you two, come on in the house. We're as glad to see you as this baby," Granny yelled.

"Yeah, right!" Gemma said.

"Parents always take a backseat when there's a new baby," Trace said.

Gemma felt like he'd just handed her the moon, the stars, and a big chunk of the sun.

Maddie went straight for Gemma, held her out at arm's length, hugged her, and then whispered, "I don't like it, but I'm not going to fight it. I'd rather see you happy than living in Ringgold and miserable. Sell your beauty shop to Noreen and propose to that cowboy, girl. He's the one."

"Thank you, Momma." Gemma hugged Maddie tightly.

"Now, give me that baby. She needs to get to know her grandma."

Gemma dressed in her signature pink boots, pink shirt, and pink hat with the gold lucky horseshoe hat pin. She ate a hamburger from the rodeo grounds that afternoon. She cheered from the sidelines when Trace rode and scored higher than any of the other riders. Now it was her turn, the last bronc rider in the PRCA Finals. The crowd was already on their feet whistling and screaming. She swore she heard her mother's voice above all the others. She felt the bronc's muscles protest when she dropped down into the saddle.

"Give it all you got, boy. Trace has eighty-two points and I need one more than that." She jammed her boots down into the stirrups, measured the rein, touched her hat pin, got ready for the mark out, and nodded.

The time had come.

Rein in hand.

Determination in her heart.

"Go get 'em, darling!" Tracc yelled from the bottom of the chute.

She smiled and remembered the first time he'd said that. That night she'd been ready to make coyote food out of him. Tonight, she could have kissed him.

Everything stopped and she was in a vacuum again. Even the dust out in the arena was afraid to succumb to gravity and fall back to earth. Like always, the noise of crowd hung above the arena like a layer of foggy smoke in a cheap honky-tonk, but Gemma couldn't hear it.

Three rodeo clowns stepped away from the gate. The chute opened and a blur of white topped with snatches of hot pink whirled around the arena whipping up dust devils in its wake.

Time moved in slow motion. She could hear the crowd going wild and the announcer's excitement, but the roar of blood racing through her veins kept all of it at bay. And then the eight seconds were done. The rescue rider slipped an arm around her waist and she slid off the side of the bronc with grace. They rounded up the horse and she stood in the middle of the arena, waving at the fans all on their feet giving her a standing ovation.

"And that brings the bronc riding to a close. Gemma O'Donnell from Ringgold, Texas, had just shown that mean bronc who is boss. The judges are tallying up the scores and Gemma has to have eighty-three to beat

Trace Coleman. One more judge and we'll have the winner of the Million Dollar PRCA saddle bronc riding event of the year. And here it is, in my hand, cowboys and cowgirls. Let's give it up one more time for Gemma O'Donnell, the only woman contestant in tonight's PRCA finals," the announcer said.

Gemma's knees were weak, but she stiffened them up and kept waving at the crowd.

"The total score for Miss Gemma O'Donnell is eighty-one points. Trace Coleman is our winner, but that's one cowboy who'd best be wiping his brow because he almost did not beat this little lady. Gemma, please stay right where you are. We will pause for a few minutes before the bull riding because we have a special event right now. Mr. George Strait couldn't be here in person, but I've got his CD so he's going to sing and our brand-new bronc busting champion would like to dance with you in this very arena."

A hush fell over the crowd as "I Cross My Heart" played over the loudspeakers. Trace came out from the side of the arena and held out a hand to Gemma.

"May I have this dance please, ma'am?" he asked.

She melted into his arms as George sang that she'd always be the miracle that made his life complete; that as they looked into the future, that they would make each tomorrow be the best that it could be. And that if along the way they found that it began to storm, that she had the promise of his love to keep her warm.

Gemma let the dam loose and the tears flowed. The song ended, but the background music kept playing. Trace stepped back and dropped down on one knee right there in front of thousands of people and said, "Gemma

O'Donnell, I love you with my whole heart. Will you marry me?" He popped open a red velvet box that held a sparkling diamond ring right in the center.

She said, "What if I had beat you?'

"Song was ready. George was going to sing. I was going to propose no matter who won," he said.

She nodded and said, "I love you, Trace. Yes, I will marry you!"

"She said yes," the announcer said. "Let's hear it for the newly engaged couple!"

They could have heard the applause all the way to Ringgold, Texas, when he put the ring on her hand, stood up, and bent her so far back for the kiss that she lost her hat. George Strait began singing the song all over again as he picked up her hat, settled it on her head, scooped her up in his arms, and carried her to the sidelines where he sat down with her in his lap.

All she could hear was the whoosh in her ears that she heard when she put everything else out and rode out of the chute on the back of a wild bronc. She laid her head on Trace's chest and the steady heartbeat brought her back to reality, one beat at a time.

"When?" she asked.

"When what?"

"When do we get married?"

"That's up to you. Tomorrow. It's all just paperwork. We're already joined by heartstrings, darlin'."

"Well, we are in Vegas and the whole family is here."

"Really?" he asked. "One question first. Did you let me win?"

"Hell, no! I gave it all I had. I was going to win and buy Teamer's ranch and propose to you," she said.

There was enough family, friends, and rodeo folks to fill Cupid's Wedding Chapel where Jasmine and Ace had gotten married. Cash walked Gemma down the aisle. She wore a white velvet dress and a white hat with illusion streamers flowing down her back from a bow at the back of the brim. Her lucky horseshoe was pinned on the ribbon twined around a pink and white rosebud bouquet, and her lucky pink boots had been shined.

"Trace is a good man. I just wish you'd buy a ranch closer to Ringgold," Cash whispered as he led his daughter down the short aisle.

"I love him, and Daddy, home is Goodnight, Texas," she whispered.

"I know, baby. You'll just have to come home to Ringgold real often or your momma will have me hauling her to your place every other week. She's fallen in love with that baby girl."

"Haul away." Gemma laughed.

"Who gives this woman to be married to this man?" the preacher asked when they reached the front of the chapel.

"Her mother and I do," Cash said.

In fifteen minutes the preacher pronounced them husband and wife.

"You may kiss your bride," he said.

Trace did a Hollywood kiss that rivaled the one in the arena. "I love you, Mrs. Coleman."

"I love you," she said.

Cash stepped up to the microphone and said, "Thank you all for attending. The reception is at the Bellagio and starts in one hour. There's food and dancing and I understand there'll be lots and lots of pictures taken. I'm supposed to tell you all that Jasmine had a nine-pound baby girl this morning. She tried to get Ace to charter a plane so she could be here and he'll probably be in hot water for weeks because he said no."

One week before Christmas, Trace brought a six-foot cedar tree and set it up in the corner of the living room. He looped the lights around his arms and walked around the tree while Gemma placed them in just the right spot. Holly had just that week learned to sit up all by herself, so she watched wide-eyed from her quilt pallet, and when the lights were plugged in and blinking she giggled like only a delighted baby can.

Then Trace looped the tinsel around his arms and Gemma worked it over and under the tree limbs. Next came the ornaments and then the silver tinsel icicles. Gemma stepped back and looked at it with a critical eye.

"I'm becoming my mother. I've seen her do this dozens of times," she said.

"What next?" Trace asked.

"The topper," she said.

"It's still in the box," Trace said.

Gemma shook her head. "Not that one."

"Why?" Trace asked. "It's only been used one year. Is there something wrong with it?"

"Yes, there is."

She opened a shoebox and took out a homemade gold construction paper horseshoe with *The Coleman Family* written in red glitter.

"Put this up there. I told you when we went to Vegas I had no doubt in my mind that I would be a winner. And I am. You got the title and the ranch. I got you and Holly, so I won the best prize of all."

Trace wrapped his arms around her and tipped her chin up with his forefinger.

"I'm amazed by you, Mrs. Coleman."

She pointed to a huge ball of mistletoe with hundreds of berries hanging right above his head. "I'm the winner, cowboy, and my Christmas wish is for Santa Claus to bring me another child by next Christmas."

"Yes, ma'am," Trace drawled. "I'm not Santa Claus. I'm just a cowboy, but I'll be glad to do my best to make that happen."

New York Times bestselling author Carolyn Brown
makes her first foray into women's fiction in

The Blue-Ribbon
Jalapeño Society Jubilee

Available March 2013 from Sourcebooks Landmark
Read on for a sneak peek!

IF PRISSY PARNELL HADN'T MARRIED BUSTER JONES
and left Cadillac, Texas, for Pasadena, California,
Marty wouldn't have gotten the speeding ticket. It was
all Prissy's damn fault that Marty was in such a hurry to
get to the Blue-Ribbon Jalapeño Society monthly meeting that night, so Prissy ought to have to shell out the
almost two hundred dollars for that ticket.

They were already passing around the crystal bowl
to take up the voting ballots when Marty slung open the
door to Violet Prescott's sunroom and yelled, "Don't
count 'em without my vote."

Twenty faces turned to look at her and not a one of
them, not even her twin sister, Cathy, was smiling. Hells
bells, who had done pissed on their cucumber sandwiches before she got there, anyway? A person didn't
drop dead from lack of punctuality, did they?

One wall of the sunroom was glass and looked out
over lush green lawns and flower gardens. The other
three were covered with shadow boxes housing the
blue ribbons that the members had won at the Texas

State Fair for their jalapeño pepper entries. More than forty shadow boxes all reminding the members of their history and their responsibility for the upcoming year. Bless Cathy's heart for doing her part. She had a little garden of jalapeños on the east side of the lawn and nurtured them like children. The newest shadow box held ribbons that she'd earned for the club with her pepper jelly and picante. It was the soil, or maybe she told them bedtime stories, but she, like her momma and grandma, grew the hottest jalapeños in the state.

"It appears that Martha has decided to grace us with her presence once again when it is time to vote for someone to take our dear Prissy's place in the Blue-Ribbon Jalapeño Society. We really should amend our charter to state that a member has to attend more than one meeting every two years. You could appreciate the fact that we did amend it once to include you in the membership with your sister, who, by the way, has a spotless attendance record," Violet said.

Violet, the queen of the club, as most of the members called it, was up near eighty years old, built like Sponge Bob Square Pants, and had stovepipe jet-black hair right out of the bottle. Few people had the balls or the nerve to cross her, and those who did were put on her shit list right under Martha, a.k.a. Marty, Andrews's name, which was always on the top.

Back in the beginning of the club days, before Marty was even born, the mayor's wife held the top position on the shit list. When they'd formed the Blue-Ribbon Jalapeño Society, Loretta Massey and Violet almost went to war over the name of the new club. Loretta insisted that it be called a society, and Violet wanted to be called a club.

Belonging to a club just sounded so much fancier than saying that one belonged to a society. Loretta won when the
vote came in, but Violet called it club anyway and that's
what stuck. Rumor had it that Violet was instrumental
in getting the mayor ousted just so they'd have to leave
Grayson County and Loretta would have to quit club.

Marty hated it when people called her Martha. It
sounded like an old woman's name. What was her
mother thinking anyway when she looked down at two
little identical twin baby daughters and named them
after her mother and aunt—Martha and Catherine?
Thank God she'd at least shortened their names to Marty
and Cathy.

Marty shrugged, and Violet snorted. Granted, it was
a lady-like snort, but it still went right along with her
round face and three-layered neck. Hell, if they wanted
to write forty amendments to the charter, Marty would
still do only the bare necessities to keep her in voting
standing. She hadn't even wanted to be in the damned
club and had only done it because if she didn't, then
Cathy couldn't.

Marty slid into a seat beside her sister and held up
her ballot.

Beulah had the bowl in hand and was ready to hand
it off to Violet to read off the votes. But she passed it to
the lady on the other side of her and it went back around
the circle to Marty who tossed in her folded piece of
paper. If she'd done her homework and gotten the numbers right, that one vote should swing the favor for Anna
Ruth to be the new member of the club. She didn't like
Anna Ruth, especially since she'd broken up her best
friend's marriage. But hey, Marty had made a deathbed

promise to her momma, and that carried more weight than the name of a hussy on a piece of paper.

The bowl went back to Violet and she put it in her lap like the coveted jeweled crown of a reigning queen. "Our amended charter states that only twenty-one women can belong to the Blue-Ribbon Jalapeño Society at any one time, and the only time we vote a new member in is when someone moves or dies. Since Prissy Parnell got married this past week and moved away from Grayson County, we are open for one new member. The four names on the ballet are: Agnes Flynn, Trixie Matthews, Anna Ruth Williams, and Gloria Rawlings."

The charter also said that when attending a meeting, the members should dress for the occasion, which meant panty hose and heels, even though that wasn't in the fine print. Marty could feel nineteen pairs of eyes on her. It would have been twenty, but Violet was busy fishing the first ballot from the fancy bowl.

Marty threw one long leg over the other one and let the bright red three-inch high heel shoe dangle on her toe. They could frown all they wanted. She was wearing a dress, even if it only reached mid-thigh and had black spandex leggings under it. If they wanted her to wear panty hose, they'd better put a second amendment on that charter and make it in big print.

God Almighty, but she'd be glad when her great-aunt died and she could quit the club. But it looked like Agnes was going to last forever, which was no surprise. God sure didn't want her in heaven, and the devil wouldn't have her in hell.

"One vote for Agnes," Violet said aloud.

Beulah marked that down on the minutes and waited.

Violet enjoyed her role as president of the club and took her own sweet time with each ballot. Too bad she hadn't dropped dead or at least moved to California so Cathy could be president. Marty would bet her sister would get those votes counted a hell of a lot faster.

There was one piece of paper in the candy dish when Beulah held up a hand. "We've got six each for Agnes, Trixie, Anna Ruth, and two for Gloria. Unless this last vote is for Agnes, Trixie, or Anna Ruth, we have a tie, and we'll have to have a run-off election."

"Shit!" Marty mumbled.

Cathy shot her a dirty look.

"Anna Ruth," Violet said and let out a whoosh of air.

A smile tickled the corner of Marty's mouth.

Saved, by damn!

Agnes was saved from prison.

Violet was saved from attending her own funeral.

The speeding ticket was worth every penny.

Trixie poked the black button beside the nursing home door and kicked yellow and orange leaves of fall away as she reached for the handle. She heard the familiar click as the lock let go and then heard someone yell her name.

"Hey, Trixie. Don't shut it. We are here," Cathy called out.

Trixie waved at her two best friends: Cathy and Marty Andrews. Attitude and hair color kept them from being identical. They were five feet ten inches tall and slim built, but Cathy kept blond highlights in her brown hair and Marty's was natural. In attitude, they were as different as vanilla and chocolate. Cathy was the sweet twin who loved everyone and had trouble speaking her mind. Marty was the extrovert who called the shots like she saw them. Cathy was engaged, and Marty said there were too many cowboys she hadn't taken to bed to get herself tied down to one man.

Marty threw an arm around Trixie's shoulder as they marched down the wide hall. Trixie's mother, Janie Matthews, had checked herself into the nursing home four years before when her Alzheimer's had gotten so bad that she didn't know Trixie one day. Trixie had tried to talk her mother into living with her, but Janie was lucid enough to declare that she couldn't live alone and her daughter had to work.

"Congratulations, darlin', you did not make it into club tonight. Your life has been spared until someone dies or moves away and Cathy nominates you again," Marty said.

"Well, praise the Lord," Trixie said.

"I know. Let's string Cathy up by her toenails and force-feed her fried potatoes until her wedding dress won't fit for even putting your name in the pot." Marty laughed.

"Trixie would be a wonderful addition to the club. She wouldn't let Violet run her around like a windup toy. That's why I keep nominating her every chance I get," Cathy said. "Anna Ruth is going to be a brand new puppet in Violet's hands. Every bit as bad as Gloria would have been."

Trixie stopped so fast that Marty's hand slipped off her shoulder. "Anna Ruth?"

"Sorry." Cathy shrugged. "I'm surprised that she won and she only did by one vote."

Trixie did a head wiggle. "Don't the world turn around? My momma wasn't fit for the club because she had me out of wedlock. And now Anna Ruth is living with my husband without a marriage certificate and she gets inducted. If she has a baby before they marry, do they have a big divorce ceremony and kick her out?"

"I never thought she'd get it," Cathy said. "I don't know how in the world I'm going to put up with her in club, knowing that she's the one that broke up your marriage."

Trixie paled. "Who's going to tell Agnes that she didn't get it again? Lord, she's going to be an old bear all week."

"That's Beulah's job. She nominated her. I'm just damn glad I have a class tonight. Maybe the storm will be over before I get home," Marty said.

Cathy smiled weakly. "And I've got dinner with Ethan back at Violet's in an hour."

"I'm not even turning on the lights when I get home. Maybe she'll think I've died." Trixie started walking again.

"You okay with the Anna Ruth thing?" Marty asked.

Trixie nodded. "Can't think of a better thing to happen to y'all's club."

"It's not my club," Marty said. "I'm just there so Cathy can be in it. I'm not sure Violet would let her precious son marry a woman who wasn't in the al-damn-mighty Blue-Ribbon Jalapeño Society. I still can't believe that Violet is okay with her precious son marrying one of the Andrews' twins."

Cathy pointed a long slender finger at her sister. "Don't you start with me! And I'm not the feisty twin. You are. I can't see Violet letting Ethan marry you for sure."

"Touchy, are we? Well, darlin' sister, I wouldn't

have that man, mostly because I'd have to put up with
Violet." Marty giggled.

"Shhh, no fighting. It'll upset Momma." Trixie
rapped gently on the frame of the open door and poked
her head inside a room. "Anyone at home?"

Janie Matthews clapped her hands and her eyes lit up.
She and Trixie were mirror images of each other—short,
slim built, light brown hair, milk chocolate-colored
eyes, and delicate features. Trixie wore her hair in a
chin-length bob, and Janie's was long, braided, and
wrapped around her head in a crown. Other than that and
a few wrinkles around Janie's eyes, they looked more
like sisters than mother and daughter.

"Why, Clawdy Burton, you've come to visit. Sit
down, darlin', and let's talk. You aren't still mad at me,
are you?"

Marty crossed the room and sat down beside Janie
on the bed, leaving the two chairs in the room for Cathy
and Trixie. It wasn't the first time Janie had mistaken
her for Claudia, the twins' mother, or the first time that
she'd remembered Claudia by her maiden name, either.

"I brought some friends," Marty said.

"Any friend of Clawdy's is a friend of mine. Come
right in here. You look familiar. Did you go to school
with me and Clawdy?" Janie looked right at her daughter.

"I did," Trixie said.

Janie's brow furrowed. "I can't put a name with
your face."

"I'm Trixie."

Janie shook her head. "Sorry, honey, I don't remember you. And you?" She looked into Cathy's eyes.

"She's my sister, Cathy, remember?" Marty asked.

"Well, ain't that funny. I never knew Clawdy to have a sister. You must be older than we are, but I can see the resemblance."

"Yes, ma'am, I didn't know you as well as…" Cathy paused and said, "…my little sister did, but I remember coming to your house."

"Did Momma make fried chicken for you?"

"Oh, honey, I've eaten fried chicken more than once at your house," Cathy said.

"Good. Momma makes the best fried chicken in the whole world. She and Clawdy's momma know how to do it just right. Now, Clawdy, tell me you aren't mad at me. I made a mistake runnin' off with Rusty like that, but we can be friends now, can't we?"

Marty patted her on the arm. "You know I could never stay mad at you."

"I'm just so glad you got my letter and came to visit." Janie looked at Trixie and drew her eyes down. "You look just like a girl I used to know. It's right there on the edge of my mind, but I've got this remembering disease. That's why I'm in here so they can help me." She turned her attention back to Marty. "You really aren't mad at me anymore?"

"Of course not. You were in love with Rusty or you wouldn't have run off with him," Marty said. They had this conversation often so she knew exactly what to say.

"I did love him, but he found someone new, so I had to bring my baby girl and come on back home. How are your girls?" She jumped at least five years from thinking she and Claudia were in school to the time when they were new mothers.

"They're fine. Let's talk about you," Marty said.

Janie yawned. "Clawdy, darlin', I'm so sorry, but I can't keep my eyes open anymore."

It was always the same. On Wednesday nights Trixie visited with Janie. Sometimes, when they had time between closing the café and their other Wednesday evening plans, Marty and Cathy went with her. And always after fifteen or twenty minutes, on a good night, she was sleepy.

"That's okay, Janie. We'll come see you again soon," Marty said.

Trixie stopped at the doorway and waved.

Janie frowned. "I'm sorry I can't remember you. You remind me of someone I knew a long time ago, but I can't recall your name. Were you the Jalapeño Jubilee queen this year? Maybe that's where I saw you."

"No, ma'am. They don't crown queens anymore. But it's okay. I remember you real well," Trixie said.

—◆◆◆—

Less than half an hour later, Trixie parked beside a big two-story house sitting on the corner of Main and Fourth in Cadillac, Texas. The sign outside the house said *Miss Clawdy's Café* in fancy lettering. Above it were the words: *Red Beans and Turnip Greens.*

Most folks in town just called it Clawdy's.

It had started as a joke after Cathy and Marty's momma, Claudia, died and the three of them were going through her recipes. They'd actually been searching for "the secret," but evidently Claudia took it to the grave with her.

More than forty years ago Grayson County and Fannin County women were having a heated argument over who

could grow the hottest jalapeños in North Texas. Idalou
Thomas, over in Fannin County, had won the contest for
her jalapeño corn bread and her jalapeño pepper jelly
so many years that most people dropped plumb out of
the running. But that year, Claudia's momma decided
to try a little something different, and she watered her
pepper plants with the water she used to rinse out her
unmentionables. And that was the very year that Fannin
County lost their title in all of the jalapeño categories
to Garvin County at the Texas State Fair. They brought
home a blue ribbon in every category that had anything
to do with growing or cooking with jalapeño peppers.
And that's the year that Violet Prescott and several other
women formed the Blue-Ribbon Jalapeño Society. That
next fall, they held their First Annual Blue-Ribbon
Jalapeño Society Jubilee in Cadillac, Texas.

The Jubilee got bigger and bigger with each passing
year, and people started marking it on their calendar a
year in advance. It was talked about all year, and folks
planned their vacation time around the Jalapeño Jubilee.
Idalou died right after the first Jubilee, and folks in
Fannin County almost brought murder charges against
Claudia's momma for breaking poor old Idalou's
heart. Decades passed before Claudia figured out how
her mother grew such red-hot peppers, and when her
momma passed, she carried on the tradition.

But she never did write down the secret for fear that
one of the Fannin County women would find a way to
steal it. The one thing she did was dry a good supply
of seeds from the last crop of jalapeños just in case
she died that year. It wasn't likely that Fannin County
would be getting the blue ribbon back as long as one of

her daughters grew peppers from the original stock and saved seeds back each year.

"If we had a lick of sense we'd all quit our jobs and put a café in this big old barn of a house," Cathy had said.

"Count me in," Marty had agreed.

Then they found the old LP albums in Claudia's bedroom, and Cathy had picked up an Elvis record and put it on the turntable. When she set the needle down, "Lawdy, Miss Clawdy" had played.

"Daddy called her that, remember? He'd come in from working all day and holler for Miss Clawdy to come give him a kiss," Marty had said.

Trixie had said, "That's the name of y'all's café— Miss Clawdy's Café. It can be a place where you fix up this buffet bar of southern food for lunch. Like fried chicken, fried catfish, breaded and fried pork chops, and always have beans and greens on it seasoned up with lots of bacon drippings. You know, like your momma always cooked. Then you can serve her pecan cobbler, peach cobbler, and maybe her black forest cake for dessert."

"You are making me hungry right now just talkin' about beans and greens. I can't remember the last time I had that kind of food," Marty had said.

Trixie went on, "I bet there's lots of folks around here who can't remember when they had it either with the fast-food trend. Folks would come from miles and miles to get at a buffet where they could eat all they wanted of good old southern fried and seasoned food. And you can frame up a bunch of those old LP covers and use them to decorate the walls. And you could transfer the music from those records over to CDs and play that old music all day. You could serve breakfast from a menu and then a lunch buffet. It would make a mint, I swear it would."

That started the idea that blossomed into a café on the ground floor of the big two-story house. The front door opened into the foyer where they set up a counter with a cash register. To the left was the bigger dining area, which had been the living room. To the right was the smaller one, which had been the dining room. Down past the checkout station was another room to the left that seated sixteen people and was used for special lunch reservations. It had been their mother's sitting room, and their dad's office, right across the hallway, was now a storage pantry for supplies.

Six months later and a week before Miss Clawdy's Café had its grand opening, Trixie caught Andy cheating on her, and she quit her job at the bank to join the partnership. That was a year ago, and even though it was a lot of work, the café really was making money hand over fist.

"Hey, good lookin'," a deep voice said from the shadows when she stepped up on the back porch.

"I didn't know if you'd wait or not," Trixie said.

Andy ran the back of his hand down her jawline. "It's Wednesday, darlin'. Until it turns into Thursday, I would wait. Besides, it's a pleasant night. Be a fine night for the high school football game on Friday."

Trixie was still pissed at Andy and still had dreams about strangling Anna Ruth, but sex was sex, and she was just paying Anna Ruth back. She opened the back door, and together they crossed the kitchen. He followed her up the stairs to the second floor, where there were three bedrooms and a single bathroom. She opened her bedroom door, and once he was inside, she slammed it shut and wrapped her arms around his neck.

"I miss you," he said.

She unbuttoned his shirt and walked him backward to the bed. "You should have thought about that."

"What if I break it off with Anna Ruth?"

"We've had this conversation before." Trixie flipped a couple of switches, and those fancy no-fire candles were suddenly burning beside the bed.

He pulled her close and kissed her. "You are still beautiful."

She pushed him back on the bed. "You are still a lyin', cheatin' son-of-a-bitch."

He sat up and peeled out of his clothes. "Why do you go to bed with me if I'm that bad?"

"Because I like sex."

"I wish you liked housework," Andy mumbled.

"If I had, we might not be divorced. If my messy room offends you, then put your britches back on and go home to Anna Ruth and her sterile house," Trixie said.

"Shut up and kiss me." He grinned.

She shucked out of her jeans and T-shirt and jumped on the bed with him. They'd barely gotten into the foreplay when a hard knock on the bedroom door stopped the process as quickly as if someone had thrown a pitcher of icy water into the bed with them. Trixie grabbed for the sheet and covered her naked body; Andy strategically put a pillow in his lap.

"I thought they were all out like usual," he whispered. "Marty will murder me if that's her."

"I did too. Maybe they called off her class for tonight," Trixie said.

"Cadillac police. Open this door right now, or I'm coming in shooting."

Trixie groaned. "Agnes?"

Andy groaned and fell back on the pillows. "Dear God!"

And that's when flashing red, white, and blue lights and the mixed wails of police cars, sirens, and an ambulance all screeched to a halt in front of Miss Clawdy's.

Trixie grabbed her old blue chenille robe from the back of a rocking chair and belted it around her waist. "Agnes, is that you?"

"It's the Cadillac police, I tell you, and I'll come in there shooting if that man who's molesting you doesn't let you go right this minute." Agnes tried to deepen her voice, but there was just so much a seventy-eight-year-old woman could do. She sounded like a prepubescent boy with laryngitis.

"I'm coming right out. Don't shoot."

She eased out the door, and sure enough, there was Agnes, standing in the hallway with a sawed off shotgun trained on Trixie's belly button.

The old girl had donned her late husband's pleated trousers and a white shirt and smelled like a mothball factory. Her dyed red hair, worn in a ratted hairdo reminiscent of the sixties, was crammed up under a fedora. Enough curls had escaped to float around the edges of the hat and remind Trixie of those giant statues of Ronald McDonald. The main difference was that she had a shotgun in her hands instead of a hamburger and fries.

Trixie shut her bedroom door behind her and blocked it as best she could. "There's no one in my bedroom, Agnes. Let's go downstairs and have a late-night snack. I think there are hot rolls left and half of a peach cobbler."

"The hell there ain't nobody in there! I saw the bastard. Stand to one side, and I'll blow his ass to hell." Agnes raised the shotgun.

"You were seeing me do my exercises before I went to bed."

Agnes narrowed her eyes and shook her head. "He's in there. I can smell him." She sniffed the air. "Where is the sorry son-of-a-bitch? I could see him in there throwing you on the bed and having his way with you. Sorry bastard, he won't get away. Woman ain't safe in her own house."

Trixie moved closer to her. "Look at me, Agnes. I'm not hurt. It was just shadows, and what you smell is mothballs. Shit, woman, where'd you get that getup, anyway?"

Agnes shook her head. "He told you to say that or he'd kill you. He don't scare me." She raised the barrel of the gun and pulled the trigger. The kickback knocked her square on her butt on the floor, and the gun went scooting down the hallway.

"Next one is for you, buster," she yelled as plaster, insulation, and paint chips rained down upon her and Trixie.

Trixie grabbed both ears. "God Almighty, Agnes!"

"Bet that showed him who is boss around here, and if you don't quit usin' them damn cussin' words, takin' God's name in vain, I might aim the gun at you next time. And I don't have to tell a smart-ass like you where I got my getup, but I was tryin' to save your sorry ass so I dressed up like a detective," Agnes said.

Trixie grabbed Agnes's arm, pulled her up, and kept her moving toward the stairs. "Well, you look more like a homeless bum."

Agnes pulled free and stood her ground, arms crossed over her chest, the smell of mothballs filling up the whole landing area.

"We've got to get out of here in a hurry," Trixie tried to whisper, but it came out more like a squeal.

"He said he'd kill you, didn't he?" Agnes finally let herself be led away. "I knew it, but I betcha I scared the shit out of him. He'll be crawling out the window and the police will catch him. Did you get a good look at the bastard? We'll go to the police station and do one of them drawin' things and they'll catch him before he tries a stunt like that again."

They met four policemen, guns drawn, serious expressions etched into their faces, in the kitchen. Every gun shot up and pointed straight at Agnes and Trixie.

Trixie threw up her hands, but Agnes just glared at them.

"Jack, it's me and Agnes. This is just a big misunderstanding."

Living right next door to the Andrews' house his whole life, Jack Landry had tagged along with Trixie, Marty, and Cathy their whole growing-up years. He lowered his gun and raised an eyebrow.

"Nothing going on upstairs, I assure you," Trixie said, and she wasn't lying. Agnes had put a stop to what was about to happen for damn sure.

Trixie hoped the old girl had an asthma attack from the mothballs as payment for ruining her Wednesday night.

"We heard a gunshot," Jack said.

"That would be my shotgun. It's up there on the floor. Knocked me right on my ass. I forgot that it had a kick. Loud sumbitch messed up my hearing." Agnes hollered

and reached up to touch her kinky red hair. "I lost my hat when I fell down. I've got to go get it."

Trixie saw the hat come floating down the stairs and tackled it on the bottom step. "Here it is. You dropped it while we were running away."

Agnes screamed at her. "You lied! You said we had to get away from him before he killed us, and I ran down the stairs, and I'm liable to have a heart attack, and it's your fault. I told Cathy and Marty not to bring the likes of you in this house. It's an abomination, I tell you. Divorced woman like you hasn't got no business in the house with a couple of maiden ladies."

"Miz Agnes, one of my officers will help you across the street." Jack pushed a button on his radio and said, "False alarm at Miss Clawdy's."

A young officer was instantly at Agnes's side.

Agnes eyed the fresh-faced fellow. "You lay a hand on me, and I'll go back up there and get my gun. I know what you rascals have on your mind all the time, and you ain't goin' to skinny up next to me. I can still go get my gun. I got more shells right here in my britches' pockets."

"Yes, ma'am. I mean, no, ma'am. I'm just going to make sure you get across the street and into your house safely," he said.

Trixie could hear the laughter behind his tone, but not a damn bit of it was funny. Andy was upstairs. The kitchen was full of men who worked for him, and if Cathy and Marty heard there were problems at Clawdy's, they could come rushing in at any time.

"Maiden ladies my ass," Trixie mumbled. "I'm only thirty-four."

About the Author

Carolyn Brown is a *New York Times* and *USA Today* bestselling author with more than sixty books published, and she credits her eclectic family for her humor and writing ideas. Her books include the cowboy trilogy *Lucky in Love*, *One Lucky Cowboy*, and *Getting Lucky*; the Honky Tonk series with *I Love This Bar*, *Hell Yeah*, *Honky Tonk Christmas*, and *My Give a Damn's Busted;* and her bestselling Spikes & Spurs series with *Love Drunk Cowboy*, *Red's Hot Cowboy*, *Darn Good Cowboy Christmas*, *One Hot Cowboy Wedding*, and *Mistletoe Cowboy*. She was born in Texas but grew up in southern Oklahoma where she and her husband, Charles, a retired English teacher, make their home. They have three grown children and enough grandchildren to keep them young.